REA

ALLEN COUNTY PUBLIC LIBRARY
3 1833 03226 9133

Y0-ABY-972

Thus Doctor Mallory

Thus Doctor Mallory

Elizabeth Seifert

G.K. Hall & Co. • Chivers Press
Thorndike, Maine USA Bath, England

This Large Print edition is published by G.K. Hall & Co., USA
and by Chivers Press, England.

Published in 1997 in the U.S. by arrangement with
Blassingame-Spectrum.

Published in 1998 in the U.K. by arrangement with
Ralph Vicinanza Literary Agency.

U.S. Hardcover 0-7838-8303-X (Romance Collection Edition)
U.K. Hardcover 0-7540-3123-3 (Chivers Large Print)

The text of this Large Print edition is unabridged.
Other aspects of the book may vary from the original edition.

Set in 16 pt. Plantin by Minnie B. Raven.

Printed in the United States on permanent paper.

British Library Cataloguing in Publication Data available

Library of Congress Cataloging in Publication Data

Seifert, Elizabeth, 1897–
Thus Doctor Mallory / by Elizabeth Seifert.
p. cm.
ISBN 0-7838-8303-X (lg. print : hc : alk. paper)
1. Physicians – Middle West – Family relationships — Fiction.
2. Large type books. I. Title.
[PS3537.E352T48 1997]
813′.52—dc21 97-30536

To

Mother and Dad

Chapter One

The house was warm and very neat. Chairs had been rearranged in the parlor; the shades were raised. The house smelled of roasting chicken instead of flowers. It seemed that everyone had conspired to obliterate the last trace of the dead.

Aunt Mabel took off her hat with a sigh. "Well!" she said briskly. "We'll have a good dinner, and then see what is to be done. John, you'd better change your clothes and see if there is enough wood and coal."

Three neighbor women were working in the kitchen. Pies were set on the window sills. Pots and pans steamed on top of the range. Mrs. Martin was putting red preserves into glass dishes. Strange dishes. Food, dishes, and table linens had all been brought in by the neighbors.

Changing into his overalls, going out to the shed for armsful of wood, his brain numb, his heart heavy in his chest, John remembered a phrase from an English lesson. "Funeral baked meats." The festivities, the bustle, in his mother's kitchen was more like a party than anything John had ever known in that house. It was more like a church supper. He edged around the table in the living room, set with stacks of plates, piles of napkins, and silverware.

"They'll all have to eat cafeteria — there ain't places to set 'em down," Mrs. Martin told Aunt Mabel. "It was a lovely funeral, wasn't it? I don't know when I've seen things go nicer. I guess you Colbys are all good managers."

John filled the base-burner with fresh coal. Did it make any difference that they were almost out of hard coal? What became of a fourteen-year-old boy if nobody wanted him? Last summer John had tried awfully hard to get a job — he ate a lot; his mother said he wore out so many shoes. What happened to a fourteen-year-old boy?

Nobody was watching him. He slipped into the stairway and up to his room. Here the air was like cold water. He lay down on the bed and rolled up in the comfort. He was hungry, and frightened.

No one missed him at dinner. No one called him until the tables were being cleared and the women in the kitchen wanted more water.

2

Isabelle was pretty sure Aunt Mabel was the most important one in the family. Still, she did not know. It would be safer to be nice to everyone. Mamma had always said that you got more by being nice than not. She used to say that to John when he would get one of his independent streaks. Poor Mamma.

Isabelle was sorry Aunt Mary and Uncle Brooke had not come. They were the rich ones. They lived in St. Louis. Aunt Mary was

Mamma's youngest sister, and had married a rich man much older than herself. They were the ones who had paid the rent. Once, when Isabelle was just a little girl, Aunt Mary had come for a two days' visit; she had been pretty. She had yellow hair, like Isabelle's, and used gardenia perfume. Uncle Brooke had come to fetch her home. He was big, and his kiss tasted like cough medicine — the wild-cherry kind. John said that was wine, but Isabelle did not care. He had smelled richly of cigars, too.

Isabelle knew that the family would have to take care of her and John. She had heard the aunts talking about it. Well, any of them lived in bigger places than Brownsville, and had cars. She would not care to go where there were a lot of cousins — but she would have to make the best of things. When Aunt Beryl asked her if she could bear being separated from John, she had looked sorry and said she guessed they could not be too particular. Aunt Beryl had patted her shoulder and said she was a good girl.

At dinner Belle waited on the uncles, saw that they had a place to put their plates. Men hated holding food in their laps. She passed cream and sugar for their coffee. She did not smile. She thought her sad, pale look was becoming. When someone would ask her if she had eaten, she would say softly that she was not hungry. So Aunt Mabel fixed her a plate with white meat and a piece of liver, and lots of gravy on her potatoes, and she poured cream on the piece of apple pie she selected as the biggest and juiciest.

She made Isabelle sit down in the Morris chair and eat her dinner. "You'll be sick, darling," she said tenderly.

And after dinner Isabelle was not allowed to help clear the table, nor wipe dishes. "The poor child looks like a ghost," somebody said.

The men put on their hats and walked around the yard, smoking and talking. The aunts helped get everything cleared up, thanked the neighbor women, and told John to sweep the kitchen and check the fire in the range. Isabelle would bet he had not eaten a mouthful of dinner. Sulky thing!

When they all gathered in the parlor, John hunched up on a stool by the door and looked cross. He really was a handsome boy with his shining, curling brown hair. His gray eyes were pretty, too, when he looked at you instead of at the carpet, as he was doing now. John was smart. He was in his third year at high school, and only fourteen.

Aunt Mabel set a small table by her chair and put a tablet and a pencil on it. She looked like a schoolteacher about to outline a history lesson. Aunt Mabel was the eldest of the sisters.

She said she did not mean to take any authority that someone else might want, but somebody had to start things. She was prepared to stay in Brownsville a few days to get things attended to. To close the house and settle any bills there might be. John lifted his head when she said this and looked at her. Isabelle was relieved when he did not declare that the Mallorys paid spot cash for everything, when he did not speak.

Aunt Mabel said that the furniture and things would have to be disposed of. The family could take anything they would like to have to remember Kathleen by; but she would sell most of the things, and the money could go toward the funeral expenses.

"Brooke said he'd pay that," Cousin Clara said, her voice stifled by the fearful cold she had.

"Yes, but I don't think he should."

"Well, he can, and never feel it. And Mary said, since she wasn't able to come — She told me to see to it that it was done that way, Mabel. She won't like it if I don't."

"Well, I had thought we'd proportion it according to the way we've been helping Kathleen."

"The furniture won't bring much," said Uncle Oliver. "What keepsakes there are should go to Isabelle and the boy."

"Ye-es," Aunt Mabel agreed. "Though I would like Kathleen's sewing table."

Again John lifted his head. The drum-topped table, with its little spindles for thread, its little curved drawers for buttons and things, had been his Grandmother Mallory's.

"You always pick the best things," Aunt Grace said spitefully. "I think anything of value should be kept for the children."

"All right. I asked for opinions. And I am

getting them." Aunt Mabel's face was red, and her eyes were angry.

Isabelle looked up at her. "You keep it for me," she said softly.

John coughed.

Aunt Mabel's good humor was restored. She smiled at Isabelle. "All right, darling. Now, since that is settled, what about the children?"

There was a little embarrassed silence. Feet were scuffled. Cousin Clara sneezed.

"Oh! Excuse me!" she gasped. "I have such a cold! Mary said that if there were no other plan, she'd take Isabelle."

The aunts evidently had known of this offer. Isabelle had not. The suddenness of this glory — to live in Aunt Mary's house, to be rich! She almost forgot, and squealed her joy. Almost, but not quite. She just put her handkerchief to her eyes to hide the excitement she was afraid might show there.

"I think any of us would be willing to care for dear little Isabelle," Aunt Mabel said. "But Mary can gave her so much more, and she has no children of her own."

"She said," Cousin Clara explained, feeling the importance of being Mary Wielande's spokeswoman, "that Isabelle could take the place of the little daughter she lost. The baby, you know."

The aunts looked at one another meaningfully, and nodded.

"Anyway," Cousin Clara said, "Mary said she'd take Isabelle. She said I could bring her back with me. Would you like that, Isabelle?"

Isabelle folded her handkerchief. "Yes, Cousin Clara. If we have to break up, I'd rather do it now."

She must not let them know that she wished she could start being rich Aunt Mary's little girl this very minute!

"Poor child," Aunt Mabel said kindly. "But you'll like it in St. Louis. Make friends. Have pretty clothes."

"Oh, yes," said Cousin Clara. "Mary and Brooke thought that if Isabelle did come to them they'd want to adopt her — have her take their name, you know."

Isabelle Wielande. Isabelle liked that. She would be a brand-new person, not at all the girl who wore dresses made over from the aunts' old ones, and cotton stockings. "It's all right," she said meekly.

"You're a lucky girl," Cousin Clara told her firmly.

Isabelle looked at her. She did not like Cousin Clara very well. "Do you live with them?"

"I live in St. Louis. I work in your Uncle Brooke's office. He's been very kind to any of Mary's family who needed help. He paid your mother's rent for ten years, you know."

"He didn't have to!" John cried hoarsely. "We didn't ask anybody to help us!"

Everybody looked at John. Isabelle felt her cheeks go red with shame for him. Mamma had always said that John must put his worst foot forward. And just now, when he could do himself so much harm . . .

"You're just a boy," Aunt Mabel said forgivingly.

"Well, what about him?" Aunt Grace asked. "Now that you've got Isabelle sitting on a silk cushion like a Pomeranian pup, what about John?"

This time the silence was longer, and very still. Nobody looked at anybody else. John sat with his head bent to his chest, and picked at the patch on the knee of his faded overalls.

"I can get a job — can take care of myself," he mumbled.

"I don't think we can ask Brooke . . ." Cousin Clara began.

"Oh, no!"

Isabelle was glad they were agreed on that. John did not fit into the picture she was making of her new home. Of course, she wanted John to be cared for, and he would be. Somebody . . . Oh, yes! "Last summer," she offered timidly, "Mamma had a letter from Uncle Ben." She paused before the amazed, hurt look John sent toward her. Mamma had said that Uncle Ben was one to get a blind mule to do his work.

"Uncle Ben Colby?"

"Pa's brother," the aunts told each other.

"For goodness' sake! What did he say, Belle?"

"Well, he said that he had a chicken ranch — or something — in California, and that if John was a strong worker and a good boy —"

"Belle!"

"Mamma said before she died, John, that the plan would take care of you — if the worst came to the worst." She had meant if none of the aunts wanted John. And none seemed to.

"She was feeling bad about dying and leaving nothing for us," Belle explained to Aunt Mabel.

"What did Uncle Ben say?"

"He said — I think I know where the letter is — that he could give John a home and send him to school."

"Until I'm sixteen," John said bitterly. John wanted to be a doctor, though he knew very well that would never be possible.

"I'd hate to have to work for Ben Colby," Aunt Beryl said.

"Hush! John can't expect to get a living without work. He's almost a man. Men have to work. You understand that, don't you, John?"

John got to his feet. He stuck out his chin and pulled his lips into a tight, thin line. "I'm not afraid to work. I'd a sight rather earn my living than get it like — like a Pomeranian pup!"

With a sound suspiciously like a sob he turned and went out through the porch door, slamming it hard behind him. The aunts looked at one another and shook their heads.

Chapter Two

From the first, Belle made no mention of John to her new family, to her new friends. She doubted if vague, pretty Aunt Mary or busy Uncle Brooke remembered that she had a brother.

Those first weeks were strange to the girl, and it took her every minute to concentrate upon and try to assimilate all this strangeness and not seem awkward and ill at ease in her new surroundings. Aunt Mary was like Isabelle's mother in one thing: she thought appearances were important. Belle thought they were, too. From the first, she and Mrs. Wielande were in accord on that subject.

Just the same — in spite of her native gift of poise — Belle, raised as she had been in a very small town, knowing almost none of the graces of pleasant living, found that she must constantly be on the alert to see and learn the little details that made up the whole of her new life. Little details, but all-important. The way one used a finger bowl or left a napkin beside her plate marked one's breeding too quickly. Aunt Mary, she knew, was pleased that Isabelle needed so little instruction in these matters.

Belle, learning so much that was new, often in

an agony of spirit lest she reveal her humble beginnings to her new friends, found little time to think of John. He wrote to her, on cheap tablet paper. She did not answer very many of John's letters. Twice she sent him a five-dollar bill at Christmas.

Belle was as smugly content in her new home as a cat with a saucer of yellow cream. Still — at first — things were not exactly as she had figured they would be. For one thing, there were no silk stockings showered on Belle. Even her "good dresses" were very simple. For school she wore a uniform. Plain as plain! Still, all the girls wore the same thing. Belle lost no time in learning that smart things were usually simple things, and that the fetish of the rich and well-born is to be "smart." She stopped regretting the frills. She could be as ashamed of a secret longing or impulse as if she had carried the mistake to fulfillment. Belle wanted to be *right,* even in her thoughts.

She learned quickly because of this longing and docility. She even suppressed the thrill she sometimes felt at finding herself a rich girl, the pampered daughter of Mr. and Mrs. Brooke Wielande. She never forgot to be sweet to Aunt Mary about her new things, but there were thrills that had to be concealed. It would not do to let anyone know, the first months, that she found it thrilling to eat breakfast in the little blue and silver sunroom, served by a maid in a gray dress and a cap and apron that were like frilled tissue paper. One must not show how exciting it was to have a butler — a real, live one — help her into her blue chinchilla coat, hand her her gloves — plain brown ones, with fur cuffs — and open the heavy front door for her; nor how especially exciting it was to have Lee, an honest-to-true chauffeur, open the car door — a black limousine — tuck the plaid rug over her knees, and then drive her to school, the back of his capped head showing through the front window glass. Belle wondered if the people she passed — people in cheap little cars, the throngs of boys and girls going on foot to the public schools — admired and envied her.

The thing was, she quickly realized, not to show the thrill you felt in these everyday things, like maids and bath salts and satin eiderdowns. Also, you must not show superiority because you had them.

It became increasingly hard for Belle to remember that she had ever lived any other life than the one which was now so completely filling her days. Brownsville, the little frame cottage, the made-over dresses, chapped hands in winter — all seemed as remote as some wild happenings Isabelle might have dreamed. Indeed, Isabelle might have succeeded in forgetting them altogether if it had not been for Cousin Clara. Isabelle avoided Cousin Clara when she could.

She did not know why she disliked this faded, middle-aged woman, except that this plain-spoken cousin of her mother could disturb the calm complacency of her days. Being with Cousin Clara was as it would have been to wear one of her shabby old dresses to Smith Institute.

Cousin Clara always asked her about John. She was always remembering Belle's father — a handsome young man who had married Kathleen Colby at the end of a ten days' courtship and had broken his neck riding an unruly horse, leaving his two orphan children and his widow dependent on the aunts and Uncle Brooke. All things considered, Belle wondered why Cousin Clara should seem to have admired Jack Mallory. She was obviously paying John a compliment when she said he was like his father. "But you're pure Colby, Belle. No doubt of that." And no compliment intended.

2

Isabelle always thought her friendship with Ellen Conte was the luckiest thing that ever happened to her. Really, in a way, luckier than being adopted by Uncle Brooke. It was more or less inevitable that Uncle Brooke should adopt his wife's orphaned niece. But there were two hundred girls at Smith, any one of whom Isabelle might have chosen as her best friend.

Isabelle told Aunt Mary about her new friend at Sunday luncheon. "I think she's rather poor now, Aunt Mary. Her father's died, and her mother has to work. And Ellen has to tutor, too. Not French, but Latin, like I do. And arithmetic. She says she's always been dumb in arithmetic.

Would Miss Shannon charge more to teach two of us?"

Mary Wielande smiled at her niece. "I'm afraid so, dear. Not that it would matter, but often one can't tactfully offer to pay for such things. The poor are always full of pride. What did you say the girl's name was?"

"I wouldn't want to hurt her feelings. It would be fun, though, if we could have our lessons together. Her name is Ellen Conte. C-o-n-t-e. But you don't say the last *e*."

"Conte? Jules Conte's daughter?"

"I don't know. Her father's dead."

Mary looked at Brooke, busy with his veal cutlet. "Wasn't Jules Conte's wife Marguerite Briand, Brooke?"

"Eh? Yes, I think so. Conte died last year. T.B. From the war. Fine fellow. Shame. Old family. I hear he didn't leave much."

Aunt Mary nodded. Smiled at Isabelle. "Ellen must be a very nice girl, darling. Both her mother and father were of the old St. Louis French families. Her father went over and fought with the French army right from the start of the war. I saw him once after he came home. He had been wounded and was soliciting war loans, or something. So handsome in his blue uniform. Ellen's mother was V. P. Queen her debut year. You must bring her home with you someday. Ellen, I mean. I'm glad you two are friends."

Well, poor or not, Ellen was the only girl at Smith — so far as Isabelle knew — whose mother had been a Veiled Prophet's Queen. Isabelle was more determined than ever that she and Ellen should study together under Miss Shannon.

That afternoon Mary Wielande took Cousin Clara for a drive in the Packard. She told, rather smugly, about Isabelle's new friend. "Clever of her," she laughed, "to pick the very nicest girl in the whole school."

Clara could not afford to be as blunt with Mary as she was often inclined to be. "What sort of kid is she? Sometimes these bluebloods aren't too attractive."

"Oh, she must be. Isabelle hadn't an idea who she was. So she must be personable. Isabelle was asking if she couldn't pay for the poor child's tutor."

"If Brooke couldn't, you mean. And I don't imagine Jules Conte left his widow actually a pauper."

"No. I don't suppose he did. Still, I hear — Brooke told me this — that she is starting up a real-estate office. The thing that tickles me is Isabelle's good taste."

"I suspect she had a tip. She's a sly little puss. And a dreadful snob, if you ask me."

"Which I didn't," Mary pointed out. Then she laughed good-naturedly. She was really pleased at Isabelle's discernment. "I'm afraid I'm a snob, too, Clara. I find it much more pleasant being with the right people than with the wrong. Isabelle is really a lot like me. I'm glad that she is."

"You couldn't do a sly thing if you tried."

"I'm not sure that I like your calling Isabelle sly. She tries to please. But that's charm. I love her being charming, Clara. It is always an asset. Just as much a one as being pretty. Isn't she pretty? You'll have to admit she is."

"Oh, I guess she's pretty enough. Especially in the fine clothes you buy her."

"I love buying them. It's like dressing a French doll. I — you know, Clara, when I offered to take Kathleen's little girl I did it from a charitable impulse. I was ready to do the best for the child, however unattractive she might prove to be. I was going to work awfully hard at being kind to an unfortunate orphan. Really, I was in quite a stew of good works. But when I saw how pretty Isabelle was, and how dear she was about everything we did for her, it was quite a relief. I expect my charitable impulse was beginning to wear thin already. I get fearfully bored doing good. I'm glad I didn't have to go on being unselfish and kind. The whole thing is really working out very well.

"And that makes Brooke pleased, too. He'd rather have adopted the boy, you know. To teach golf, I suppose, and the fine points of bootleg liquor."

3

Marguerite Conte never knew Isabelle very well. She became accustomed to seeing the two girls constantly together, to knowing that if Ellen were not at home she surely would be at Wielandes'. It was a natural thing for girls to chum so.

Isabelle was a pretty thing, and popular. She would have her own beaux. The time of debut balls was coming, all too swiftly, when Ellen's mother would need to wonder if her daughter would have enough men to go round. Isabelle, as a best friend, would be an asset. The child had nice manners and seemed content with the more harmless, conventional diversions. She served as something of a check to Ellen's occasional willful impulses. Her debut year, the Wielandes would entertain lavishly for their daughter. Ellen would share these honors if the close friendship persisted. In return, small, select luncheons and teas would adequately balance the Conte side of the ledger. Yes, the alliance was a good one, looked at in cold blood — as Marguerite Conte must now look at most things.

Ellen became as much at home in the Wielande household as was Isabelle. She even called Mr. and Mrs. Wielande "Uncle Brooke and Aunt Mary." But then, such familiarity was natural to her in homes she visited as familiarly as she did the Wielandes'. She often complained to Isabelle that she was related to half of St. Louis.

"The fusty half," she giggled.

Isabelle sighed. "You don't know when you're lucky. I've no one in the world but Aunt Mary and Uncle Brooke."

"Not anybody, Isabelle?"

"Oh, a stray cousin or two. Not anyone my own."

She gave no thought of the hurt this statement

would have caused John. He still considered it his obligation to serve his bondage of youth and debt, and then assume his rightful responsibility for his sister.

"Remember, too," Isabelle continued plaintively, "I'm only adopted."

"You're their own niece. You told me you were."

"Yes, but not really their daughter. That's why I don't call them Mother and Father." The Wielandes had never suggested that she do so.

"They are perfectly grand to you," Ellen pointed out. "Even better than a real father and mother. They give you everything."

Isabelle knew that this was true. They did give her everything. Summers at exclusive girls' camps. Her registration at Miss Ferriss' school in Connecticut — she and Ellen would be roommates there. Probably a year of travel in Europe with Mrs. Slocumb. She and Ellen would be debs together, and maid of honor at each other's wedding. Nothing, nothing, the two girls solemnly vowed, should ever come between them to mar their undying friendship. Isabelle knew she could count on Ellen's loyalty from now on. A promise meant a lot to Ellen. Being her best friend was like an infusion of St. Louis' "best blood" in Isabelle's own veins.

Chapter Three

John dreaded the trip to California, hated the journey in its every detail. He was unfamiliar with trains. He was afraid to leave the coach to buy food; he was certain that the two dollars in his pocket would melt in the terrifying atmosphere of the diner. He was uncomfortable in his hot, gritty clothes, ashamed of sleeping in the indecent publicity of the chair car. He was notional and finicky. He knew that he was, and knew that a boy in his position had no right to such fastidious ideas. He hated the journey; he hated California, bright and hot and strange. He was prepared to hate Uncle Ben.

John and a foreign-looking fellow with two live roosters in his hand were the only ones to get off at Villa Franca. The train barely hesitated at the small, neat station. The town seemed like any of a dozen they had passed that morning, clustered stucco buildings, a bright red chain store, and the broad ribbon of the new highway going off into the sunlight.

Fighting his shyness, John asked for directions and started out along this road, carrying his suitcase with his sheepskin coat folded under the straps. The highway led through the main business street. Soon the stores gave way to houses.

Little bungalows with screened porches and patches of very bright green grass in front of them, and incredible flowers in bloom. Now and then John saw a palm tree. They must be that, but they seemed rather scrubby.

Everything was very clean, except for a fine powdering of yellow dust which showed on bright cars parked along the curb. The air was thin and clear, the yellow sunlight really hot. John's heavy clothes became oppressive; he switched the suit-case back and forth from hand to hand. Once he stopped and put the money he had left — almost a dollar — into a folded handkerchief and tucked it inside his undershirt, held firmly against his skin by his belt. He could not have explained his action.

The little houses gave way to larger ones, with big yards, sometimes inclosed by wall or fence. Shrubbery and flowers took on a more formal note. The last of these big homes was an ornate frame house, its porches of pinkish wood, un-painted. On the wooden gatepost was a faded sign. "James Hayes, M.D. Physician and Sur-geon." A brindle bulldog came galloping down the driveway and cocked an inquiring head at John.

"Hello, dog," John said. The big animal reared up against the gate and wagged his stump of a tail. John ventured to put his hand out and scratch the hard white forehead. "Good boy," he said approvingly. The dog went along inside the fence as far as he could accompany John. When

John looked back, he could still see the pink and white muzzle pressed through the pickets. The boy smiled. He had made, he thought, a friend.

Now his road led between small truck farms. Tiny houses, each with its garage and tank for water. And neat little square patches of vegetables, half of which John could not identify. Fruit trees, always, if only a few of them, close to the house. The men working in these fields looked dark and foreign. Not like the blond farmers of Iowa who, at this time of year, would be sitting behind their stoves. Once John saw a woman and two small children bending over a row of plants, picking green leaves — it must be spinach — and filling tall baskets. Not a weed nor a bit of wild grass showed anywhere. There were not many animals, either. Chickens, and a dog or two. But not many cows. And not a single horse. Nor were there any barns. Just a small shed, sometimes, besides the garage.

A strange country.

2

For some minutes John had been aware of the filling station ahead of him. In a country so flat only a turn in the road could have concealed anything so bright. So bright, and so ugly. For nearly half a mile he could see the huge sign on the main building. "Gas. Oil. Cabins. Eats. Ben Colby, Prop."

A square frame building with a deep portico and half a dozen pumps were mustered along the road, all painted a bright yellow and red. Behind the building were wire runs and small sheds, white chickens in unbelievable numbers. Then Uncle Ben did have a chicken farm. Not such a big farm, but certainly lots of chickens. Over beyond the main building John could see several small houses. He could not think of another name for the bald, ugly structures. As he came up to the filling station, he counted six of these buildings, one larger than the rest. "Baths and Comfort," read the sign above the door. John coughed. A couple of cars were drawn up between the cottages, and there was a heavy-looking trailer truck pulled under the big trees which shaded a dusty croquet ground and horseshoe pitch. Two elderly men sat in tilted chairs under one of these trees, and smoked and talked. John could smell potatoes frying. He looked into the office of the station. A fat woman was behind the restaurant counter, talking to a boy in green coveralls that had "Ben Colby" embroidered across the shoulders.

John looked again toward the two men. He was not going to let Uncle Ben know he was afraid; he lifted his shoulders and approached the men with his chin out. "I'm John Mallory," he said clearly. "Is one of you Mr. Colby?"

Both old men dropped the front legs of their chairs and regarded the boy over the tops of their spectacles. There was not much to choose between the two old coots. The one with hair — stiff gray hair parted in the middle — took his pipe from his mouth.

"I'm Ben Colby," he said. His voice was not low, but it had a faint, whispering undertone that sounded odd. "I been expecting you the last day two. John, eh?"

"Yes, sir."

"You look like a real strong boy. Pale, though."

John knew he was not pale, but he had felt so himself among the browned skins of California. Uncle Ben stood up and came close to the boy. He had a fresh-colored face, clean-shaven except for a small mustache the same strawlike gray of his hair. Like old, dead straw that has seen many winters' snow and rain. His face was deeply wrinkled, and his small gray eyes, behind big, gold-rimmed spectacles, seemed to smile. He was not so terrifying as John, for some reason, had feared he would be.

The other old man rose and started down the path to the highway. "I guess I'll be going along, Ben. Must be close to dinnertime."

"Yes. All right, Mr. Peters. You come back." Both he and John watched the man until he was well across the road and out of earshot. "This town wants to know your whole business," Uncle Ben informed John.

John nodded, and shifted his shoulders in his coat. "It gets pretty warm out here for January," he said uneasily.

"Yes. We're having a warm spell. Some mornings it's nippy. Not like Iowa, though."

"No." John felt a swift nostalgia for the blue-rimmed snow of an Iowa winter morning.

"Yes, sir, you're a right pert boy. They wrote me you was only fourteen."

"I am. I'll be fifteen in June."

"Pass for sixteen easy, right now. Was your pa a big man?"

"I don't remember." John's mother had never talked of Jack Mallory to his children.

"Yes, I'm sorry now I told folks you was only fourteen. Come I could let on you was sixteen, wouldn't no busybody expect me to send you to school."

"I — I like to go to school."

"You do, eh? Smart in your lessons?"

"I make good grades. I'm doing mostly third-year work. Except in Latin."

"Latin. Well, I want to know. Latin. Not much help cleaning out chicken pens and filling gas tanks, Latin won't be. Yes, I figure you've had just about all the schooling you'll need."

John felt fear wash over him like cold water. Dared he remind Uncle Ben that he had promised two years of schooling? He kept silent. Uncle Ben turned his smiling gaze toward the shoe-box cabins behind the filling station. "What do you think of my tourist camp?" he asked.

"I — I guess it's very nice. I don't know about such things. We — we didn't have a car."

"No. Mabel wrote you was poor folks. I got a right nice little camp here. Tourist trade getting bigger all along. Few years I'll build me a big center building with stoves and washtubs. Some people don't have no homes but their automobiles. And then there's my idea of serving fried chicken instead of hot dogs and such. People take on to that. Most anybody'd rather pay a quarter for a big piece of home-fried chicken than a dime for a bun and a wienie. Especially if you ain't got the hot dogs. You get pretty tired touring around eating hot dogs day in day out."

John nodded, but said nothing. As hungry as he now was, any food seemed appetizing.

"You know anything about chickens?" Uncle Ben asked.

"I — a little. We kept about a dozen hens, and raised some little ones every summer."

"Fiddling business. I keep five hundred fryers out in them pens right along. Don't mess with eggs. Buy chicks and raise 'em to eating size."

John looked at the narrow runs, the small, whitewashed houses.

Uncle Ben hitched at the top of his baggy trousers. "I guess we'll go get a bite of dinner. You got overalls?"

"Yes." Patched ones, already too tight in the seat.

"You better change into 'em. You kin have Elmer's cot in the lean-to. I'm firin' him this afternoon."

John picked up his suitcase and went toward the largest of the frame buildings, following the direction indicated by Uncle Ben's pipe stem. He stood aside to let a fat woman tourist come out of the washhouse. She giggled self-consciously, and twitched at her skirt.

There were only two windows in the wash-house — small ones, high up in the end walls. As the door was kept shut, the air of the place was fetid with the smell of sewage and wet wood. Water dripped in the shower on the side marked "Gents." John tried to tighten the faucet — the gasket must be rotten. The lean-to, which contained Elmer's rumpled cot and his few clothes hung on pegs against the unpainted board wall, was probably intended for tools. Its sloping roof made the tall boy bend his neck as he changed to a blue chambray shirt and his overalls. He folded his suit and put it into the bag, which he shoved back under the bed.

Elmer met him on the path to the filling station. He would have shoved against John, but the younger boy side-stepped neatly.

"You'll be sorry you ever came here," Elmer told him darkly.

John was sorry — had been for some time — but he made no answer.

He found Uncle Ben seated at one of the tables in the station, and the fat woman giggling behind the counter. "This is John, Bertha," Uncle Ben said indistinctly. "Give him something to eat."

Bertha put some canned beans on a plate and set it in front of John. There were rolls on the table and a small pat of butter. The woman brought a thick plate which contained two very pink cookies. "I guess he's hungry," she said apologetically to Uncle Ben.

"You don't want to spoil him," Uncle Ben warned, taking one of the cookies.

The beans were heated only half through, but John ate every one of them. The rolls were stale, and the butter proved to be margarine.

"You want coffee?" Bertha asked him.

"I'd rather have milk, please."

"He don't drink coffee," Uncle Ben said. In the years John stayed at the station he was never offered coffee a second time. Nor did he ever have milk there. That served to the lunch-counter customers was canned.

"You needn't fix your mouth for chicken," Uncle Ben told him pleasantly. "We ain't in the business to feed ourselves chicken, are we, Bertha?"

"No, sir. Is John going to clean the chickens for me?"

Uncle Ben filled his pipe and leaned back against the bench. "Yeah, I gotta tell him what his work is. Gener'lly I tend to the pumps. I like to visit with all the people comin' through, an' I like to keep a check on things. So I us'ally give the gas and oil. 'Course, come a customer wants his car washed, I'd let you do it. I'm gittin' along. I don't relish real hard work no more. Bertha here cooks and tends to things here in the lunchroom, but she don't us'ally get time to dress the chickens. You can tend to that every morning. Then, it'll be your job to keep the houses and runs clean, and feed the chickens. Day or two, right at first, I'll show you how to do. Odd times, you can kinda slick up around the camp. The human creature is about as filthy as chickens. Drop their dirt where they ben standin'."

John made no comment. He had expected hard work here at Uncle Ben's. He would make an honest effort to do all that was expected of him.

"The way I figger," Uncle Ben continued, "you ought to be wuth about five dollars a week, if you work steady. An' that ought to cover your meals here, and what cloes you need. Leastways, you'll have to fit your needs to that amount. I don't aim to be allowin' you more. Since you're a relative, I'll give you your roof and bed free. What cloes you got?"

John told him, ashamed of the poverty the list revealed. "My suit is almost new."

"It's a-gittin' small on you. Better sell it, I guess. You won't need nothin' better'n overalls. Come these wear clear out, ye can wear Elmer's coveralls. They look snappy and are good advertising."

"But — for school I can't wear overalls." John felt as if he were swimming against a whirlpool.

"Oh, yes. School. Well, now, I tell you, John. 'Course there ain't no reason you can't wear overalls to school. There's a lot worse things than a pair of clean overalls. I don't figger your five dollars a week — providin' you earn that much — will run to much in the way of swallow-tail coats and striped pants." The old fellow giggled at his flight of fantasy. "But, about school, now — won't hardly be worth while your going any more this year, will it? Term's half over, I'd say."

In June, John would be fifteen. If Uncle Ben would only give him schooling until he was sixteen . . . John took a firm grip on his courage. "I can't miss a whole term of school, Uncle Ben. In a public place like this, people will know if I'm not in school."

Uncle Ben looked at him. His little eyes glittered. "Stubborn, ain't ye? Well, we'll see. You work right hard this week, and we'll see if you can spare time for school. Mornings, maybe. First thing, you'd have a good two-mile walk. There, and back."

"I shan't mind the walk," John assured him. "What do you want me to do now?"

Uncle Ben showed him the pen of chickens ready for the pan. Uncle Ben killed one by stepping on its neck and pulling off the head. He left John to kill five more. After he had gone, John hunted until he found a hatchet. Bertha gave him a bucket of hot water, and he sat on the back steps to pick the chickens, trying to think.

He brought the limp yellow corpses inside so that Bertha might show him how to quarter them for frying. She was a big blond woman, probably in her middle twenties. She smelled of grease and body sweat. Her flowered house dress was split under one arm, and her big breast bulged against the tear.

"Do you live near here?" John asked her.

"Me? I live here in the station. My home's down near Long Beach. I got a married sister there. She's married to a sailor. He's machinist mate on the hospital ship. She has an easy time."

"Is Long Beach near the ocean?"

"Sure. Right on it."

"I've never seen the ocean. I want to. Sometime."

"Be careful, don't cut the gall. You ought to run away an' be a sailor, if you love the sea."

"I don't know that I'd love it. I just want to see it."

"Sailors have an easy time. Regular pay, and they don't work too hard. Your uncle'd love me telling you to run off." She giggled and looked over her shoulder.

Now and then a car stopped out in front, but they had no customers beyond an occasional demand for cigarettes.

"Don't ever snitch any smokes," Bertha warned John. "It'd set your uncle wild."

"I haven't begun to smoke. Have you worked here long?"

"About a year. My sister says she don't see how I can stand it. Him so old and all. I tell her a girl ain't in danger of gettin' into trouble with an old man."

John kept his eyes on his work. Slowly the significance of what Bertha had said worked into his mind. The dirty, filthy . . .

3

John worked harder all that week than he had ever done in his life, and John's life had never been an easy one of idle days and soft living. He rose at dawn, and worked until the station lights were turned off at midnight. He dressed chickens until the ends of his fingers were cracked and bleeding. He cleaned chicken houses, and raked the pens. All his life the peculiar stench of the fowls could turn his stomach. He learned to stretch a sack of lime into as much whitewash as Uncle Ben thought it should make. He scrubbed the floors of the cabins. He washed blankets and his own overalls. He slept at night on his hard bed, his nostrils filled with the sourness of the washhouse. Once he dragged his cot out of doors, and Uncle Ben endeavored to whip him. He said John had tried to shame him before folks. John evaded that indignity by stepping beyond the old man's reach until, stuttering with rage, Uncle Ben threw the length of rope to the ground and screamed that John should have nothing to eat that day. Bertha sopped a roll in the grease of the chicken skillet, and John wolfed it down in two mouthfuls when he brought the chickens in to the counter.

Bertha knew that the food Uncle Ben allowed him was only a part of what the boy needed. She would save odd bits of food in a cracker tin kept in full sight on a shelf behind the stove. John would empty it when he got the chance, gratefully eat the half of roll left on a customer's plate, and gnaw the thin edge of a chicken wing some better-fed person had spurned. His empty stomach cured his distaste for leavings. He tried to do little extra things for Bertha, though his own duties left him little enough time.

Bertha herself warned him that he mustn't seem too friendly with her. "The old fool's apt as not to get jealous. He knows you're nearly a man grown. But if he ever goes into town . . ."

John chose to be innocent of the promise she held out. "He never goes into town," he said.

It was true that Uncle Ben never went out of sight of his pumps. He greeted each car that drew to a stop at the station. He visited familiarly with each casual stranger, talked intimately with the tourists who stayed in the cabins for a night or so. He was a big talker, Uncle Ben was. He had a fund of odd bits of information, probably secured from all these travelers, and there was no subject on which he would not venture an opinion. It seemed to John that his lack of knowledge was more prominently displayed than any real information he might have. His faulty grammar, his gross display of ignorance and prejudice, grated on the boy, unhappy and nervously sensitive at this time. He was bitterly ashamed of his uncle, wished often that the fatuous old fool would be stricken dumb.

It did not take John the full first week to discover how Uncle Ben was regarded in the community. Not that the town's contempt for his meanness, his braying self-confidence, ever bothered Ben Colby. His was a brassbound spirit. People who snubbed him, those who attempted to insult him, he was quite sure were the people who rankled with envy of him. At least once every day John heard him declare that some people can't 'bide a smart man, can't bear to see anybody get ahead just by hard work. Uncle Ben was well satisfied with Ben Colby.

Knowing all this, knowing that he would have to wear the hateful name embroidered across his shoulders, John approached his uncle late on Sunday afternoon. "If . . ." he began, hating this business of deferring to a man he despised. "I've done all my work. I thought I'd change my clothes and walk into town, find out where the high school is. I'll be starting there tomorrow."

Uncle Ben took his pipe out of his mouth and looked at it. The pipe was a small one, the bowl carved into a rough semblance of a man's head. Uncle Ben was very proud of that pipe. "So you've done all your work," he repeated. His breathy, whispering voice, the deep wrinkles beside his eyes, could seduce a stranger into thinking he was a kindly old fellow.

"I — I thought it would save me time tomorrow. Bertha says she has plenty of chickens, and I've raked the pens."

"Ye might take the hose and wet down the platform," Uncle Ben suggested. By the platform he meant the square of concrete under the station portico. John had swept it that morning.

Uncle Ben stopped to service a car and tell the driver that Warren Harding looked to him to be a right smart fellow. John filled the radiator and wiped the windshield. There was a child in the car who asked for a drink. John brought a glass of water from the lunchroom. The mother thanked him and, as they were about to drive off, tried to give him a coin. John refused it courteously.

He watched the car drive away and turned to meet Uncle Ben's furious eyes. "No, thank you," he mocked angrily. "It was nothing. I'm a rich boy, an' we don't sell sody pop or nothing. We just give away ice water free. An' we don't want no pay neither!"

John bit his lip. "I hate tips," he said stiffly.

"You hate tips. Charity, I guess you call it. Well, what kind of a name have you got for what you take from me?"

John went to the corner of the building and unreeled the hose. Uncle Ben could continue on this subject for hours. John knew the futility of offering the arguments on his side. From now on he would swallow his pride enough to take tips — when Uncle Ben was not around. John's chances of earning any hard cash here at the station seemed slim.

"An' on top of that you want to dress up and walk into town. Git yourself a girl, I reckon. An' go to school tomorrow. Guess you think you're pretty fine."

John thought that he was just one degree higher than a worm. He sluiced the cement into a square of brown dampness.

"Well, ye ain't goin' to dress up. I'm a-goin' to sell that suit. Any goin' into town you do, you'll do in overalls."

John remembered his mother's efforts, her sacrifices, to present her children to the world in decent garb. Overalls on Sunday, or worn to school, would have been indecent in her sight. In the past John had sometimes resented his mother's overemphasis on the need for proper clothing. He saw now that what she had really been struggling for was a dignified place in the social scheme. A blue serge suit for her son, an organdy dress for Belle, had been symbols of the respect she demanded for her family.

Ben Colby had no use for respect. "I don't know as you're going in to school so bright and early tomorrow morning," he persisted.

John turned off the water. Wiped his hands on a rag he kept in his hip pocket. "Let's get this straight, Uncle Ben. You've given me a home. And you've promised to send me to school. You call it charity, and perhaps that's true. But I know this much: if you had taken a strange orphan boy out of a home, you would have been obliged to send him to school. I'm ready to work as hard as I can to earn what you give me. But I'm going to school, and I'm going tomorrow."

Uncle Ben knocked his pipe against the oil rack. "Well, I never said I wasn't going to send you to school, did I?" he cried testily.

4

True to his word, John went to school the next morning. He had arisen at dawn, killed and dressed six chickens, cleaned the pens, and fed the squawking, silly birds. Then he took a bucket of cold water into his cubby — he dared not use the tourists' shower — and scrubbed himself from head to heel. He brushed his hair as flat as it would go. He dressed in clean overalls, the old blue ones he had brought from home. He tied a necktie under his blue collar. Sometime yesterday evening Uncle Ben had taken his suit and his white shirts and his heavy coat. But John still had his dark blue sweater, only half wool, but it would keep him fairly warm. This morning had a tang of frost in the air. The grass beside the chicken runs had crackled under his feet. He buttoned his small supply of money — eighty-nine cents — into the pocket of his shirt, along with the stump of a pencil. He devoutly hoped the school would supply books. He went into the station by the back door. Bertha was warming her hands against the coffee urn.

"Cold, ain't it?" she asked. "You going to school?"

"Yes. Where's Uncle Ben?"

"Out and around. He's cross as a poisoned pup this morning. I wrapped up two rolls for your lunch. You won't be able to come home."

"I thought maybe I could arrange my schedule so I could get home early."

"You stay there full time, if he don't catch on.

Do your studying there. He won't give you no time or peace here."

John knew that was true. "Do you know where the school is?"

"Yeah. You can see it as you go into town."

"A big white building with a green roof?"

"Naw, that's the college."

"College? In Villa Franca?"

"Yeah. I don't know much about it, only your uncle has pups every time he has to pay taxes and knows part of it goes for the college. He ain't got much use for book learnin'. I guess he figures he got along pretty well without it."

John was glad to get away without encountering Uncle Ben. As he walked briskly down the highway, his thoughts were busy. Bertha seemed to think that Uncle Ben was a successful man. Successful in what way? He had his own business, but lived so meagerly it amounted to pauperism. Nor had he ever known, or desired, better things. He himself thought that now he had reached the peak of endeavor. It seemed a warped sort of success to John which brought a man neither respect nor friends.

John looked with new interest at the white buildings of the college. He must find out more about that. Perhaps, by some miracle, he could one day attend classes there. After high school — if he could do his pre-medical work at this college — Oh, he was completely crazy! Why did he not resign himself to being Uncle Ben's nephew, and cut his coat to suit his cloth?

The big bulldog was out in the fenced yard when he passed. Lying in a patch of early sunlight, curled into a ball. He opened one eye as John went by. John smiled. He was a good dog. The curtains of the big house were drawn. John pretended that the doctor had been out all night on a call, and now his family was being very quiet while he slept. Next to being a doctor, it must be fine to have one in your family.

5

The school was bigger than John had expected. Still, Villa Franca had fifteen thousand people. It looked like a fine school. There was a big athletic field out behind it. Tennis courts. There was no sign of pupils this early. But the main door stood open, and a janitor in blue denim was polishing the door handles. John approached him.

"I'm a new pupil. Can you tell me where the principal's office is?"

The man did not look up. "Straight through — door on the landing."

John stepped confidently through the wide doorway. He felt how wonderful American schools are, how wonderful it was that every boy could claim his share in them. These marble steps, this wide hall, and the big, clean windows were John's! He sniffed the air with pleasure. Damp sawdust, a little dust, chalk — it all went to make up a heavenly atmosphere.

His cheeks were pink and his eyes aglow when

he came to the principal's office. He had forgotten that he wore patched overalls, and that he could buy little except a pencil and tablet in the way of school supplies. The ground-glass doorpane said "L. E. Arndt. Principal." John knocked and, at a murmur from within, opened the door and entered.

The room was sparely furnished. There were no shades at the big windows. Some filing cabinets, a chair before the desk, and one behind it. In the latter sat a woman. Yes, a woman. Her thin white hair was drawn sleekly into a knot at the back of her head. Her face was round and pink; she wore eyeglasses attached to a black ribbon. She wore a tucked, mannish white shirtwaist, with links in the stiff cuffs and a small black tie under the collar. A woman.

"I . . ." John gulped. He had not expected a woman. "I'm John Mallory. I've just come to California. I want to enter school."

The woman nodded. "Sit down."

She took a card out of a desk drawer and unscrewed the cap from a thick red fountain pen. Her hands were strong, but smaller than a man's hands would be. Her voice was husky, she spoke shortly; but John was in no way afraid that she would be unkind. Mr. Crawford, the principal of the Brownsville school, had given him a letter. John took it out of his pocket and held it toward this woman. She swung around in her chair and held the unfolded sheet to the light. John looked at the little bronze statue of a football player that served as a paperweight.

"Humph!" John started a little at the sound. He could feel the package of lunch in his pocket. "You look older than fourteen."

"Yes. I know."

"Fine big boy — you'll catch up to your height. Play football?"

"No . . ." He hated to say "ma'am." Saying "sir" was different. He did not know why.

"My name's Miss Arndt."

"Yes, Miss Arndt. I — I never had time to play. I guess I could. I won't have time now, either. I work after school."

"Do you? Mr. Crawford says you do very well in school."

John made no reply. Again he was grateful that he had advanced so rapidly. "I'll have to graduate before I'm sixteen," he blurted.

Miss Arndt took off her glasses and looked at him. "Why?"

"I — Uncle Ben won't send me to school after I'm sixteen."

"Who's Uncle Ben?"

"I'm an orphan. He's my great-uncle. Mr. Ben Colby. He runs a filling station out on the highway."

"I see. You work for him?"

"He — Yes."

"Colby's is beyond the city limits," Miss Arndt commented.

John's heart shook. "Would there be tuition?"

"Ordinarily, yes. A small one."

"He — he won't pay tuition for me. He — he'll only send me because the law would make him. He — he's sort of old, and doesn't think a boy needs schooling. School."

"I see. You don't agree with him?"

"Oh, no! I want to go to school. I have to!"

"Have to, eh? That makes things different. About the tuition."

John was too shaken to wonder why it should. "Do I — Are the books and supplies furnished?"

"Yes. Nearly everything. Everything you'll need. Now, let's see. You're taking too heavy a course, John. Trying to do it in three years? I see. What are you preparing for?"

"I — probably I can't — I'd like to be a doctor."

"I see. That's a long study, and expensive."

John hung his head. "I know it. It will probably take me all my life; but I'll do as much as I can, when I can. Maybe things will be so I can work my way through the higher schools."

"Yes, maybe they will. You could do your premedic right here in Villa Franca."

"At the college? I wanted to ask about that."

Out in the halls John could have heard the scuffle of feet, the hum of voices which presaged the start of another school day. No one interrupted Miss Arndt. "It's not the best school in the world. I mean, it isn't Leland Stanford. But the chemistry department isn't bad; that will be the main thing you'll need for premedic. And the degree would be accepted almost anywhere. It's a township school, and the tuition would be small. A hundred dollars a year would send you to school."

John sighed. "I haven't a hundred cents."

"You could be saving something out of what your uncle pays you, maybe earn a little extra."

"No. He says I don't earn my food and clothes. He doesn't pay me any money."

Miss Arndt bent over the schedule card she was filling out. She made unintelligible sounds in her throat. "We have a cafeteria here," she said. "You could work behind the counter at noon. For a hot meal every day. We have to get several boys and girls to help us out. We don't make a profit on the lunchroom; we can't afford to pay them cash. It won't be necessary to have your uncle's permission."

John, angry at the betrayal, felt tears hot in his eyes. "Thanks," he murmured.

Miss Arndt handed him the card. "I don't think you'd better try a language until next fall, John. Get used to things here. You can begin it here, and go on with it in college." Her china-blue eyes twinkled behind her glasses.

"Yes," said John stanchly. "I could do that."

"If you walk four miles every day, you can be excused from gym. Take that hour for study. Save your carrying books home."

"Yes, thank you." There had been no need to explain his home conditions to this woman.

"Another thing. Are those the only clothes you have?"

John went hot, went cold. "Yes. I — Yes."

"Why I ask — about two years ago the boys here in school got funny. Wore overalls to school, and no socks. Wouldn't shave. It was pretty bad. We passed a ruling that overalls were prohibited."

John drew his lips back against his teeth. "I — as I told you — I have to go to school. But I won't have anything better than overalls."

The woman's kind, shrewd eyes held his steadily. "You won't?"

"No. After these are gone, I'll have only the station coveralls."

"You hate that, don't you, John?"

"It isn't their being *overalls* — yes, I hate it. I — but I *have* to go to school."

"Yes. Do you know where Dr. Hayes' place is, out on the highway? It's a half mile or so from Colby's."

John's eyes sparkled. "Yes! There's a dog!"

"There certainly is. Tut. King Tut, no less."

John laughed, and Miss Arndt smiled grimly. "Well, Jim Hayes is my brother-in-law. I'm old-maid aunt to his children. All grown now. But I live there. Our China-boy is getting old — he needs some help now and then. You could earn some school clothes that way — change at our house, if you'd care to."

"I — I don't know how to thank you."

"Don't try. Come on, now. I'll start you out in school."

6

During the next years John Mallory felt that he was two persons, had two separate bodies which he occupied turn and turn about. At the station, wearing the hated green coveralls, submitting to Uncle Ben's petty tyranny, working harder than his strength could sometimes endure, his hands were torn, his senses sickened with the debasing work he did. He felt humiliated there, inferior to the scrubbiest tourist who stopped for gas. He went about his duties — Uncle Ben saw to it that every hour was filled — with his head down between his shoulders, his voice restrained to the necessary monosyllables. He stayed away from the front of the station as much as possible. Once, the first weeks of school, a girl classmate had called out gaily to him from a passing car. Uncle Ben had used that incident for hours of sarcastic ranting. John, afterward, tried to keep fully occupied in the cabins and chicken runs.

He never got a penny from his uncle. Occasionally a tourist tipped him; once John found a dime on a cabin floor he was scrubbing. He hoarded these coins in a tobacco sack tied around his waist. He would have stolen, would have short-changed Uncle Ben — he had tempered some of his rigid ideas of honesty — but he had no access to the cash drawer. Uncle Ben trusted no one with money. John did not blame him; he would have cheated the old man if he could. It was blackly humiliating to know this, as humiliating as it was to wear the branded coveralls which were the only clothing provided for him. Now and then Uncle Ben grudgingly bought him a new pair of cheap, heavy work shoes. They were always too big, because John had outgrown the first pair before they fell off his feet. When John asked his uncle for money to have his hair cut, he was told to let Bertha do it. Dr. Hayes paid for John's barbering.

Dr. Hayes was kind in many ways. John knew that he stood ready to do much more than John was free to take. He was a little round man, with a sweet smile, and a mop of curly gray hair. John soon learned that he was the town's most successful, most popular, physician. He had a fine suite of offices in town, and was on the staff of the local hospital. But he seemed the most leisurely of persons. Almost every morning when John came in the side door to change his coveralls for the decent, plain clothes Miss Arndt secured for him, Dr. Hayes would call from the breakfast table: "That you, John? Come in and have a cup of cocoa. Wong knows I don't drink the damn stuff."

John knew, as well, that Wong made the cocoa especially for him. At first, shyness made him silently accept the cup of creamy goodness, and eat the wheat cakes or scrambled eggs. He had not known how to refuse. Besides, he was always so hungry. The big dinner he ate at school helped a lot, but Dr. Jim said a kid emptied his stomach within two hours. John told him solemnly that he surely did.

When John came back in the afternoon, Dr. Jim would be down at his office; but usually Wong came trotting along the hall with a couple of big apples, or a handful of molasses cookies. "Doc'r Jim say you maybe bring in li'l wood fireplace." Or, "Doc'r Jim say you give Tut big play. He all time too damn fresh."

The small tasks John performed at Hayes' were always of a nature to permit his prompt arrival at the station. It was understood that Uncle Ben clocked his return from school. John lived in constant fear that Uncle Ben would discover his double life. He grew sick at the thought that he might someday be deprived of all this — his breakfasts in the big, sunny dining room, his friendship with Dr. Jim and Miss Arndt. They treated him as if he were a real person, listened with respect to what he had to say. His small triumphs at school made them proud. Miss Lillie's tart tongue meant nothing — she scolded John and Dr. Jim with equal fervor. These two elderly people served to bolster the boy's self-respect, which conditions at the station might have undermined. They preserved John's belief in decent men and women.

Once Tut's sharp teeth tore a long rent in John's coveralls. He mended it as best he could, but Uncle Ben saw the tear. John told him, only, that a dog had done it.

"Whose dog?"

"One — down the highway a piece."

"That big brute of Hayes', I expect. Ever he comes around here I'll shoot him at sight. Guess you'll have to eat light this week to make up that suit."

He meant that John would have no supper except, perhaps, a hard, stale roll. John could bear that, but he was swept with fear lest sometime Tut might follow him home. Uncle Ben must not find out about Hayes! He must not.

When, at the beginning of vacation, Dr. Jim offered John a home for his usefulness about the place, John bit his lip and refused. "I want to, Dr. Jim. You'll never know how much I want to. But — he's my guardian. I'm afraid he could make me stay with him, and I'd rather he didn't know about you. About the things you do for me."

Dr. Jim looked at the boy long and steadily. "I understand, John. If he ever abuses you, let me know, will you?"

John agreed, miserably ashamed that even Dr. Jim should have to know about the festering sore that was his Uncle Ben. He hated to make that decision. He felt that heaven itself would be approached if he could have come to live in the big frame house, be always with these gracious, kindly people. But he knew that Uncle Ben must, indeed, have some legal claim upon him, else Dr. Jim would have protested John's decision to stay at the station.

7

School was fine. If there were any snobbish reaction to his relationship with Ben Colby, John was never aware of it. His fine scholarship was quickly recognized in the classrooms. He had no time for clubs or sports. Doing without these things, which, as a normal boy, he wanted so achingly, cruelly disciplined his spirit. His biggest recreation was the noon hour. John was nothing of a snob; but, even so, he quickly saw that a job behind the lunch counter was a coveted position. The boys and girls who worked there were ones who needed the little financial boost, but they were also attractive people. John shared his post behind the milk bottles and cups of cocoa with the vice-president of the senior class, Betty Mason, a pretty, dark-haired girl who lived in Villa Franca because her father "had lungs." Betty told John it was a shame he could not get to some of the school parties. She asked his advice about her "dates." She accepted his judgment, without question, on who was a "good guy" and who a "sad pill." John wished he could have had dates with Betty. Big for his age, he had all the normal adolescent's longings and dreams. He wanted to know girls. Not the sort who came to the station cabins. Some of them were not so bad, but their being at the station revolted him. He rejected anything connected with the hated place.

John might have been popular. He got to know everybody there at the lunch counter. Their friendly greetings were as comforting, as sustaining, as the big trayful of lunch he sat down to the last ten minutes of noon hour. Soup, liver and bacon, a baked potato. Pineapple salad, cup custard, and a bottle of milk. John knew how good and nourishing the food was. When he heard boys and girls complain of the things offered on the day's menu, or saw them leave food on their plates, he wished he might be able to tell them how hungry he got over Saturday and Sunday, how he was dreading the long summer vacation with a dread that clutched at the pit of his stomach. He wondered, sometimes, if he had not come to think food unduly important. He suspected that food was one thing you valued most when you did not have it.

8

John, in his isolation from true companionship, was having a lot of time to think these days. Problems that might not have appeared to him if he had maintained his safe, dull life in Brownsville now showed up in his brain. Working in the chicken pens, raking the fine gravel of the runs, whitewashing the low walls, scrubbing the floor of an empty cabin, John had plenty of time to consider things. Why people were as they were — why some of the tourists made the services John gave them a shameful, degrading thing; why some could accept the same service and seem grateful for it, could make John feel that he was rendering it as a part of a manly duty and job; why, at school, one teacher seemed to draw so much more out of a class than another could do. He wondered about differences of opinion on the same subject. About differences of likes and dislikes in food. Did food taste the same to all palates? Was salt the same sort of salt on everyone's tongue? How could anyone know surely that it was? He wondered about a friend of his who was color-blind. Dick was quite frank about his distinction, and freely answered John's interested questions. John wondered if, perhaps, the lenses of the eye in a color-blind person were not finer, did not filter light rays more completely, than those of the ordinary eye. In shades of purple and brown, Dick could distinguish red and green tones that seemed negligible to John.

Uncomfortable in his man-made surroundings, dreading the hours he must spend in his airless bed cubby and the minutes in the grease-saturated lunchroom, John grew to a fuller appreciation of nature's gift to mankind. He wondered at the winter in Villa Franca, the clear, thin air, the warm, glistening sunlight by day, the snappy, tingling starlight after dark. In March, when the rains began, they, too, were a delight to him. They were not like the rains of Iowa. They lasted longer, for one thing. They were so very — so very *wet*. Moisture seemed to come up from the ground as well as down from the sky. There was no lightning or thunder. Just wetness everywhere. The distant mountains disappeared completely; little streams of water ran along the edges of the highway. None of these Californians complained of the rain. They counted each recorded inch as a miser counts another dollar put away. And when the rain stopped, the sky was gorgeously blue again, with fleets of clouds sailing overhead, all canvas-spread to the warm breeze. The stars came out again at night, close and intimate. The roadside, all untended fields, burst into bloom — little bright flowers that made a warm, smiley feeling touch John's heart. The truck gardens were bursting with greenness.

John had come to know, and nod to, the Italian families who lived along the road. Dirty, lazy dagos, Uncle Ben called them. John knew they were nothing of the sort. He knew that the poorest of these people worked harder than did Uncle Ben, lived a much warmer, happier life.

It was among these people that John achieved his first patient. One morning he was hailed by one of the women as he walked by on his way to school. Her little boy had somehow caught his leg under a gasoline drum which had rolled off its supports. John rescued the child, and fetched Dr. Jim.

He always thought of the Alberni boy as his first "case." All the time the child's leg was in a cast, he would stop in for a minute each morning. Dr. Jim must have thought something of that sort, too. When the Albernis paid their bill, which they did promptly, being thrifty folk, and prideful, Dr. Jim gave John two crisp one-dollar bills.

"Your share as consultant," he said brusquely.

John felt queer. "I —"

"Don't argue with me, John!"

John laughed. He was not afraid of Dr. Jim when he shouted. "I — I wouldn't. I just wondered where I could keep these. Uncle Ben —"

"Take 'em, eh?"

"He might. He'd think they belonged to him."

Dr. Jim looked around the big dining room. Got up, his napkin stuck between the buttons of his vest and trailing out behind him like a small sail. At a look, John followed him into the darkened living room. Dr. Jim took a vaselike object from the far end of the mantel. It was urn-shaped, and made out of polished wood. He showed John how the top unscrewed, leaving a small egg-shaped opening within.

"My boy used to keep things in here he didn't want his sister to find. You might use it for a bank. It won't bear interest, and it might burn if the house did. On the other hand, you could put your money into the bank downtown; and if the officers were scamps, you might lose it there. So take your pick, fire or human nature."

When Belle sent John five dollars the next Christmas, he put it away in the wooden vase. The occasional coins he secured at the station went into his cache. He had few pressing needs for money. The main thing was to save for a year at college. Two years. Three. Slowly he would somehow get his degree.

9

If John had retained any doubts about Uncle Ben's actual intelligence, they would have been dispelled during the months of summer vacation. During those long three months of summer, no longer eating the good food provided at Dr. Jim's and at the cafeteria, denied milk, and even fruit which was so cheap in this abundant land, and working as hard as he did, John lost weight quickly, his cheeks became hollow, and he looked taller even than he actually was. It seemed absurd that Uncle Ben should not notice the change, nor seek a reason for it.

John wondered how Bertha stayed so fat. He knew that she ate a large share of the canned beans or corned-beef hash she opened and heated for him and Uncle Ben. He knew that she fried the chicken giblets and ate them herself. Once in a while he would see her drink pop, with some generous tourist paying for it. Uncle Ben kept a close check on the candy bars and peanuts, but perhaps he gave Bertha some of these delicacies.

Bertha was still friendly, but not quite so much so as she had been at first. She probably was more than half convinced that John's ignoring of her advances was due to distaste rather than innocence. John's mother had always called the boy squeamish. The more filth he worked with, the more fastidious he became. Because his hands must so often handle the muck of the chicken yards, must be in soapy scrub water so much, he was overly particular about bathing his body and brushing his teeth. He shamelessly stole baking soda and salt from the kitchen for the latter rite, and saved bits of toilet soap left behind by tourists as carefully as he saved his pennies in Dr. Jim's urn. Bertha had no charm for him. The fact that she could endure companionship with Uncle Ben made her repulsive to John.

John also came to despise the tourists because they would listen to, and tolerate, Uncle Ben. Perhaps the old fool's wrinkled face, his small gray eyes that seemed to smile, fooled these casual acquaintances for the duration of their brief stays. Perhaps, too, the time was too short, or their own knowledge too superficial, for them to detect the spurious nature of Uncle Ben's freely voiced wisdom.

Where, John asked, emphasizing his thoughts with vicious scrapes at the rods of the chicken roosts, where did Uncle Ben get all his information? Where had he learned so much about road engineering? Because he ran a second-rate filling station on a road? Where had he acquired so much authoritative knowledge about the Japanese menace to the Pacific coast? Because for forty years he had clerked in a grocery store in San Francisco? He had never traveled, he did not read, he had nothing but the most elementary of educations. Why should such a man set himself up as an authority on every matter from medicine to metaphysics? Why should other people listen to his empty-headed pronouncements?

One thing was sure. John was always going to

be sure of his facts before he would set out to instruct and inform others.

10

Summer went by, and it was September again. John returned to school without raising the issue with Uncle Ben. The old man contented himself with sarcastic remarks about its being a poor house that could not support one gentleman. He hoped his educated nephew did not learn so much that he would not know how to scrub a floor or mix mash for the chickens. John was painfully acquiring a hard shell of indifference against Uncle Ben. His irony slid off the boy's consciousness like water off a tar roof.

John resumed his friendship with Dr. Jim and Miss Arndt and Tut and Wong with a joy that was uncomfortably close to tears. Dr. Jim noticed how thin the boy was, made him come up to his office after the first day of school, take off his shirt, and let the doctor thump and listen to his chest. Made him get on the scales, and swore at the reading.

"Doesn't he feed you, son?"

"Yes. Not — He says I eat as much as I'm worth. That's not an awful lot."

School went by too fast that year. John had a horrible, crawling fear that it was to be his last year of school. He tried to clutch at the speeding days and make them last. His classmates talked of college and jobs. One boy was pretty sure of an appointment to Annapolis. Some of the boys were going to Stanford or Berkeley. Dick Mason was going to specialize in geology at the Villa Franca college; most of the class would continue there. Ray Small's father was going to make him study medicine. Ray was rebellious; he wanted to work at one of the new airports, study aviation. Dosing roupy chickens, John toyed with the idea of changing places with Ray.

Premedic, medical school. At least a year's internship. Nine years. White coats, rubber gloves, the tingling smell of iodine and ether which sometimes clung to Dr. Jim. Of such things is Elysium made. John had nearly ten dollars saved in his urn. The first semester's tuition would be fifty dollars. There would be books to buy. Uncle Ben was already talking of the things John could do around the station when he no longer "wasted eight hours a day at school paid for by the sweat and self-denial of hard-working taxpayers." Small hope that Uncle Ben would even furnish *time* for John to go on to school.

Perhaps because they knew how hopeless the project would be, Dr. Jim and Miss Arndt said no more about college to John. John treasured their continued kindness and friendship as he treasured the things he was learning in school, to be remembered and thought about when his whole life became a waste of chickens and splintery cabin floors.

Graduation time drew near. John was to be given Senior Honors; but John would not be on the stage to receive them with his diploma, just as he would not attend the Junior-Senior Banquet nor the final Senior Dance. It hurt, not having all these things. He wanted to have them, to have a best girl; wanted to buy her sodas at the Greek's, to kiss her after a class party. He wanted those things just as he had wanted to go out for football, and to play tennis on the hot, bright courts. He wanted to dance with girls in frilly dresses; he wanted to be chums with Dick Mason, going home with him after school, sitting with him through long spring evenings, talking.

John could have none of these things. He could not let himself think about them too much. He was grateful to Dr. Jim and Miss Arndt that they never tried to secure these impossible things for him; did not encourage him to try for them, to kick against the pricks.

John might have braved Uncle Ben's wrath and sarcasm in order to graduate. But, somehow, he could not bring himself to sit there on the platform, looked at by the eyes of the town. The school kids had grown used to Ben Colby's nephew. But their parents would look at him curiously, and would probably tell one another that the fine garments he wore belonged to Jim Hayes' son-in-law. John could not go out and flaunt himself on a brightly lighted stage, parade himself across that platform when his name was called.

He could not tell Miss Arndt that he would not be there. His throat swelled with shame, and probably tears, at the mere thought of doing so and having to face her shrewd, understanding blue eyes. It would seem as if he made a bid for further pity and help. He just would not go.

At rehearsal he took his place in the procession and sat in the chair marked with his name. His absence Friday night would make Dick walk alone, and his empty chair would show up like a pimple on a boy's nose. Miss Arndt would not notice his absence until she had read his name aloud, and there would be a horrible empty pause. People would nod and look at one another. That would be bad.

John must write a note and give it to Wong to deliver to Miss Arndt at supper, too late for her to hunt him but in time for her to adjust things at the auditorium. He would try, too, in the note, to thank Miss Arndt and the doctor for all they had done. He felt like bawling to realize that his friendship with them was over.

11

Wong gave Miss Lillie the little folded paper when she came downstairs, dressed for the evening's festivities. Her frock was of heavy white silk — silk sent to her by Dr. Jim's son, Robert, who was a surgeon in a Chinese hospital. The blouse was as plain, as severely tucked and collared, as the starched shirtwaists she wore to school; the skirt was as tubular, as much like a pair of man's trousers, as a woman's skirt may be. That the costume was of silk, that her Oxfords were of white buck, was the only concession she made to the convention of dressing for evening.

She adjusted her glasses and stepped out upon the porch to read the note. She read it twice, her face flushing a bright pink. She took off her glasses and polished them with her large white handkerchief. She went up the broad stairs again, and directly into her brother-in-law's room.

Dr. Jim, the tails of his white shirt hanging halfway to his knees, was struggling with a tight buttonhole. "Lillie? You might knock."

"Why? I never have knocked at your door. I haven't been shocked yet. Here, I'll fix that — you'll get it all smudged."

"Hands . . . clean . . ." Dr. Jim gasped, tipping back his head so that she could adjust the pesky thing. "What's the matter?"

"Hold still. Had a note from John. He's not coming tonight."

"Not — going to graduate? John?"

"He'll get his diploma. He knows that. But — here. Read it."

Dr. Jim unfolded and read the note, Miss Arndt peering over his shoulder.

Dear Miss Arndt:

I am very sorry to tell you that circumstances beyond my control make it impossible for me to attend the graduation exercises tonight. I desire to take this opportunity to thank you and Dr. Hayes for your many favors during the past eighteen months. I hope I shall see you both from time to time in the future.

Very sincerely yours,
John Mallory.

Dr. Jim coughed. He took off his spectacles and wiped them. He coughed again. He started for the bathroom, muttering that he needed a glass of water. Miss Arndt sat down in his old leather rocking chair and waited.

"That's the way I feel," she said when he returned.

"If he were my son . . ."

"Get dressed. We haven't a lot of time. Wong will be waiting for us. He isn't your son. Your son is in China. And your daughter is a society lady in Glendale. John Mallory is the grandson of that —"

"Nephew. Grandnephew."

"Just as bad."

"It isn't. Blood strain much thinner."

"I don't want to cast any aspersions on John's grandmother, but I'd bet John hasn't a drop of old Colby's blood."

Dr. Jim snorted. Glared suspiciously at the watch he was winding, and tucked it into his pocket. Picked up his coat and put it on. "Let's go down to supper."

Wong, in his white coat, was standing patiently at the dining-room door. "Suppah all velly damn spoil," he said cheerfully. "Miss Lil' all doll."

"Miss Lillie's what? What the devil are you trying to say, Wong?"

"He means I'm dressed up. Dolled up. You don't keep abreast of modern slang, Jim."

"Not as Wong talks it, I don't. What the devil is this, Wong?"

Wong looked amazed. "Sweet bleads. Same as Doc'r bring home. Only salad, not cleamed. So all damn hot."

Miss Arndt nodded to him. "That's a fine idea, Wong. Dr. Jim should eat more salads."

"Don't like mayonnaise. Looks like —"

"Jim! If you only wouldn't bring your profession to the table! You needn't eat the mayonnaise. Now. What about John?"

Dr. Jim made a great business of selecting and buttering a slice of bread. He pushed the mayonnaise off his salad and picked out all the bits of green pepper. He put milk and sugar into his coffee and stirred it around and around. Miss Arndt watched him as she would have watched a Freshman trying to evade some charge of misdemeanor.

"I — I guess you know how I feel about John, Lillie."

"I think I do. Tell me — why isn't he sitting with us here this very minute? Living in this house?"

"I'd like it well enough," Dr. Jim said slowly. "He's a fine boy. Smart. A gentleman, and he'll make a fine doctor someday."

"He won't, cleaning chicken roosts for Ben Colby."

"No-o."

"Couldn't we adopt the boy, Jim? He's only sixteen."

"We can't so long as Ben Colby gives him a home."

"Hah!"

"Technically it is a home. Or unless John would bring charges of neglect and cruelty."

"Last fall, when he came back to school, the boy was half-starved."

"He was. But he didn't say he'd been hungry."

"No. He never says one word against his uncle. But you and I know —"

"What all Villa Franca knows. That truth isn't a pretty spot in John's consciousness, Lillie."

"He's as mean as — as — Couldn't we bribe him to give us John?"

"Not if he thought we wanted John very badly. I offered John a home last year. He refused."

"But you didn't go to the uncle."

"If I had, and he'd refused, it would have ended anything we might have been able to do for the boy, Lillie."

"Ye-es. Is he hard up? Ben Colby, I mean."

"I don't know. He has the reputation of being close. Miserly. Certainly he doesn't waste anything on John. But old man Peters told me —"

"Peters!"

"He's a drunkard, and a fool, but he does know Ben Colby. He says Colby is a sucker for any invention or wildcat stock a tourist may mention to him. Someday, he thinks, he'll be a millionaire. Meanwhile he hasn't much cash on hand."

"He sounds crazy."

"He is crazy. Not asylum-crazy, just off balance. I suspect John knows that better than you or I do."

"You'd think he'd run off."

"He might, some day. But John is a shrewd boy. He knows that the station is at least a base of operation, a place from which he may be able to realize his ambitions. Unless things get too thick . . ."

"I hate his living there. He works too hard. His hands are always scarred and torn. That mean old man, and that fat woman — Something will happen to John. It would be our fault."

"The very distaste for the place, the things he sees there, will protect John's spirit, Lillie. Physically he's a strong boy."

"But his school — his future —"

"Yes. That must be taken care of. I'll have to figure a way."

"I have the money, if you haven't."

Dr. Jim smiled at her. "We both have it. And the desire to finance John's education. But I'm thinking of the boy. I do that, more and more, as I grow older. See the other fellow's side. You and I could make a doctor out of John, and feel good about doing it. But you know the boy. He's been taught that he must work hard for a little. If we offer him tuition and books and time for his schooling, he may take them. The temptation will be great. But he'll know that, sometime, he'd have to repay the debt."

"Not to me, he wouldn't."

"He would to anybody. John Mallory is a person who can't take a gift. No such thing exists in his life. You've seen that. You saw it when you figured out a way for him to earn the secondhand clothes you give him."

Miss Lillie nodded, her pink face stern.

"Well, anything we do for John we'll have to wangle in much the same way. It won't be easy. I think, without any doubt, I can get him a scholarship at the college. But the time, the freedom — that's the important, and the difficult, thing. We'll have to buy that somehow from Ben Colby. He isn't obliged to give John any more schooling, and the old duffer knows it. But I'll find a way if I have to blackmail him."

Miss Arndt got up from the table, smoothed the front of her white skirt. "I must be getting along. Blackmail might not be a bad idea. There isn't anything I wouldn't do for John."

"I know. But, just as I say, ready as we are to give — we don't want to burden the boy's future with a debt to us. Not any sort of debt. Sometimes, you know, a kindness can be too great. We'll help John where we can — offer him the opportunities our wider experience knows about. He wouldn't be John if he didn't want to pay his own way, stand on his own feet. He'll get to the top. Don't you worry."

Chapter Four

John was scrubbing the washhouse the day Dr. Jim drove up to the filling station. He saw the coupé hesitate at the pumps, then come on around the driveway that the cabin patrons used. John recognized Dr. Jim's car. He could not believe that Dr. Jim was in it. His first impulse was to go out and greet the doctor. Perhaps something was wrong at home. He saw Uncle Ben go slowly toward the car. John dropped to his knees again, dipped his hands into the pail of dirty water. Better wait. If Dr. Jim wanted him, he would be called. John would finish here, then get about painting the chicken houses. He had not had much breakfast. The smell of this place made him dizzy.

He was cleaning chickens, still worrying about Dr. Jim's long visit with Uncle Ben, when — so swiftly that John was not aware of his approach and could do no more than rise to his feet — Dr. Jim stood fairly over him. Dr. Jim was able to wink elaborately at John before Ben Colby came shuffling up. John's lips turned up a little at one corner, and his eyes glinted. He made no other sign.

"This is my niece's boy, John," Uncle Ben explained to Dr. Jim.

"How are you, John?" said the doctor gravely.

"Quite well, thank you."

In contrast to Ben Colby's thin whine, the boy's voice struck Dr. Jim as that of a gentleman. Firm, resonant, without being at all loud.

"Dr. Hayes wants about six chickens to take home with him, John," Uncle Ben went on importantly.

John looked down at the limp bodies on the newspaper he had spread out on the step.

"I'll take live ones," Dr. Jim said. "My China-boy can clean them."

"I'll be glad to do it, sir."

"I wouldn't be able to use them all at once. Better get me live ones."

"Yes, sir. Fryers?" He looked at Uncle Ben.

"Best we got," said Uncle Ben. "I'm gettin' rid of the chickens fast as I can. The dang things stink so it drives off trade. Ain't goin' to mess with lunches no more."

John stared at him. What on earth . . .

"I'm goin' to fire Bertha, too," the old man chuckled. "Yes, sir. Be quite a change around here. Build some more cabins. You'll have a chance to learn the carpenter trade, John. I always say, Doc, if a boy has a trade . . ."

John looked at his hands. The fingertips were rough and calloused. He had a hard streak of scar tissue along the end of one, where his knife had slipped and cut to the bone. Cleaning chickens was no work for a boy who meant to be a surgeon. Carpenter work, for a novice, would be little better. Dr. Jim was talking.

". . . too big a boy to be cleaning chickens and scrubbing floors for his keep, Mr. Colby. My sister-in-law — she's principal of the high school — told me that your nephew was a bright boy. I could get him a job in town at a man's wages. Are you going on to college, John? At the hospital we usually have one of the students taking care of the night desk."

John looked at him helplessly. The color came and went in his cheeks. What was he supposed to answer? He was new at this business of double talk.

Uncle Ben spoke up hastily. "I guess John ain't got no kick coming. I took him in when he hadn't any home. I've fed him, and give him food and shelter. I won't turn him out on the town, nor on you neither, Doc, as long as he works hard and seems to try to do right."

Uncle Ben's voice sounded angry, hurried, and a little fearful. John looked at Dr. Jim. His blue eyes seemed to hold reassurance. John drew a deep breath. Whatever it was Dr. Jim was up to, John could trust him. "I'll go get the chickens," he said quietly.

2

John stood and watched the old coupé until it disappeared down the road. Somehow he was frightened. He felt as if his world had changed. How, he did not just know. For so long he had dreaded a meeting between Dr. Jim and Uncle

Ben that its happening meant disaster of some sort. That the catastrophe was not immediately evident made it all the more frightening. He could feel undercurrents push against him. The ground beneath his feet trembled and slipped; he did not know where firmness and stability lay. He felt the burden of his youth, the shackles of his inexperience, press upon him. What should he do? What could he do, now, for John Mallory? Did these older men, behind their masks of friendliness for each other, expect him to see the game they played? Was he, too, a player? If so, what was his move?

He looked up and met Uncle Ben's small twinkly eyes. They were like those of the rats that looked at John from the corners of the chicken houses. "Doc Hayes is a big bug in these parts, John. It don't never hurt you to be nice to the big bugs."

"I — suppose not, Uncle Ben."

"I guess Dr. Hayes is a right smart man. Town talks about him and his sister-in-law living together in that big house, but maybe there ain't no harm in it. An' if there is, I guess Doc ain't no more nor human. You don't know nothin' about sech things, John. Leastways, I hope you don't. Poor boy, and all. But come a man gets able to support himself it's natural he wants a woman around. Doc's wife died about fifteen years ago, I hear. Her sister had been livin' there with the family. It wasn't much mor'n natural Doc should keep her there instead of takin' up with somebody else. I guess he's a real busy man. I do think, though, they coulda found time to git married."

John looked at his uncle. He felt anger and disgust swell in his throat, set the blood in his brain on fire. The muscles in his upper arm tightened, and he saw his right hand knot into a hard, hammerlike fist, lift itself . . .

Uncle Ben saw it, too. He stepped back, and his pipe fell to the ground. He bent over and picked it up with fumbling fingers. He mumbled something in his throat and scuttled away. John stood on the cinders and looked at his hand. The knuckles were white and hard; the cords in his brown forearm were like wire rope. Slowly he opened the fingers and looked at them. He was strong. He could have struck his uncle. Killed him, perhaps. Sweat broke out on his forehead. He had not known that he could get so angry, that the muscles of his body would respond to any such reflex action as to . . .

Uncle Ben had been frightened. John laughed — a short, ugly sound back in his throat — to remember those trembling fingers, those hurrying old feet. John leaned against the tree and laughed aloud. A clear, ringing, hearty laugh — as a man laughs when he has gone a struggling, climbing journey and, at the end of it, drops his heavy pack from his shoulders, sees before him an open path. John Mallory never again must know the fear, the craven indecision of childhood. He was not free. Few people in this crowded world are really free. But he had attained a man's right to respect and consideration, even though that demand be backed only by a strong right fist.

He went back to the station and began to clean up the mess of feathers from the chickens he had picked. Uncle Ben and Bertha were quarreling. John could hear them through the thin walls of their bedroom. In spite of himself, John's thoughts contrasted that blowzy apartment — its cheap iron bed with dust in rolls beneath it, Bertha's dirty hairbrush and the movie magazines lying around — with the sleeping quarters at Dr. Jim's. Dr. Jim slept out on a screened porch on a high iron bed with box springs. Wong put fresh sheets on it every day, and the blankets were khaki-colored, scratchy woolen.

Miss Arndt had a big room on the south side of the house, with windows on three sides shaded by Venetian blinds whose varnish had been scrubbed to a dull gold softness. Her walnut bed stood in an alcove; the spread was a gay India print of the loveliest colors John had ever seen. The walls of her room were a solid mass of books. Old books, new books, novels, histories, nonsense verse. Bright bindings and gay jackets stood in friendly harmony with rubbed, hand-tooled covers.

Dr. Jim's whole house was filled with warmth and sunshine and cleanliness. Stretches of bare, polished floors. Faded colors of a chintz-covered chair. A jade bowl on a mahogany table. Roses spilling out of a blue pottery pitcher. A wood fire snapping on a wide, swept hearth.

Such were the things John wanted. Wanted in his life. Not just to see and touch; he wanted to have them for his own, to live with them. He wanted to know about music, to know it thoroughly and completely. He wanted to develop his own judgment and taste about it. He wanted familiarity with all fine things. Ridiculous things for a boy in his position to dream of. He knew that, just as he knew how ridiculous it was for him to dream of a John Mallory who wore a surgeon's gown and mask and worked with skill under the blue lights of an operating room. But he wanted to be such a surgeon, and he wanted to know about some of the fine things he had read of in his books at school. What was a Sarouk rug? What was Coleport china, and Alençon lace? He wanted to see and touch these things. He wanted fineness and beauty in his life with a desire that ached in his bones like fever.

3

For a week strange things happened at the filling station. John wondered if Uncle Ben had sold the place. Or had he gone a little mad? That last thought came when he saw Uncle Ben, after hours of noisy quarreling with Bertha, give the woman some money — several bills taken from the dirty roll of them Uncle Ben kept in his shirt pocket. John was called in to help Bertha pack her belongings into pasteboard boxes. He paid little attention to her tearful recriminations of his uncle. He, too, wondered where she would go now. What she could do. She was not young. She was fat and untidy. She was not much of a cook. What did women of her sort do with their lives? John did not know, just as he had never known what thoughts filled Bertha's head when she was working. When John worked, his thoughts whirled. Big thoughts, little thoughts. How much energy was there behind the patience of the men who, for centuries, had studied and charted the stars? Why did chickens and birds need to tilt their heads back when they drank water, yet seem able to swallow food in the ordinary, muscular way? What things did Bertha think about?

Uncle Ben secured her a lift to town on an oil truck. John had a last glimpse of her ponderous limbs climbing into the high seat. Uncle Ben bade him take down the sign advertising fried chicken. After this, the station would sell only packaged foods. He went on endlessly about the dangers a restaurant proprietor was exposed to. Ptomaine, actual or imagined, was a risky thing to monkey with. They would sell the big coffee urn. Sell the chickens. Uncle Ben hunted up a newspaper to find the price quoted on chickens. A day or two later a truck drove up and took all the silly, screeching birds away. John was glad to see the last of them. Whatever lay ahead could not be worse than chickens.

Then men came and talked to Uncle Ben,

and measured, and walked around, and talked again. John had been set to tend pump while these negotiations were carried on. Uncle Ben was figuring on new cabins and washhouses. He wanted the chicken pens and the old washhouse torn down, the lumber used in the new buildings. It took a lot of talk. The various men who came out to talk to Uncle Ben never failed to tell John, as they drove away, that old Ben Colby was a close trader. They seemed, grudgingly, to admire the quality. John grimly endured his uncle. He had lost all ability to grant him any virtue.

In the evenings Uncle Ben drew strange pictures on odd bits of paper. Plans for the new cabins, he told John. As well as the boy could judge, they were to consist of pairs of cabins, built in a fond semblance of towers, joined by an arched shelter for a car. There was to be a semicircle of these buildings with a square, tessellated washhouse at either extremity. Then, in the foreground of the horseshoe was to be a big building. It was to contain a kitchen and a central recreation room, and was to be marked with four towers. The buildings were to be of stucco, then showered, so John gathered, with stones. The stones were important. Loads of them began to be delivered at once. John was set to work with hammer and crowbar to tear down the chicken runs and houses. The ground, he was told, would be sprinkled with lime and covered with fresh gravel. Uncle Ben said he was going to plant some young trees to make a grove. John was to build an outdoor fireplace. They were about to encourage tourists who wanted to sleep in their own tents. Occasionally a car would come along with a crude excrescence hitched on behind. Trailers, these things were called, some of them pretty ingenious in their housekeeping arrangements.

One day John was called to unload a mass of canvas and short poles from a truck. Tents, Uncle Ben told him. Bought, secondhand, from a Boy Scout troop. John was to put them in order, set one up and begin sleeping in it. That way people would know this station was a good place for tent tourists to stop.

John's tent was small. He set the poles carefully, laced the sides strongly. He scrubbed the ground sheet and bleached it in the hot sun. When he moved his canvas cot out of the lean-to into the warm canvas room, he felt that some hidden power was working for his personal good. Whatever Uncle Ben had up his sleeve to do, there would be compensations. He took some boards from the chicken pens and made himself a rough table. Placed on it his razor and old toothbrush, and his broken comb. Last winter one of the washhouse mirrors had been broken. Uncle Ben had mourned it for a week. Still mentioned the disaster. John had salvaged a corner of the glass and now, after some effort, managed to fix it to the wall of his tent. He made his bed neatly, surveyed his new home with pride.

At night he could lift the door curtain, watch the stars.

Uncle Ben offered no comment on John's new home, nor did he, in John's presence, enter the tent. Uncle Ben was a man of affairs these days. Busy, bustling, important. For want of better audience — after the tourists had withdrawn to their cabins for the night — he would tell John something of his plans.

"Business warrants it," he told John, "I'll put me in a pit and do car greasing."

"You'd have to have a helper for that," John told him.

"You could do it."

"That work takes an expert. I'm not very good at mechanics."

"An' don't want to get your hands dirty," Uncle Ben sneered. John looked down at his hands. "A boy dependent on me for his food and shelter oughta be willing to do most anything I ask him to."

"It isn't a question of being willing, Uncle Ben. I just don't think I'd make a good mechanic." He was remembering what Dr. Hayes had said about his being able to earn a man's wages. "Perhaps I could get a job somewhere, and you could get a mechanic for what you pay me."

He had not intended sarcasm, but his words sounded that way. Still, the statement was fair enough. He drew his body erect and faced his uncle. Let him be angry.

John was aware of himself as he stood there

under the bright lights of the pumps. Aware of his tall, lean body; his strong, straight limbs; his slim hips; his firm, hard waist. His shoulders, his arms, his strong and big-knuckled fingers. He was aware of his feet in the heavy, clumsy shoes, his garments against his skin. He felt his thick crest of dark hair, his lean cheeks, his deep-set gray eyes.

Uncle Ben was looking at him curiously. "Well, if that ain't gratitude for you."

"I don't know whether I owe you gratitude or not, Uncle Ben. I feel that I've earned everything you have given me. And now —"

A car drove up and pulled into the station. John went over to the driver, a young woman. Dark hair, pretty white teeth. She wore a thin sweater of a soft, light green.

Her voice was cool and clear. She was like one of the pictures cigarette companies pasted to the billboards along the highway. Lovely, impersonal, unreal. John took the hose and filled the gas tank. He took a cloth out of his back pocket and wiped the windshield. He did not look at the girl, who was watching him. He put water into the radiator and opened the shiny black hood.

What was it he was about to demand of Uncle Ben? Wages? School? What was it he wanted? Manhood and a recognition of his personality, but he must not be vague and foolish-sounding. Uncle Ben must need to respect his demand, whatever it would be. John must make it clear that he was asking no favor, just the right to get what he could earn.

The girl gave him a five-dollar bill. John handed it to Uncle Ben. He was not allowed to open the cash register. But he took the change and went back to the car. The girl took the bills, left the change in the palm of his hand. Her fingertips brushed his hand as she gathered up the money. John looked at her. She smiled. His eyes held steady.

"Thank you," he said gravely.

"O.K." She lifted a slim little hand in a gesture of farewell, a gesture which was friendly. John put his hand down into his pocket. The coins jingled a little.

"She tip you?" Uncle Ben asked suspiciously.

"Yes. Thirteen cents."

"Going to keep it, are you?"

John hung the hose more firmly on the hook. "Yes. I earned it. She wouldn't have tipped you."

That was true. The tip had been for John's youth and his clean good looks. Uncle Ben sat down in his chair and tilted it back against the wall. John took the broom and began to sweep the platform.

"So you think you're a man, eh?" asked Uncle Ben.

"Yes. At least, I think I'm worth more than the five dollars you claim to spend on my food and clothes each week."

"You get your bed."

"Even so. I knew a boy at school who earned seven dollars a week working at a drugstore after school and on Saturdays. And he didn't work as hard as I do."

"You're a great grumbler, John."

That was untrue. John kicked at a lump of sticky dirt with the toe of his shoe.

"A poor boy can't be afraid of hard work."

"It isn't the hard work, Uncle Ben. I just think I earn more than you give me. Or I could, somewhere else."

"Oh. You're remembering what Dr. Hayes said to ye, ain't ye?"

"Yes. Partly that."

"You think 'cause a pretty girl looks at you wise, you're a man. Well, you ain't. You're just a half-baked boy, no experience, no training. What could you do to earn a living? Tell me that, huh?"

"Any number of things. I could pick fruit for more than I get here. But, Uncle Ben, if you'd pay me — even a little — so that I could save it . . ."

"What for?"

"I want to go to school. To college."

"Oh. So that's it. On my time, huh?"

"It wouldn't take any more time than I used for high school. I'd work hard before and after school." His voice shook, and he stopped. Uncle Ben must not know how much he wanted this thing. Perhaps he could get a scholarship. If Uncle Ben got ugly, he would run off. Make a living somehow.

Uncle Ben took out his pocketknife. The handle was shaped like a woman's leg, and there was a picture of a naked girl printed on it. A poor knife, but it did to scrape a pipe bowl. John watched him, his throat dry. "I've almost a notion to let ye try to earn your own way, John," the old man said in his breathless, whispering voice. "You think I ben treatin' you hard. Well, I don't sleep in no bed of roses my own self. This station jest about makes a livin' for the two of us. And then there's the indebtedness to pay off. Now, I've borrowed more to make these improvements. Figger, with luck, I'll do that another five years or so. But I won't if I have to pay you big wages."

"I'm not asking . . ."

"You're asking cash, ain't ye?"

"Well — yes."

"And cash is what I'm scarce on, John. But I'll tell you what I'll do. You're a good smart boy. We don't always see eye to eye; but I'll give it to you, you're smart. All Colbys is smart. Well. You know I'm going in debt about three thousand dollars right now to improve the business. Way I figger it should pay for itself come five year. Come five year, you'll be a man. Twenty-one. Come five year I may be dead. I wouldn't figger on that if I was you, but anyway you'll be twenty-one. Now, here's my prop'sition. You go on workin' for the next five years, like you ben doin'. Cleaning up around the place, makin' yourself useful. What with the chickens gone, you won't hardly be kept busy; but, anyway, I keep on feedin' and housin' and clothin' you. And if you do that faithful, for five years, or until I die if I don't make the whole time, and don't ask for no cash wages, I'll heir you this prop'ty."

John leaned against one of the pillars and thought. Even if it was down on paper — and five years was a long time to wait. He heard the cars zoom along the highway; he looked at Uncle Ben. The old man had a shrewdness of a sort. A mean, calculating sort. He would not hesitate to cheat an inexperienced boy. He was taking tribute of five years of John's life. And Dr. Hayes had given John the message that he was worth a man's wages. Should be getting them.

"I'll think your proposition over, Uncle Ben. First, though, I'd like to see if I can find another job. Maybe — Dr. Hayes — a job where I could go to school, if only part time."

"Still being ungrateful for the last two years, huh?"

"No. You were bound to send me to school until I was sixteen. I earned, paid for those years, anyway."

"What do you want more schooling for? If I'd heir you this station, you wouldn't need Greek and any ology to run it."

John stopped before he told his uncle that if he ever inherited the filling station he would sell it the minute it became his to dispose of. He felt his jaw square with stubbornness. "I'll stay here — on your terms — if you'll give me the same time off I've been getting to go to school."

"Oh, you will! I guess so! Work hard at some job for eight hours a day, and come home too tired to do more than eat your meals."

"No," John agreed. "That wouldn't be fair. I meant, I'd use part of those eight hours to go to school — if I can get a scholarship. I think I can. And the rest of them, and summers, trying to earn the money for my books. I'd give you six or eight hours of work every day, Uncle Ben. I'd clean the cabins, and wash blankets and things, just as I've always done."

This bettered the terms Doc Hayes had specified in his bargain with Ben Colby. He had said that John was to be given eight hours a day free for his pursuit of schooling in return for a five-year loan of twenty-five hundred dollars. Also that Colby was not to demand more than four hours' work at the station from the boy.

It was like the fool John was to be ready to work extra hard from gratitude. He thought that he had argued all these concessions from Ben Colby. Didn't guess the terms had all been decided on that morning Jim Hayes had come to the station, and later put down in black and white — even to Ben's obligation to send John into Hayes this next Monday morning.

"Well, now, I tell you, John. I know you think I'm a hard-hearted old devil. I ain't never made over you much, I'll admit. And I'll admit, too, I think this school business can be overdone. I ain't had a whole lot of schoolin' myself. Got a heap more outa buckin' the world than I ever did out of books. But, still, times change. There's folks that think the more schoolin' a man gets, the more he's wuth. Maybe they're right. But you seem to want to try. I can't pay for your books nor no college-boy cloes. If you think you can earn your keep here, and then git out and hustle an eddication for yourself in eight hours a day, why, I guess it's up to me to let you try it. Ye may be able to do it. I dunno. But jest let me warn ye not to bank too heavy on what Doc Hayes said the other day. He was talkin' business with me, an' 'twas sorta natural he'd try to please me by sayin' something nice to my nephew. They's people think that's the way to do business. I don't get fooled none, an' you mustn't. Just the same, you go round to Doc Hayes Monday mornin' an' tell him I sent you. You tell him what it is you want to do and see what he says."

John sighed. His whole body seemed to slump. Had he really won this fight? He was not worried about Dr. Jim. But was Uncle Ben planning some new humiliation, some hateful trick? "Do you care if — if we put that down on paper? About the hours — and my inheriting the station?"

He was sure there was admiration in Uncle Ben's little eyes. "That's a good thing to do in all business, John. You write it out."

4

John was aware that the bit of paper he carried down the highway with him on Monday morning was an unusual document. Probably Dr. Jim would laugh at it. But he did not care. It meant a certain amount of freedom to John, and he felt good about possessing it. He felt good all over.

The early sun was hot on his head and shoulders. He could feel it burning his bare left arm. He wondered if Dr. Jim would get him work to do. Would he advise him about applying for a scholarship? Yes, Dr. Jim would do both of those things. Miss Arndt would help, too. The tone of the note she had sent with his diploma had been kind and encouraging.

As John opened the gate, Tut struck him full in the stomach like the wadding out of a gun. John grunted, and laughed at the grinning, capering dog. "Good old Tut! Glad to see me, are you? Get down, you crazy pooch!"

He scratched the hard head and rubbed the soft, clipped ears. Pushing Tut away, he went up the steps to the side door. Through the screen he could see Wong fussing around the breakfast table. John could smell coffee. Should he knock? Or go in, as he had always done? Go in, of course. Wong would screech like an owl if John made him stop his work to answer the door.

"Hello, Wong."

Wong looked up. "Missa John. Doc'r Jim be down two three minutes. He have baby all night. Get him bath clean shirt. You sit down. I make cocoa."

"Don't do that. I've had breakfast."

Wong looked at him suspiciously. Came around the table and prodded John's midsection with his clean yellow fingers. "What you have?" he asked scornfully.

"Oatmeal." Every morning John had oatmeal. It was cheap, and easy for Uncle Ben to eat with his odds and ends of broken teeth.

"I fix cocoa," Wong repeated with firmness. "An' eggs. Two eggs. An' bacon." He trotted out, still talking.

John laughed, and went over to chirrup to the canaries in the big cage at the window. He heard the doctor's step and turned, smiling.

"Well, John! Glad to see you. Sit down — eat breakfast with me. Ring for Wong, will you?"

John laughed and pulled up a chair beside Dr. Jim's. "I've seen Wong. He's out in the kitchen cooking everything in the house for me."

"That's fine. Wong likes to cook for young people. Lillie nearly breaks his heart by sucking an orange for breakfast."

"I came . . . I didn't think about its being breakfast time."

"Don't ever waste time on apologies where none is due, John. I guess you came to talk business with me, and knew I'd be most free at breakfast time. And you were right. I was up all last night. Saw to things at the hospital before I left there."

It always gave John a little shiver of excitement when Dr. Jim made even a casual reference to his profession. The boy was like a devout worshiper who touches divinity by glimpsing some sacred relic.

"I did come to talk business, Dr. Jim. I — I've talked Uncle Ben into letting me try to earn the money to go on to school with."

Dr. Jim worked busily at his grapefruit. Wong brought half a one to John, and he tasted it with delight.

"Did it take some persuasion?" Jim Hayes felt pretty sure that Ben Colby would not have told the boy about their queer financial deal.

"Yes, sir, it did. You helped a lot by telling him I ought to be getting a man's wages. Uncle Ben is old-fashioned. He thinks I have had all the education I need to run a filling station."

Dr. Jim put on his eyeglasses and studied the eggs on his plate. The bacon was pink and curly. A silver-covered dish disclosed a stack of toast dripping melted butter. John sighed.

"I wish I didn't like food so much," he murmured.

"Be a funny boy if you didn't have an appetite. An abnormality. Keep it, John. Don't be a hog, but always have a healthy interest in food. It's one of man's blessings and harmless pleasures."

"Not when . . ." John stopped, and stirred his cocoa into rich swirls, like brown marble.

"What?" Dr. Jim asked. "What did you start to say?"

"I — only that an appetite is a nuisance if — if you're poor."

"Yes, that's true. That's true enough. Did you tell your Uncle Ben you didn't mean to run a filling station?"

"No, I didn't. Because I may have to. Perhaps I shan't be able to do what I want. That's what I want to ask you about. If you think it will be crazy for me to try to be a doctor, I guess I'd better spend the time I have on something practical. Five years won't be enough . . ."

"What five years?"

John told Dr. Jim about his contract with Uncle Ben. He had to speak frankly if he were to ask the doctor's aid. He let Dr. Jim read the agreement. Dr. Jim took a long time to do it, because the boy's clear handwriting, his terse, economical phrasing, meant more to him than the actual context. At that, the thing made him hot under the collar. That snide caterpillar, Ben Colby! As for the inheritance, Dr. Jim, remembering unmistakable *arcus senilis,* doubted if the old man would live five years. He might. But maybe he would not.

"You want to take care of this, John."

"Yes, sir. I thought I'd put it in my bank."

"Your bank? Oh, yes. Got some money in there?"

John fetched the wooden vase. Spilled the contents out upon the tablecloth. He separated the several bills from the coins, added to the latter pile the change the girl in the Buick had given him Saturday night. He smiled ruefully at Dr. Jim. "Not a whole lot," he said. He touched the coins. "I stole these."

Dr. Jim looked at him. "Tips? I'd trust you with anything I have. Your Uncle Ben — Well, now, let's see. You asked me if it would be practical for you to plan to study medicine."

"Yes, sir. I know how long it takes, how expensive it is."

Dr. Jim waved away these difficulties with a flip of his pink hand. "The point is: do you really want to be a doctor?"

"Yes, sir. Yes, sir, I do."

"Why?"

"Well —"

"I mean, do you want to be a doctor because I am a doctor, because I have been friendly to you and live in a big house? Do you, perhaps, think that doctoring is the way to personal profit and prestige?"

John looked at him with amazed, hurt eyes.

"I must tell you, John. You'll find this out if you enter medical school. Nine-tenths of the doctors become doctors, not from idealistic reasons, but because they think a doctor is a pretty fine sort of social and economic person to be. Doctoring isn't all ideals. By Godfrey, no! For his own protection a successful doctor ought to be something of a businessman. But — well — that's why I ask you why you want to study medicine. Your row is going to be harder to hoe than most. You ought to want what's at the end of it for pretty sound reasons."

John nodded. He must be sure. He had no time to waste. "I — I've wanted to be a doctor all my life, Dr. Jim. I — this is hard to say. I couldn't ever say these things to anyone else.

"I've always been poor. My father was killed when I was only five. And my mother had to work hard, had to take charity from relatives. It was hateful, that charity. What I've had to take from Uncle Ben has been hateful, too. Back home, in Iowa, people were kind enough. Sometimes they gave Mother clothes to make over for my sister and me. We had to take such help. I hated it. Then — once I had a cough. It hung on and on. Mother tried to get me well. She was fine, my mother. She worked hard. She wanted us to be decent and self-respecting. But she hadn't any money to pay a doctor, nor to use for medicine. She worried about my cough. I expect she had cause to. Anyway, one day I was bringing in the coal and I got to coughing so hard I had to set the bucket down and lean against the fence. We lived on the corner, and the doctor's buggy came down the little side street. He stopped and asked me what I was doing for that cough. Then he told me to stop at his office on my way to school next morning. He acted cross, and I was afraid not to stop. He gave me a big dose of nasty medicine. Cod-liver oil, I think. He said I was to stop every morning or he'd send the health board after me. His office was in an old store building, and it had brown linoleum on the floor. He kept his pens and his pipe cleaners in a broken skull on his desk. He chewed tobacco. I don't guess he was a very fine doctor, but I worshiped him. He was the first person who had ever given me anything I didn't feel ashamed for taking. A person who could do that — a doctor — was what I wanted to be.

"When my mother got sick — she died of cancer of the throat — I told old Dr. Boettcher. He came to the house. When my mother told him not to come again, he pretended to get mad and said it was as much as his reputation was worth to let a woman be sick in the town. Did she want everybody in the place doubting his ability? And a lot more like that. So Mother let him come; and although she was a religious person, she told me — she couldn't talk much at the end — that a doctor is the one person on earth who gives without charity.

"It's been the same with you, Dr. Jim. You've done for me, and befriended me, when I guess the thing I needed most in the world was a friend. I — I want to be a doctor."

Dr. Jim stirred his coffee, cold now, and dead-looking, stirred it round and round. "A doctor is a man before he is a doctor, John. You could still be that sort of man . . ."

"I think if I were that sort of man, the way I'd spend my life — my profession — would be helping the greatest number of people. Maybe a preacher does that, too. I want to be a doctor."

"Well, then, I expect you'd better be getting about it."

John sat looking at a spot of sunlight on the white tablecloth. Dr. Jim had said that solemnly. And it seemed to John as if his words cleared away the last obstacle. Nothing, now, would prevent John Mallory from becoming a surgeon. The faint breath of carbolic soap that came from Dr. Jim's body and clothes was like the fragrance of incense which swings about a neophyte's head. "I'm going to work hard," he said. "It won't be my fault if I fail."

"You won't fail. Not if I can help it. Why, good Godfrey Hannah! I told you that one-tenth of the doctors go into medicine from a hard case of ideals. We don't want to reduce that average by keeping you out of the profession!"

John looked at Dr. Jim and laughed. "I'll get over being young," he promised.

Dr. Jim snorted. "Yes, I'll bet you will. Well, now let's get down to cases and see what we have to work on."

"Not much. Five years' time and seventeen dollars. Do you suppose I could get a scholarship? Miss Arndt spoke of a student loan fund."

"Keep borrowing for the last resort. But there are scholarships. One in science that I think I can get for you. You'll want a B.S. for medical school."

"Four years from now I'll have that worry. By that time I'd be almost of age."

"You can't get into any good medical school until you're twenty-one."

"Can't I?"

"No. It's a good rule. Especially for you — it'll let you take five years for your college course here, give you a little extra time to earn the cash you'll need. Books and lab fees run into money.

But you could earn most anything you'll need summers, and odd hours school term."

"Do you think I can find a job, Dr. Jim?"

Dr. Jim got up from the table, went over to the window, and pulled a shade straight. "If I get you a scholarship, I should have first chance at your services."

"Of course. If you'll really let me work."

"I'll make you work. I told Ben Colby I could use you." He stopped hastily and fished for his handkerchief.

John came around the table and looked into his face. He was taller than Dr. Jim. "Somehow, I think you've managed all this, Dr. Jim. I was thinking I'd finally done something for myself, but it doesn't matter. If things turn out well, and you're not disappointed in me. I don't know how you did it. Probably you threatened Uncle Ben with the health authorities. I don't know why you did it, either. Except — I know how it is about wanting to do things for people. I feel something like that about getting able to take care of Belle."

"Who's Belle?"

"My sister. She's living with an aunt in St. Louis. They are quite rich. They take fine care of Belle. But someday I want to do for her. She's only fourteen. Someday we'll be together again."

"Sure you will. Maybe you'll go to medical school in St. Louis. There's one of the best schools in the country there."

"Is there? Tell me about it."

"Some other time. Got to get to work now.

You make yourself useful around the place. Where's that paper?"

"What paper?"

"That contract with your Uncle Ben. I'm going to have it certified. Your medical education is in that paper; we don't want to play careless with it. I don't trust Ben Colby any further than I could throw — er — ahem!"

John flushed. "He can't be trusted. There's nothing to prevent his making another will."

Jim Hayes frowned mightily at his hands, holding the paper. "I stand ready to back you, John, if you'd ever have — er — trouble with him. Just as I'd give you a home, if you'd take it."

John wished he knew what to say, how to show his gratitude and love. "I — I'll cut the grass. Do you think Wong will let me work inside the house? I can wax floors, and clean wallpaper, and —"

"I'll pay you ten dollars a week. You draw up one of these contracts for me, too. I don't want to be liable if you work yourself to death."

5

John wasted no time fretting at the discovery that he had not independently and masterfully brought about this change in his condition. He was shrewd enough to realize that experienced guidance in this business of becoming an educated man might save him some considerable waste in time and money. He hoped that if he had been thrown on his own resources he would have acted creditably. But for the next few years it was pleasant to know that Dr. Jim and Miss Arndt stood behind him, ready with advice and praise and criticism where it might be needed. It was almost like having a family. It was the thing that kept him on at the station, enduring Uncle Ben's ugliness, working too hard. In some way this unpleasant life had led him to Hayes', would probably continue to lead him where he wanted to go. He saw too many boys on the road who had cut loose from home and family stricture. A boy did not get far alone. John was timid about tempting fate. He could stand things at the station. They were hard, but they were not hopeless.

He was learning a lesson he would need. To be busy all day, and to be pleasant while he worked. Six hours of sleep did him as well as ten, had to do him. When he came to serve his apprenticeship in hospital work, he could brag that, as a boy, he had learned to sleep intensively, each minute in bed counting for two.

He had a strong, healthy body, and Wong's abundance of good food helped to keep him well under the double load he was carrying. He had little fun, had no time to play. These essentials he reserved for the future — just now he was busy with other things.

Conditions at the station were changing, just as the appearance of the place had done. John was growing up, had attained enough maturity, enough self-assurance, to withstand Uncle Ben. Or perhaps it was Uncle Ben who was changing.

Still mean, still niggling and cruel in his outlook on life, still the fount of gross lack of knowledge bountifully spouting, John no longer was afraid of him.

Now John wore the clothes Miss Arndt gave him back to the station and hung them in the tent when he changed to his coveralls. Uncle Ben looked at the duck and flannel trousers, at the white shirt or the sweater. Sometimes he made sneering comment. John had heard him explaining to a tourist that the clothes were charity gifts from a fool old-maid schoolteacher in town. But he made no move to touch the things.

6

It seemed to John that Uncle Ben was getting older very rapidly now. He was still active about the station, still as voluble in his interchange of opinion with the tourists. Still as faultfinding with John. But there were things . . . His limbs had seemed to shrink within the tubes of his wrinkled, shapeless trousers. The bones of his skull stood out more prominently. His little wicked eyes held a new light — as if the flame behind them trembled a little. Did old people, who knew their lot of days was nearly used, begin to fear death? In the flush of his youth it seemed to John that old people should have lived their lives fully, and in the final years should be able to face death with a sort of resignation, if not peace.

At any rate, Uncle Ben seemed to fear something, and John wondered if it might not be death. John's mother had been fanatically religious, as punctilious in her churchly observances as she had been to satisfy all social demands. She had not wanted to die. Perhaps because of the children she must leave behind her. But, when she did contemplate her future life, it had been grimly. Heaven, in its actuality, had not risen before her as a place of waiting glory and ecstasy. It was rather a place of atonement, perhaps of punishment.

Uncle Ben had no religion. Yet he, too, was cross and fearful about dying. Perhaps it was just to assume that he regretted to leave his worldly goods behind him. In a way, his case was as John's mother's had been. The thought of the world he left, or was about to leave, could cloud his promise of deep sleep as it had dimmed the glory of heaven for Kathleen Mallory. Wondering about this, as he wondered about so many things, John debated whether the fault lay in the heaven a person stored up for himself after death. Did it not rather — did one's peace of mind — not depend on the life he builded toward the time of transference?

John did not know. There was so appallingly much he did not know. A man grown, studying geology and zoology and ancient history at the college. A man six feet tall, with a resonant voice, and strong, virile limbs — he had never smoked a cigarette; he had never seen any picture show except the occasional films shown at school; he had never done more than speak casually to any girl; he had never played a game — football, baseball, tennis — he was a queer, one-sided person. He could read *Romeo and Juliet*, and sit dreaming over the pages. But what did he know of women and love? The only women he talked with were Miss Arndt and the various female persons who came to the station camp.

Not that these women were unaware of John as a fine male creature. Ordinarily he was unconscious of the appeal he made to them. He was always so busy "at home." It only took up time when little girls, not over fourteen, tagged his heels, or when big girls asked him to rub sun-tan lotion on their backs. He had no time for such nonsense. Uncle Ben might know he had none.

But one evening a carful of young girls — they said they worked in a knitting mill — drove into camp and engaged two cabins, and made countless demands on John for help in unloading their baggage, for help in making their bunks, for help in lighting the stove in the kitchen. It was John, John, all evening. Would he bring their Victrola over from their cabin? Would he help move this heavy chair? He did not dance? But he must learn! Right now! John had work to do, but he smiled and spoke pleasantly — did the things they asked as quickly as possible. He saw Uncle Ben hovering around, supposed he was seeing that the new guests were comfortable.

When he had finally evaded the girls' insistence that he learn to dance, and was going on about his work, Uncle Ben called to him from where he sat on the platform. "Git them girls to bed yet?"

"They're in the recreation room. They're full of pep."

"I see they are. I see they are. Noisy as a bunch of grackles."

"They don't mean any harm. They've got this old car, and a two weeks' vacation. They're out to have all the fun they can."

"One or two of 'em ain't bad-looking."

John had not noticed. A tourist, to him, meant just so much floor space to clean, another pair of blankets to air or wash. He went over to the first pump, prepared to empty it for the night.

"Let it be. Let it be," his uncle said testily.

"It's after eleven."

"Anxious to git me to bed, ain't ye?"

John made no answer. He did not know, nor care, when his uncle went to bed. He felt that he himself should go to his tent by twelve. He must get up at six.

"Set down on that cheer."

Lately the way his uncle said certain words — "set" and "cheer," for instance — put John's teeth on edge.

John tilted the chair back against the wall of the station. It was a warm night, with the sky like dark blue plush, dusted thickly with little stars. His uncle was talking, leaning forward in his chair, his face pink, his eyes glittering.

"Ye don't want to mess with no girl here at the station. Come you got to have one, do it outside. Bring trouble to both of us come you git a girl here, and she set up a holler she ain't willing you shoulda done it."

John stared at his uncle. "I don't know what you mean," he said coldly. He felt as if, without warning, he had touched some hidden mess of filth.

"I mean, I ain't likely to be held responsible if you catch a girl out somewheres, but come you do it here on my prop'ty . . ."

John's face must have shown the dumbfounded amazement he was feeling. "I've never touched a girl in my life," he blurted.

His uncle gaped at him. "Don't you lie to me, John Mallory!"

"I'm not. I wouldn't."

Still the old man looked. But now his eyes took on an expression that made John's flesh prickle and his cheeks go hot. An expression of curious wonder, of envy, of salacious pleasure — a horrible expression. John wanted to cry out against it, to run away from it.

"Well, now, maybe you ain't," Ben Colby said, with a pleasantness that was like the touch of a sour dishrag. "You ain't only a boy, was when you came here. I guess you ain't had the chance. I guess, too, I stand in the way of father and mother to you, to tell you an' teach you."

John got up out of his chair. He was afraid — afraid of the light in his uncle's eyes, afraid of the words on his lips. "Don't . . ." he said soundlessly.

"Set down, boy. Set down. 'Tain't but right you should learn about bein' a man. Ef there's one critter on God's earth I feel sorry for, it's a man that's got to let some woman teach *him.* Now, they's all manner of men, an' they's all manner of wimmin. You can't set no hard and fast rule about . . ."

John sat there on the green painted chair and stared at the lights above the nearest pump. He should have run away. He must not listen now. Things were not like that. Women were not. Nor men. He could ask Dr. Jim. There were decent people. There were. Boys like Dick Mason and himself. Sweet, clean girls. Dick's sister, Betty. And Belle. He could ask Dr. Jim. Dr. Jim said the human body was the most wonderful, the most beautiful, thing on earth. A doctor needed to respect that body; he dedicated his whole life to its service. Not a body such as Uncle Ben knew and spoke of.

The old, feverish, creaking voice went on and on. Waves of slime and muck washed over John, staining his flesh, choking his mouth and nostrils until he fought for air, until his limbs grew hot and heavy, and his blood labored in his veins.

He struggled to rise, to stand. His face was flushed, a lock of hair hung down over one eye. He wanted to curse his uncle. Words came from odd corners of his brain, words he had heard Uncle Ben use in anger — odd, meaningless profanities such as a boy, passing men on the street, picks up and stores away in his mind.

These words clogged John's mouth. He swallowed them with an effort, turned, and left his uncle sitting there, grinning, still talking.

7

To an average boy John's life would have been one of unbearable hardship. But it did not matter too much to John. His medical degree was, to him, such a shining goal that he did not grudge the tremendous bodily effort he must expend to attain it. The hard, unpleasant tasks at the station, the dull, dragging hours with his uncle, slipped from his consciousness the minute he set foot on the smooth, clean highway that led to Dr. Jim's and his real life.

In this life were all the things that John thought of as "swell." Thinking of those things helped him do his work at the station, helped him not to mind the toilet bowls he scrubbed, the trash departing tourists left behind them. He could remember his friends at school, Dr. Jim's brusque kindliness. He could, wearily at the end of a long day, rake the driveway smooth and clean, and smile to remember Wong chasing Tut with the potato masher because the dog had jumped with muddy paws up against his clean afternoon coat of snowy linen. Wong had not had a Chinaman's chance of catching Tut.

John could remember the hours he worked with Miss Arndt in her garden. Miss Lillie raised flowers as intensively as she did everything else. The results she had were magnificent, even for

California, but it took a good deal of work. John's strong back and arms were a great help.

They made a strange pair, the stiff old woman and the tall, slender boy, his young limbs still awkward with their rapid growth, his curly black hair blowing in the wind, his face and arms burned a rich brown by the hot sun. Miss Arndt would find herself watching John with wonder and delight. A little sadly, too, sometimes, to see the eager light in his gray eyes, to hear the enthusiasm in his voice. He was like a beautiful book, fresh from the binders — not of much use unless it were read and handled. John must live and be hurt. Still — his youth was so achingly perfect.

Miss Arndt's gardening costume was as severe as her school one. Of white linen, as a concession to the California summer, but stiffly starched, high-collared, firmly cuffed. On her head, completely hiding her face, she wore a wonderful sunbonnet. It had been made by her mother, she told John. You could not get such bonnets nowadays. John thought she was probably right. But not even the lavender ruffles, the full cape which swept her shoulders, could make Miss Arndt look feminine. Dick Mason declared that, in it, she looked like a huckster's horse. John could never in his life see a strip of clean straw matting without recalling Miss Lillie's kind, pink face under the poke of that bonnet.

It was with Miss Lillie that John acquired an ability to talk well and interestingly. A gift he was to value in later years. Dr. Jim said the two of them did more talking than they did gardening. Well, they did talk. Both of them. About everything on earth. The things John "wondered" about. Sometimes, to his delight, he discovered that Miss Arndt had pondered these things, too. They talked about books and the people who live in books. They talked about the places Miss Arndt had seen in her travels over the world. John thought he liked that subject best. He could smell the yellow clay of China. The mosquitoes of Canadian glaciers stung his flesh. One hot day he stood on the approach to Mary's Bridge in Vienna, smelled the crisp cold of the shoveled snow, felt his cheeks tingle with the frost that made halos around the clustered light standards. He saw the bronze griffon; he heard a violin.

"Will I ever go to Vienna?" he asked passionately.

Miss Arndt crumbled dirt with her pink fingers. "If you're a doctor, you're likely to. Jim says a man can learn more in the clinics of Vienna than anywhere else."

"I'll go then," John said with confidence.

Miss Arndt gave an approving rap on the little flowerpot. "You'll go," she agreed. "You'll get what you want from life."

John sat back on his heels and chewed the sour, green stem of a geranium. "Do you believe that a person plans his life? Or that fate does it?"

"Fate! A weak man's excuse for failure!"

"Maybe. But, look. It wasn't my fault that I

came out here to California, and that you and Dr. Jim helped me start to be a doctor."

"It wasn't your doing that you came to California. If you had stayed in Iowa, you would still have learned doctoring."

John shook his head. "I'm not so sure. Mother — maybe she would have been harder to get around than Uncle Ben. Because she was kind to me. Good, I mean. I think, as soon as I was through high school, I would have had to get a job to take care of her. I really like bucking Uncle Ben. It would have been different with Mother. Besides, I wouldn't have had you and Dr. Jim to help me."

"There would have been someone else. Your old lady Fate would have found somebody."

John bent over the geraniums. "Maybe sometime I can tell you and Dr. Jim how grateful I am."

Miss Arndt got up from her knees, stiffly, grunting. John held up a long arm, and she steadied herself against his hand. "I'm getting old. And fat," she gasped. "Let me tell you something, John Mallory. And I mean every word I say. Don't be grateful! It's a humiliating, inferior way to feel. Be friendly; do for your friends the things you can, and accept similar service from them. But don't be grateful. Think to yourself: Would I, in Dr. Jim's position, do as much for another boy? Would I enjoy doing it?"

John looked up at her, and his eyes began to

smile. "You're swell, Miss Lillie," he said earnestly.

She glared at him. Not for worlds would she have shown pleasure in his compliment. "Well, I wish you wouldn't take my claw."

John grinned and pulled the little hand-cultivator out of his pocket.

One day their talk turned to sex. Miss Arndt forgot by what winding paths they had arrived at the matter. A matter which seemed to hang heavy on John's consciousness. Her years of teaching had given her a good idea of the adolescent's point of view. Sex, she knew, was a big item with the young. In nature's scheme it was a problem on a level with food and shelter. She respected the importance of the subject.

It took very little time and talk to uncover the stain Ben Colby had left on the bright blade of John's youth. This was the first time John had ever evaded her eyes, had tried obviously to turn the talk into other channels. Miss Arndt was sorry. When she thought that John's shame might have been caused by things he had seen at the station, her blood boiled. Literally, she could feel it humming in her veins. Her first impulse was to go forth and do murder — talk more plainly than was her brusque wont. Uncontrolled anger was a luxury Miss Arndt thought too rich for her nature. It had no place behind a school principal's desk, nor here in her garden.

"John," she said, her rough, heavy voice sounding a little strained.

"Yes, Miss Lillie?"
"How old are you?"
"Sixteen."
"Yes. I'm sixty-three."

John set a stone carefully in line and packed sand around it firmly. He was glad Miss Arndt was changing the subject.

"I'm sixty-three," Miss Arndt repeated. "When I was a little girl, when I was your age, sex didn't exist. Chickens laid eggs, and mares had colts, and my mother had babies — but there wasn't any sex."

"We talk about it too much now," John said. His eyes still would not meet hers.

"Maybe we do. The pendulum swings hard. I think, like some other natural processes, it isn't a parlor topic. Oscar Wilde thought women ought never to eat in public. He said it was such an ugly thing to do."

John's lips drew in at one corner. It was not a smile. He was horribly tense. Tension may warp a man's whole nature.

"But my point is: in my childhood, in Oscar Wilde's time, now, back in Adam's day, sex itself was pretty much as it is, and always will be. A bodily hunger and appeasement."

John sighed. If older people would only let the young . . .

"Some people have gross table manners, and are filthy in various ways. Some people are gluttonous in their hunger for food; some will eat food under any conditions. Some seek it out with a finicky distinction of flavor and variety. One is as much a beast for food as another. Sex is an appetite."

John knew about appetites.

"You know history, John. You and I have talked of the men and women in history, people we admire. Your choice of heroes has seemed to be the human sort of fighter. The Crusader for right or knowledge. Yet, always, the likeable, real person rather than the one-sided genius. Well, John, real, human people have always had the real, human appetites. You're a boy. You've grown fast, and sometimes the very length of your limbs is a burden to you. For a time the fact of your sex will be an awkward, unmanageable thing. Those other men felt that, too, no doubt. John Paul Jones probably fell over his own feet when he was sixteen, and lay awake at night worrying about his own body."

John looked at Miss Lillie. "How — did you know?"

"Why shouldn't I? Because I'm an old maid?"

"No. But you're not a man."

"Do you think women haven't bodies and appetites, John Mallory?"

John's cheeks went a dark, painful red.

Miss Arndt's blue eyes flashed. "There's nothing shameful about being an old maid! Likewise, there's nothing shameful in being a married woman with a dozen children in the house. Both conditions are natural."

John nodded. He was feeling better. "I — it's

talking so much about things, sometimes . . ."

"I know. But remember: for every unclean mind there are dozens of decent, natural ones. I wouldn't want you to be the hateful sort. I'd feel rather sorry if someday — oh, fifteen years from now, perhaps — you didn't come across a girl that you liked and wanted to be with, and then began to want to love, and then did marry and love. I want you to live a happy, full life, John. Look at all things sanely. Don't get a warped viewpoint on any subject. Certainly not on sex."

John nodded, and Miss Arndt began to talk about Black Leaf 40. John was giving himself a hard, swift kick, and feeling rather good about doing it, too. Here, when he should know better than anyone how specious was Uncle Ben's information on any subject, he had let the old dodo lecture him about sex, and had taken every word for inevitable truth. Darn Uncle Ben! He didn't know any more about this subject than he did about irrigating Death Valley. When he expounded the latter subject, John laughed to himself and forgot what was said. When he had told John about — Well, John would forget the whole thing. As Miss Lillie said, John had a good many years still; if he knew anything about the study of medicine, he was due to learn a good many things in these next years. Things Uncle Ben would not know how to pronounce.

8

One night Dr. Jim and Miss Lillie sat on opposite sides of a snapping fire, reading and dozing as people past sixty do at the end of a busy day. The down-cushioned chairs were soft, the fire rosily warm against their shins. They had a pleasant consciousness of the wet fog which pressed against the windows.

Dr. Jim folded the last section of the newspaper, took off his spectacles and put them into the old-fashioned case. He rubbed his eyes and sat looking at the fire. "Lillie," he said abruptly.

Miss Arndt put her finger between the pages of her book and looked up. "Yes, Jim?"

"I sold John down the river this afternoon."

"You took him to the hospital."

"He tell you?"

"No, but I had an idea."

"We've lost him, Lillie."

"I don't see why we should."

"There's a boy who gives his whole soul. John is going to be a dyed-in-the-wool surgeon, Lillie. Anything outside of surgery will get absent-minded attention from him."

"Is that a desirable thing?"

"So far as surgery is concerned, it is the ideal thing. As for John, he may miss a lot in life."

"The right girl to love would balance all that. I know he must have been excited about the hospital. Tell me."

Dr. Jim chuckled. "I took him in the back way, where the receiving room is. That corridor smells pretty stout. But John loved it. He keened his nose like a beagle; you could see him scenting the wind. It wouldn't have surprised me if he'd bayed. His eyes fairly sparkled, and his breath came quick. I could see his hand tremble. I introduced him to Gilfoyle, then took him to the superintendent's office. Miss Bean. Smart woman. She saw John's excitement. Agreed to let him work four hours a day to suit his school schedule."

"She'd want to please you, Jim."

"Yes, to some extent. But she liked John. So did Gilfoyle. Between them they fixed it so he could have the scrubbing of the operating rooms."

"Oh, Jim, not —"

"John was thrilled. He knows how important cleanliness is in an operating room."

"I know. But scrubbing! It's such a waste! John could do better work. All he does is scrub! At the station, the porches here, and now at the hospital!"

Dr. Jim rubbed his jaw. "Well, scrubbing won't hurt him. It won't last. He'll go into more dignified work. Just now, a little muscular —"

"It's not the muscular part. Scrubbing, Jim — down on your knees — it's humiliating, degrading work."

"It is, if you make it that sort. John doesn't look at it that way. He has considerable pride of spirit. And to him, scrubbing is only a means to an end. An end which seems very much worth while. So he accepts the chance to scrub, and with good grace. You see, Lillie, John, on his knees on the operating-room floor, can see quite plainly the time when he will stand at the surgeon's position beside the operating table."

Miss Lillie smiled grimly into the fire. "At the risk of being as sentimental as you are, I'll admit that it makes growing old easier to have your accumulated money and experience link you to the young."

"Yes. The handing on of the torch. Immortality. After we are dead, and John has forgotten us, every life Dr. John Mallory saves will be saved because you and I lived here in Villa Franca and took a fancy to a big-eyed, hungry boy."

Miss Lillie nodded. "That's true. Only, John won't forget us."

"The young do forget the old, Lillie."

"They do. It's right that they should. But the winds which blow between John's youth and our age are not too cold. John will remember us."

9

True to Dr. Jim's prediction, John did not long continue scrubbing the tiled floors of the operating rooms. In less than a month he was taken to the laboratory and given the job of washing and keeping the glass and the instruments there. By summer he was back in the operating rooms, responsible for the cleaning, the sharpening, the sterilizing, of all surgical instruments. The sterilizers themselves were in his charge; he saw to it that the dressings cabinets were fully stocked, that the supply of sterile linens was always up to quota. It was a responsibility for a seventeen-year-old boy. John cared for his work with reverence.

He wore white trousers and white shoes around the hospital, and a fresh linen jacket every day. The nurses and doctors called him Johnnie. Found him willing to help where and how he could. Occasionally he did a bit of orderly duty; the patients found him pleasant and interested.

He had a great deal of authority over the instrument cases and the sterilizers. Only Miss Bean or the head surgical nurse could take a scalpel or a packet of gauze sponges without John's permission, and they had to leave a memorandum on his file. He learned the name of every sort of instrument, bandage, and dressing. His innate curiosity made him find out their applied uses. In a very short time he knew, without being given detailed orders, the various things which would be required for the more common operations.

Dr. Gilfoyle bragged of John to Dr. Hayes. "He's a born surgeon, Jim. And he told me last week that the bistoury I used was old-fashioned."

"It is," Jim Hayes chuckled. "They've improved on bistouries a dozen times since you began to use that one."

"I can still repair a hernia with it," Dr. Gilfoyle retorted.

The next hernia section he had he asked John

if he would like to watch the operation.

John looked at the chief surgeon, and his face went white.

"Come on, if you want to," Dr. Gilfoyle said casually.

John wanted to. He wanted to so badly that his limbs shook with eagerness. But he was afraid. He recalled all the tales nurses told of their first operations. John did not want to be a nuisance, perhaps get sick at the sight of blood. Someday, with a class of medical students, he would see his first operation. But now, alone — He checked the knives, the forceps, the clamps, the scissors, in the sterile trays. He counted the towels, the sheets, the aprons and gloves and masks. Cotton, sponges, gut. Iodine, alcohol. He stripped off his rubber gloves and went to help the nurses bring in the cart. He helped lift the heavy man to the table. He adjusted the anesthetist's shield. He took the cart out into the hall and stayed there beside it. The "special" came out through the flapping doors; John could smell ether, sweet, tickling his throat. Slowly he pushed the cart down the hall. Dr. Gilfoyle would not ask him again. He would think John had not wanted to stay. He *had* wanted to. It was only — the first time . . . Doctors did not think of the *person* on the table. To them it was a case, a problem. Blood was not blood, but a handicap of the game they played with such deadly seriousness. John must acquire this detached, impersonal point of view. A surgeon had to have it.

He would be afraid of his work if he did not. His own imagination would tear him to pieces.

Dr. Gilfoyle probably knew this patient as well as John did. But just now — there in that white room — Dr. Gilfoyle was a surgeon, not a man. Dan Ryan was not the jovial traffic cop known to the whole town; he was an operative field exposed through the hole in the surgical sheet. A problem of ruptured muscles and strangulated tubes.

Next time John would stay.

Next time he did stay. Without invitation. Dr. Gilfoyle's eyes twinkled with understanding to see him there behind the brass railing. A Caesarean section did not come up every day. John would have been a fool . . . He sat forward on his stool and watched the gloved hands go in and out under the cone of blue-white light. He recognized the sureness and the swiftness of their movements. Once, when an assistant fumbled in his choice of forceps, John's fingers stretched out in a little reflex motion, as if he would hand the instrument to the surgeon. His own muscles knew how delicately the surgeon's fingers gauged the depth the knife must cut, his own hands held the placenta and handled the baby with a touch so light as not to have bruised the most fragile of surfaces. When the child cried, John knew the satisfaction of a life saved, of injury averted.

After the operation he was tired with the fatigue of a big job well done. He knew, also, physical contentment. Thinking about the experience, he remembered the excitement and drama of the moment. He hoped an operating room would always hold drama for him. But he had felt no sense of strangeness, nor fear, nor horror. Nothing had shocked him. He had been able to admire the surgeon's skill, but he had not wondered at it. Certainly Dr. Gilfoyle was skillful; the nurses and the assistant had, of course, worked like cogs in a finely geared machine. They had studied and trained — all the surgeons and doctors from ages back had worked and experimented and dared toward this morning in the operating room at Villa Franca.

John tried to tell Dr. Jim something of how he had felt. "I felt, Dr. Jim, as if I belonged there. As if I were home. It sounds silly — but I felt as if I'd been roaming around in the dark, and now I've come in to light and home. I was happy there. I want to go back. As soon and as often as I can."

Dr. Jim nodded. "I understand."

He did understand. He watched John a little wistfully these next months. Jim Hayes was a good all-round physician, his keen insight into human nature serving him even better than did his medical training. He had never felt the inspiration John felt. He envied John. Not his youth — Jim Hayes had lived his life well and honestly; he would waste no time now wishing he might do it over. But he wondered if John had not caught a spark that for Jim Hayes had gone unnoticed. Had it ever been there for men like Jim Hayes? Dr. Jim, the son and grandson of physicians, had been dedicated to medicine from birth. He could not remember ever feeling the passion for science which glowed in John's gray eyes. John would not wind up simply the most popular doctor in that part of California. He would not care whether people liked him or not — he would be the kind of doctor to try new things, to blaze new trails. Dr. Jim envied him the adventure.

Before he ever attended a class in medical school, John acquired a thorough knowledge of hospital practice and operating-room technique. No chance word was too trivial, no experience too unimportant, for him to snatch up and store away in his file of medical lore. He was scrupulous about observing the definite limits of his work; but nothing prevented his learning, wherever and however he was given the opportunity. While testing urine and making routine blood slides in the lab — as he was later permitted to do — he began the work that twenty years later was to make him known as an authority on blood infections.

It was a matter of seizing his chances. The essential thing was his love for the hospital. He had for the place the caressing affection men usually reserve for women. He went through his day — his work at the station, his hour or so at Hayes', his schoolwork — all bent on the four hours he would spend in the hospital. That was the end and purpose of all existence. There he lived and breathed. There he had no fears, no doubts. Whether he shaved the belly of a beery bum for an emergency appendix, or sealed the spinal fluid of a meningitis victim, everything he did had definite meaning.

Dr. Jim saw the assurance with which he walked the hospital halls, heard the confident ring in his voice, saw the intentness of his eyes. In the hospital John was a man full-grown.

10

The days at college, the five years, went quickly. John's mind was the sort to make a feast of knowledge. Shakespeare, biochemistry, scientific German, were all as stimulating to him as the smell of bacon on a crisp winter morning. It was during this time, too, that he discovered and developed his ability to play the piano by ear. An experience which made up to him, somewhat, for the bodily outlets denied him — the playing of games, dalliance with women. Those were things John, healthy young animal, envied other men for having. Their experience was a locked door to which he had as yet no key. He would know them some day. It was John's destiny to acquire things slowly.

11

The summer John's own class of friends graduated from college — Dick Mason and all the boys and girls he had known for so long — that June,

Dr. Jim's granddaughter, Mattie, came to visit in Villa Franca. Mattie was sixteen, a pert, spoiled girl. Her parents had gone to Europe, but she had preferred staying with her grandfather. John knew immediately that her chief reason had been the smooth-spoken youth who drove over from Hollywood each Sunday, and he would have liked to spank Mattie for pretending that "touring Europe" bored her. He contented himself with calling her Infant, telling her when she had put on an intolerable amount of lipstick, and laughing aloud at her story of an innocent, but thrilling, encounter with Ramon Novarro.

"Was he thr-rilled, too?" he asked. Mattie sprang at him with curved fingers, like sharp-edged claws. John caught her wrists in his strong hands and told her to behave. "I'm in a hurry."

Miss Lillie decided to give Mattie a party. All John's friends were invited, and he found himself listening to Mattie's plea that he come, too.

"I don't ever go to parties," he protested. "I can't leave the station at night."

"I think you're silly to stay at the station. Granddad does, too."

"Uncle Ben needs me. He's getting old."

"But — just one evening?"

"I haven't any party clothes."

"You have the white pants you wear at the hospital. And your suit coat. That's how the boys will dress. Please, John?"

John wanted to go to the party. He had never had one with his friends. In another year they would be separated. Some of them working out of town, some married. John himself would not be here after another year. He would be somewhere working on a full-time job, saving for medical school. He wanted one party.

"Granddad thinks the Victrola would be enough music for dancing — he let me buy some keen new records. But it would be kinda nice, too, John, if you'd play."

So that was why she wanted him. Her grandfather's hired boy, whom she could order around. "I'll see if I can arrange it," he said, his voice stiff with hurt.

"We'd pay you for playing," Mattie said, eager to please him. She really admired John.

John glared at her. "Try it," he challenged her. "I'll slap you till the paint comes off in flakes."

"Oh!"

"If I come to your silly little party, it will be because I want to."

He looked very young as he stalked away from her. Mattie thought he was "cute," with his shiny gray eyes and red cheeks.

John asked for, and got, the afternoon off at the hospital. Miss Bean, who weighed two hundred and thirty pounds, said anyone could have knocked her over with a feather. Johnnie had never done such a thing before.

John went back to the station at noon. Told his uncle that he would do up his work early, because he had an engagement for the evening.

"Girls, I bet," Uncle Ben said with satisfaction.

"Just an engagement," John repeated, reaching for the box of soap powder.

That evening, when John was nearly dressed, his uncle lifted the flap of his tent and came in. It was the first time John could remember his uncle's being in the tent with him.

"Were you going?" Uncle Ben asked, going toward the bed.

John swung the chair around. "Sit here."

"Bed's good enough."

"Sit on the chair."

Uncle Ben sat on the chair, his lips working with silent peevishness.

John fussed with his new tie. He knew Uncle Ben was taking in his freshly ironed duck trousers, his white shoes.

"Where you going?"

"Dr. Hayes'. I'll be back around midnight."

"Party? Dancing?"

"It's a party. I don't know how to dance."

"Jest an excuse to hug the girls. Guess you could manage that."

"I don't know. I've never tried." John knew the very coolness of his tone maddened Uncle Ben. He did not care. He reached for his coat.

"Kinda fixy, ain't ye?"

John made no answer. There was no point in working Uncle Ben into a stew, and have him go out to the tourists and tell them a lot of stuff about his nephew. Made himself out quite a martyred old man, Uncle Ben did.

"You mighta asked me if you could go," Uncle Ben whined.

"I might have. I came home early and did my work. I'm getting pretty old to have to ask permission. . . ."

"Old, and independent. That what you think?"

"Something of that sort." John wound the inexpensive wrist watch Miss Lillie had given him last Christmas.

"Let me tell you something, John Colby."

"Mallory. John Mallory." Either Uncle Ben was getting childish and forgetful, or he guessed that John would have hated to be named Colby.

"Let me tell you one thing. The fust is, that you're a poor boy. Ye're jest as poor as a boy can be. Ye ain't got nuthin'!"

Uncle Ben's voice rose to a thin scream of hatred and anger.

"I know how poor I am."

"Well, what you don't know is that for poor folks there ain't no sech thing as being independent. There never will be. Every bone and muscle in your body has been built by the food ye've et, and ye've owed that food to somebody else. Ye've owed it, and ye always will owe it. Ye ain't ever ben independent, John. Ye ain't now, standin' there in them white pants that old whore give ye. And ye won't ever be. Jest remember that!"

John ducked under the tent flap and went out into the soft and comparatively silent night.

12

The day before, John had helped the Chinaboy hang lanterns on the wide porches of the big house. But he was unprepared for their beauty as they swung in soft, rosy globes against the darkness. Girls in pale, fluttering dresses moved across the lawn. Music — "Only a Rose" — came in gentle waves of beauty to his ear. A party was beauty, was grace, was happiness. A few children pressed their faces against the pickets of the fence. The little Alberni boy stepped aside to let John open the gate and go in.

"Hi-ya, ice-cream pants!" the boy yelped.

John grinned. That, too, was being grown-up and going to a party.

His friends were frankly amazed at his presence, and just as honestly glad to have him there. Betty Mason and Mattie wanted him to dance. Wanted to teach him how to dance.

"I'd spoil the party," he assured them.

He changed records, and fetched a shawl for Miss Lillie so that she could stay out on the veranda and watch the fun. He sat at the piano and played dance tunes for nearly an hour; then, in some manner, he was playing songs, and the boys and girls clustered around him, or sat out on the porch steps and in the shadowed swings, everybody singing. Even Dr. Jim sang. John saw him, standing with his arm around Mattie's waist, singing "Oh, Suzanna." It was fun. Without John it would not have been as much fun.

Then it was time for supper, and John helped

the boys serve at the table in the dining room. Big plates, a napkin, a fork, a spoon. A heap of Wong's delicious chicken salad made with salted almonds. Pickles and olives. Soft little sandwiches made with cream cheese and walnuts. "Haven't you some without nuts? They hurt my teeth." John looked with disbelief at the complaining boy. Were there things a boy of nineteen could not eat? Little puff shells filled with lobster mayonnaise. Molded roses of strawberry and pistachio ice cream. Too perfect to eat. Too delicious not to eat. Cups of coffee, or glasses of iced cocoa or lemonade. Some piggish ones took all three. Betty Mason came and helped John dip lemonade. It was, she said, like the cafeteria. Betty was a grand person.

When nearly everyone was served, Miss Arndt ordered the two to fill plates for themselves and go off somewhere and eat. "I have a scandalous appetite," John confessed to Betty, heaping his plate.

"I know it," she said. And they laughed.

Walking warily, they went out the side door and down to the bench under Miss Lillie's rose arbor. Tut came to them, and John fed him bread from one of his sandwiches. Tut was not hungry; he lay down with his chin on John's shoe. John could feel his hot breath puffing against his ankle. He sat very quietly so as not to disturb the old dog. "Funny nobody found this bench," he told Betty.

"Miss Arndt said we weren't to go into the

flower garden. Thought we'd spoil things. We're all about fourteen to her."

"I guess so. But she's swell."

"Oh, she is. I used to be afraid of her."

"Were you? I never was. She's bossy. And sounds cross — it doesn't mean a thing."

They ate busily, hungrily. They could hear the others laughing and talking over at the house. Once a girl screamed out in a noisy exaggeration of mirth. John frowned.

"Girls do that so you boys will notice them," said Betty calmly.

"Well, we do. Ought you to give away lodge secrets?"

"A yell like that is no secret," Betty giggled. She had forgotten a napkin. John shared his with her. "It's a grand party," she said.

"Yes. It is."

"Fun. But not rowdy."

"I — don't know much about parties."

"You've had to work hard, haven't you, John?"

"Oh, well, I'm an orphan. It's different when you have folks."

"Yes. Dick and I both earn something. It hasn't hurt us. It won't hurt you. I mean, it hasn't."

"I hope not. Dick leaves next week, doesn't he?"

"Yes. We'll miss him."

"Pretty grand, his getting into the Government geological department."

"I know it, but we'll still miss him. You're

going to study medicine, aren't you, John? Then are you going to help Dr. Hayes?"

"Goodness, I still don't know how I'm going to arrange the medical-school part. Cost better than fifteen hundred dollars. Even if I don't eat, or wear shoes."

"My. How will you manage, John?"

"Well, I'll have to get some sort of job, save every penny I can. I'll probably be the world's oldest medical student. You'll see me in Ripley's pictures."

Betty laughed, and touched his hand with her soft, brown paw. John covered it with his other hand, marveling at how small and boneless hers seemed. Betty had on a thin, ruffled dress. Pink. But out here it looked soft and gray, like the roses. Her hair was a dark smudge above her face and white throat. John considered the creamy oval of her face, her soft brown eyes, her full, rose-colored lips. Why, he wondered, did women paint their lips a hard, brilliant scarlet? Or were men — other than himself — attracted by such lacquered artificiality?

Back at his old trick of "wondering," John realized that the girl beside him was very sweet. As sweet, and as familiar, as Miss Lillie's roses and pretty-by-nights, whose fragrance hung on the soft darkness like a cloud. John's right arm drew her closer; her head tucked into the hollow of his shoulder; a soft feather of hair clung to his cheek. They sat there, very still.

"Jo-o-ohn! Come and play!"

It was Mattie, up on the porch. John sighed. Betty looked up at him. In the dusk he could see the gleam of her smile. He bent his head and kissed her. Her lips — a girl's lips — were soft. Sweet. Warm, and at the same time cool. He had not known . . .

He gathered up their dishes and followed Betty back to the house. She went along the path to the front veranda; John went on to the kitchen, and put his plates and cups into the dishpan.

"Oh, there you are, John," Miss Lillie said from the pantry doorway. "Would you want to play again?"

"Yes. Of course. The eats were grand, Miss Lillie."

"Thanks for the opinion of an expert," Miss Lillie said shortly. John laughed and, passing her, went on to the parlor and the piano. He saw Betty dancing with Mattie's friend from Hollywood.

13

Walking home along the empty highway a little after midnight, John thought about Betty and the kiss. Betty was like a sister to him. Like Belle would have been if they had stayed together. But the kiss had not been the sort that a brother gives a sister. Without its having any definite urge or promise of passion between them, it had certainly been the kiss a man gives a woman. It was the first time — John had had no idea that a girl's lips were — well, like they were. Nor that her body would be so soft under his hands. John had had no idea. His mind had known about sex, the hard, ugly things known as the Facts of Life, the scientific evasions he had learned in biology. But his lips, his hands, had not known that a woman's skin is soft and silky, that her lips and breasts are frighteningly soft.

John was glad that he had kissed Betty. The kiss had meant nothing. It had meant *everything.* It meant that he was a man, strong and tough. Far off he could glimpse a world of beauty and tenderness — a world where women like Betty dwelt, and would admit the men they thought fine enough. John had now another thing to dream about, to work toward. He was suddenly impatient to be out and about this business of building his life. Building it for himself, with his own effort, under his own guidance. He resented the year that still bound him to the station, the college, Dr. Jim, even to the hospital. He was marking time, a time paced by others. A slow, dragging pace.

Oh, he was grateful to Dr. Jim. God knew he was! But he was eager to be free of these older people who had helped him. Eager no longer to need their help. He wanted to take the reins in his own hands, to turn the horse's head straight ahead, and to urge life into a brisk trot.

Chapter Five

The next winter was the coldest, wettest, John had known in his years in California. Native sons explained the unusual weather to each other and were quick to resent the casual comment of an outsider. Each morning John carried armsful of wood to the fireplaces in Dr. Jim's house. The tourists complained of the damp and the cold in their unheated cabins. The hospital took on a new stink from the round blue oil heaters put into the rooms.

Dr. Jim, working too hard, fell desperately ill with pneumonia. John was a strong right arm to Miss Lillie in this crisis. Her sturdy spirit was shaken to realize that death could come so close. She determined to retire from teaching; she and Dr. Jim would do some of the things they had been planning to do. Go to China to see Rob's family, before it was too late.

2

"Come I'd git sick you wouldn't play wet-nurse to me," Uncle Ben complained when Dr. Jim was better and John was at the station for his usual duties and hours.

For the last year or two Uncle Ben had seemed to get thinner, more bloodless. His old voice dripped venom ever more constantly. This last year a tourist occasionally complained to John about the old man's hatefulness. "The only reason anybody would put up with the old coot is because this is the cleanest tourist camp in the country."

Still, John was not at all prepared, one morning late in April, when he went to his uncle's room to see why he did not come for breakfast, to find the electric light burning and the old man slumped on his knees beside his bed, dead for many hours. John was shocked to know him dead. He was still more shocked to know that he had lain there all night, unnoticed, uncared for.

Dr. O'Connor assured the coroner, and John, that death had been instant, from cerebral hemorrhage. John hated it — he had been within call. He might at least have straightened those bent old limbs.

Miss Lillie went with John to the cemetery. There were flowers from John's friends. John looked at them curiously. He wished he might mourn his uncle. Wished that someone might mourn him. These friends, these flowers, were tributes to John. A man who so lived that no person could find a sincere word of regret at his going was dead, indeed. John was sorry.

Bewildered a little, too, at the change which necessarily came to his life. Mechanically he attended the last weeks of classes at the college. He had to hire a man to tend pump; it seemed incredible that Uncle Ben's chair on the platform was empty. Regretfully John gave up his job at the hospital. "We'll always have a place for you, Johnnie," Dr. Gilfoyle told him kindly. When John graduated, the staff gave him an expensive microscope. John wished he need not think of the gift as another hundred dollars acquired toward the expenses of medical school.

He went over Uncle Ben's meager belongings. Burned his empty old shoes, his shabby clothes, the pipe with the head carved on the bowl. He found records of lottery tickets Uncle Ben had bought, packets of worthless stock. He found the paper which told him of Dr. Jim's loan to Uncle Ben and the agreement between the two which had provided for John's years at college.

His face went white. Bitter anger at this unneeded proof of his uncle's meanness, white with new gratitude for Dr. Jim's help to himself. How could he ever pay such a debt?

"He's spent thousands of dollars on me," John told Miss Lillie. "I want you to tell me how — whom to go to — I want to deed the station to Dr. Jim."

"Did your uncle leave you the station?"

"Yes. It's mine."

"Free of debt?"

"No. There's a mortgage. And this." He held out the soiled bit of paper.

"Jim's a long way from being well, John."

"I know."

"I'd hate anything to happen to prevent our

sailing the first of July."

"Yes."

"He's counting big on seeing Rob and his grandsons. It — it would worry him, hurt him, if you made a fuss about this, John."

"But, Miss Lillie, it's so much! So much money! He's done enough for me that I've known about. You both have. But thousands of dollars!"

"You've earned most of it back, John."

"My clothes. My meals. What the hospital paid me. But not this twenty-five hundred." His voice was stern, stubborn.

Miss Lillie nodded. John was no fool. She admired his fine integrity. "According to the agreement, that debt has paid itself out."

"So far as Uncle Ben was concerned. Yes. Not for my part." His jaw set firmly. Miss Lillie smoothed her linen skirt.

"John, will you do something for me? Two things?"

"Well . . ."

"You can do them. This thing is between you and me. I'll tell Jim about it when he's stronger. Maybe someday when we're sitting in the court of Rob's temple, with the wind blowing cool over the Wall of China and a little dwarf cedar tree standing in its blue jar, black as an etching against the blue and gold Chinese sky. I'll tell him then. Tell him that you know of this debt. This debt of honor. That's the sort it is, you know, John."

"Yes, Miss Lillie." He was feeling the cold

wind of China, too. He could hear a little bell ringing.

"Well, I'll tell Jim that you've assumed the debt, and that someday when the opportunity comes for Dr. John Mallory to repay that debt, when your chance comes to save his career for some young medical student or doctor, you'll pay it back. Jim will think it a fine bargain, John. You know he will. Jim is a sentimental old fool, and we have to humor him."

John tried to smile. His eyes were very dark.

3

John sold the station the week after Dr. Jim and Miss Lillie sailed for China. He had not been ashamed of the tears he shed on Tut's brown coat when he watched their sedan disappear down the highway. He took the old dog back to the station with him, where the big brindle died a month later. John felt there was not much left of his old life in California.

He stayed on at the station, working for the new owner, until the end of August. He had a sizable bank draft to put into his wallet with his tickets to St. Louis, his letters to the medical-school dean from Dr. Gilfoyle and the president of the college. He had some decent clothes in a presentable suitcase, a boxful of books, and his microscope.

If he could find any sort of job in St. Louis, he was assured of his medical education. The draft would cover a little besides tuition fees.

John would not ask Uncle Brooke for more than a job. Perhaps Belle would know of something, some work he could do.

4

When John reached the smoky Midway of the station in St. Louis, he realized that his definite planning had gone only so far. He set his bag on one of the yellow varnished seats and pondered the situation. The term at medical school would not start for another month, but he would have, according to his letter from the dean, to take an "aptitude test." That had better be arranged for immediately. Then he wanted to see Belle. See her for his own sake, and hers. Also, Belle would probably be able to give him all sorts of advice about getting a job, about finding some cheap place to board. John knew he could not afford the school dormitory.

The noise of the Midway, the hurrying feet, the excitement of people going on journeys, the noisier excitement of people coming home from trips and vacations — all this was confusing and delightful. He liked the immensity of the place, the long stretches of dark stone floors, the iron gates and posts that soared up into the murky darkness of the beamed and girdered roof. He liked the blue lights that burned in the dusk, making it as tangible as a fold of aged velvet.

The air was warm — even hotter than that of Villa Franca. John wiped moisture from his hands and upper lip when he went to the telephone booth to call Belle. He found the number easily. "Brooke Wielande, r. 5328 Lindell Blvd. Ca. 2613." The girl at the switchboard said the *Ca.* stood for Cabany. She called his number, and indicated a booth. John put in his nickel. A man's voice was saying, "Hello, hello?"

John gulped. "Hello. I'd like to speak to Belle Mallory, please."

"You must have the wrong numbah!" The receiver clicked in his ear. John went into the Midway again. He had not had the wrong number. He had been writing to that address for years. How . . . Oh, yes! How dumb he was! Belle was not Belle. She was Miss Isabelle Wielande. He had been writing to that name for years, too. Years in which Belle had grown into a young lady. He looked back at the phone booth. He decided not to approach the cool impersonality there at the board. He would check his bag, get something to eat, then try again.

It was ten o'clock. He was hungry. Dozens of people were eating in the big restaurant. Ceiling fans flapped overhead. The train caller's meaningless howl came through a screening over the counter. The floor was tiled, blue and white, like Dr. Jim's bathroom. The high, arched windows were sooted with train smoke. The tables had clean white marble tops. Old-fashioned. John liked them. He ordered a nice compromise between breakfast and lunch. It was pleasant to pay for the meal out of his own pocket. He was not rich, of course. Dr. Jim had advised him to put his money into a checking account in a Federal Reserve Bank, pay his medical-school fees as they came up. And pray for rain, John added for himself. God knew the little hoard would have to grow.

Asking his way at the information desk, he started down Market Street in search of the bank. Whew! St. Louis was hot. Dirty, too. At least, here at the station. Olive Street was not much better. Old buildings, getting higher as he walked east. He might have taken a streetcar. Twelve blocks. He would walk.

He could have loitered all day before the plate-glass windows of the department stores. He called himself a hick, and grinned as he tipped his head back to see the whole of a shining new skyscraper. He looked with wonder at the mannequins displaying wares of "The August Fur Sales." He had lost familiarity with a climate that could veer from the shimmering heat which burned his shoulders today to a winter cold which would make these fur wrappings welcome.

The bank was huge, cool, hushed. John had the service of one of a row of youngish men seated at glass-topped desks. "Mr. Leary," said the name plate. Mr. Leary was, perhaps, forty. A little fat, beginning to be bald. He wore Palm Beach trousers, glistening tan shoes, and a snowy white shirt and brown tie. In ten minutes he had John's story — the part of it that told him how much money John had and what he wanted to do with it. He was friendly, impersonal. Attended to John's small business with a kindly briskness.

John ventured to ask Mr. Leary for directions to the medical school. Mr. Leary gave him a small booklet that was a guide to St. Louis. He took a red pencil and marked John's route on the streetcar map. Mr. Leary was a nice chap.

In the vestibule of the bank was the booth of a pay telephone. John found another nickel, went inside, and closed the door. His gray eyes sparkled to note that a light went on as the door closed. As Uncle Ben would have said, a nifty idea.

He called the Wielande number, and the same male voice answered.

"May I speak to Miss Isabelle?"

"Oh, Miss Isabelle is out of the city. Who is this calling, please?"

Need he be so shocked that anyone would expect "Miss Isabelle" to be in the city in August? "Can you tell me when she will return?"

"We are not expecting the family to return for another month. Who is this calling, please?"

"John Mallory. Thank you very much."

Well. At least he could not try to see Isabelle before he went to the medical school. He went out on the street, stood in the shelter of the tall gray-stone building, and studied the guide. Quite a large section was given over to the Boone Hospital Group and Lincoln University Medical School. There was even a plot of the buildings. Whew! No wonder Dr. Jim had said it was a fine place. If it could make room for John, he would have a fine springboard for his dive into the medical profession.

He walked the block to where he could catch the proper streetcar. He let one come, take on passengers, and go off without him. He had never ridden on a streetcar. He was not sure he knew how it was done.

But he was ready when the next car came, and mounted the platform with confidence. "I want to go to Boone Hospital," he told the conductor, who took his quarter and gave him a handful of odd tinny coins in return.

"Put a token in," the man said. "Transfer to Taylor." He punched a strip of drab paper and gave it to John. John found a seat near the door and examined the transfer and the tokens. The car moved swiftly and noisily. The air through the barred windows was cool against his face. John looked eagerly out of the window. Too much to see to get more than a general idea that St. Louis was much bigger than he had expected. Definitely it was a big city. The people on the streets and here on the straw benches of the car, the very buildings, had a withdrawn, impersonal, urban appearance. John must not expect small-town interest and patronage here. He must learn to get along on his own, just as he had learned to ride the streetcar.

He was beginning to get a little uneasy about the length of the journey — no doubt he had passed his transfer point — when the conductor called out, "Change for Taylor!"

He showed John, too, the corner where he must await the other car. A good thing he did — John would not have had the slightest idea of what to do, nor in what direction to move next.

St. Louis must be a prosperous city as well as a big one. Out in this neighborhood there were fine homes, trees, wide streets. Nursemaids in smart uniforms walked their charges in the shade of the buildings. To the southeast, if John had not lost his sense of direction, he saw two huge gas tanks. Round, and painted a shiny red and black, their bulk seemed a symbol of the city itself. Big, bright, ugly, strong.

But there was nothing ugly about the bigness of the Boone Group. Not that John could see the entire thing from the sidewalk where the streetcar left him. Not that he could take in more than a general idea of these clustered golden buildings towering up into the hot blue sky. There were awnings spread at the west windows. He could see white beds and wheel chairs on some lofty screened porches. Patches of green lawn with hoses jetting arcs of spray, and little round green trees. Wide doorways, and bright cars parked along every inch of curbstone. Way up at the top of one of the buildings a little plume of steam flaunted itself like a banner flying.

John walked along the street. He felt about two inches tall, shadowed by these immense piles of yellow brick and white stone. The size of the place stunned him. The smokestack alone, over there across the street, was higher than the hospital at Villa Franca.

Over there, too, not so high, not so tremendous, were the medical-school buildings. That was proper. Start 'em small. Let 'em work up to the ten-story hospitals and clinics. John waited his chance and went across the street.

5

By midafternoon John was out on the street again, with his first trimester of medical school embodied in a receipt in his pocket and an empty stub in his new checkbook. Nearly three hundred dollars gone, but that did not matter. John was enrolled in medical school. He was one of the eighty-two men accepted out of about three hundred applicants. What was more, the dreaded aptitude test had resolved itself into about a hundred questions from the dean. That gentleman spoke approvingly of John's recommendations from the school and hospital in Villa Franca. John could begin school the twenty-fifth of September. He would need white coats and lab aprons.

When asking for his address, the dean said regretfully that the dormitory was full. John must find a place near. His hours at school would be long. Nine to five, three days a week. Probably two afternoons free. A good student used them for lectures and clinics.

John asked, flushing, about the possibilities of

getting a job, say in the evenings, for his room and board.

The dean gave him a mild, and unneeded, lecture about the rigorous work facing a medical student.

"I know, sir. I'm a little pressed for money. I have tuition and fee money. But — somehow, sometime — vacations, perhaps, I'll have to earn my room and board, and clothes."

"Family?"

"No, sir." John told him about the money he had inherited from Uncle Ben. He had, of course, no claim upon Uncle Brooke.

The dean mentioned scholarships John might apply for, though he admitted there would be dozens of men before him. He mentioned a student loan fund. John remembered Dr. Jim's advice about borrowing.

"If I could get a job — in or near the hospital — I've had experience — I'd do anything, sir."

The dean looked at John. He seemed a kindly person, interested in John as a potential doctor. "As a matter of policy, Lincoln does not encourage the medical students to work at an outside job. We strive for a very high standing in the school. We are able to pick and choose our students so as to maintain that level. Your free hours, most of your summer vacations, could profitably be spent on your clinical clerkships and electives."

Did he mean that the school had no place for a poor man? John looked at the man with dismay.

"Perhaps you would advise me to wait — to work for a year or two — until I would have the money I'll need."

"You say you have enough for tuition and fees?"

"Yes, sir."

"I'd enroll now. I'd work as hard at my studies as I could. There are certain prizes. Sometimes you could get a small pay-job in certain of the clinics. If you are an exceptional student, there are sometimes tutoring opportunities. Also, you could give blood. You look strong. Oh, yes! You must go around to the students' physician and arrange for your physical examination. And put your name in at the registrar's desk as a student who needs financial aid. She — the clerk there — can give you a list of places to room, too. I'd eat at the school refectory. If I were you, I mean. The food is monotonous, but sustaining and well balanced."

John smiled. "I could work in the dining room," he suggested.

The dean reached for his telephone. Obviously he considered his business with John finished. "No," he said. "As a student of medicine, as a doctor-to-be, you have a certain professional bearing to acquire and maintain. It's one of the burdens of the profession. But you'll make it, Mallory. I'm sure you will."

John wished he could have been sure. Was the dean right about the sort of job a student could hold, or just snobbish? Certainly there had been a warning behind his words. John must not take on any job that would take him away from the medical school. Not very far away. It looked as if he would have to live on capital for a while, bone hard, and hope the ravens flew his way.

The registrar's clerk was pleasant, told him to keep in touch with her. She had lots of calls for students. She gave him a list of boardinghouses, indicated the addresses that sounded best to her. She told him how to find the students' physician.

That gentleman was out. But his eyeglassed nurse made an appointment for John to be examined at nine the next morning. Gave John a slip to that effect. By now John had a lot of slips. He had become, too, Mallory, J., 32. The 32 must mean his year. He would get his M.D. in 1932. He hoped.

By night, tired and a little discouraged, John was established in a small front bedroom of a flat on Euclid Avenue. A tiny, hot room over the front vestibule but, at that, the nicest room John had ever lived in. The narrow iron bed had a clean, striped spread and a hard pillow in a snowy case. There was a faded, clean rag rug on the floor. The wallpaper was striped pink and white. There was a golden oak dresser, a small oak rocker that brought John's knees up to his chin when he sat in it. There was a tiny closet for his clothes, and John had the use of a small, immaculate bathroom at the end of the hall. The long window of his room opened out upon a little balcony with an iron railing.

John's landlady, a smiling little woman, said she usually rented the room to one of the nurses from the hospital. But women made so much mess, always washing things. She was going to give men a try. John paid her three dollars and a half in rent for the first week, and went downtown for his suitcase and his box of books.

6

The first weeks went swiftly enough. John passed his medical examination and was allowed to put his name and type on the list of blood donors. In the refectory he met other students, some of them working on assistantships. He put his name down for such a job, and on every scholarship list he could find. He heard about a job at the central post office, but the hours were from nine to two at night. Common sense told him he could not undertake such a thing.

He put out a frightening sum of money for whites and the instruments he would need at the start of school. Later there would be other, and more expensive, things to buy.

He found that he had the run of the hospital halls and operating rooms. He learned to check in his name. All these hours of observation counted. He spent a good many hours in the psychopathic wards, thought for a time that he would make that his field. There was heart work, too. So much to challenge a man.

He grew familiar with every corner of the big medical center. The drone of the amplifiers became so customary to his ears that the noisy outside streets seemed oddly silent without it. He grew impatient for lectures to start. He was spending a lot of money and not getting anywhere. Eating as carefully as he could, saving on clothes, it cost him ten dollars a week, every week, to live. When he would use a white coat every day, his laundry bill would be worrisome.

He wished, too, that Belle would come home. If she delayed until classes started, he would be too busy to see a lot of her.

September was hot. Unusually so. There were two weeks when the nights were as hot as in mid-July. John, who liked to walk in the park, saw whole families sleeping on newspapers spread on the grass. His own bedroom was like an oven.

Mrs. Schuler told him to leave his hall door open, to let the air circulate. "We ain't going to look," she said.

There was a lot of infantile paralysis. One whole floor of Children's Hospital was quarantined. John got his first call to give blood, a direct transfusion. He was carefully masked before he was allowed to enter the operating room. He knew, too, that he was going to hate taking the money. He stood only too ready to help a suffering child.

But the clerk told him not to be silly. Either the family could pay or there was a fund. Boone Hospital was heavily endowed. There were lots of funds.

John went to the school library and read all he could find on infantile. He attended a series of lectures offered the practicing doctors of the city. Incurable diseases were a challenge. Before he was through, John hoped he could do something about this scourge of childhood. Was there significance to the fact that the amount of infantile was increasing?

John was getting to know St. Louis. With the aid of Mr. Leary's guidebook he roamed all over the place. He visited Shaw's Gardens, and the lily ponds in Tower Grove Park. He wished Miss Lillie could be with him to see that. He knew every inch of Forest Park; he imagined that the bears in the zoo pits had come to know him and his jelly beans. He explored downtown St. Louis. The old Courthouse, where the stench of slave auctions still hung in the air; the old Cathedral that was like a bonneted, white-haired lady riding on the seat of a garbage truck. He found the levee and the slow-moving brown Mississippi. He went back to the levee again and again. In the very early morning, with the sun rising red out of the smoke clouds of Illinois. He went there at noon, when the shadows were marked in startling contrasts of black and gold. He went there at night, with a moon overhead or with rain falling softly. The old cobblestones under his feet, the huge span of the bridge, the shadowy boats tied up at the dock, let him imagine he was in another country. Antwerp, perhaps. Folkestone on a foggy night. On the levee old St. Louis lingered.

He saw it in the names over the old brick warehouses and stores. French, Spanish, German — all fused into a mellow harmony that pleased John's ear as the blended smells of molasses and coffee and tobacco pleased his nose. There was a knowledge of hidden power under the slow-moving surface of the brown river, just as there was knowledge of hard muscles under the brown skin of the stevedore who slept in the shadow of the bridge. John sensed that power, and was thrilled by it.

He wished he had some friend to share his delight in the levee, and be thrilled as he was the first time he saw Soulard Market. Why, the very name, Soulard, was exciting!

7

John had, from time to time, called the Wielande home and asked for Belle. Mrs. Schuler let him use the phone whenever he wished. Along about the fifteenth of the month the masculine voice — John felt as if the owner were an old friend by now — told him that "Miss Isabelle" would return tomorrow. John hung up the receiver, delighted. He would give her a day to get unpacked and settled, then he would go out to the house. He had discovered the place on one of his walks. An ornate, red-brick building, with white flower urns on the stoop and an iron grille protecting the front door. Well, John knew that Brooke Wielande was a rich man. But Belle was still his sister.

Mrs. Schuler told him, the next afternoon, that he had had a call from the hospital. John expected that meant blood, and went right over. If this kept up, he would about make expenses. He was lucky to be a general blood type.

Again it was for a child. A boy facing an amputation. John was able to talk to the big-eyed kid, to cheer him up. He was able, too, to realize the miracle of blood transfusion. The boy seemed to blossom with health under his very eyes. "Good-by, John," the lad called back happily, as the cart was wheeled out. Poor kid.

John sat on a stool, a little dizzy, while the intern bandaged his arm. They had taken a lot.

"You ought to take up pediatrics," the young man said.

"I'm registered for surgery."

"You have a way with kids. Lots of men don't."

"I'll think it over."

"You do that. Better take it easy tonight. You might have a headache."

"O.K."

John did have a headache. The first he ever remembered having, and he went to bed early. Traces of it lingered next morning, and he ordered black coffee when he went to the refectory for breakfast. A good many students were at the school by now, a pleasant, rollicking bunch. All of them inclined to be friendly with John.

John's knees still felt wobbly, so he went to the park and sat on a shady bench. He would wait until afternoon to go to see Belle. And he thought he would not attempt the clinic at Children's this morning. He guessed it was just as well the intern had said he must wait at least six weeks before giving blood again. Still, the money helped. He ought to write to Dr. Jim. He and Miss Lillie had decided to stay the winter in China, and then come home by way of India and Europe. It seemed strange to think of the big house in Villa Franca standing empty, Miss Lillie's roses unpruned.

John felt better by noon, and ate a good lunch. He was able to listen with interest to the talk at his table. One of the students — a second-year man, John thought — was being very funny about a laboratory course in physiology, where, John gathered, the students themselves were the subjects of experiments. One started, the man gravely assured John, by scraping the inside of his cheek, and ended up by drawing lots to see which member of each team should have his leg cut off. "To see what the reaction will be."

John buttered a roll and looked at the second-year man. "The greenness around my gills," he said pleasantly, "is due to a bucket of blood I lost yesterday. I expect they don't amputate many legs on the students around here. So far as I can see, sitting down isn't encouraged."

The other men at the table laughed. When he left the table, Barngrove, the talker, came up and linked his arm through John's.

"Mallory, isn't it?"

"Yes."

"Live at the dorm?"

"No, I don't. I have a room down on Euclid."

"I see. What's your school?"

"You won't have heard of it. A small college in California."

"Near Hollywood?"

"Not close enough to help any."

Barngrove laughed. He was a likeable chap. "What are you doing this afternoon?"

"I'm busy, I'm afraid."

"O.K. I'll see you around."

"Yes."

John went back to his room and bathed and shaved. He had decided that two o'clock would be a good hour to call on Belle. Early enough that she would be at home, but well past lunchtime. He had been wearing his light clothes during the hot weather; but today he got out his new brown suit, polished his brown Oxfords, took out a fresh white shirt. His tie was a shade lighter than his suit, and his felt hat matched it exactly. John studied himself critically in the mirror and decided that he looked well enough. He thought he was not a handsome man, but he was tall and clean-looking. He did not think Belle would be ashamed of her brother.

Belle had used to be a lot like their mother, likely to put undue emphasis on outer appearances. John admitted that, up to a certain point, such an attitude was right. Certainly cleanliness and good grooming were important.

John was not too much awed by the Wielande

mansion, nor by the fact that the door was opened by that hitherto mythical creature, a butler. John wanted to see his sister. A plateglass door and a striped vest would scarcely be enough to stop him.

He asked for Miss Isabelle and gave his name as John Mallory. Afterward he wondered why he had not identified himself as Belle's brother. It would have saved a lot of hurt and trouble. Just now he was wondering if he should not have asked for Aunt Mary instead of Belle. But it was Belle he wanted to see.

The man — the butler — showed him into a shaded room, the chairs and divan covered in white muslin, and disappeared. But he came back immediately and said Miss Isabelle would be right down. He whisked the sheets off two chairs, murmuring that the family had only just returned. He offered John cigarettes, which John refused with a smile. He sat down on one of the rose-colored chairs and prepared to wait.

The house was very still. As if no one were in it. Yet there was, John knew, the butler chap, and Belle, and a maid in black and white he had seen moving about in the dining room on the other side of the wide hall. There were no smells, either. Dr. Jim's house always smelled of something pleasant. A chicken Wong was roasting in the kitchen or a bowlful of roses Miss Lillie had brought in. Maybe this place would smell, too, once the family had got fully settled in.

Belle made him wait about ten minutes, then

she came running down the stairs and into the room. She closed the wide door behind her, and turned to face, and look at, John.

"Why, John!" she said in a pretty, tinkling voice. Then, more warmly, and she smiled, "Why, John!"

John stood and looked at her, holding her hand. He did not remember ever having kissed Belle. He had not, he knew, when they had left each other. But now she evidently expected him to do it. He bent and touched her cheek lightly. She smelled, and tasted, of perfumed face powder.

For a long minute, then, they stood smiling and looking at each other. Belle, John thought, was a pretty girl. Woman. Taller than he had somehow expected her to be. She had an exquisite, immaculate look that he admired. Her hair was still a lovely pale gold, cut short and waved softly, close to her head. Her skin was very white and fine. She had a lovely color on her cheeks, and her lips were bright red. Some of that was make-up, of course. Her eyes were the rich brown he remembered; her eyebrows arched perfectly away from her little straight nose. She wore a plain, short dress of yellow linen, with a demure round white collar close against the base of her throat. Her shoes were flat-heeled white Oxfords such as the nurses wore. Or something like them.

"How tall you are, John!" she cried. "And good-looking!"

John felt his cheeks redden. It seemed impossible that this girl was his sister. "I — You've changed, too, Belle. A little."

She laughed. She had a pretty laugh, and pretty teeth. "Goodness, I should hope so! After all Uncle Brooke has spent on me. What are you doing in St. Louis, John?"

"Didn't you get my letter?"

"I haven't heard from you in a long time. Our mail never did catch up with us. I've been in Europe since May. Traveling with Mrs. Slocumb."

Evidently the name should have meant something to John, but it did not. "We've a lot to tell each other."

"I know. And I'm so busy. I tell you — I'm supposed to exercise an hour every day; we could walk in the park. Or would you want to do that? You might come back at another time when I'm not so rushed. It's just now, coming home, and only two weeks left . . ."

"I'd like to walk," John said, to still her chatter. It had little meaning for him. He would be busy, too, in another week.

Belle fetched a small yellow hat, white gloves, and a wire-haired terrier on a braided leather leash. The dog seemed more a part of her costume than a pet. Isabelle did not care much for the dog, it seemed to John.

"I must be back by three-thirty," she said solemnly, as they went down the steps.

"All right." They began to walk slowly along the wide sidewalk. Occasionally — quite often, in fact — Belle spoke to someone, and John would lift his hat. She chattered about Europe, and John told her briefly about Uncle Ben's death and medical school.

"Did he leave you a lot, John?"

"Not enough. I hope I can get some sort of job. I — I hate to ask this, Belle, but do you suppose Mr. Wielande . . ."

Belle frowned. "Uncle Brooke? Well, you see — oh, he's grand, John. Perfectly grand. But he's done so much for me. I could ask him, though."

"I'm not asking him for anything but a job," John said stiffly. His head was beginning to buzz again.

"I know. But if he knew you were my brother — he has spent so *much* on me, John. And he isn't very well. He's having his teeth pulled, and that makes him cross and miserable. You see how it is, John?"

Frankly John did not. Perhaps it was his head that made her words seem confused and irrelevant. But just then they met friends of Belle's, walking in the other direction. Belle stopped, and John took off his hat.

"Mrs. Howe. John Mallory. Miss Howe."

John dipped his head and said, "How do you do?" and then just stood while Belle chattered to the women about her trip and the perfectly vile crossing, and some party, and some Queen, and was Isabelle a Maid? "Oh, of course. It's a bore, but I suppose I must." She had her dress but was not sure herself just what it was like. She had selected several. "Patty, are you going to Trudy's luncheon? I hope they don't have meringues. I'm sick of meringues. I'll see you there. Good-by, darling. Good-by, Mrs. Howe."

John nodded again, and put on his hat.

"Did you see? She had on satin slippers?" said Belle.

"Who did?"

"Patty Howe. In the afternoon. It just shows what nobodies they are."

She seemed outraged. John laughed aloud. "What difference does it make?" he asked.

"Why, John! Oh, well, of course, you can't imagine all the details there are to being social."

She went to some lengths to explain the social system to John. She was, he learned, to make her debut that year. John thought all this chatter about satin slippers, and V. P. balls, and first- and second-year girls quite silly. But he liked watching Belle's pretty, animated face while she talked. He was proud to be walking along beside her, to know he was her brother. He was glad that she need have no other thought in her little yellow head except parties and clothes.

"It's going to be grand having you here in town," she told him when they turned again toward home. "You're awfully good-looking, and an extra man is a treasure!"

"You're a funny kid, Belle," John laughed.

"Don't call me Belle. I really don't like it. Promise me, John. You belong to me. My invitations come first."

"I'm your brother," John reminded her seriously.

"Oh, yes, but —" She took his arm and looked up at him. "I was wondering — no one knows I'm your sister — perhaps we needn't mention it?"

"But why? Unless you are ashamed of me?" If she were, quite completely, that would be that!

"Oh, John, I'm not! It's quite the other way. I — you'll think I'm silly, but I'd rather people would think you were a conquest than a brother. Do you see? Brothers have to be nice to their sisters. But — do you see?"

She probably was afraid he ate with his knife. "I'm afraid I don't." His head was thumping now, and his knees felt funny. He should not have walked so far, perhaps.

"Then there's Uncle Brooke. I want you to understand about that, John."

"Yes," John agreed. "So do I."

"Well, now, there are several points. In the first place, for years and years he's been helping Aunt Mary's family. Mother, and me, and Cousin Clara. He's paying for an operation for Uncle Archie right now."

"I'm not asking him to give me a thing, Belle."

"I know. That's the point. I'm *sure* you don't want to claim anything because of our relationship. But if he knew you were a relative, he'd immediately think you *were* asking, and take out his checkbook. On the other hand, he's fearfully fond of me. He isn't demonstrative, but I can tell. If he thinks you are a very good *friend* of mine, he'll be interested and want to help you."

"Do you think he would give me a job?"

"He might. What sort of job do you want?"

John hesitated. He did not know. Back in his mind had been some vague idea of helping in Uncle Brooke's house as he had done at Hayes'! Take out ashes, he supposed, his lip curling in self-disgust. He realized that he *had* been counting on Uncle Brooke's offering him a home, and Belle was afraid he would do just that. She did not want John in the Wielande home, just as she had not wanted him there seven years ago.

"I don't suppose there'd be anything," he said stiffly.

"He's a broker. Perhaps he could invest your money. People are making just scads of money on investments, John."

"Yes, I've heard. I'm not much of a gambler. Haven't the guts, I expect."

Belle tucked her white-gloved fingers into the bend of his arm and smiled up at him. She had pretty, appealing ways — she was not consciously selfish, John knew. He smiled down at her.

"I am glad you're going to be in St. Louis," she told him. "I'll invite you to some of my parties, and you can meet my friends."

"Hey! Hold on! I'm a busy man. Once school starts . . ."

Belle giggled. "You seem so grown up to be going to school."

"Medical school isn't the grades."

"I know. I'll be proud of you when you're a doctor. Dr. John Mallory. But you'll have time for some parties. Evenings, anyway."

"I'll be busy," John repeated stubbornly. "You see, Belle, if I mustn't ask Uncle Brooke — if I can't work at some job, I'll almost have to get a scholarship. I mean, work extra hard for top grades. All the students are pretty darn good. It isn't going to be easy."

Belle frowned and jerked the terrier away from a fascinating wad of paper. "I hate to hear you talk about working hard. It makes me remember all the things I've tried to forget. Mother, and Brownsville . . ."

John frowned, too. "Are you ashamed of those things?"

"Well, yes, I am. A little. Anyway, they aren't pleasant memories."

"Perhaps. I expect you are ashamed of me, too. Ashamed that I am poor and have to work."

"No. I told you — I think you are good-looking, and nice. Men who have to work — especially for something like medicine — that's all right."

"You're a snob."

"Well, maybe. But you shouldn't care. So long as I like you and want you to come to my parties. Give me your address, John. I want to put your name on Aunt Mary's list."

"I told you —"

"You don't have to come to everything. But I expect you could manage tea some afternoon, couldn't you? It's the only way I'll get to see anything of you, John. This winter I —"

"I could think of ways to arrange our seeing each other. If you wanted to see me. Besides, won't Aunt Mary upset all your silly schemes? Won't she recognize me?"

"You've changed."

"I mean the name."

"Oh. No-o. I don't think she will. Not that it would really matter. But I'm sure she won't. She's bad about names. Vague. Gets them wrong. Once — years ago — I heard her tell someone that Mother had married a man named Joe Malloy. You see? Honestly it'll be sort of fun, fooling people."

"Who will you tell her I am?"

"Who?"

"Aunt Mary. When I come to *tea* some afternoon. Which I probably won't do."

"Oh. Why, just John Mallory. You're a medical student at Boone. That will be enough."

John did not like it. He saw right through Belle's silly, snobbish schemes. He felt he was not unattractive enough to warrant such a reaction. He was not, of course, a rich man, nor did he know anything about the social rigmarole she evidently thought was so all-important. But he did not have *bad* manners. He — Still, he loved Belle; he wanted to be with her. She was all that he had in the world. He admitted that his plans for making a home for her had been a little high-flown, but he did not want to lose his chance for some sort of companionship with her. He guessed he could agree to her silly plan. She was just a kid. She would grow up someday and laugh at her own foolishness. Meanwhile John would let the matter slide. Probably Aunt Mary would recognize his name. But he did not go to tea at Wielandes' that week, nor the next.

8

John was busy now, with school opening, lectures and laboratory hours beginning. Too busy to worry about Isabelle's strange behavior and snobbish fears. When two cards came for the Veiled Prophet's Ball, and a note from Isabelle explaining that they would admit him and a friend to the balcony, where he would not need to dress, John snorted, and stuck them in the pocket of his leather notebook cover, and almost forgot them.

But the next Sunday's paper was full of the V. P. parade and ball. Isabelle's picture was in the rotogravure section. John looked at it carefully, tore it out, then trimmed it neatly and studied it again. A posed portrait — Isabelle looked like a million dollars. Pretty as she really was, the photographer had made the most of her blonde beauty posed against a shaded background. The picture made John think of the single diamond pendant he had seen displayed in one of the Locust Street jewelers' windows. Walls of glistening mirrors, dark blue velvet draped with studied carelessness, and that single perfect jewel laid there. So was Isabelle displayed, her head slightly tilted, her perfect lips parted in just the faintest promise of a smile, her dark, simple dress chosen carefully. Just so she appeared the most beautiful, the most desirable. "Miss Isabelle Wielande, daughter of Mr. and Mrs. Brooke Wielande. She will make her debut at an elaborate ball on Christmas night."

John sighed and pushed the clipping away. He had better study his anatomy, and let social doodads worry along without him. The picture was still there on the table when Barngrove dropped in before lunchtime. He picked it up and studied it critically. "Tasty baggage," he decided. "If you find something more to your liking, I'll bless the lady with my interest."

John reached for his necktie. "She's a little out of our class, I'm afraid."

"Know her?"

"Yes."

Barngrove raised an eyebrow, and looked again at the picture.

"This V. P.," John said hastily, "must be quite a blowout."

"Oh, yes. We're a little old for the parade. I remember my dad holding me on his shoulder to see it. That was when horses pulled the floats, and they used gasoline torches. Smelled swell. Now it's all electric, and you don't get the same atmosphere. Besides, it's your own feet hurting. It always rains."

"What about the ball?"

"I hear it's good, too. You have to be a big shot — or work for one — even to get a ticket for the nigger heaven. One time when I was in high school I went down and watched the ritzy dames cross the sidewalk. I froze my ears in that rarefied climate."

John laughed. Barngrove was a good scout. "I've been given two tickets to the balcony. If you'd like to go along — just to see the Queen crowned —"

"Say, what is this? You aren't old St. Louis' left-handed son, are you?"

"Nothing like that. I'm a distant, very poor — and very well-concealed — relation of one of the big shots."

Barngrove let it go at that, and Wednesday night he and John boned together in Pete's room at the dorm. Then, about nine-thirty, they started for the Coliseum. John did not need Barngrove's finger to show him the limousines that were whizzing along Kingshighway, revealing exciting glimpses of silk hats and pale satin evening cloaks. There was even one man in full dress on the streetcar. John decided that a long-tailed coat deserved better than a perilous anchorage to a streetcar strap. Barngrove said maybe the guy was a waiter.

9

The Coliseum was a huge place. Even Barngrove had a little difficulty in finding the door that would admit them. But finally they were inside. John supposed the place was used for all sorts of shows, including animal. They went down confusing concrete runways and climbed a mile of spiral iron stairs. Their balcony was crowded. John despaired of getting a seat, or seeing more than a small corner of the lower floor. But Barngrove was resourceful. He picked his objective, then persuaded people on the first and second tiers to slide a little more closely together on the concrete steps. He told John to sit down quickly before they relaxed.

"You'll have a swell case of steatopygia," he said in John's ear.

John grinned, his eyes busy.

The big circular hall was decorated in violet and gold. The lower floor itself was empty except for an occasional gentleman in evening clothes with a wide ribbon across his shirt front. Down to John's right a dais had been erected with three throne chairs upon it. There were rows of chairs, covered in pale gold satin, curving away from the throne. The lower circle of boxes was already well filled with men and women in evening clothes. Now the gentlemen ushers began to conduct girls and women to the satin-covered chairs. "Maids and Matrons," Barngrove whispered. John nodded. Beside the Matrons, poised, graceful, serene, some of the Maids seemed pathetically awkward and bony. John searched eagerly for Isabelle, but did not find her.

The hall was full now, every seat taken. The

lower boxes were crowded with men and women, expensively, elaborately dressed. The perfume and flowers alone, Pete whispered to John, would run a good hospital for a whole year.

The orchestra was now playing a march. John's fingers itched to thump out those rousing chords on ivory keys. Four pages in white satin — slim girls of probably twenty or so — came to the front of the platform, lifted long golden trumpets, and announced the entrance of the Past Queens. The Maids and Matrons all rose from their chairs. Everyone in the hall looked toward the doors.

Now the Prophet sat upon his throne. He seemed fabulous, indeed, in his rich, flowing garments and mysterious veil. Last year's Queen sat at his left hand, a dark-haired girl in light blue.

The pages lifted their trumpets; the herald held aloft his scroll.

"His Majesty, the Veiled Prophet, summons to rule for one year over the Court of Love and Beauty, his Queen . . ."

A sharp tingle of electric excitement sparked through the immense, crowded hall. The woman next to John edged forward on her seat. John's hands felt moist.

The Queen's name meant nothing to him. Vera Ahnheim.

"Beer," Pete whispered in his neck. "Near beer since prohibition. Oceans of suds."

John took out his handkerchief and wiped his

hands. The Queen had a mass of curly dark hair; she seemed very handsome from this distance. Her dress glistened as if made from diamonds. Her train, of white velvet edged in ermine, swept out in a tremendous circle behind her. She knelt before the Prophet; she was crowned; she turned to face her applauding subjects. Her monstrous bouquet of orchids trembled piteously.

The Special Maids were summoned. The Fourth Maid. The Third Maid.

"Miss Isabelle Wielande!"

Isabelle did not tremble. Isabelle did not have trouble with her long train as the Fourth Maid had. John felt himself grinning like an idiot. But he was so proud! He wanted to tell Barngrove, tell the woman next to him, that this tall, slim, golden-haired girl was his sister. No one would believe that that glorious creature in silver and blue could belong to him!

The Second Maid seemed inconsequential after Isabelle. She was fat, and she stumbled on the steps. Her face was too flushed. She smiled too much. John looked again at Isabelle's icy poise, her calm assurance.

"The First Maid: Miss Ellen Conte."

"She shoulda been Queen," John's neighbor declared with conviction.

Even as Maid she was receiving a tremendous ovation. John found himself smiling, clapping. He looked closely at the girl. Not regal like Isabelle, but she was having a swell time. John liked her. He clapped harder.

"A-ha! Jack's girl friend!" said Barngrove.

John bit his lip. Yes, the sort of "girl friend" he would pick — down there, a hundred feet down — a girl in a gown of white lace, wearing a court train of gold-colored velvet bordered in soft, dark fur, a jeweled tiara in her hair.

And John — up here on a stone seat, the greenest of medical students, less than a dollar in his pocket, no friends, no position — Barngrove might well be sarcastic.

But that did not keep him from turning his eyes, again and again, to this copper-haired girl. He watched Isabelle, too, but somehow the other one — Ellen — kept swinging into focus. There was something about her . . .

Critically he observed the men with whom she danced. He felt happier when she favored the gray-haired, the bald-headed — until it occurred to him that the very young might, like himself, be also the very poor, the very ineligible. This debutante business was a matrimonial venture, he felt quite sure.

Miss Ellen Conte danced well. Her dress had little inserts of pleated chiffon at the hem; the ruffles looked pretty swirling out as her black-garbed partner swung her around. Most of the women — a lot of them — danced with their faces close to their partners' — too close. His Ellen did not. Her proud head was flung back. She was laughing, having a good time.

John wished he knew how to dance. He wished he might get to know a girl like that one. Perhaps she was Isabelle's friend. Perhaps, by swallowing some of his pride, by going to one of Isabelle's damn teas, he might meet this swell girl.

Chapter Six

John was able, when so inclined, to keep a pretty accurate and detailed idea of Isabelle's activities during this winter. Any newspaper he might pick up would be fairly sure to have her name in one paragraph or more of the society column. He grew used to seeing her picture — some new, formal pose, or a news photographer's snapshot taken at the horse show, a football game, a Junior League luncheon. Belle gave John one of the portraits taken of her in her Special Maid's gown and train. John put the big folder into a drawer, hidden between his shirts. Opened, on top of his dresser, it obscured the best part of his mirror. Besides, Mrs. Schuler might be embarrassingly curious. Barngrove, he knew, would be too interested. John liked Pete Barngrove, but he did not relish Isabelle's name being subject to the sort of gossip that flourished in the medical school. The time had passed, he realized, for claiming her publicly as his sister.

He saw her, but not often. She was busy, and so was he. Lectures and laboratories took more time than they would seem to when written down on a schedule. John "boned" hard, in the library, and at home in his room of nights. He attended as many operations and clinics as he could manage.

In November he got a job of sorts, assisting the instructor in anatomy. This gentleman was the son of a rich and old St. Louis family. John suspected that, had he been poor and forced to work, Hugo Marke would have been a brilliant surgeon. As it was, he maintained his place on the Boone Hospital Staff by lecturing the freshman medics three times a week. Usually he came dawdling into class, late, carelessly dressed, perfunctory in his discussion. Once, however, he became interested in some muscular pains induced by hyper-nervousness — scarcely a subject for a first-year anatomy class — and the men stayed ten minutes past the bell listening to him, fascinated and enthralled. John knew he was a genius, actively disliked his not using his God-bestowed gift to its full advantage.

This clever, careless man possessed a store of the vilest stories John ever hoped to hear. "If Marke ever tells you the same yarn twice," Barngrove told him, "walk out on him. You're being cheated."

One time Dr. Marke came to class dressed to the nines — a fashion model from the top of his tilted silk hat to the tips of his gray-spatted, patent leather shoes. He perched the topper on the head of Horace, the muscle-man, settled his gray trousers with a careful hand, smelled the gardenia in his buttonhole, lifted an eyebrow to the class, and remarked that they were being allowed to gaze upon the correct, the fashionable, thing in wedding guests. From there he went on to quote the *Ancient Mariner* — inaccurately — and thence to tell a vile anatomical joke. Dr. Marke was drunk.

It was this man, however, who paid John five dollars a week to take the roll call at lectures, keep the records of laboratory hours and work of the class, and grade the occasional quiz books. John was grateful, but he still did not like Dr. Marke.

Once John met the man at Wielandes'. He could not say what had led him finally to accept Isabelle's casual invitation to tea. This particular Thursday afternoon it was snowing. John thoroughly enjoyed his walk through the park. He stopped and watched the youngsters skating on the small, shallow lake where last summer they had held toy-boat regattas.

His cheeks tingled with the cold when he came into Wielandes' warm house. It was entirely too warm, and the cocktails of that period smelled all too much of the anatomy vats. It was not surprising to find Dr. Marke in this atmosphere, but John disliked the familiar way his hand lay upon Isabelle's waist. Because he himself had no facility with social small talk and casual manners, John never came to like the meaningless, fashionable use of "darling" and "sweetheart," the men's bad manners, their overplain talk, their light gestures of affection and intimacy. He did not like Hugo Marke's being near his sister. Evidently he showed how he felt.

The girl seated at the tea table raised her brows above eyes like the bluest leaves of the wood violet. "Isabelle thinks you should be polite to people named Marke," she chided gently.

John's heart plunged. He knew this girl — he had looked down on that coppery hair; he had been noticing her pictures in the papers. "You don't like him!" he challenged.

"Oh, but you mustn't follow my example. Me, I'm society's problem child."

John had to grin, then, and let her fix him a cup of tea — which he did not want. But the least thing Ellen Conte's hand had touched . . . He accepted the green and gold cup and saucer, the tiny napkin of linen and lace. He took a sandwich from a plate of them and moved over to a window. Hot dog! He was in society, balancing a cup of tea like an old hand, or — so he hoped. The sandwich was good but very small. If he knew the ropes, he could make a meal. Some of those pretty cakes and a handful of salted nuts. Today, he had better be wary. He had accomplished one thing. He had seen Ellen face to face, had even spoken to her! He watched Belle, greeting newcomers, bringing them to the tea table, moving from group to group. Gosh, he was proud of her. She was as poised and assured as if she had never eaten at a kitchen table covered with dark green oilcloth nor worn panties made of washed flour sacks.

The butler brought his tray up to John, and lifted an eyebrow invitingly. John shook his head. The amber drinks looked good — however they might smell — but he would stick to tea.

When he had first arrived, Belle had introduced him to Aunt Mary, beautiful, white-haired, and — Isabelle was right — vague. She now brought up a tall, horse-faced woman and smiled brightly at John. "Edith, this is John Manley, a friend of Isabelle's."

John ate salted nuts and listened to Edith talk. He decided that keeping the relationship a secret might have its points. People would evidently say to him what they really thought of the Wielandes and Belle. This Edith-person wondered why Mrs. Wielande should be so quaint as to serve tea. Nobody drank it. She — Edith — would just have cocktails. Maybe even beer. St. Louis men liked beer. With a debutante on your hands it was important to attract the men. Mr. Manley knew, did he not, that Isabelle was an adopted daughter? Pretty, but no family. Lucky there was so much money.

Edith drifted on to somebody else, though she had not seemed discontented with John's silence. John did not mind standing alone. It had never occurred to him before that Isabelle — and he — were without family. In Edith's specialized sense of the word, of course.

He shrugged and wondered where Ellen had got to. He looked around for Belle and found her. He liked to look at her prettiness. She had charm and grace. She greeted each person warmly, and people seemed genuinely glad to see and speak to her. She had turned her attentions now to an old lady, seated on the divan. Belle brought her a cup of tea and filled a plate with sandwiches and cakes. She sat beside the woman and held the plate on her knee. The dowager ate and drank hungrily, licking the frosting from her old fingers with a frank tongue. John watched the tableau, not knowing that he smiled.

"Isn't Isabelle wonderful?" someone asked at his elbow.

John started, and turned to look at the girl who stood there. "Hello," he said. "Yes, she is." This Ellen popped up . . . He felt all hands, distinctly out of place.

The girl frowned a little, then she laughed. She had a nice laugh, pretty, sparkling teeth, and a little dimple at the very corner of her mouth. "I'm afraid I've forgotten your name," she said frankly. "I'm bad that way. Isabelle would never do such a thing, would she?"

"Oh, no," John assured her earnestly. "She wouldn't."

"Do you? Forget names?"

"Always. Isabelle is about to disown me."

The girl laughed again. It was a merry little chuckle. "Isabelle has so many virtues," she complained admiringly. "The way she covered up your glare at poor Hugo Marke. And, now, the way she is with old Mrs. Carter. She always is nice to the right people. She can't really *like* them."

"I can't manage that, can you?"

"Never. I'm nice only to interesting people. People I like."

John shook his head solemnly. He wished he knew how to *talk*.

"I'll bet you aren't any better. Are you, now?"

"No, I'm afraid I'm not."

"Why I ask — you see, if I discover enough of your faults, I may remember your name."

"You won't," John assured her. "You've never heard it."

She looked up at him, unbelieving. "Oh, but — I'm sure I have. I'm sure I know you very well. Don't I? Please don't tell me I've picked up a man?"

John laughed aloud. People near turned and smiled at the two of them. Belle, tied to horrid old Mrs. Carter, looked across at them. Ellen and John were having a grand time over something.

"Can't I get you some tea?" John was asking this jolly girl — she was like a russet apple, all soft, warm tones of rose and amber. She had sparkle; she had tang.

"I don't want tea," she told him. "But I would love about ten sandwiches."

"Ten sandwiches it is," said John, starting off.

She seized his coat sleeve. "Oh, no. Aunt Mary would think you were crazy."

"I'll tell her they are for the starving Armenians." He went on to the table and picked up a large plate of small sandwiches. Mrs. Wielande did not so much as glance his way. Ellen had moved into the window embrasure, and John put his plate on the cushioned seat between them. "There you are!" he said triumphantly.

"Oh, how grand. I never get enough sandwiches at teas, do you? They are always so small, and so good."

"Is Mrs. Wielande really your aunt?"

"Oh, not really. I call her that because of Isabelle, you know."

"I'm afraid I don't. I really am a stranger, you see."

"Honestly? What is your name?"

"John Mallory."

"John Mallory." She said it reflectively. "How very nice. Nice and plain and strong. Like good baked beans with a sugary crust. Or simply chewy molasses candy."

John leaned against the window frame and laughed again. He had a hearty laugh. People, hearing him now, smiled to one another.

"I'm that way about names, aren't you?" Ellen asked.

John had never met, nor seen, such a jolly girl. Such a genuine sort of person. He had known she would be that sort, from his first glimpse of her at the ball. He felt as if he had known her all his life. He felt, too, as if he had opened a new book and, having read the first fascinating page, could not bear to put it down before he had read on and on. How could he feel both ways at once? As if he knew her completely, and at the same time as if he could never know enough about her?

"Take Helen. That's tomato bisque. Paul is steak and mushrooms. Ann is hot gingerbread with butter."

"And I'm baked beans."

"*Good* baked beans."

"What's Isabelle?"

"The name? Or the person?"

"Aren't they the same?"

"Not always. But Isabelle — I think she's strawberry mousse. I like it, don't you?"

"If it's what I think it is, I do."

The girl laughed again. "You've got a grand line," she told him.

"So have you."

"You mean — all that about names?"

"Yes. Still, people are rather like things to eat. I myself thought you were like a juicy apple."

"Oh, heavens!" They laughed together, not noisily, but with great merriment.

Isabelle murmured something to Mrs. Carter and came across the room. "I'm glad you two have found each other," she said sweetly. "Isn't John grand, Ellen?"

"Yes, he is. Where have you been hiding him?"

"He's my well-concealed past." She ran her hand under his arm; he held it in his own palm. Her hand was tiny, and white and soft. His own hands, clean enough, were big and scarred. The nails filed short. He realized that Ellen Conte was watching him.

"Are you," she asked, "Isabelle's past?"

"I suppose so. All the past she has. Wouldn't you think she could do better?" He heard the relief in Isabelle's giggle. He felt new shame that she should have denied her brother. John should have come out and told this grand girl — Isabelle could not have done a thing about it — he should have set things straight right at the start. Now there would need to be explanations. He wished he had not come near Wielandes'. His discomfort showed in his face. "I — I'm crazy about Isabelle," he told this other girl unhappily.

She smiled, nodded, and jumped to her feet, brushing crumbs from her brown velveteen skirt. Isabelle still clung to John's arm. "I'll have to be going on," Ellen said. "We're calling on Aunt Philomene Coquin tonight. She's threatening to give a luncheon for me, Isabelle. If she does, don't accept. I'm warning you."

Isabelle laughed. "Don't be silly. I'd as soon refuse a bid from Queen Mary. Good-by, darling. Call me in the morning."

John watched the girl stop beside Aunt Mary, bend and kiss her cheek. He watched her walk out of the room, a straight, proud creature, with amber hair curling out from under her little brown hat, a fine lace collar lying weblike against her brown jacket.

"Are you two friends?" he asked Isabelle.

"Ellen's my very best friend."

John nodded. "That's fine. She's a swell girl. If you'd tell her I am your brother, she might be my friend, too."

Isabelle patted his arm. "Your chances are better if I don't tell her," she said gaily.

"I don't see why."

"You wouldn't. But you can take my word for it, they are."

When John was leaving, Isabelle called to him to wait. "I have to go down on Maryland for a fitting," she said. "I'll take you home in the car."

She led him back through the hall. He helped her into her silky, fur coat, knelt and put her slippered feet into fur-topped galoshes. They went out the side door and got into the back seat of the town car.

John tucked the fur robe around Isabelle's knees. "He needs it more than you do," he said, nodding toward the chauffeur in his unprotected seat.

"Lee? Don't be silly."

"I'm not silly. I hope you buy him good heavy red flannels."

"He has a good job and knows it," Isabelle said indifferently. "Light me a cigarette, John. These gloves . . ."

John complied, his face stern. "Have one yourself," she suggested.

"Thanks, I can't afford it."

"Oh, John!"

"I can't. Fifteen cents a day means a meal to me."

"You're cross today."

"I'm sorry."

"You were rude to Dr. Marke, too."

"I loathe the man."

"Didn't you say he was a teacher of yours?"

"He is. And I work for him. Do his dirty, detail work. I still loathe him. He knows it, too."

Isabelle puffed a veil of smoke at the low, velvet ceiling of the car. "Yes, I suppose he does. Don't you think you're making a mistake, John?"

"If you knew what sort of man he is . . ."

"I do know. Better than you probably think is nice for me to know. Still, John, he has important family connections, and in the school he is in a position to help you. If you are as poor as you claim to be, I'd think you'd realize how important a little diplomacy, to the right people, can be."

John turned and gazed out of the car window at the flying snow, the dark trees, the street lamps blossoming rosily in the mist. "I can earn what I need, Belle. I won't toady. To anyone."

Belle sighed. She thought "diplomacy" was a legitimate profession. Certainly it had taken her where she wanted to be. "John, dear," she said patiently, "I'm not asking you to go against your principles. I'm not even asking you to be nice to Hugo Marke. I think myself he's rather awful. But — you know, yourself — you've told me about the doctor in California who did so much for you — he didn't do all that because you were rude and independent, did he?"

Dr. Jim. He and Hugo Marke did not belong to the same species. Isabelle's way of arguing was that of a child. Or to a child. "It's not the same sort of thing at all. I liked — admired — Dr. Jim because he was — what he was, not because I hoped to get anything out of him."

She sighed again. Her effort toward patience was obvious, and a bit irritating. If she tried, further, to show John the policy of liking the right, the advantageous, people, he told himself that he would get out and walk. But she did not. The hospital buildings loomed before them, looking like a gigantic peep show, their myriad tiny lighted windows twinkling through the snow.

"Did you get a card for my dance?" she asked.

"Yes. I can't come. I haven't the clothes."

"Ellen Conte is to be honored with me; she's my best friend. I could see that you liked her. I want you to come, John. An extra man I can count on. Would you let me give you a dress suit for Christmas, John?"

John looked at her. "They cost like the devil."

"I have plenty of money. Uncle Brooke . . ."

"I know. They're grand to you, Isabelle. I suppose I should be grateful."

"You should. Oh, John, please do this for me. Other girls have cousins and uncles —"

"And you have a brother you're ashamed of."

"I'm not. Would I ask you to my dance if I were ashamed of you?"

He supposed she would not. And he had been

nasty about Marke. She seemed to want him at her dance. . . . Reluctantly he consented to go to the tailor's. Ellen would be at Isabelle's dance.

2

Just before Christmas John found a note in his mailbox asking him to call at the registrar's office. Probably some lab fee that had been overlooked when he paid his second-trimester tuition. He hurried through lunch. The clerk told him that the registrar himself wanted to see him, and John went on to the inside office.

"Did you want to see me, sir? I'm John Mallory."

The man looked up, took off his glasses, smiled. "So you're John Mallory? Sit down. You're older-looking than I'd pictured you."

John put his notebook on the floor and crossed his knees. "The conventional answer to that, sir, is that I've had my worries."

The registrar laughed genially, and tried to balance a pencil on the ends of his fingers. "Clichés. Ah, yes. They get better with the years, but they still smell of the rubber stamp. I believe a medical school is a particularly fertile field."

"Yes, sir." What in time did the man want? John had anatomy dissection at one o'clock. The early men got the best stiffs.

"Er — Mallory — I have you down on my list of students desiring financial aid. Your first trimester grades put you up at the top of the freshman list. That is very gratifying."

"Why, it is to me, too, sir. Thank you."

"Yes. Of course, a man's grades are taken into consideration. If we can only help a part, we want to help the best. Also, good standing usually indicates an honesty of purpose."

"Yes, sir." On the other hand, John might have argued, a man worrying about finances may not do his best work. He said nothing.

The pencil fell to the floor, rolled under the desk. John got down on his knees and fished for it. He wanted to tell the registrar to stop playing with the thing.

"Er — thank you. John, do you like Jewish cooking?"

John stared at the man in wonder, and some alarm. Surely the medical school would not have an insane person . . . "I don't know that I've ever eaten any, sir."

"It's not bad food. Just different."

"I usually can handle any food available," John said pleasantly.

"Good appetite, eh?"

"Excellent!"

"Do you know the Heidemans?"

John frowned. The name was familiar.

"The Heideman Laboratories," the registrar suggested.

"Oh, yes, sir. Some of the students . . ." John stopped short, his cheeks flushing.

"Exactly. Some of the students send their analyses there. The sort that — if they ever get their M.D.'s — will meet every tricky diagnosis by consulting a specialist. Yourself, for instance. Specialist, I mean, naturally."

John made no answer. Of course, the faculty must know what was going on.

"Dr. Heideman has a very fine commercial laboratory," the registrar went on equably. "He lectures in the chemistry department at Lincoln. He is an authority in his field. His wife is a scientist, too, but her health is bad. Fine people, both of them. But orthodox Jews, and the cooking does run to the sweet-sour."

John waited. He supposed the registrar would eventually make his point.

"Do you know Lundgren?"

"Not personally." Lundgren was a third-year medic. Bad curvature. Humpbacked.

"He's left Boone. We couldn't persuade him that a man of his — er — handicaps — should attempt nothing more than laboratory research. I believe he plans to be married. And study in the East."

"Oh." The marriage part shocked John. Lundgren's curvature was of the congenital sort. The least knowledge of medicine should make it clear to him that he had no right to marry. Besides, the man was physically repulsive. His hands . . .

"Er — yes," the registrar agreed with his thoughts. "The Heidemans have been kind to him. They live in an apartment in the laboratory building, you know. It's two blocks south of Orthopedic. They usually have a medical student living with them in their home. He helps Dr. Heideman with his personal lab work, helps him write his lectures and scientific articles, helps Mrs. Heideman, too. She writes for home magazines, lately. Quite brilliant in dietary chemistry, she is. They'd give you room and board for what help you'd be to them."

John sighed sharply. He had thought the registrar would go on all afternoon about these Heidemans. "Me, sir?"

"Yes. If you can eat Jewish cooking. Lundgren has left. They told me this morning they'd take on another student. Fanny came herself. You can go over and talk to her after you're free this evening."

John got to his feet. He really could not sit down calmly. "They'll give me room and board? Are you sure?"

"I'm sure. But you can ask 'em. The laboratory has the name over the door. The apartment entrance is to the left of the vestibule. And don't take any slush in on Fanny's carpet. You're going to be late for lab."

John ran. This meant a cool five hundred dollars a year to him. He would make it now, barring too heavy lab breakage.

3

He went to see the Heidemans late that same afternoon. He was soon to get so familiar with the strange odors of that household as not to notice them. That first evening, coming in out of the smoky cold, they all slapped him in the face, full force. Alcohol, iodine — God knows what not — from the labs. Gas from the Bunsens, hot rubber, the smell of the animal cages.

And in the house — ushered therein by a round little woman wearing a black wig — the smell of furniture polish, burning candles, something cooking in vinegar, perfume from a huge urn filled with blood-red roses, the smell of his own damp overcoat.

Little, dumpy Mrs. Heideman, coming in and looking up at him. Little, bearded Dr. Heideman, only glancing at John, watching anxiously to see if he pleased "Fanny."

"Papa, he is a nice one, huh? So big. So red in the cheeks. *Gemüthlich,* no?"

"So fort." The little doctor twinkled at John. "You'll try it?" he asked.

"I'd like to. If you think . . ."

"It's what Fanny thinks, in this house. You'll learn that."

"I meant — the work."

"*Ach,* that! You can do that easy. Chemistry you have, no?"

"Yes, sir. I understood there was some writing."

"Can you typewrite?"

"No. I can learn."

The two Heidemans looked delightedly at each other. "He can learn!" they chorused.

"John is it? The name?"

"Yes, sir. John Mallory."

"Do you speak German?"

"I can read it. But I've never tried to talk."

"So, so. Only a little is needed to talk, to understand Fanny when she talks." He winked elaborately at John.

Fanny slapped his arm. "Ha! And to understand the Herr Papa when he gets mad! Come, now, I show you your room."

John followed her. She was short and round. She wore a heavy black woolen dress, white stockings, and broad-toed, flat-heeled black Oxfords — they looked like boy's shoes. Her thin gray hair was unevenly bobbed.

John's room was a large one, overlooking the street. There were three windows, reaching from ceiling to floor. Mrs. Heideman cautioned him solemnly about falling out. The bed was wood, with two feather mattresses, and a red and white crocheted spread. There was a massive dresser and chifforobe. A heavy oak table with a reading lamp and a microscope. John would have his own tiled bath.

"I feel like a prince," he told Mrs. Heideman, and she laughed and blushed like a girl.

"Papa and I sleep in this other room, here. We're old-fashioned. We sleep together. But we have no *Kinder.*" She giggled naughtily. John liked her.

"Beyond is dining room and kitchen, and the room for Berta and Karl. They are married. Then the front room, you saw that. You like it, huh? You stay?"

John looked at her. "I'll be glad to."

"So! We are glad, too. When do you come, John? Soon?"

"Any time. I have to get my things at Mrs. Schuler's."

"I send Karl *mit*."

Mrs. Schuler was sorry to lose John, though her room was never empty for long. John, she told her friends, was such a nice boy. Always washed out the bathtub and hung up his towels.

John, eating *Hasenpfeffer* that first evening at Heidemans', and *Strudel*, liking them and loosening his belt a notch, knew that he had fallen soft again.

"You must let me earn my keep," he told the doctor seriously.

"Nu, Nu," the scientist growled over the bowl of his porcelain pipe.

4

John was never sure whether the work he did at Heidemans' paid for his board or not. John was the last student they ever kept. He lived there nearly four years.

He did do some work. There were nights when he and the doctor worked very late in the laboratory. There were several experiments and tests he and the doctor carried out together over several nights and weeks and months. John kept a neat and efficient record of the doctor's tests with serums, even when the actual work was done by the paid technicians of the laboratory. Occasionally, in emergencies, John made the reports of analyses. The police work of the laboratory was fascinating, the testing of blood and fabrics; but John liked best the serum work. He ventured to bring out the records and blood smears he had begun to keep at the Villa Franca Hospital. He and Dr. Heideman talked absorbedly of the serums someone would one day discover for the incurable diseases.

He learned to use the typewriter, not fingering correctly, but he was accurate and had fair speed. He couched the doctor's articles in more fluent English. He typed the speeches and lectures the little Jew was so often called upon to make. He typed Fanny's articles, too. He discovered that she had a timid flair for poetry. He urged her to send some of these beautiful fragments to magazines. When the first of them was accepted, she and John did a war dance around the dining-room table, with the doctor beaming approval and Berta running around closing windows lest someone hear the disgraceful racket.

Fanny bought John a stethoscope with that first check. "Better I would like to buy you some loud shirts," she told him. "But I know you doctors. You like your little playthings, no?"

John lifted the instrument reverently from its case. "I — Fanny — you don't know what this means. I can't thank you . . ."

She stood on the tips of her broad shoes, pulled his head down, and kissed his cheek. "There.

Now, we're even. I guess not many girls have done that, eh?"

"No."

After that John always kissed Fanny when he entered or left the house. Even when guests were present. She liked his doing it. So did the doctor. "John," they would say, "he is a nice boy."

John knew, if only in a vague way, that the doctor took comfort in the young man's presence in the house when he had to be away on his frequent trips. Sometimes he went to make speeches. Quite as often he went to give expert testimony at some trial, or to give an illustrated lecture before a famous clinic. Not a few important serums had been developed in the Heideman Laboratories.

Lately, because of Fanny's poor health, the doctor had been refusing these invitations and opportunities which took him out of town. But with John in the house at night, with John there to talk to Fanny, to be fussed over and planned for, the doctor felt free to pursue again this important branch of his profession.

Fanny, of course, did fuss over John. He told her she would make him as fat as a pig. She retorted that he must, in truth, be Jewish. He took so heartily to the orthodox cooking. She mended his clothing. She sent his dirty linen to the laundry. Even his white coats were put in with the huge piles from the laboratory. On a cold day she was not above stooping suddenly and hoisting the cuff of his trousers to see if he had on heavy socks.

John laughed at her, but he could not resent these attentions. Once when he did catch a slight cold, she cared for him as solicitously, he declared, as if he had been six weeks old, with the croup. In return he was very kind to her. He honestly liked her. Dr. Heideman never found on John's lips the tolerant smile for Fanny's idiosyncrasies that sometimes appeared on the faces of other medical students when Mrs. Heideman chose to attend some lecture at the school.

John knew that she was eccentric. He knew also that she possessed a brilliant mind, which might be that of a genius. The students could laugh at her stumpy, waddling figure. The students did not know her.

The staff doctors did not laugh at Fanny Heideman. John was to meet, at one time and another, a great many famous men in the Heidemans' fussy living room. They none of them laughed at their hostess.

Homely, untidy, she was. Without any of the conventional feminine charms. Yet John Mallory was never, in all his life, to know a woman so truly loved by so many men.

She suffered, at rather frequent intervals, from terrific nervous headaches. They prostrated her, against her strongest intentions; and when the beating, pressing pain had left her, she was as exhausted as if she had been seriously ill for weeks. John's small attentions, little kindnesses, added to the doctor's rumbling solicitude, made these periods of torment as easy as they could be for the brave little woman. Pain, a living, breathing monster, dwelt there in her brain. John's firm, cool hand, his steady eyes, were a great comfort to her.

"He will be a good doctor, Papa," she'd whisper contentedly.

"Aber gewiss!"

5

There was often music in the Heidemans' apartment. John at the piano, Fanny's cello, the doctor's violin. John was made to learn his "pieces" in the proper key. His facility was admired, but a flashy arpeggio could not conceal a false note from the Heidemans. Sometimes other friends came in, and the little orchestra grew to impressive proportions. To every newcomer Fanny would tell how John used to play Rubinstein's "Melody."

"In *A* is it," she declared. "The maestro would turn in his grave."

The music was fun. The talk was even better. Good talk. Shoptalk. With John an eager listener, and sometimes an accepted contributor. His little story of the hen-medic in the anatomy lab was laughed over, listened to, just as courteously as was Dr. Heideman's account of the four-foot slab of concrete roadway that had been sent, intact, to the laboratory to have the stains upon it analyzed and thereby bring a murderer to justice.

John learned a lot in these sessions. "As much

as I'm learning in school," he wrote Miss Lillie.

Sometimes he went on short trips with the Heidemans. His second vacation he accompanied the doctor to a six weeks' clinic at a famous Eastern medical school, assisted with the lectures and demonstrations.

6

Fanny was openly jealous of Miss Lillie Arndt those times John mentioned his old friend. Especially so when he made no effort to conceal his delight over the box she and Dr. Jim sent him for Christmas.

"You like her better than me, huh?" Fanny asked.

John tried, in the bungling fashion of men, to tell one woman how different the other was. "Oh, she's a lady," Fanny decided, hurt indeed. But she brightened when John succeeded in reminding her that Miss Lillie was in China. "She and Dr. Jim were kind to me — just as you and the doctor are kind to me."

Her jealousy amused John even more when he decided that Miss Lillie was also jealous of Fanny. "You mustn't let that Jewish woman mother you into forgetting your old friends, John." Women were queer, John thought. As if any loyalty he might give Fanny need be taken from the amount he owed to Miss Lillie.

Once, Fanny asked John if he had a girl. They were sitting in front of the little coal fire waiting for the doctor to be ready for supper. It was streaming rain outside. When the doctor had come in from the university, Fanny had ordered him to take a warm bath and put on dry clothing. John sat with one of his heavy medical books open on his knee. Fanny was knitting something purple.

John started to say that he did not have a girl. Then, "I have a girl I'd like to have," he said, laughing at his own syntax.

"What kind of girl is that, *Mein Schatz?*"

"Well, I mean I'd try to make her my girl if I thought she would wait ten years for me."

"Ten years is not so long."

"You know it is long, Fanny. And she is so lovely, every man who —"

"Ah, yes, but how does she feel? Huh?"

"I don't know. You see, I don't really know her very well. I'd like to. She's the sort of person I'd like to be with a lot, to know very well. But the only reason I see her at all is that she's my sister's friend." He stopped and hastily picked up his book.

But Fanny's attention was alert. "Sister? You have told me of no sister."

"I — well, I should not have told you now."

He avoided looking at Fanny, who was, he knew, staring wide-eyed at him. "I am imagining things much worse than are possibly true, John."

Yes. She probably was. So, first enjoining her to secrecy, he told her of his separation from Belle, and the reasons Belle had brought forth for keeping their reunion a secret. He stressed

Belle's reluctance to seem to ask Uncle Brooke for anything for John. "I am sure she is not ashamed of me," he said, all the more firmly because he was not sure.

"She should not be," Fanny agreed. "And I think maybe she was right not to ask your uncle. You really did not need his help. If you see her, it is all the same. When you are on your feet, you'll owe no man a thing, and you can go to him as good as he is."

John laughed ruefully. "The thing is — I feel that good now. But Belle — Belle doesn't agree."

"She is young, and a woman. Is it not strange your uncle does not recognize you, and your name?"

"I've not seen him. The name — he is an uncle only by marriage. They've probably not spoken to him of me, anyway. He's been ill. Belle has been very busy all winter making her debut. Goodness, you can't imagine how hard she works at having a good time."

"Is she pretty?"

"Belle? Very pretty. Slim, and very blonde. Not at all like me."

"*Ach,* that is too bad. And her friend — this girl of yours?"

"Oh, she is lovely, Fanny. Not smooth and polished like Belle. Ellen is just — well, lovely. Her hair is a light brown, a little blonde, a little red. She parts it in the middle, but it's curly and doesn't stay parted well. Something like mine." He smoothed his own obstreperous hair. "She has blue eyes. Really blue. With an almost black circle around the iris. She — oh, she's too good for me, in every way. I know that. But she's the only sort I'd ever want — way out beyond my reach. Too good."

Fanny frowned over a knot in the purple yarn. "You are better than you think, John," she said placidly.

"So far as I go. Which isn't far. Ellen has so much. Her looks. Her family — the oldest families in St. Louis. Money. Not rich like Uncle Brooke, but they have plenty. Much more than I'll have for some time. I — I have nothing, Fanny. If I slide through medical school, I won't have a penny change."

Fanny nodded, her fingers busy, her eyes on her work. "Money. It is a lot. But it is not everything. What you have, even your rich Uncle Brooke could not have given you."

"What have I?"

"Well, you are a pretty man." John knew that her idiom differed from the English one. Still, he snorted disdainfully.

"Yes, you are pretty. Tall, strong-looking. Your gray eyes are nice. Your hair. People like to look at you. That is important to a girl. Then, John, you are so *nice*."

"How do you mean? That I'm a prig? For all you know, I don't raise hell because I haven't the price. I can't even afford to smoke."

"I don't mean that kind of nice. I mean you, yourself, are nice. You are solid good, clear through. You are gentle. You speak gently. Your eyes are gentle, your hands. You are calm, quiet. Serene, is it? Your eyes are steady and calm. People trust you. These things, also, are in your character. Besides, you will advance in your work. You will be a fine doctor. I know this from your record at school, but also because I know you are a person who can work hard for whatever he wants. You work hard. Everything you do, you do with all your strength. That is a fine quality, John. You do not waste time and effort."

"I haven't ever had any time to waste," said John soberly. "What about my faults? I suppose I have some?"

"Oh, yes," Fanny agreed readily. "That you do not know how to waste time and be a little naughty is a fault. You do not know how to play. You do not make friends with people your own age. And you are stubborn."

"Yes. My mother used to say I was."

"But — maybe for you that is not a bad thing. All great men need strength and stubbornness. Otherwise they do not stand straight against the high winds. You have to work hard to go the places you want to go. You have to be stubborn about holding the ground you gain. You also have another fault. You judge all people by yourself; you judge their actions, their thoughts, by what you yourself would do and think. So — you misjudge."

"If all people were honest and sincere . . ."

"Ah, yes. That would be fine. But they are not."

"It would be simpler."

"It would so. But some people are not strong enough — not stubborn — to walk the straight path. Others, they love to scheme, to trick, to confuse. It is called cleverness."

John shook his head. "It seems a lot of bother."

7

John could scarcely have avoided speaking of Ellen, thoughts of her were so constantly in his mind. He knew, quite simply, that he loved her. Knew, too, of course, what small chance his love had to reach more than friendship with her. So he cherished each word, each minute, he had with her. A few brief sentences in the Wielande drawing room. Her gay appraisal of him the night of Belle's magnificent debut ball, when John appeared for the first time in evening clothes. He pirouetted proudly before her and Belle. Recounted gravely, as the tailor had done, the fine points of his figure for wearing tails.

"I need hardly any padding on the shoulders," he said seriously. "And I have no hips. That is important. Even more important than a flat waist. Because there are corsets, you know."

"Why, John!" Belle squealed modestly, but Ellen cocked a contemplative head.

"You're right," she said. "Most men do have hips. And they really shouldn't. John, you are a success. Emily Post says that the test of a gentleman is whether he looks well in tails. Or, if she didn't, she should have."

"You really think I look well?"

"Oh, I certainly do. Blue-blooded, in fact."

"All because I haven't hips. Which, when you come to think of it, isn't a bad place for an overabundance of common stock to be."

The two of them had gone off in gales of laughter, and Belle had been a little confused by their nonsense. This unexpected gayness of John's — when he was with Ellen — she neither understood nor liked it.

8

One rainy afternoon he met Ellen on the street. She was wearing a belted blue reefer and had a blue beret pulled down over her hair. There was a drop of rain on the tip of her pert nose.

"Oh, John, do you like to walk in the rain?"

"Love it." He had on his high-laced boots and his leather jacket, an old cap of Dr. Heideman's pulled down to his ears. He had spent the best part of the afternoon watching a plastic surgeon cauterize a man's mouth. The smell had been . . . Plenty of the medics and dents had passed out. John had not, but the cold and rain were a welcome change.

He swung into step with Ellen, choosing to go where she might be going. Eventually that road led to the glittering little stucco shop — Marguerite Conte, Inc. — where Ellen's mother conducted her tidy little business of finding, remodeling, furnishing homes for a select clientele. Ellen and her mother had an apartment over the shop. Cleverly ultramodern, the apartment was. John, feeling too roughly dressed, looked about him curiously.

Marguerite Conte was a gracious lady in platinum-gray satin, her hair a lustrous, sculptured white about a face as lovely and girlish as Ellen's. She told Ellen that she would be late for her dinner engagement. Was very charming to John Mallory, but managed to get him back on the street in less than ten minutes.

However, a week later Ellen called him at Heidemans' and invited him to drive with her and her mother out to their "real home" in the country.

John met them at the shop at noon on Saturday. Mrs. Conte, beautiful today in russet tweed, asked him to drive the car. Ellen sat beside him and told him what roads to take. John suggested taking the ladies to luncheon, but Ellen said no, Maum Bette would have something ready.

The roads were clear, but there was a soft padding of snow on the fields and woods. Ice blocks moved sluggishly in the Missouri River. "When it gets warmer, we'll come out here for a picnic," Ellen promised him. "I'll bet you don't have much fun at your solemn hospital."

The Conte house was an old building of worn, soft brick, painted red, then faded to a velvety rose color. It stood, stiff and square, at the end of a double row of elm trees. Ellen bade John drive around to the rear of the house. Here the building expanded into two wings inclosing a bricked courtyard. There were porches out here, too — verandas — upstairs and down. One of them had been screened and must be a delightful place in summer, shaded by giant honey locusts, commanding a wide view of the river at the foot of the hill.

John could detect, under the snow and the careful coverings of straw, traces of a formal garden. Round flower beds, neatly bordered with tilted bricks. Rose trellises and arbors. A long grape arbor. He looked again at the strangely beautiful old house, serene, simple, strong.

"Do you like it?" Ellen asked him, watching his face.

"Yes. Much better than your tricky apartment."

The two women exchanged glances and laughed. "The apartment's my show window," Marguerite Conte told him. "I've never got around to decorating *Les Grâces*."

John, carrying several bundles into the house, tried for a translation of the name. He had not studied French. They — Ellen and her mother — told him to explore while they "tended to things." John spent a happy hour, peeping into high-ceilinged rooms, a parlor with pink roses on the carpet, full-length mirrors framed in gilt, fragile chairs of a velvety rosewood upholstered in pale apricot brocade. He tiptoed through a hall with wallpaper the color of weak tea, and having faded brown steamboats depicted at regular intervals. He went up the gently sloping white stairway; the handrail was lustrous, dark, and slick to his fingers.

He looked in at lofty bedrooms, shuttered windows reaching up from the floor; big, testered beds, two of them with unpolished maple trundle beds pushed beneath them. He smiled gently at wonderful "toilet sets." One of them was blue, with garlands of pink roses. One was white, with rust-colored scenes of the first Philadelphia exposition. There were little cane-seated rocking chairs. A fearsome, tailless hobbyhorse pranced in one bare room. Had Ellen ridden it as a child?

He came downstairs again and made his way to the brick-floored kitchen, where two black women, their heads tied in white kerchiefs, chattered to Ellen and her mother and stirred things cooking on the big range. Ellen introduced him to the two negresses — Maum Bette and Missouri — as Doctor Mallory. To John's startled glance she explained, "I might as well start calling you that. These two keep their habits."

Mrs. Conte was arranging short-stemmed pink roses in a round crystal bowl. She looked up at John and smiled. "Ellen's plans seem to encompass the future, don't they, John?"

"I hope so," he said fervently. Happiness filled his veins like beaded wine. Marguerite Conte saw it glow in the depths of his eyes. Her slim white hand touched his arm briefly. John looked at her gravely, then gathered up the florist's box, waxed paper, and string. Lifted the lid of the stove and put the litter into the fire. Automatically he checked the draft. Maum Bette giggled.

"You sure must have a range in yor house," she told him.

"We did. I've never eaten bread as good as my mother baked in it."

They ate a hearty dinner in the dining room golden with winter sunlight. Stewed chicken and rice, rich with gravy. Dandelion greens that Mrs. Conte said Maum Bette had gathered last spring on the hillside and canned. Apples, boiled in a pink sirup until they were delicate globes of frosted glass. Tiny biscuits, brown and crisp outside, white and feathery within. Wild-strawberry preserves, as clear as ruby glass. Mrs. Conte told how the Russians used such preserves to sweeten their tea. And, finally, baked caramel custards, with great wedges of fruit cake, moist, rich, delicious.

John, to his dismay, kept remembering Uncle Ben and Bertha, the stale rolls and canned beans of the station lunchroom. He made himself attend to the gay talk of the two women, glad that Miss Lillie had widened his conversational horizon to include an intelligent recognition of the things they mentioned. Any subject served them. The newest purchase of the city's Art Museum. The chrysanthemum show of last fall. California weather. The best place in St. Louis to buy socks. The *bombe glacée* served at the Claridge in London.

John's eyes wandered over the glass and silver and china so lavishly displayed on the huge sideboard, on the tea table, on the shelves of the towering china closet. All sorts of china and silver and glass. Massive cut-glass vases and punch bowls. Slender crystal compotes. Brandy glasses that were as tenuous as bubbles. Terrific hand-painted plates. Three teacups of thin white porcelain lined with glowing coral. An old, heart-shaped bonbon box of china painted with violets. Silver tea services and trays. Old. A little tarnished.

Seeing his interest, Mrs. Conte pointed out two Chelsea-figurine candlesticks. A bowl of rose-colored glass, its upper curved surface incrusted with gold. A nice piece, she told John. She opened a cupboard door and brought out a silver contraption. "It was my grandfather's," she said, laughing a little. "It was a traveling set. See: knife, fork, spoon. Even salt cellars and napkin ring. This let him, when traveling about the country, always have the refinements of life to which he was accustomed. Hotels in that day were apt to be primitive."

"You have so many lovely old things," John said shyly.

"Yes. We have. Also some pretty awful old things. But, when they've belonged to your own people, they have value, if not actual beauty. *Les Grâces* is my one extravagance, John. I could have sold it many times. I could make it more comfortable, more modern, for my own use. Or I could weed out the junk and have it all beautiful. I like it the way it is."

"So do I," said John soberly.

Maum Bette's son had kindled a fire in the "sitting room," and they went there after lunch. "We ought to run a foot race after that fruit cake," John declared.

Mrs. Conte sat down at the secretary desk; John spied a paperweight made of three balls of clear glass supporting an apple of a flawless turquoise blue — a lovely thing. He balanced it in his hand and murmured over it. Mrs. Conte laughed. "You've a nice taste," she said. "Collectors have told me that is the finest thing in this house."

John looked long at the globes of glass, held their smooth surfaces to his cheek. "It's simple," he marveled. "If I ever steal anything from you, this will be it."

"I cut my teeth on it," Ellen told him. "I love it, too."

The furniture in this room was partly modern. Ellen explained that the old horsehair just had been unendurable when winter underwear ceased to be boiler plate. There were several deep chairs, and a down-cushioned couch covered in flowered chintz. And there was a piano which was twin sister to the one out at Hayes'. John yelled to recognize it — a Jesse French it was, too! — so that Mrs. Conte blotted the check she was writing. Blushing, John explained his excitement.

"Do you play, John?" Ellen asked.

"By ear. I understand it's something to be ashamed of."

"Wouldn't that depend on how well you play? Let's hear you."

John adjusted the stool to his height, dusted the yellow keys with his handkerchief. Ellen, laughing hard, told him Maum Bette would scalp him alive if she would see him. He played "You're the Cream in My Coffee." He played "My Little Gypsy Sweetheart" and " 'Swonderful," Ellen murmuring the words at his shoulder. "I can't sing," she confessed regretfully.

Then, because modern music did not seem at home here with the paperweight and the funny, frowning photograph of Ellen's grandmother at the age of three, John's hands dropped into the heavy opening chords of the "Waldstein" sonata. He liked Beethoven. The music seemed to express for him the things he desired in life. Pride. Happiness.

He was smiling when he swung around on the stool, to find Ellen and her mother sitting together on the couch before the fire.

"Thank you, John," said Mrs. Conte, smiling at him.

"I'm afraid I've kept you from your business."

"You rested me. I came out here for a rest. You play well, John."

"I play pretty loud," John amended. "I don't know a whole lot about music. I mean to learn someday."

"People with your gift scarcely ever learn to play well by note."

John carefully closed the piano. "I didn't mean that. I mean — I want to learn about harmony, and composers. What makes fine music fine."

Ellen groaned. "Harmony! I took lessons all my life, John. Now, when I sit down to play, the only thing I can do is 'Les Glissants,' around and around — the piano lifts its leg and kicks me. Hard."

"I do have to write some checks," Mrs. Conte laughed. "You two children run outside and play for an hour."

They wandered down the hillside toward the river. The wind was cold, but somehow the sunlight held a promise of spring. John found some ice flowers at the foot of a walnut tree, and showed them to Ellen. Told her how they were formed by the snow melting, then being frozen again and forced up through the crevices of the ground as beautiful orchid-like crystal flowers.

"Oh, I must tell Mother!" Ellen cried.

"Your mother's grand, Ellen."

"Isn't she? She likes you. I'm so glad. She can be very *grande dame* with people she doesn't like."

"I can't imagine her being like that."

"She won't be, with you. She really likes you. I'm glad."

"Why? I mean, what makes you think she likes me?"

"Oh — lots of reasons. Your playing. She likes spontaneous, sincere things. And she likes your admiring our house. Most people we bring out here laugh at our tin bathtub. Even the things they do compliment they patronize."

John looked out across the river, sparkling with a million diamonds in the sunlight. So it had looked to the Indians. So it had looked to the first Briand who chose this site for his home. "I think it is — wonderful," he said simply. "Maybe those other people — the ones who laugh — have seen something better. I never have."

9

John was never to forget that first day at *Les Grâces*. All his life certain things — the "Waldstein," violets painted on china, a room fragrant with roses and wood smoke — would be able to give him again a breath of the happiness of that day. There were to be other days at *Les Grâces.* The days they spent together there added to the special quality of his friendship with Ellen.

True to her promise, one bright Saturday during Lent Ellen called John at seven o'clock and asked if he would go on a picnic with her and Isabelle.

"Try and stop me!" he shouted. "What shall I bring?"

"Oh, Isabelle and I will get things. We'll meet you in front of the medical school at twelve. We're taking Izzy's roadster."

It was a fine party. John built the fire neatly. Gathering small twigs, he stopped, rapt, to watch and listen to a cardinal on the top branch of a hickory tree. No other song could be so piercingly sweet, no other feathers so gorgeous. "Ke-vitch, ke-vitch, ke-veeee!" he mocked, coming back to the girls. "Redbirds are Russian. Did you know?"

They laughed obligingly. "Is it true that the birds in California don't sing, John?" Ellen asked him.

"Haven't you ever been to California?"

"I have. But I never make anything of my opportunities."

"Well, I don't think I did, either. Now you've asked me. But I'm sure some birds sing." He carefully balanced the coffeepot.

Ellen bade him cut long sticks for the kabobs.

"Ka-what?" he asked, opening his knife.

"Didn't you ever make kabobs when you were a Boy Scout?" she asked, showing him how to thread the wedges of pork and veal and onion on the long sticks he brought back.

"I wasn't ever a Boy Scout," John told her cheerfully. "When I was that age, I was cleaning chicken pens for a living."

Isabelle coughed, suddenly and not too naturally. "The smoke — from the fire — chokes me," she explained hurriedly. "Ellen, are you going to the occupational-therapy rooms every morning during Lent?"

It was obvious to John — and probably to Ellen, who was no fool — that she meant to change the subject. Isabelle was constantly afraid that John might dwell upon the fact that he had been poor, was still poor, and had had to work hard. She feared even more that she would be linked to his grubby existence. She seemed unable to forget that her dazzling social position had been built on a very flimsy foundation. John wished she would be more sincere, simpler, franker. She would be happier, he thought. Still, maybe not. Isabelle was truly most content when putting on a show, staging an act.

He wished, then, that she would let him be honest. She admired Ellen Conte, all the things Ellen did and had. Could she not see that Ellen was honestly friendly with John? His poverty and obscure background bothered her not at all. Why, then, could Isabelle not claim John as her brother, now that he had established his behavior and conduct as socially acceptable? John wished there need be no sort of deception between himself and Ellen.

Clearing up the litter from their lunch — Isabelle had gone over to the car for her compact — John said, deliberately, to Ellen: "Your mother knows that I'm poor, doesn't she, Ellen?"

"Mother? I don't know, John. It wouldn't make any difference. There are plenty of poor Briands, you know. Heavens, I should say so!"

John was never with Ellen but what she asked him to play the piano. Either the little ivory-tinted grand at the apartment or the square Jesse French out here at *Les Grâces*. So, when they went back into the house to wash and warm up a little before their drive back to the city, John went to the instrument and began to play. He was not through the first chorus when he looked up to see Isabelle standing there staring at him, her cheeks pink, her eyes too bright.

"What's the matter?" he asked, letting his right hand twiddle out some runs.

"I didn't know you could play. You never told me." She sounded angry, hurt.

"You never asked me." John attempted the humorous.

"Where did you — I mean, Ellen knew you could. You've told her. You've been out here before. You've had lots of good times together. I can tell. The way you laugh and joke."

John swung around on the stool. "What's the matter with her?" he asked Ellen.

"I don't know. But it sounds as if she might be jealous."

"Oh, no!"

"Yes, I think she is." They were discussing Isabelle in much the same tone that he and his working-buddy discussed a specimen in lab.

"But she can't be, Ellen. She's —" He looked up and met Isabelle's still, warning eyes. He felt a shiver of distaste. "She's — even you can never take Isabelle's place with me." Agh, he was a spineless worm! If Isabelle thought he had any idea of clutching to her social skirts to get himself anywhere in the world — well, she need never fear that he would put any claim upon her in that respect!

Ellen was answering him, her tone light and bantering. "Dearly as you love me?" she asked.

"Dearly as I love you," John replied seriously.

Her eyes dropped and her cheeks went rosy. "Oh," she breathed.

It promised nothing, John told himself, driving back to town. Girls of Ellen's sort talked that way to men. Men called them darling, and meant nothing.

10

Mrs. Conte came into the apartment late that afternoon and found Ellen curled up on the window seat, looking out into the dark street, seeing nothing. "Daydreams, darling?"

"Yes."

"Did you have a nice trip?"

"Wonderful. Lunch was good. John liked the kabobs. He says he gets hungry for pork, being orthodox so much of the time. He lives with a Jewish family. He likes them, but he told some funny stories about them. He — Mom, John's swell."

"Yes. I like him."

"I mean — he's particularly swell. He's so honest. You know, Mom, that paperweight he likes?"

"Yes, dear." Mrs. Conte ran her fingers through her hair. She was tired.

"John's like that. You know — it's just glass — but it is beautiful, fine, because it is so clear. John is like that."

Mrs. Conte smiled. "Yes, dear. You'd better be bathing, hadn't you?" She, too, thought John Mallory was fine. If Ellen should be serious, and wanted him — The family would think she ought to marry within the sacred circle. Briands, Contes, Coquins, Loisels. People bred as fine and brittle as their own cherished Sèvres teacups. Even Felix, the best of the approved lot, was not half so handsome, so strong, as this unknown John Mallory. "Why don't you wear your blue taffeta, darling? Aunt Philomene thinks taffeta becomes a *jeune fille.*"

Ellen kissed her mother. "You're sweet," she said shyly. She knew that Marguerite would stand beside her against any family feeling there might be against John. Of course, that did not mean everything was fine. Isabelle would have to be reckoned with. Ellen wondered if she ought to ask Isabelle outright, "Do you want him?" Only — if Isabelle said yes, Ellen did not think she could bear it.

Turning the hot water into the tub, reaching for the violet bath salts — Aunt Philomene liked violet scent on *jeunes filles,* too — Ellen squeezed out a luxurious tear at the picture of herself being maid of honor at the marriage of Isabelle Wielande and Dr. John Mallory.

11

John was far too busy to essay the social education close companionship with Isabelle would require. Except for Ellen, he had no desire to mingle with Isabelle's social friends on his present basis. He had too much pride to go where she felt he had no business to be. Therefore, he really saw very little of his sister, from choice and from need. His days were full, his leisure hours few. He wished things might be different. He still felt that he and Isabelle belonged together.

Wishing to do his full part, he would agree to respond to some such demand as she made the evening she called him and asked him to fill in at one of Aunt Mary's dinners.

"It will be dull, darling, but I'll put you next to me. Aunt Mary is at her wit's end. This lawyer — Mr. Hogue — was in a car smashup at three o'clock this afternoon. The hospital just called. It's too late to get anyone else. You will come, won't you? White tie, darling. Shall I send the car?"

"I'll walk." To that small extent he would maintain his independence. He had an histology quiz next morning for which he should study. But he dressed cheerfully enough. If Isabelle tried to tell him which fork . . . Uncle Brooke would be there, and John admired his Uncle Brooke. He did not like Aunt Mary so well. Too often she looked — and sounded — like Uncle Ben Colby. Sometimes Isabelle did, too. They both had a greediness for social preferment, and a smug satisfaction in the rightness of their own opinions. John hated his criticism of Isabelle. He wished he might love her, do for her.

Mrs. Conte sat on John's left. Ellen, she said, was at a hockey game.

The dinner was a large one. Forty guests, John counted. Older folk, mostly. The men were paunched and wheezy, or very thin, their eyes yellow with senility. Very rich. The women were gowned in velvet and satin and lace. Black, purple, crimson. High-bosomed, big-armed, elaborately jeweled. Mrs. Conte's cream lace gown had no back, nothing above the armpits except shoulder straps of small velvet pansies. Because she was slim, her arms round and slender, she looked more fully clothed than the old woman across from John who had a cloud of tulle drawn up under the chin.

The dinner was elaborate. Brooke Wielande was known as a gourmet; his dinners were famous. There had been cocktails in the drawing room, reverently made. A square bottle and a round bottle brought in on a gleaming tray. Absinthe counted out in exact drops. John was reminded of the rapt attention of a superpharmacist. Caviar dipped out of a bowl of hollowed ice, clinging to the spoon, plopped on squares of very hot toast. John did not like caviar on an empty stomach. He was not a gourmet.

The long table was spread with a lace cloth. Italian filet, Mrs. Conte murmured to him obligingly. She confessed it was a pleasure to have an excuse to take verbal account of the appointments. Social indifference was a real trial to her. Her other neighbor was a man of importance.

She gave a good part of her time to John.

The service plates were of ivory queen's ware. The goblets at John's plate were of amethyst glass. There were ivory candles, tall and slim, in amethyst candelabra. John thought of the seven-branched candlestick burning in Fanny's bedroom. Pink lilies in low dishes. Lowestoft bowls, said Mrs. Conte.

There was a delicious soup; clam, John was sure. Chicken, he thought. A spoonful of rich clotted cream put into its hot thickness. There were ripe olives and crisp little celery hearts. Then some sort of bird. Quail? Partridge, Isabelle murmured reverently, and Mrs. Conte laughed. Anyway, it was served on toast, with a sort of goo made of the giblets. Rich. Tiny molds of purple grape jelly. John confessed that he had always liked jelly with chicken. Brown little puffs that were potatoes. Plain, common, delicious string beans, tiny as tiny, cooked in butter. The dessert was frozen fresh pineapple, served elaborately on long silver platters. There was wine, too. John's array of glasses had been filled from time to time. Neither Isabelle nor the servants seemed to approve of his abstinence.

John talked blandly to Isabelle, and he talked happily to Mrs. Conte. Nothing he could do would shock Mrs. Conte, he felt sure. Almost anything he said or did was likely to upset Isabelle. It almost made him want to do something outrageous. He was vaguely aware of other conversations going on around him. The woman across was telling in detail of a cure she had just taken at some Austrian *Bad.* John wished he might question her professionally. Even he recognized that some pleasures were not practical in society.

At the end of the meal the women did something he had only read about up to now. They "withdrew." John parted the tails of his coat and sat down again in his chair, shook his head at the footman's offer of cigars or cigarettes. He watched another man bring him a big glass with a small amount of golden liquid at the bottom of the crystal globe. He watched the guests swirl this stuff in the glass, smell it, drink it slowly — like a child taking a nasty medicine, he thought, smiling. A small, dark, ugly man across the table saw his smile.

"You do not care for brandy?" he asked, his German accent as thick as Dr. Heideman's.

"I don't know. I've never drunk any. I may not have a head."

"It is as well not to find out on this brandy."

"I'd say you had a very fine head," the gentleman next to John offered. A tall, bony gentleman, with a face as craggy as a rock.

"That is a great compliment," the little dark man told John. "Do you know Mr. McIntyre? He is a photographer. A great one. He takes only interesting people, he says."

John smiled. "Then it wasn't necessarily a compliment. Almost any marked type would interest a photographer."

Mr. McIntyre nodded approval. "That is true. What Dr. Silverman meant was that I choose only to photograph types of character. Just at present I am stalking him as a type of —"

"The late tertiary period," Dr. Silverman supplied, chuckling.

John's cheeks were red. "Are you Dr. Mark Silverman, sir?" What this man had not done for deaf children!

"I am Mark Silverman. Marcus, till my daughters grew up. Who are you?"

"My name is John Mallory. I'm a student at Boone Medical. I —"

"John Mallory. I've heard of you."

"Oh, you couldn't have. I'm only in my first year."

"Brooke Wielande spoke of you — and you are the boy who lives at Fanny Heideman's, aren't you? I hear you've begun to prepare a thesis on convalescent-blood serums for infantile."

John colored. Several other men — these rich, elderly, important men — had turned to listen to the famous little ear specialist. "I — yes, sir. I'm interested in serums."

"Ha!"

Brooke Wielande had risen from the far end of the table. At the door Dr. Silverman placed a hand on John's shoulder. "Come and see me at the Institute," he invited. "I mean that."

Back in the drawing room, most of the guests going eagerly to the bridge tables, John tried to tell Isabelle what a thrill it had given him to meet the great Dr. Silverman. Did she know how much he had done for deaf children?

"Yes, I know he is wonderful," Belle said seriously. "I'm glad you met him. He's on the staff at Boone, isn't he? He may be able to do a lot for you. I'd be nice to him."

John was nervous, excited by the strangeness of the dinner party, the wonder of having spoken to the great ear specialist. He let his irritation at Belle's inevitable formula show itself plainly. "That's all you think of — be nice to people if you can get something out of them. I hate back-scratching, Isabelle. I hate your thinking it is the thing to do."

Isabelle frowned. "Don't shout. You've behaved yourself very well — and, as for back-scratching, your wonderful Dr. Silverman accepted this dinner invitation only because he is trying to get a hundred thousand dollars out of Uncle Brooke for his precious Institute."

John stared at her. Evidently she was speaking the truth. "Well," he said sulkily, "even if he is, Mr. Wielande could not give his money to a more worthy cause!"

Isabelle patted his arm, smiled sweetly. "I'll tell Uncle Brooke you said so," she murmured. "He likes you so much I'm almost jealous."

But John had come to the point where he discounted everything Isabelle said.

12

John had first met Brooke Wielande at a Sunday-afternoon symphony concert. The Wielandes had, of course, a season's box, supported the orchestra as a matter of social obligation. St. Louis, as a whole, is a musical town. And though Aunt Mary and Isabelle cared little for music, they had at their command a bright patter of conventional phrases, and usually attended the Friday-evening concerts. But, Belle told John, nobody ever went to the Sunday pop concerts. She meant nobody of her social sort. He smiled at, and accepted, her offer of a card which would let him use their box whenever he wished.

He enjoyed the fine music, and the young artists who appeared as soloists at these concerts. He read his program assiduously, was gravely critical of accent and interpretation in the music's performance. He liked the dingy old Odeon where the concerts were held. The dark red walls, the uncomfortable seats, the full horseshoe of boxes placed companionably close to the first floor — the "parquet." He liked the audience, largely made up of women, schoolteachers, students, but there were occasional groups of young men who argued hotly during the intermission. The subscribed boxes often had parties of children — boys and girls in their teens, who came with their governesses — obviously children of rich and cultured families. John heard French spoken to them, and German. They were nicely behaved children. The boys wore dark suits with broad white collars. The girls had round little hats on their prim braids and curls. Nearly all of them wore orthodontic wires.

John felt not at all lonely there in Box M. In fact, he was a little startled to find, that Sunday, a portly gentleman sitting in his own favorite corner. John hung his blue overcoat beside the gentleman's superlative fur-lined garment in the vestibule. "How do you do?" he said, coming out to take one of the chairs in the box.

The man lifted heavy eyelids. He was too fat; he did not look at all well. He grunted, and closed his eyes again. John studied his program. They were going to play the *New World Symphony*. This porcine friend of the Wielandes should not spoil it for John. Why did people of that sort come to concerts? Or, imbedded within that mountain of flesh, was there an ear for music? John turned the page. The second half of the program was to be Tchaikovsky. That would please the children. John liked drums, too. The soloist, a violinist, would play Saint-Saëns. John sighed. A very nice afternoon was in prospect. He watched the cellists come in and tune their instruments. The percussionists fiddled with their little screws and valves. John liked the noises of the tuning orchestra. He wondered if anyone had ever attempted — say — a concerto, using those strange harmonies?

"Damned if I can place you!" Suddenly his companion burst into speech.

John started. "I — I'm sorry I don't know you,

either. Miss Wielande kindly lets me use the box on Sunday."

"Ha! Haven't met you, have I?"

"I don't think so, sir. I'm John Mallory."

"Like music?"

"I do. Do you?"

"Used to. Don't hear much any more. Don't like dressing up for it. Hate opera. Do you?" He talked in a series of puffy grunts.

"I — I've never heard any opera."

"Don't. Unless it's the best. Even then it's terrible. If you could listen, and not have to see the tenor's legs and the prima donna's wig. Good idea to broadcast it. Best song in the world is in an opera. Wolfgang's aria in *Tannhäuser.* I'm Brooke Wielande."

John sighed. The man was odd. Abrupt. Forceful. Interesting. "Are you, sir? Isabelle said you'd been ill." He'd told his name. If Uncle Brooke chose to claim relationship —

"Have. Pulled out all my teeth. Said I'd feel better. It's a damn lie. Got out of a lot of parties, though. Isabelle's a pretty girl, isn't she?"

"Lovely. I expect you're proud of her."

Uncle Brooke grunted.

In the fifteen-minute intermission he heaved himself out of his chair and was gone from the box for nearly half the time. John read about the *Nutcracker Suite*. When Uncle Brooke came back, John automatically got to his feet until he was seated — the elderly man smelled of tobacco and alcohol. Whisky, John supposed. He was no connoisseur of liquor in the bottle or on the breath. Mr. Wielande settled himself ponderously and peered up at John. "You just come to St. Louis?"

"Yes, sir. I'm attending medical school at Boone."

"Are, eh? Why?"

John felt at a loss. "I — well, because I want to be a doctor, I suppose."

"Good enough reason. Messy business, isn't it?"

"Not if you like it."

"Expensive way to go to school, isn't it? I had a doctor tell me his education cost him twenty-five thousand dollars."

"I expect he was justifying a big fee. I'm hoping to do it on a little less than two thousand."

"Two thousand dollars? That's not much money these days. Expect to make it on that?"

"I hope so. It seems like a fortune to me. I've always been poor."

"Have, eh?"

After the concert John helped the unwieldy gentleman into his topcoat, and walked beside him down the long entrance hall. "Place will burn up like a bale of straw someday," Mr. Wielande declared. "Hope nobody's inside. They'd roast like pigs. Can I give you a lift?"

The doorman was calling, "Mr. Wielande's car. Mr. Wielande's car!" The early dusk was smoky, cold, damp. John turned his coat collar up behind his ears. "I think I'll walk. I'm glad to have met you, sir."

"John Mallory, eh? See you again. Good night!"

John watched the long blue car slide away from the curb. "One of the richest men in St. Louis," someone said aloud at his shoulder. John liked Brooke Wielande. He was, finally, glad that he had been able to meet him on an equal footing, not seeming a poor relation asking for help. Isabelle had been right. Besides, John was sure that Brooke Wielande had recognized the name of John Mallory.

13

It was spring. After long hours in the biochemistry lab, and just as long ones in the dissecting room, John thought he had never known so beautiful, so fragrant, a spring. He loved the warm sunlight; he loved the soft, dark nights. One evening in April he found Ellen free and asked her to walk through the park with him. It was raining, softly, steadily. They skirted the lagoons and came up the long, curving, glistening road to where the Art Museum glowed at the top of its high hill.

"Isn't it beautiful, Ellen?" John asked, looking out across the velvety darkness.

"Yes," she agreed. "People in cars never see anything. If we were driving, we'd be afraid we'd skid."

"And we wouldn't smell the rain. Spring in the city is lovelier even than in the country. In California they don't have spring. Not really. The being glad that the cold and ice and snow is gone. The new greenness and cleanness."

"Poetry, John?"

"Sort of Gertrude Steinish."

"There are violets out in the country. Redbud, and dogwood."

"They are all here in the park, too. I can smell 'em. I can smell the grass growing, and the soot being washed off old St. Louis' nose, up there."

"If I had my piano, I'd play 'Rustle of Spring,' and you could do an adagio down the hill. Into the lagoon."

John giggled, too. With Ellen his stiff sobriety, his too mature gravity, dropped from him like a discarded coat. "I'm feeling swell," he admitted. "I'll tell you a secret. I've won the Hill Prize in anatomy. I could talk an hour on the pain it's given Hugo Marke to see me win that prize. And, besides, I've been given a scholarship that will cover my next three years at medic."

"Oh, John! How wonderful!"

"Wonderful? Girl, if you only knew! It's so many things. The money. And the knowing I'm good at this work. And — in years to come — my record. Oh, Ellen, I'm so excited I — I think I'm going to kiss you!"

She put up her face like a docile child. John bent and kissed her cheek. He kissed her lips, cool and wet with the rain. He held her to him for one golden, blissful minute. "Ellen . . ." he said shakily. "I guess — I guess I *am* excited. We'd better go home."

14

The dean had enjoined secrecy about the scholarship. The award, he said, would be duly announced at the university commencement exercises in June. But John told, besides Ellen, Fanny Heideman.

She was not overly surprised. "Once now they do what they should do, John."

"I was surprised," John admitted. "There are so many fellows asking for it."

"Do they do better work than you do? Do they go to so many clinics and operations and extra lectures? Do they?"

"Well, I don't know. But there is one thing, Fanny. I don't want you to misunderstand my saying this — I'm awfully fond of you and the doctor — but, with my tuition paid, I'd have money, I think, to care for my other expenses now."

Fanny put on her gold-rimmed glasses and picked up a magazine. "If you like us, why do you want to leave us, huh?"

"I don't. I just thought it would be only fair to give this chance to some other student."

"You and your conscience! Making everybody unhappy. We don't want some other student. We are used to you."

John smiled. He went over to the small table and uncovered the typewriter. A spark came into his eyes. "Then perhaps I could pay you board?"

"Du lieber Gott!" Fanny cried. "Now! I tell you how you can spend your money. Such a lot I bet

it is! You can buy yourself some decent clothes. A gray suit and some blue shirts and dark blue ties. One day I see you standing talking to a pretty girl — *ein hübsches Mädchen* — she was all in silk, a fine fur on her shoulders. How do you look? Like a bum!"

John's cheeks went red. "Did I really, Fanny?"

"You need some new clothes," she maintained stoutly. "And you stay here. Else the Herr Papa, he won't go to Cleveland next week."

John nodded. "O.K. I'm glad enough to stay." He grew busy with the lecture he was typing for Dr. Heideman. Fanny hoisted herself out of her low chair, came across the room, smoothed her hand over John's hair. He looked up at her and smiled. "You knew all along about the scholarship," he accused.

"The Papa told me. We are both very proud. As you say, there were many who wanted it."

"I know. I still can't see . . ."

"The dean told Papa that they had fifteen names on the list — from all the classes, of course. The committee had many meetings. It was Dr. Silverman who pushed your name the hardest."

"Dr. Mark Silverman?"

"Yes. He said he had met you at a dull dinner. That you did not drink, nor know more than the old men. And that you were a protégé of Brooke Wielande and had been responsible for his giving a very large sum of money to his Institute for the Deaf. Dr. Silverman was chairman of the scholarship committee."

"Oh. I thought I'd earned it — by hard work." He *had* backscratched.

"Do not be a *Dummkopf,* John. You got on the list by hard work. Having a good personality will never hurt you when you are a doctor. Do not call it luck, either. A good personality grows. The things a little boy does, the way he grows, makes the kind of man he becomes. Each thing you have ever worked for, wanted so hard that you've gotten it, is to blame for Dr. Silverman's liking you at that dinner."

"All right, Fanny. If you say so."

"I know it is true. How do you know the rich Mr. Wielande?"

"I told you. He is my uncle. He adopted my sister."

Fanny's mouth made a round *o* of surprise. "That one!" she said softly. Her eyes were thoughtful when she returned to her chair. John's sister must be a foolish girl. But she had not, really, hurt John by her foolishness. She had, rather, cheated herself and Brooke Wielande. Though, in all likelihood, this award would be the rich man's indirect way of helping a deserving nephew. Should she say so to John? Later, perhaps, it would be wise.

15

John stayed in St. Louis that summer, serving as clerk for the children's clinic. There were students, envious of his getting the scholarship, who claimed that he had played smart to the dean, who was a child's specialist, by going in so strong for pediatrics. Barngrove, who was doing a similar job in the G. U. clinic, told John to spit in their eyes. Doctors, he claimed, knew more ways of being jealous than members of any other profession. They started young, too.

Ellen and her mother were away all summer. Mrs. Conte was furnishing a summer "cottage" at Rye, and then they had six weeks in Ireland. "You'd love it," Ellen wrote John. "It rains all the time."

Isabelle and her foster parents spent the entire summer in Michigan, at the resort where the Wielandes owned a large home, as did many of their St. Louis friends. Isabelle wrote only once to John. Missing her, he regretted some of the harsh thoughts he had entertained about his sister the past winter. Raised soft, as she had been, of course her point of view would be different from his own. Next year he'd try for a truer companionship with Isabelle.

Quickly school opened again, and John was a second-year medic, busy with physiology and bacteriology. He felt that the scholarship obligated him to harder work, the best of grades. His hours were long.

Ellen returned and brought John a piece of rock she declared was a chip from the Blarney stone. Isabelle came home; but when John phoned her, she told him she was busy — she would call him back.

After lab one Friday — dinner was always late on Friday evenings at the Heidemans' — John walked over to the Conte shop and rang the bell of the apartment. The correct little maid took his hat and overcoat, and showed him into the living room where Marguerite Conte sat before the fire. She smiled to see John. "The place is a mess," she said. "We're decorating."

John looked around at the familiar light green walls and bone-white furniture. "This all looks nice," he said lamely.

"You know you don't like it. You said so one time."

"I said I liked *Les Grâces* better."

"Yes, that is what you said. A Victorian young man, I am afraid. You won't want a drink?"

"No, thank you. Are the new things to be Victorian?" He and Ellen's mother got along famously.

"Indeed, they are not! My best show window? I have sold the apartment as it stands now to a fat-faced automobile dealer and his bride."

John looked again at the pretty Empire room. "How will you manage?" He was intrigued by people who formed their homes complete in the brains and taste of a stranger. If he ever had a home, it should be built tenderly about things he bought and admired himself.

They spent a pleasant half hour discussing the way this apartment would be transplanted to one out on Clayton Road. Mrs. Conte brought out her cardboard mats on which she was working out a new scheme for herself and Ellen. She and John talked happily about concealed lighting, a color scheme of gray, wine, dusty pink. John suggested a touch of clear jade. "A coffee set, perhaps. And a bowl of white flowers. Lilies."

"John! You're an artist! I had thought of low glass bowls filled with pink and red carnations, wedged in very tight, you see, in circles."

"Or dead-white bowls. Where is Ellen?"

"Serving at Vera Ahnheim's tea." Marguerite looked curiously at John. "She should be home any minute. She has a dinner engagement."

"I thought second-year girls retired into oblivion."

"It's a gradual process. There are always announcements, and bridal dinners and things. Ellen is to be bridesmaid twice before Christmas. She's popular."

"Don't I know it? I never see her."

Mrs. Conte was called to the telephone. She gave John the folded evening paper as she went to answer it. He was staring at the large picture on the first page when Ellen came in from her tea party, excited, glowing, her arms full of flowers. John got to his feet, his eyes blank and dazed.

"Oh," Ellen said. Her smile faded. "John?"

He dropped the newspaper upon the table. "I — it's all right. I guess I'm a little winded."

"You didn't know?"

"Did you? Before the party, I mean."

"Oh, yes. Isabelle wrote me from Harbor Point. I supposed she had told you."

"You'd think she would, wouldn't you?"

"It — hurts you, John?" She could see that it did. John's eyes were black with hurt. At the minute Ellen would gladly have given him to Isabelle to see that hurt gone.

"It does hurt — to read it in the newspaper, along with all the strangers in St. Louis."

"She should have told you. I expect she was so excited — she looked so pretty this afternoon, John. Only, you won't want me to tell you how pretty she was. I haven't much tact."

John plunged his fists deep into his pockets and took a short turn across the floor. "I know she's pretty. And if she's happy — why, that's all right, too. That will be fine. It's only — Do you like this Ahnheim fellow?" John did not. The man was fat, and so blond he seemed bald. No visible eyebrows. But one always noticed the thick blond hair on the backs of his hands.

"Oh, Kurt's all right. Isabelle should know what she's doing. She's level-headed, sensible."

"Do *you* like him?" John demanded.

"I wouldn't marry him, if that's what you mean."

"It is. Why wouldn't you?"

"Well, he's horribly spoiled. And I like my own way. I shouldn't get on with his sort. Isabelle will. She has a lovely disposition."

John nodded. His lips were drawn into a thin, tight line. "I see what you mean. I also remember how stinking-rich the Ahnheims are."

"Ah, John."

"It's all right." He patted her shoulder. "I expect she'll get around to making me think she's not treated me like dirt. You'll be maid of honor, I suppose?"

"I don't know. Vera might be. Kurt might want that."

"It's what Kurt wants now, isn't it? I'll be going, Ellen. Your mother said you had an engagement."

"Come back, won't you, John? Often?"

16

On his table at Heidemans' John found a charming little note from Isabelle telling him of her engagement to Kurt Ahnheim. "You know how nice he is, John, dear. Uncle Brooke and Aunt Mary are so pleased."

They, of course, had a better say than her brother about whom Isabelle should marry. And — what could John have said about the man? Only that, to him, he seemed overly physical, not a little stupid, and, as Ellen had admitted, rather badly spoiled by being the only son of the Ahnheim Brewery millions. Also, John knew, the horsy young man was considered a great social catch, in many ways the best in St. Louis. Isabelle could be considered lucky. Perhaps she was lucky.

17

Two weeks after announcement had been made of Isabelle Wielande's engagement to Kurt Ahnheim, the market crashed. The disaster was so immediately felt to be a great one that even John realized it. The Heidemans had lost to a large extent, were to lose even more. By the end of that year the laboratory force had to be cut. John was able really to help the doctor now, after classes.

Brooke Wielande was reported seriously ill. His business had been wiped out, Isabelle told John. Uncle Brooke had lost millions. And millions more for other people, John supposed. Still, the specialist and nurses in attendance on the sick man did not look like abject poverty to John. The butler still opened the front door; the limousine and Isabelle's new coupé stood in the driveway of the Lindell Boulevard mansion.

Isabelle, too, was going blithely on with her plans for a large wedding in the spring. Two maids of honor — tactfully she could have both Ellen and Vera — eight bridesmaids. A honeymoon in Hawaii. They could not get just the house they wanted, so they were building a new home out in swanky Dardenne Village.

"I'm glad the Ahnheim fortune wasn't in stocks and bonds," Isabelle told John frankly. "If prohibition is repealed, they'll be richer than ever. Anyway, they have their money protected, you can be sure."

She was, too, a little smug about having snared

Kurt before the market crash. Rich young bachelors would be scarce now. John hated her self-satisfaction until he recognized her feeling as being similar to his own sense of gratitude that he had the scholarship safe in his possession. There would be a great many more medics asking for help now. He supposed it was everyone's proper instinct to protect himself first, to be glad if he himself were safe. He need not feel lofty about Isabelle. It was certainly the instinct of the female to make as fine a nest as possible for herself and her young.

Chapter Seven

The Contes felt the pinch sharply, and at once. With them it was not a matter of getting along with two cars instead of four. Mrs. Conte had had some money — a rainy-day fund — in stocks, but most of their assets were in the properties she handled. She had many chances to sell homes, now, but no one came forward to buy. Rich people were always slow paying their bills. The summer cottage she had done at Rye, way last summer, had never been paid for, while she herself felt obligated to pay the bills for furnishings and draperies, had already paid the labor charges.

She and Ellen were ensconced in their shiningly new apartment, while the "fat-faced automobile dealer" canceled his order for the old *décor,* having decided to live in his father's home until things looked better.

Mrs. Conte was worried. John came in one evening and found her hanging gauze curtains of dusty pink in the curving bay window of the living room. He made her sit down in one of the new armchairs, took off his shoes — he would have to stand on the gray-upholstered window seat — and hung the draperies himself, Ellen assisting.

"Thank you, John. That was a real help. I am sick about getting these new things." It was then that they told him how bad their affairs were. "I haven't lost so much real money," Marguerite told him. "It was just money I thought I had, and was living on."

"I'm going to help Mom," Ellen told John. "I mean, really help. I'm sure I can attend to the shop."

"And what would become of the girl you have now?" John asked her.

"Oh. I hadn't thought of that. But there must be some way. I want to work. Even if this hadn't happened, I meant to work. I'm not a deb at heart, you know. I never was."

Mrs. Conte smiled. "Contacts count in a business like mine. Your debut was probably a good investment. You have lots of friends. In time they'll be marrying and buying homes. They'll still have some money. Or get more. The market may go up as quickly as it went down."

"You shouldn't count on that," John told her.

"How old are you, John?"

"Twenty-two."

"You seem so mature. Experienced."

"I've had to make my own way. It makes a difference. I've never thought it was anything to be ashamed of."

"It certainly is not. And it does make a difference. It gives a man — or a woman, either — a strong inner core that a carefree childhood may deny him."

John sat looking at his big, scarred hands. Not so rough and stained any more, but they would always show the years of scrub brush and chicken pens they had known. The nails had been mashed, the fingers cut and torn. Sensitive, strong hands — they would never be beautiful ones.

"If it were only Ellen and I," Mrs. Conte mused, her gray eyes on the glowing fire. Ellen sat curled up beside John on the red velvet love seat. She was fastening little silver buttons to what looked like the bodice of a blue velvet dress. John liked to watch the way she frowned over the threading of a needle. He liked to watch the play of her slim white fingers against the rich fabric. "We're such a large family. So many aunts and cousins and elderly uncles. They've all come to me with stories of their losses. I'll have to help them. How, I don't know. Unless . . ."

"Now, Mom," Ellen protested. "You promised."

"I know I did. And I won't be sentimental. You see, John — just last week — I had another offer for *Les Grâces*. Almost as big an offer as I've ever had. I'm pretty sure it's my obligation to sell it."

John was horrified. To him it was as if she had considered trafficking with Ellen. "That seems dreadful," he said inadequately.

"Doesn't it? Like betraying a trust. Still, John, *Les Grâces* is only bricks and wood and old furniture, long gone out of date. Aunt Philomene,

Uncle Pierre, the cousins — they're very precious flesh and blood. They're alive. They're my own. I — I can't let sentimental attachment for *Les Grâces* blind me to the fact that they'll need warmth and food and care."

John nodded. He valued Mrs. Conte's talking so frankly to him. She was a proud person. She would not have spoken of these intimacies to everyone. He studied her problem with all the care he could give to it.

"Isn't there someone else, besides you —"

"Uncle Beau," Ellen spoke up.

Her mother frowned. "She means Dr. Beaumont Watts. He has a good practice. He'd help. His money is really his wife's, and his son's. You know Felix?"

"Yes. How many are there who need help?"

"Oh, about ten. They've had a little income, each of them. They have their little apartments; they are not extravagant people. The French are not. But they like their little prides and refinements. They have to put on a brave front to the world. The young people of the family — there are still a few — can probably manage. But old Uncle Pierre is as frail as white porcelain. Cousin Briand Loisel is deaf. They must be cared for."

"Couldn't you — This is only a suggestion, but I know a little money can go a far way. If you'd take them all out to *Les Grâces,* one fire, one roof, would shelter them all. You have that colored family to do the hard work. Wouldn't enough of your — your relatives — be able to do what else was needed? Make beds, dust, do some of the cooking? What sewing there is. The men could have a garden; there are fruit trees on the place. There is so much room."

Ellen and her mother looked at each other, their eyes shining. "We could, Mom!"

"We certainly could! And they'd love it. They'd love being at *Les Grâces*. It means a lot to them, too. Oh, John!"

"Can't you just see Cousin Briand bringing in his first lettuce? And Uncle Pierre putting paper bags on the grapes?"

"Yes," Mrs. Conte laughed. "And Aunt Philomene washing the teacups, and darning the lace curtains in the parlor. Oh, John, we never would have been practical enough to think of this! What do you charge for your ideas?"

John colored. "I — I don't have enough of them to set up in business. I — I'd hate to see you sell *Les Grâces*."

"I know you would." Happily she went to the desk, began making lists and plans.

More frequently, after that, John went out to *Les Grâces*. He was an "old friend," trusted and admired by the family. Not an eligible suitor for Ellen, naturally, but a *brave* young man. The twittering aunts taught him a little French. They knit bedsocks and wristlets for him. He helped the "gentlemen gardeners" pick peas in the spring, and transplant iris roots in the fall. He was even asked to climb up on the roof and replace a slate that had been blown loose. He had saved *Les Grâces* for the Briands — they gave him much more credit than he felt was his due — and he had a rightful interest in the place.

2

John had not been asked how he felt about Isabelle's becoming engaged to Kurt Ahnheim. Isabelle knew that he was hurt, discontented, about her marriage. She took time to coax and cajole him prettily about being jealous of Kurt.

"I'm not," he retorted. "But, by rights, I should have some part, some say, in this."

"You can't have anything against Kurt, John, dear. Except that he is a rich man and doesn't work."

"I haven't anything against him. It's you marrying him, and you should be worrying about his being dull and stupid. But, anyway, if I were choosing for you, it would be something better. Then — there's this. I am your older brother. I should be allowed the gesture of 'giving the bride away.' "

Isabelle patted his cheek. "Silly, stubborn John. Uncle Brooke is the correct one to give me away. Goodness, he's earned that much, all the years and money he's spent on me."

John frowned. "I know. It wasn't my fault that I was only fourteen when Mother died. But, now, in a few years, I could care for you, Isabelle. It's what I've planned for. You don't have to marry Kurt."

Isabelle widened her brown eyes. "But, darling,

I *want* to marry Kurt. I don't have to marry anybody. Don't you suppose other men have asked me? Don't you suppose Uncle Brooke would still feed me? He's given me a nice trust fund, you know. He feels as if I'm really his daughter. I love him. You like him too, John, I know. You wouldn't want to hurt and upset him now, when he's sick, and has had so much bad luck."

Well, she was right, or had, as usual, been able to make herself appear to be right.

After promising himself that he would not go near, John cut lab and went to the wedding. Afterward he was glad that he had done so.

He had sent a gift to Isabelle so extravagant that the paying for it had salved his pride a little, much in the way biting on an aching tooth can seem to give a little relief to the sufferer. But he made sure that Isabelle would not be ashamed of his gift. She could boldly display those goblets of Swedish glass, as beautiful as frost in the sunlight.

The wedding was large, important, beautiful. The great church was lighted by hundreds of tall white candles in high candelabra along the aisles, banked among the roses and lilies in the chancel. A vested choir sang. Guests, beautifully gowned, fragrantly perfumed, rustled in and knelt and sighed and whispered discreetly. The men held silk hats on their striped knees and looked uncomfortable.

The bridesmaids, Ellen Conte and Vera Ahnheim, wore frocks made "quaintly" long, and looked sweetly virginal in poke bonnets of shirred chiffon. Isabelle was a tall, slim sheath of loveliness in her white satin, and a "rare old family veil of Alençon lace." Whose rare old family, John never discovered.

He listened, unheeding, to the stately service. His thoughts were busy, trying to make himself feel that the bride was Isabelle, a creature of flesh and blood, his own sister whose baby face he had washed a thousand times, whose arithmetic problems he had done to keep her out of trouble at school. He could not make her seem real. That beautiful person, that lacquered loveliness, was a doll in one of Vandervoort's elaborate window displays. She was wound up to stand, and kneel, and bow her head. She had no ears to hear the bishop's beautiful voice, no sense of touch lingered in the hand she placed in Kurt's. She could not feel the ring; she would not know the ecstasy of love.

Slowly, unwillingly, John began to hear Uncle Ben talking about sex. "Some wimmin is cold. They don't feel nothin', and they ain't no comfort to a man." John jerked his head impatiently. That was all dead and buried behind him. Such thoughts had no place in this shadowed, fragrant church, just as Uncle Ben would have no place in, no knowledge of, the world in which Isabelle lived. Sex, love, all emotions, to Uncle Ben had been animal-like. In Isabelle's world, living was gracious and beautiful. Wealth and culture meant time and careful planning toward such a life. Such a life Isabelle had deliberately built for herself, excluding all earthy things as she had excluded her past — and her brother. John had come to the point where he no longer cared if he were excluded. It seemed no longer to matter or be important.

3

Before the wedding John had gone to the Wielande home one evening, found that Isabelle and her aunt were dining out, and asked if he might, perhaps, see Mr. Wielande. From Uncle Brooke, John was always aware of friendliness and genuine liking. Both men had found it unnecessary to discuss who John was, or who Isabelle might claim him to be.

It was a rainy spring evening, and Mr. Wielande was enthroned in a huge leather armchair before a snapping fire. He wore a black quilted dressing gown, a white silk scarf tucked into the throat. A rug of soft, scarlet wool was laid over his knees. He was perfectly barbered and groomed. He had lost weight and looked very tired. Wine in a decanter on the low table beside him caught the firelight and glowed like some huge, crimson jewel.

John warmed his cold fingers at the fire before shaking hands with the sick man. "A doctor's trick," Brooke Wielande commented. "How are you, John?"

"That isn't the way to train a young doctor. You must leave that question to me. But the answer is: I'm very well, thank you."

"You look it. Wish I could wear a thirty-inch belt."

"You've lost weight."

"Yes. At ten thousand dollars an ounce. Have you had dinner?"

"Yes, I have, sir."

"So've I. Feed me a nursery supper at five o'clock. So I'll sleep better. What'd you have?"

"Hasenkuchen."

"Shut up, damn you!"

John laughed, put his hands behind his head, and stretched his feet toward the fire. He liked this dark-paneled room with its touches of crimson and gold in the bindings of books on the shelves, the leather armchairs, the carpet.

"Play the piano, don't you?"

"By ear." John had learned to make that qualifying admission to people who knew music.

"Know any Strauss waltzes? Not the 'Danube.' Beautiful, but I'm tired of it."

John went over to the small grand, pushed the bench back to suit his comfort, and began to play. Playing with the Heidemans, he had learned a good many German waltzes. He saw the tired lines in Brooke Wielande's face grow fainter; his whole body seemed to relax and rest. John let his fingers stray to the Chopin "Prelude in A." Brooke Wielande smiled.

"That's what I thought love was like, when I

was about your age, John," he said dreamily.

"Did you find out that it wasn't?"

"No-o. But I found out that two people hardly ever sing their love song to the same tune."

"Oh." John came back to the fire. "Perhaps," he said hesitatingly, picking the words he would use, "perhaps the disharmony we have learned to accept in jazz music makes love, too, seem different these modern times."

"Doesn't. Modern people just have come to accept shoddy in place of good sheep's wool. Jazz isn't as good as Chopin's harmonies. Modern love — marry for excitement, to find out what it's like, and divorce if things get too bad — that isn't love. Abelard would have had none of it."

John nodded. "It's not too easy, being young in a modern world and having outdated ideals."

Brooke Wielande looked at him sharply. "You don't strike me as a person who would abandon an ideal because maintaining it would mean a little difficulty."

"I'm not. I hope I'm not. But it's a little sad to see dead ideals lying around, unburied, unmourned. In my profession these dead ideals smell pretty rankly."

"Yes, I should imagine so. On top of that you're fretting because Isabelle is marrying a brewer's son."

"Well, yes, I am. Are you satisfied, sir?"

"I've been trying to figure what claim Isabelle has on you, John."

"I —"

Uncle Brooke's soft white hand stopped him. "I know. I know. I meant, what claim she had on your continued affection and loyalty. I've had to decide it was her beauty, her being a lovely woman. And the trouble with us men, John, is that we see a beautiful, delicate woman and we think she ought to be put up on a shelf with other fragile bric-a-brac. That idea is a mistaken one, of course. Most beautiful women can stand more than a hand-hammered brass bowl. I guess Kurt will be good to Isabelle. Better than some of these blue-blooded youngsters around here. I can even be glad — as you should be — that Isabelle didn't set her heart on marrying family. She might not have been so successful. The ranks of the pedigreed can close up pretty tight. They'll be friends with you, and let you give 'em a check for their pet charity; but when it comes to marrying, both parties will have to have great-grandpappies who came up the river with Laclede. So — maybe Kurt is the right one for Isabelle. Besides, John, wealth is a great comfort to a woman. It makes up for a lot of shortcomings in a husband."

There was no reply John could make to that. Aunt Mary had married fat, middle-aged Brooke Wielande for the comfort of wealth. John got to his feet. "I hope things will be all right. I'm afraid I've stayed too long, sir. Have tired you."

Brooke Wielande waved a white, useless hand. "No, you haven't. Come again. Play for me, and talk. I'm especially grateful to you for not telling me what is wrong with the stock market."

John smiled. "I thought you'd know," he said, and left the room, hearing the sick man's chuckle behind him.

4

Ellen was worried about the way John felt. Her mother said she was jealous, and Ellen admitted that she might be. John, she declared, was a peach.

One afternoon, up in Isabelle's sitting room, examining newly delivered articles of the trousseau, chattering idly of this and that, she put the matter bluntly up to her friend. "Do you know, Isabelle, I thought you liked John."

"John? Oh, Ellen, don't be silly!"

"I'm not. You did seem to like him. I know he adores you."

"Yes, he does. He doesn't always approve of me, but he does seem to be fond of me. But, then, John and Kurt — why —"

"I thought maybe you'd marry John." Ellen was very serious.

"Oh, why, I couldn't!"

Ellen stood up with an impatient little jerk. "Sometimes *I* don't approve of you," she declared. "I suppose you're thinking that he's young and poor. Well, John Mallory is *fine*. He's the very finest person I know. And that you know, too."

Isabelle looked thoughtfully at Ellen. "Are you in love with John?" she asked.

Ellen colored, then her cheeks went white, her

eyes dark blue and wide above them. "I — Yes. Yes, I suppose I am. I shouldn't be, I suppose."

Isabelle nodded. "You shouldn't be. Your family would never consent."

"If — My family couldn't stop me, if —"

"Yes, they could, Ellen."

"Mom likes John."

"Liking him — and letting you marry him — that's a different matter. You'd do much better planning to marry your cousin, Felix Watts. You know that's what they plan for you."

"They wouldn't interfere — they want me to be happy."

Isabelle's smile was patient. "Ellen, do you know — Has John ever told you anything about himself?"

"Why, no. No, he hasn't. But he's a fine person and nothing else would be important."

Isabelle smoothed a length of satin ribbon. "If I tell you something — something that *would* matter — would you promise to keep it a secret? Especially from John?"

"I don't know, Izzy. I don't like secrets."

"John wouldn't want you to mention this thing."

"If it's something he doesn't want me to know, don't tell me."

"It's something you ought to know. If you love him, and have any crazy idea of marrying him."

Ellen laughed shortly. "It takes two to have that sort of idea. John seems to be fonder of you than of me. We're just good friends."

Isabelle nodded. "Yes. Now you are. But John is ambitious. He has worked awfully hard to get as far as he is. He knows a doctor can use a few things like influential friends — a successful marriage — to get along in his career."

"John wouldn't —"

"I know him better than you do. What about that scholarship of his? He got that by being nice to Dr. Silverman."

"He got it by being the smartest man in the school."

Isabelle laughed. "You're the most naïve thing! Ask anybody. Ask your mother. Ask Hugo Marke. Or your own Uncle Beaumont."

"I don't need to. John wouldn't do anything so — so calculating."

"But, Ellen, there's nothing wrong with being nice to the right people for the sake of your future and your career. There'd be nothing wrong with John's wanting to marry you."

"If he couldn't have you."

"Oh, silly! I must tell you this thing about John. Only you mustn't ever tell him that I told you. Of course, he may tell you himself someday."

"You sound as if he'd been in prison."

"No. Nothing of that sort. Though in John's eyes it's almost as shameful a thing." She was speaking with great earnestness.

"All right," Ellen agreed. "Tell me."

Isabelle sighed. "To a certain extent I know how John feels. You see, Ellen, John is my brother."

Ellen snorted. An inelegant sound for the daughter of St. Louis' best families. "I don't believe it."

Isabelle shrugged. "That's why he's been able to keep it a secret. It is so incredible."

"But — how — why — what about Uncle Brooke and Aunt Mary?"

"Listen. I'll tell you. You'll see why I asked you not to mention this. It — it isn't a pretty story. I wouldn't tell it myself if I didn't think this was an emergency — that you ought to know before you get in too deep."

Ellen shivered. "You make it sound so scary — so romantic."

Isabelle smiled faintly. "It sounds that way. But living it — that's different."

"Don't tell me if —"

"We've been best friends for years, Ellen. I owe it to you — not to spare my own feelings when it's for your good.

"You see, my mother married against the family's wish. My mother's people were decent, respectable folk; some of them had money, some not. You know how families run. They disapproved of my father because he came from nowhere. He was handsome and charming — like John, they tell me — and probably married Mother thinking he would have her family behind them. Well, he died when John and I were babies. Then Mother died. John went to live with an uncle in California — it was he who left John the money to study medicine. And Uncle Brooke and Aunt Mary adopted me. John — maybe he was a little jealous that they'd chosen me — anyway, John never liked my taking the name Wielande. He has a stubborn sort of pride, you know. When he came here to school, he wouldn't say he was my brother — wouldn't claim me — and, of course, I wouldn't make an issue of it, risk a scene. So you see —"

Ellen's eyes were troubled. "But — No, I don't see anything except that he — He still hasn't made any demands on Uncle Brooke, has he?"

Isabelle smiled tolerantly. "Naturally Uncle Brooke helps him in all sorts of little ways. I think it's very generous of him — to overlook John's stiffness. John never gives him any credit or thanks."

"But I still can't see what difference it makes. Why, you told me — except to prove that John didn't want to marry you, that he's only jealous of you as his sister."

Isabelle frowned. "Do I have to say it so plainly? I told you who John is to show you how impossible it would be for him to try to marry you — when he is nobody, and has no family behind him."

Ellen tossed her head in fine disdain. "I don't see that it makes a bit of difference. He's still a fine, honest person."

"So is our butler. Ellen, can't you see —"

"You don't want him to marry me, do you?"

"No. Frankly I don't. I think it would be the greatest mistake in the world — for both of you.

Your standards, your backgrounds, are so different."

"Well, he probably won't ask me. I'm afraid he won't."

"He will," Isabelle promised. "He knows what a help your family position would be when he gets ready to practice medicine. John's been poor — he values family more than you or I would."

And again Miss Conte snorted. "I intend to go on as if you hadn't told me!"

It was only when she got home — hours too late — that Ellen recognized the fuzziness of Isabelle's reasoning, and that she recalled the day, seven or eight years before, when Isabelle had been the one to deny having any family other than the Wielandes and a stray cousin or so. Well, it did not matter. John was John. Ellen would just keep that comforting thought in mind, and forget the rest of it.

Of course, now, she knew why John was feeling badly about Isabelle's marriage. He certainly was being left out, disregarded, in the whole affair. The Saturday after the wedding Ellen persuaded him to drive out to *Les Grâces* with her. John had so little *fun*. She did so like to be with him. And with Isabelle out of the running. . . .

They visited dutifully with the aunts and uncles and cousins. John helped Maum Bette's son, Joe, put a caster back into the leg of a heavy walnut dresser up in Cousin Briand's room. But before they must go home, John and Ellen had their usual walk down the hill toward the river.

The turf was springy underfoot. Dandelions were sprinkled like coins upon the new green grass. There were violets on the slope of the hill — violets the color of Ellen's eyes — and the sunlight slanting down between the tall old trees tangled in her hair.

"I like spring," Ellen declared happily. "I don't envy Isabelle in Hawaii. Not a lot, I don't."

John's face clouded. "I wonder if she likes it."

"Honolulu's gorgeous."

"I didn't mean — just Honolulu."

"Oh. I see. You didn't like her marrying Kurt, did you, John?"

"No," John admitted. "I didn't. I wanted — something different." He bent and picked up a few sharp little stones, threw them out into the river, dimpling and clean-looking. "Of course, I'm crazy. I don't suppose I'll ever have the sort of money Kurt can give her. And she couldn't wait. It seems a deb has to marry her second year, or be a — a prairie dog, or something."

"Woof, woof! That remark certainly puts me in the kennel." His smile hurt Ellen, clear to her toes. He seemed so alone — she answered with the hope of lightening his sense of loss.

John stood looking down the river, his head up, his eyes serious. "Money is made too important a thing, Ellen," he pronounced. "People work and scheme to have it, and then, when they're rich, they don't use it for the things they thought they wanted. People with money are cheated out of a lot of things, Ellen. Take Isabelle. She's stinking-rich, now, and she'll spend her life talking to Papa Ahnheim about his blood pressure, and worrying whether Kurt is going to be peevish because his mare took only a red ribbon in the show."

Ellen gurgled appreciatively. "Papa Ahnheim wants cake and pie both for dessert," she told him. "We're being very naughty, John."

"But don't you see? Their money, beyond buying them both cake and pie, isn't worth the value people put on their having it? The Ahnheims patronize the arts. They have a box at the symphony which is used by the family of their Swiss butler. The Ahnheims buy paintings some dealer tells them are masterpieces, and then they spend their time leaning over a fence watching their prize Poland China boar. They could have as much fun on not a cent more than fifty thousand dollars."

"Yes, John. But Isabelle knew what she wanted. Or thought she did. She'll be happy. Isabelle is darling, but she isn't one to get philosophical or worry whether she's made a mistake. I can see how it must be a great comfort to be conventional, to know definitely that a rather commonplace man with twenty million dollars is preferable to — say — a John Gilbert with prospects."

John nodded. "I hope you're right. I — I love Isabelle very dearly. I want her happiness above everything else."

Ellen trudged along at John's side, content to be with him, content to let him talk, to expound his disdain for money and position. His words gave no weight to Isabelle's suggestion that John might use Ellen as a ladder to professional success and position. That was not a part of her knowledge of John. She wished only that she knew of some way to make him notice her, not as a friend, but as a girl, a woman desirable enough to make love to. Indeed, Isabelle's revelations had resulted only in a sense of revulsion toward her friend that she should so misjudge and misrepresent John's impulses. Isabelle was the climber, the opportunist, not John.

Still, Ellen must go on being nice to Isabelle, seeing a lot of her. If she had an ounce of sense, or loyalty to her mother — poor Mom was having trouble enough these days. The commission to decorate Isabelle's new home was a godsend. The Ahnheims might prefer red plush, but they did pay their bills. Besides, Isabelle had given the entire matter over to Mrs. Conte. She had been one person not to welsh on a promise given before the depression.

"Of course, Mom, when she first hired you, she did it because, before October, 1929, it was the smart thing to have a home à la Marguerite Briand Conte. Ink. But now I'm pretty sure she's going on with it — out of charity."

Marguerite continued calmly to sort swatches of glazed chintz. "Pride is a luxury we can scarcely afford, my dear."

Ellen bit her lip. "I know it. I'm a beast."

"You're being very childish. And isn't there a trace of jealousy? Over John, I mean."

Ellen said nothing. There was not much she could say.

"I know that John is fond of Isabelle. I know he sees something of her — or used to. That he kisses her casually. But hasn't John ever kissed you?"

John had. Ellen remembered in minute detail. There had, first, been that rainy night up on Art Hill. John's lips had been hard against her mouth. She had felt his big, lean body tremble. She had thought he, too, had felt the passion of that kiss. For days after it Ellen had gone around in a warm glow of happiness, trailing little clouds of glorious dreams behind her. John had not kissed her again; the little pink clouds had drifted off and melted. Of course, John was young, poor, and still in school. Ellen would have to wait. Years and years. He probably felt he had no right to ask her to wait, had no right to bind her to his uncertain fortunes.

The second kiss — Ellen had given it to John. Her cheeks went hot every time she remembered it. He had been playing the piano out at *Les Grâces*. Chopin's "Nocturne in F Sharp." A simple, sweet thing. Sunlight had come through the long west windows, touching the dome of glass over the flowers on the mantelpiece, bringing to life the rosy garlands on the plum-colored wallpaper, lighting a soft nimbus about John's dark head. Ellen had put her hand to his hair. It was like a live thing, strong, clinging to her fingers. And she had kissed him, right at the corner of his mouth, where his lips had a dear little funny quirk. Her lips remembered the roughness of his close-shaven cheek.

And John . . . John had got up abruptly. Gone over to the window, away from her. Stood there, his hands pushed down into his pockets. "Don't do that!" he had said gruffly. He did not look at her. He must have known how shamed, how hurt, she had been. He had never mentioned the affair again. They had driven home, and talked all the way about some doctor who had let a man die of appendicitis because he had, suddenly, become afraid to operate, and still had too much pride to let another surgeon take his place.

Ellen remembered that kiss and, sometimes, remembering it, she almost hated John Mallory. The only explanation she had been able to make of his brusqueness — inexperienced as she was in being rebuffed by men — was that he wanted to be only friends with Ellen. And that he wished Ellen to know how he felt on the subject.

Meanwhile, of course, John was being as miserable as Ellen. He felt, more keenly than she could have imagined, his position as a green medical student, without family or money, and what prospects he had so far in the future that they seemed a very indifferent thing to offer to the choice bud of St. Louis society.

He suspected that Ellen had misunderstood his grouchiness over her kissing him that day at *Les Grâces*. But, good heavens, he did not want her being sorry for him. He did not want her patting him on the head. "Nice Fido. Lie down, Fido!"

If she only knew . . . He had to see her, and talk to her. So long as she was free, and seemed to like him, he could not give up all hope. Some miracle might occur to make her see him as different, distinctive, among other men. The depression had helped. Ellen told him that she felt obligated to help her mother now. Else she would probably have married long before this. She was popular. At dances she swung from one man's arms to another's. Three times out of four John would come to the apartment and find her gone out with some other man, or some other man — and he often enough found young Felix Watts — claiming prior rights to half of the red velvet love seat. John took his fourth time, and was grateful. He could not do a thing about the hazards of these other men. Likable, eligible chaps, most of them. It was not to be hoped that other men would not see Ellen's beauty and preciousness, and covet it. John saw it, and achingly wanted it for his own. The years he must wait were so long, so ridden with the dangers of losing her.

Chapter Eight

The years whirled along. It was spring again, and John helped Cousin Briand dig thick white stalks of asparagus. It was fall, and he tied straw around the rosebushes and caught a little blue and green lizard sunning itself on a rock.

John was a senior medic, promised internship at Boone. Only the best of the class stayed on here. Those not chosen argued that it was wiser to change one's field. Well, that was a good argument. John was glad he had been chosen for Boone. Barngrove was to be assistant resident at Boone Hospital itself. John would still see his friend. He could still have his room at Heidemans', and see Isabelle. And Ellen.

In May Dr. Heideman told John he was going to take Fanny to Switzerland for the summer. Put her under the care of a nerve specialist there. If John liked, he could go along. Dr. Heideman thought he could get him an assistantship in a clinic for tubercular-bone diseases.

John felt exactly as he had done when Dr. Jim first got him a job scrubbing floors at the Villa Franca Hospital. Well, he had been right to be thrilled with Dr. Jim's job. It had been a first step. He was justified in being thrilled now. For one who meant to be a specialist in crippled children's surgery, three months in the Kinderhof clinic would mean a step in seven-league boots.

John did not mind when Isabelle made light of this, his first trip to Europe. Ellen was amused, but she was not laughing at John. When he confessed that he had never so much as *seen* the ocean, nor been on a boat, except the big, waddling excursion steamers, she was as thrilled as he was. Together they made out lists. Lists of things he should take. Lists of things he should see in New York, of things he must do on the boat. They were taking a slow cabin boat. So much more fun than a luxury liner, Ellen assured him. And three more days at sea, John pointed out.

"I hope you won't get seasick!"

"Oh, glory! What if I am? And waste all that time!"

Of course, he wrote and told Miss Lillie and the doctor about the trip. Were they, sure enough, coming East to see him take his degree? For a year Miss Lillie and Dr. Jim had been planning that journey. John was going to engage rooms at a West End hotel. Isabelle had said he could use the Dodge. Just tell Conrad? She would be leaving the first week in June. Seeing John get *cum laude* honors with his M.D. meant nothing to her. She gave him a handsome Gladstone for a present. Isabelle's time was not fully her own. John understood that.

Ellen and her mother would be nice to Dr. Jim and Miss Lillie. John would have a great time introducing Dr. Jim to all the medical bigwigs at the hospital.

But, the last week, a letter came from Miss Lillie. Dr. Jim had had a slight stroke. It had lasted only about six hours, affected his tongue and throat. The doctors thought it safer if he would stay quietly at home. John would understand their disappointment. His graduation meant much to both of them. "We are proud of you, John. As proud as if we had scooped up the wet clay and molded you by hand. Be sure to send Jim any clippings and programs. They'll interest him. We are sending a gift by express. I shall write you again very soon."

The gift was a pin-seal medical bag, completely equipped. Fanny admired it, grudgingly, jealously.

"You silly thing," John scolded her. "You and Dr. Heideman are like my mother and father. Miss Lillie and Dr. Jim — they are like grandparents. I have room for both of you!"

"Oh?" said Fanny. "She is old?"

"Yes. They're both old. I worry about them. I haven't seen them for so long."

2

Sitting in the Field House on Commencement Day, his arms folded across his chest, his gray eyes focused on the bunting above the stage, listening to the speaker — a member of the United States Supreme Court, dignified in his voluminous robes, his voice a cellolike instrument on which he played with skill and feeling — John thought about the goal he had won today. Not the end of the game, that goal. But a goal for which he had fiercely played, which had been fairly won. Looking back, the fight did not seem to have been too hard. Both the game and its results seemed very much worth while.

Looking about him, too, at the six hundred or so young men and women here to get their degrees, he was struck by the tremendous financial investment this group signified. A million dollars would not have been a large enough value. Yet, here and now, there was not a dime's worth of tangible product that might be wrapped up and handed over a counter. Likewise, nothing — except mental failure — could ever rob these young people of what they now held in their possession. Much less could be said of other investments.

It was thrilling to have Ellen tuck her hand under his arm, to have her thin white skirts blow with the full black ones of his gown as they walked along the grass of the sunny hilltop campus. It was thrilling to have his fellow medics, afterward, tell him that his girl was a pip. She was, too. There had not been a prettier girl in that whole crowd than Ellen Conte in her white Swiss frock, a wreath of cornflowers around the crown of her floppy hat.

Then, coming back to Heidemans', conscious of a need to get about his packing, he was met by Fanny, who put a telegram into his hand. A long telegram from Miss Lillie.

The words blurred before John's unbelieving eyes. Dr. Jim? Gone? Dead? His Dr. Jim, with his sweet smile and curly gray head.

> Do not give this to John until after the exercises. Then tell him that Dr. Hayes died last night, peacefully. If John cares to come to California later my house is waiting for him, and Dr. Hayes' place in the Villa Franca Hospital. Jim willed it to him. Give him my love, tell him to consider carefully, and act as he thinks wise and best.

John looked at Fanny. "But . . ."

"Will you go?"

"To California? Oh, Fanny, I don't know. I don't know. I feel as if I had fallen into a deep hole. This changes so much."

"Yes. It changes much. Will you go?"

"I — I'll have to think. There's so much — I can't get there for the funeral. There's my job at Boone, and the trip."

"And your girl."

"My . . . Oh, Ellen. Yes, now there is Ellen."

"Perhaps you should go, John."

"I need my internship."

"Yes. You would get that in this other hospital. No?"

"Well, I suppose so. I'd like working there. With Dr. Gilfoyle. But, oh, Fanny, Dr. Jim . . ."

His face crumpled, and he turned away. Fanny quietly left the room.

John phoned Ellen that evening, briefly told her the news. Listened soberly to her words of condolence and encouragement. Ellen knew how he felt about Dr. Jim.

"I may not be going to Switzerland," he told her. "I should go out to Miss Lillie."

"To stay?"

"I don't know. Can I come to see you, Ellen?"

"Yes, of course. Tomorrow evening?"

"I — yes. I — I have something to say to you now, to ask you, before I decide."

Ellen set the phone back on its cradle. It had come. The time was now. The time which she had awaited with changing emotions for so many years. Four years. She had loved John for that long — ever since she had first met him in the Wielande drawing room. She had loved him when she had thought Isabelle had a prior claim upon him. She had continued to love him when she knew he was Isabelle's brother. She had hoped he would tell her — and, of course, tomorrow night he would tell her that before he mentioned anything else. His being Isabelle's brother had never made any difference — Ellen discounted any claim that John was kind and friendly because of her family's prominence. She and John liked each other. Just two people.

And that was the way it should be. Two people alone — no other consideration. But lately there had been some — Not Mom. Mom had not said one word. But the other members of the family had certainly begun to show Ellen that she should be marrying, and marrying suitably. Would they approve of John?

They liked him. Yes, indeed. But he had no money, no social position — even as Isabelle Ahnheim's brother, he would have no social position in the eyes of the Briands and the Contes.

Even Uncle Beau — a doctor himself, and one of the family who still had money — had told her kindly that young Mallory was very "promising." He had told her that when he and Aunt Melanie were taking her to New Orleans for the Mardi Gras, with their son Felix as a companion for her. Felix, whose grandmother had been a Coquin and who, from his mother, would inherit the Gerard Chemical Company. Family and a fortune both had Felix. And some personal attractiveness, though Ellen did not care a lot for his type, slender, blond, aesthetic.

In New Orleans he had asked her to marry him, and Ellen had promptly refused. Felix had been unwilling to take her word as final. He knew that he had the family approval. He had told her to think the matter over. And to consider her mother as well as herself. For a good many years Marguerite had been carrying the burden of Ellen — as well as that of the whole Briand family — on her tired shoulders. Should not Ellen now be ready . . .

His words stayed in Ellen's loyal consciousness. But — there was John. Surely, surely her mother would want Ellen to marry for love. Surely she would? John had prospects. One day, even Uncle Beau admitted — one day John Mallory would be famous. With her family's influence, and the Wielande and Ahnheim money —

Ellen stood and looked at the blue taffeta spread of her bed, its gleaming surface pulled taut by Justine's expert hands. Why, that was what Isabelle had meant. John would be helped — his career would be helped — by his marriage to Ellen Conte. John was too practical a person not to realize that.

He *was* practical. Almost too mature and sober in his realism, his recognition of economic values. He had shown that side of his nature to her a dozen times. And he was ambitious. Those two qualities would lead him to appreciate the advantages of a marriage to Ellen Conte. He might be asking her to marry him for exactly the same reasons that the family thought she should marry Felix. If she argued that John was justified in recognizing such advantages, why would she not be forced to examine further this matter of herself and Felix? If she could talk it over with Mom . . . But, with people like herself and Mom, there were certain things one did not say.

She could not ask Mom if marriage to John — Ellen loving him, John being friendly toward Ellen but valuing her social assets more highly than her emotional appeal — she could not ask Mom if such a marriage would be all right. Just as she could not come right out and ask Mom if she — Marguerite — really hoped Ellen would marry Felix. In neither case would she be able to put a direct question, nor would her mother be able to give a sincere, unbiased answer.

This was something Ellen must work out for herself. And it was very confusing. And sad. For years she had been loving John, and contentedly waiting for him to be in a position to announce his love for her, to claim her love for him. Now that time had come. And she did not know what she would say. Because, now, she also had awakened to the thought and knowledge that marrying is a complicated business, not simply based on a matter of "I love you. Do you love me?"

Ellen, on her part, was ready to be simple, to be honest. Whether she *should* marry John, whether she *should* marry Felix — or not — she was quite prepared to cut cleanly through the tangle of arguments and obligations, both implied and acknowledged, and to follow the dictates of her heart and her body, blindly say to John that she loved him, that she would marry him.

Her heart sang and tumbled in her breast to anticipate the joyous abandonment of such an announcement. Just she and John against the world, the family. They two making a life for themselves.

If — and her skin prickled, and her limbs went cold to think of this — if John, too, seemed to be as frank, as honest. But, of course, he would be. John was the most sincere of men. He hated sham and deception. She knew that he did. She knew him so well. Dear, dear John.

He was coming to her, to tell her that he loved her, to ask her to plan his life, a life which she would share and, therefore, had a right to plan. She could hardly wait for the joy of that moment. Having waited years, the minutes now were weighted with lead.

Over and over she rehearsed what he would say, what she would say. How she would feel — her cheeks went hot to know how she would feel. They would be married very soon — out at *Les Grâces,* probably, with the aunts and uncles to sponsor them.

But maybe the aunts and uncles would not approve.

Well, they would be married *without* their approval. It was silly for all those impoverished ladies and gentlemen to frown on John's lack of money. Only —

To most of them the money part would not matter. It would be, more, a matter of family and breeding. Well, John was as good as they were. Only, of course, they would not think so. Would not think he was good enough for Ellen Briand Conte. They would ask who his grandmother was, and his —

Isabelle. Would John tell her that he was Isabelle's brother? Surely, now, he must tell her. If he did not — why, if he did not, he was not being wholly honest with her; and if he was not wholly honest, how could she trust his declaration of love as being purely that, not fogged with the fact that she had much besides love to bring to a doctor who wanted to get along? How could she know?

The light went out of her eyes, the color from her cheeks. What if he did not tell her? Oh, he must, he must! He must be wholly honest with her. Or . . . or . . .

3

Justine answered the door that next evening with a smile for Dr. Mallory, and the information that Mrs. Conte had gone out to play bridge but that Miss Ellen was in the living room. At Ellen's request the maid brought a tray with glasses of limeade and a plate of fresh macaroons. John sat down on the love seat, and bent over to straighten the fan of paper in the cold fireplace. Ellen, oddly silent and reserved, curled up in the armchair across from him. The low coffee table was between them. Ellen murmured a message of sympathy from her mother.

John ate a macaroon and drank his limeade. Ellen held her glass in her hands, and looked at John. He had changed since she first had known him. He was, for one thing, older. He would be twenty-five in a day or two. He had learned to dress well in these four years. His well-cut, dark blue suit, his two-toned blue tie, his carefully polished dull black Oxfords, and the black silk socks were all in perfect taste. He had learned how, subconsciously, to tuck his handkerchief back into his breast pocket, and have all the little points show crisply just as they should do. He was sitting there, looking into the fireplace, frowning a little. Aunt Philomene said a man who had puckers between his eyes possessed a conscientious character.

John looked up at her with a smile. "You're a restful person to be with, Ellen."

"Which may, or may not, be a compliment," she retorted.

John smiled again, got up from his chair, bent to smell the carnations, went over to the windows, and, lifting the curtain, looked down into the street. "It was a compliment all right," he said finally.

"Well, that's something. Why don't you sit down?"

"I — Could I move this table out of the way? I can't see you. Or could you come over here?"

Ellen laughed. Secretly she was proud of her poise. "I'll move. Mother hates the furniture changed around. She says moving furniture is an undesirably feminine trait."

"Your mother is a wonderful person. Level-headed, clever — but she's thoroughly feminine, I should say."

"She'd be glad to hear you say it. She hates women who try to conceal their being women. She hates sham of any sort."

They were both nervously sparring for the proper conversational opening. John took his handkerchief again and touched his lips. Ellen reached out her hand and took it from him, sniffed at it, and gave it back to him. "Smells good," she said. "I like the perfume you use."

John's cheeks were red. "I can't help getting a little tainted," he said. "Of course, I never notice the stink myself."

"I like it, I told you. Hospital-liniment-bandages. My favorite perfume."

"I'll give you a bottle for your birthday."

"Do. John, have you decided what you are going to do? After your trip? Work here in St. Louis? Or go back to California?"

John sighed. Now he could talk. "I haven't decided. What I do would depend on what you would think best."

Ellen's heart caught, held, plunged heavily. *Make him say it! Make him say it!* "Goodness, I'm no one to advise you," she said lightly. "I don't know a thing about your profession, John. I've never been sick. I am even one of those outcasts of medical society, a person with tonsils. I —"

John touched her hand. "Ellen," he said quietly. Just so, in clinic, he was accustomed to quiet an excited child. She looked up at him, her eyes dark, her soft lips parted sweetly.

"You see, Ellen, what I do must be what you want to do, too. We could stay here, where your mother and your friends are. I can do my internship, then go in with some older doctor, be on the staff at Boone. We shouldn't be rich, but I expect I'd make a living for us. Or I could go back to Villa Franca. The town is growing fast. I could work with Dr. Gilfoyle, who knows me. We'd live with Miss Lillie — you'd love the big, old house. It has wide porches, big trees, a rose garden. You see, Ellen?"

Ellen was smiling at him. Dear John. "Is this a proposal of marriage, by any chance, Dr. Mallory?"

John's eyes widened. "Why, of course! You know that I've loved you — for years. I had to wait. I've been so afraid some other guy would beat my time!"

Ellen laughed softly, happily. "You're sweet. But you do propose very badly."

John got up, pushed Mrs. Conte's coffee table out of his way, and paced the smooth gray carpet, his hair a little wild, his hands thrust into his trousers pockets. "It's hard work. I wonder men ever do get married. They must want to, very badly. As I do." His smile was beautiful. Ellen's breath caught.

"Oh . . . John."

He came and dropped down beside her, had her in his arms. His lips were hard, questing; his shoulders, his arms, his hands, so big and strong. So warm and safe. Ellen let herself have this minute of sinking, drowning joy.

She took account of each detail, noticed each little thing, as a condemned man might notice the grass blades and the flecks of dust as he walks to the scaffold that will end all such things for him. She felt John's teeth behind his lips, the prickly smoothness of his warm cheek. Even the texture of his coat and tie; all those things she noticed and meant to remember. *He had not told her. He was not going to tell her!*

"Ah, Ellen, Ellen," John was whispering against her hair. "It's been so long — so hard, waiting. I was afraid you might not love me enough. But you do, don't you? And, now, always, we two — together, working, planning — Oh, Ellen, are you as happy as I am?"

He held her away from him, looked searchingly into her face. And to her dismay, fight them as she would, tears filled Ellen's blue eyes and ran down her cheeks. "Ellen?" John asked.

"Oh, don't make it hard for me, John, darling. I love you so. Truly, I do." She should not have said that. . . .

John smiled. Took his handkerchief and wiped her eyes, but the tears kept welling up. "Don't cry, sweet. This really isn't a sad business. Please, Ellen. It's not like you to cry."

Ellen gulped. "I — I can't stop. I — you're so sweet — and I love you so much!"

"Well, cry then, if that's what makes you do it. It's going to be a little damp, this business of being in love and getting married to a silly little nut who cries when she's happy."

"I'm not happy!"

"You're not? But — why aren't you? Are you dreading the hard lot of a doctor's wife?"

Ellen pushed back out of his arms. "Listen, John," she said with determination.

John smiled down at her tolerantly. "All right. I'll listen."

"I love you. I have for years, and I suppose I always shall. Your being a doctor has nothing to do with you and me — what I feel."

"My being a doctor? But — that's me, Ellen. I *am* a doctor. It isn't a sterile coat I take off and put on. It's me, and I'm it."

She shook her head. "Whatever you may think, your life as a doctor is a separate, distinguishable part of you, John. It's a precious, valuable sort of life, too, needing to be cared for, protected, pampered to. You would be right to do the things which would best help your life as a doctor. I grant you that. Nothing you do would be too much for it. You must serve it, as you would a shrine. And I thought I could serve it, too, help it and you, just by loving you and being your — your wife. But . . ."

She was talking too much, had already used too many words. John was looking at her oddly. But she could not stop talking. She must not let John guess that she cared more than he did. That love was everything to her — honest, sincere, frank. Nothing withheld, nothing underhand. Isabelle. She must remember about Isabelle. She must not mention Isabelle. She could not bear the hurt in John's eyes, the bewilderment. "But there are more things in all lives than just a man's profession and a girl's willingness to serve it. One must consider other things, other people." . . . She was babbling!

No wonder John looked at her so strangely. He recognized the note of hysteria in her voice; but he knew, too, that Ellen was sincere, if not in what she was saying, in her feeling that she must hold him off, repulse him. Incredible as it seemed, this was a real conflict between them. Conflict with Ellen. Ellen, of all people. John, poor devil, had no experience with human conflict, no familiarity with it. There had been Uncle Ben, of course. But that opposition John had met with cold resolve and stubborn silence. He could scarcely use those weapons on Ellen.

His mind whirled. He could feel his brain cloud and befog, as if a chemical had been dropped into a beaker of distilled water and the whole mess had become now a smoky, whirling confusion. He must think. He must meet whatever it was he had to meet, clearly, sensibly. In his work he was able to meet problems calmly. A convulsive child only stirred his mind to a more alert clarity. If he might only be able to give this matter the same poised, unruffled consideration.

Ah, but this was different. This was Ellen, stirring his senses, fighting against his desire and his love. This was a matter of human emotion and reasoning. Or lack of reasoning. It was confusing. . . .

Ellen had fallen silent. She sat back against the cushions of the couch, white, spent, looking appealingly at John, hoping that he might cut cleanly into the heart of this thing, say the one word that would test, would prove, his sincerity and his love.

John drew a deep breath. "Ellen," he said unhappily. "Perhaps I don't understand all you have been saying. It — it must be a hard thing for you to say. Birth, breeding, can never be mentioned by those who have them. That I should know. I — I was afraid I hadn't enough to offer you. But I love you so. I want you so much!"

"Don't be humble!" Ellen cried out, hurt, angry, that he should so willfully misunderstand her.

John looked up, a bitter smile on his lips. His eyes were tormented. He was remembering Miss Lillie, in her straw-faced sunbonnet, telling him not to be grateful. Miss Lillie, trying to set him right about the desires a decent man could have for a woman.

"You mustn't say a thing like that, John. It isn't like you to be snobbish!"

"It isn't like you, either, Ellen. But — what else can I think? You say you love me, but — Ah, Ellen, it would be so beautiful."

Ellen got to her feet, walked over to the window, knelt on the cushioned seat, her forehead pressed against the cool glass. "Beautiful, if it were possible," she said clearly.

John stood up. "That is all — you'll say?"

"Yes. Yes, John. The way I see things — that is the way things stand."

John stood there for a minute. Picked up one

of the little jade-green coffee cups, examined it curiously, unseeingly. He felt tears ache and burn in his throat, in his heart. "Well," he said, "I — I can't say any more. A man can offer a girl his life and his name, but if it isn't enough, it isn't enough. Good-by, Ellen."

She did not turn around nor speak. She heard him go out, close the door behind her. She saw him go out into the street, pause a minute, then stride off and away. She felt as if she might be dying.

Marguerite, coming in about an hour later, spoke softly in the doorway of Ellen's darkened room. Ellen did not answer, but, as she undressed, Marguerite was sure that she heard the girl sob.

4

John went back to Heidemans'. He undressed, bathed, turned out the light, and got into bed. He lay there, on his back, his arms folded under his head, his eyes watching the shadows which passing cars threw upon the ceiling. A fresh wind blew the starched curtains back from the window. The noises of the city came into the room in a familiar blur. John could hear the zoo lions. A few times he heard the seals bark. The seals were Ellen's favorites. Ellen.

Ellen.

The thought of her was like a knife turning against his heart. He had loved her for so long, still loved her so dearly. She was so much a part of him, of his consciousness, his thoughts, his plans. He had always been afraid he might lose her, but he had never really considered the actuality of that loss. He could not consider, could not believe in, that loss, even now.

Ellen, except for those confused words, was still over there in the apartment. Her coppery hair, her frank blue eyes, her sweet, clear voice. Tomorrow afternoon John could call her up and they could go to the zoo together and feed the seals. Nothing had changed.

Everything had changed. John's whole life. He and Ellen would never go back to Villa Franca. He would never show her the vase where he had banked his money and where their son could bank his. On the other hand, they would never rent — or buy — a little cottage out in Webster, a cottage on a big lot so that they could build later to suit their larger family. He had thought that when he went into practice Ellen and her mother would delight in furnishing and decorating his office.

What had he done to make Ellen feel that this happiness, this joy, could not be? Was there anything he might yet do to make her change her mind? Should he appeal to Mrs. Conte? Was there anyone he could ask, or go to, for advice?

Hardly. This was a matter between Ellen and himself. This was not so easy a matter as wresting an education from Uncle Ben Colby; there was no Dr. Jim, here and now, to smooth and straighten John's path. This was a harder, knottier problem — harder because John must fight it out for himself, and alone. Harder because there was nothing to fight.

Ellen loved him, but she would not marry him. John was unwilling to accept such a decision, but what argument or persuasion might he use in his own behalf? What defiance might he present against Ellen's decision?

For one thing, he was sure he did not know just why Ellen would not marry him. She had said spunkily that it was not a matter of family. He believed her, too. Still — would it do any good to tell her that, instead of being a lone orphan, he was brother to Isabelle Ahnheim, her friend, nephew to Brooke Wielande? Well, if it *would* do any good, he would certainly not tell her. He would stand, or fall, on his own personal qualities. Besides, he did not think it *was* a matter of family. He did not, either, think it was a matter of money. Ellen could have married for money, if that had mattered. She had shown a nice ability to handle financial stricture when business had been bad with her mother. Ellen did not overvalue wealth or belongings. She probably knew that John would be able to care for her in the way of necessities.

Of course, there might be family pressure upon her. Ellen was a loyal soul — but, surely, she would have told him if there had been anything of that sort, if she felt obligated to marry someone else. No. He did not think that was the trouble, either.

Then — why? He did not know. And the more he lay there and watched the ceiling, and listened to the cars whiz by out in the street, the less he knew. Some woman's idea it must be. But what? If she loved him, it could not be physical repulsion. Besides, if she loved him, why in Tom Thunder would she not marry him?

John wished his was a nature that would let him go to Ellen and shake the truth — or some sense — out of her.

He wished, after running the treadmill over and over until almost morning, that he might talk the matter over with Isabelle. Belle would know if he had some fault, or lack, of which he himself was unconscious. She had known Ellen since childhood, had been her intimate friend for years. She would know what thing it was that would let Ellen love a man, and yet refuse to marry him, to consider a fulfillment of that love. Yes, he would like to talk to Belle.

Would she, too, talk about Laclede? Agh! He would worry no longer. He would go back to California. There he would have work, and a pride in what he might make of himself and his life! A man did not *need* a woman. He only wanted her. Wanted her . . .

Chapter Nine

Since now he had given up his internship at Boone, John was especially appreciative of the opportunities offered by his three months in the Kinderhof clinic. He planned to go into the Villa Franca Hospital in October as Junior Surgeon. Dr. Gilfoyle had promised that he should do the pediatric work. He was glad that he had decided to get this specialized experience before going to California. He would feel more assured, for one thing. He was, besides, learning a great many things from these bearded doctors with their rough voices and kind hands.

The Heidemans wanted him to stop with them in St. Louis for a few days, were hurt at his brusque refusal, at his buying a ticket through to the coast. "The break has to come, Fanny," John told her. "Better make it clean. And quick."

"John . . ."

"Yes?" He caught the dark worry in her eyes, patted her shoulder.

"Are you happy about going back to this little hospital?"

"The hospital part is all right, Fanny. I am blue about Dr. Jim — but the hospital isn't so darn little but what we can do some pretty good medicine in it."

She wanted to ask him about Ellen. In three months' time he had not mentioned her name. She had fed him coffee and strudel, and hoped he would talk to her. His grave, forbidding silence had daunted Fanny. She dared not speak now. At Chicago she could only kiss him, tears in her eyes, and beg him to write, to remember them.

"Come back to us, John?" she begged him. "We need you here. The Papa and I — you have friends here. Do not forget us."

"I'll never forget you, Fanny. You know that. And you can come to see me, in California."

Fanny sniffed. "With *her* there!"

John laughed. "Still jealous of Miss Lillie? You foolish Fanny."

"Will she take care of you?"

"Lord, yes. Though one would think I would be old enough to take care of myself."

"No man ever gets that old," Fanny assured him.

John was thin. Too thin. The snows and sun of Switzerland had burned his skin brown; his eyes were light against it. Light gray, and tortured. His mouth was drawn always into a thin, tight line; his brows were leveled into stern self-control and concentration on his work, on externals. His voice was deep and steady. In three months he had hardly laughed aloud, hardly had seen the beauties which surrounded him, had noted little but the work which lay under his hand, had thought of little else.

Except at night. Except when he was alone, when his hands and body must rest. Then he could not control his thoughts, his feelings. Dropping off into a sleep of exhaustion, he would wake to the memory of Ellen, to his loneness from her.

The kindly doctors at the clinic, the Heidemans, urged him to work less hard, to play a little. But — unless he worked — tramping the decks of the boat, making himself climb one of the slopes about the hospital, wandering through the streets of the quaint town — Ellen's eyes and coppery hair went with him always, to Switzerland and back again; his arms ached with emptiness, and his nights were white with his need of her.

If the pain would get a little better — if something could make him forget, or take her place! He could not go on this way. He must go on! What a fool he had been to count on her so to share his thoughts, his life, that now when she was denied him he found his mind as empty as his bed. He must snap out of this. He must. He had work to do, a life to make for himself!

He sat now alone on the train, not reading, not seeing the passing countryside. His thoughts were determinedly fixed on what lay before him. He would not look back, regret, think of what might have been. Perhaps if he had gone on at Boone, had stayed near Ellen . . .

He owed it to Dr. Jim to take up his work where the older man had had to put it down. A man's work was the most important thing in his life. If he gave the best in him to his work, did the job earnestly and well, the other things would come. Or would not matter. John hoped.

All his life he had worked toward the day when he would be a doctor. Would be recognized as one. That day was at hand. When he got off the train at Villa Franca, he would be taking the first step on the main road of his life, the road that would probably lead straight on to the end.

John was a good doctor. He knew that he was. He had no fears about his ability. Nor of his zeal. He knew the hospital in which he would work, knew it from baseboard to ceiling lights. He knew the people with whom he would work, knew those who would be his patients. He remembered the assurance, the sense of rightful power, the Villa Franca Hospital had always endowed him with — it would still do that to him. Surely, it would?

The California sunlight was much like that of Switzerland. There was every reason to think that John could repeat here the things those Swiss doctors were doing. Porches could be built along the south side of the hospital. There were rich people in and around Villa Franca. Miss Lillie would help him get endowments for clinics and beds. If he could specialize in the various tubercular infections . . .

There were all the children of the ranchers and truck farmers, not fed properly, worked too hard when little. The mothers and fathers were kind;

they just had never been taught. John knew these people, would know how to talk to them. If he could start on the children, make them strong and disease-resistant . . .

What use regretting Boone, and St. Louis? A small hospital, a small town, could offer a single doctor as much work as his hands and skill could care for. A sick child was a sick child. John would give his life to the sick children of Villa Franca. He would keep his medical, surgical, knowledge abreast of the times. He would go to clinics regularly, read. He would use his money to buy instruments and equipment. A man without wife or family could devote all his resources to his work, could dedicate his every attribute to that shrine.

Ellen had called his profession a shrine. Ellen.

Well, Ellen was gone. And John must go on without her. He must put her out of his mind. He would put her aside from his thoughts. Only — putting her out of his mind was one thing. Putting her out of his blood, his body, was another. A man could decide, with an effort, what he would think. He had no such control over what he would feel.

2

His train reached Villa Franca after dark. Fog veiled the lights about the station, touched John's cheeks with clammy fingers. Dr. O'Connor met him, drove him to Dr. Jim's. Dr. O'Connor was glad to see him, said they would expect him at the hospital in the morning. There would be a staff meeting for lunch. The hospital had built a new wing; the staff had grown. There were two surgeons, two internists. And, now, John.

Not once did Dr. O'Connor speak of John as "Dr. Mallory." Of course, he had known John since the old days.

Miss Lillie had a cold. A strange China-boy opened the door for John, brought in his bags, took his topcoat and hat. But Wong came trotting along the hall. A wrinkled old walnut of a man, Wong. Glad to see John. He spoke crossly to the new boy.

"Damn dumb," he told John. "Miss Lil' sit by fire her room."

"Which is my room?"

"Doc'r Jim gone. You have his room, an' be careful."

John smiled at him, took the stairs three at a time, knocked lightly on Miss Lillie's door. At a murmur he turned the knob and went in. Only one lamp was lit. Miss Lillie sat in a wing chair by the fire, a rug across her knees. Her shadow danced in huge grotesque upon the ceiling. She turned her head, reached a hand for the cane which leaned against the small table.

"Don't move," John told her. "How are you, Miss Lillie?"

She clung to his hand. Smiled up at him. "I've had a cold. Don't kiss me. Best way to catch cold, kissing people."

"Is that how you caught yours?" John asked

her, hooking a little walnut stool toward him and crouching there at her knee. Her yellow old hand wandered to his hair. Miss Lillie had failed.

"Still sassy. But that sounded like Jim, John."

"Did it? It seems — strange without him."

"Yes. It never will seem anything but strange. He was a good man, John."

"Yes, Miss Lillie. He was."

"I wish he could have lived to see you come back here and take up his work."

"Yes. Only — if he were alive, I'd probably be still in St. Louis."

She scarcely waited for him to finish. Her voice was still more like that of a man than a woman, but now it was an old man's, cracked, querulous. ". . . great responsibility. Must always be guided by the thought of what Jim would have wanted you to do."

John nodded. "I'll not disgrace you, Miss Lillie. I'm anxious to get to work."

"If you ever have any doubts, I stand ready to advise you, John."

He made a murmuring sound of acquiescence. He was shocked at the change four years had made in Miss Lillie. He was sure her being through with active work accounted for some of the unfamiliar flabbiness of her voice and manner. Then, she had been sick. Her hand felt feverish. He glanced at his watch. "You go to bed, Miss Lillie. We'll have lots of time to talk now. I'm going to unpack, and turn in myself."

She agreed, and John went across the hall to

Dr. Jim's room. This was better. There was no sense of change here. Putting his shirts and socks away in the old highboy, hanging his suits in the wardrobe, John had a guilty feeling that Dr. Jim might come in from the porch and tell him to clear out. Dr. Jim's books were on the shelves, his Zeiss microscope and his pens on the flat-topped desk. His set of seven razors lay on the hutch in the bathroom. John smiled. This was like home!

On an impulse he changed his clothes, pulled on a raincoat and a cap. He would go for a walk. Take a look at old haunts, locate himself. Put himself in a proper frame of mind for work tomorrow, for his new life.

Miss Lillie's door was open a crack. He was sure he had closed it firmly. "John? That you?"

He stopped with one foot out over the stairs. "Yes, Miss Lillie. Want something?"

"What are you doing?"

"I — I was going for a little walk. I need some air."

"Oh. Well, don't be gone long. I hate to be alone at night."

John drew in his lip, rolled his eyes at the ceiling. "I'll be back within an hour. Go to sleep. Good night."

Well, this was going to be fine. This was, in fact, going to be just grand. An old woman watching him, checking — he shrugged these ungrateful thoughts away with a thrust of his broad shoulders. A little lip service to this old woman would be small enough return for all Miss Lillie and Dr. Jim had done for him in the past. If he could not bring himself to listen respectfully to her preachments and advice; if he could not give her a little companionship, and do it with good grace — John Mallory was a pretty poor sort. Miss Lillie had lived too long in a doctor's house not to know how to respect his impersonality and integrity. She would not meddle with John's profession. Let her seem to boss him in other things.

3

California's famous sun was back on duty next morning. John had set his alarm for six, dressed quickly, and gone down to breakfast. Wong brought him his grapefruit and a cup of steaming cocoa.

"Eggs, ham, come light along," he said cheerfully.

"Fine. Wong, after this, could I have coffee for breakfast?"

Wong straightened the silver at Miss Lillie's place, always set, though John could not remember Miss Lillie's ever eating breakfast. "Cocoa better for boys," the old Chinaman said then. "Coffee bad."

John laughed. Wong, too? "Do you realize that I am twenty-five years old, Wong?"

Wong nodded. "Cocoa better for boys," he agreed. "Miss Lil', you up?"

John hurried to set a chair for her. She thanked

him. "I'm much better this morning. What's all this nonsense about coffee?"

"Wong thinks I'm too young for it," John laughed.

"Fool!" Much more of the old Miss Arndt was in evidence this morning. "Wong, you're to fix Dr. Mallory whatever he asks for."

"Coffee? For Missa John?" Wong's voice was thin with unbelief.

John reached for the toast. "I may get coffee," he told Miss Lillie. "But I doubt if you ever get Wong to call me Doctor."

"Certainly he'll call you Doctor. Or he'll have to leave."

John shook his head. "We all know better than that, Miss Lillie. Well, I'm off. Oh, yes. Did you keep Dr. Jim's office uptown?"

"Jim gave up his office two years ago. I don't think I'd open an office away from the hospital, John. I expect they'll keep you busy. They've built a new wing. They have two surgeons now, and two internists, and —"

"Yes," John agreed dryly. "And me. I know. That may be an ascending scale you're singing, but I don't think so."

Miss Lillie stared at him. "Why, John Mallory!"

"Sorry. I — I guess I'm a little jittery this morning. Who wouldn't be?"

"Of course. And you surely realize that you've still lots to learn — experience, judgment — those things come only with years and work."

"Yes, Miss Lillie," he said meekly. One thing was sure. He was going to have his position at the hospital clearly defined from the start. His inherited stock in the hospital would not put him ahead of Dr. Gilfoyle and Dr. O'Connor, who owned as much. It would not even put him on their level, professionally. John hoped he would always have a fair estimate of his medical ability and status. If he were expected to start in as intern, all right! He would be intern. But he wanted the matter settled at the first.

John walked to the hospital, though Miss Lillie said he might use Dr. Jim's "new" sedan. He wanted to walk. He felt the need of some physical exertion to compensate the repressed excitement which tingled through his nerves. This was as big a thrill as his first trip to the hospital. He felt as young, as hopeful, as full of pride. For all his years of training he felt as if he might be about to open some surprise package, its delightful contents still unknown but sure to prove entrancingly satisfying. For the first time in months he felt a zest for work, felt no need to drive himself to concentration and interest. Maybe, now, things would be all right.

He squashed an impulse to take the old path around to the service entry. He made himself go boldly up the front steps, opened the heavy front door, and stepped into the early-morning sounds and smells of a busy hospital, not so large that all its professional activities are completely removed from the vestibule.

A nurse sat at the reception desk. As John entered, her telephone rang. They exchanged smiles, and John went on to Miss Bean's office — was Miss Bean still here? She was. Large and flushed, and as busy as ever. She had a few words for John, was glad to see him but conscious of the pressure on her time and attention. She mentioned the staff luncheon. Both operating rooms were busy. Hospital was ninety-three per cent full. John had a smile for the accuracy of her figures. John had better wait in his own office for a probable call. "You're taller, Johnnie, but you haven't changed."

"I hope I've learned some things."

"Well, I hope so, too. Your office is down the hall, beyond the lab. Your name is on the door. Here's your key. Don't lose it."

John grinned as he left her. It was evident that, four years to his credit, he was still the old Johnnie to these people. Miss Bean really should not call a staff doctor by his first name. Here was the lab, where he had washed test tubes and run simple analyses. His office had been the old metabolism room. And, by George, it still was! His name was on the door. "Dr. Mallory." Looked fine, too. Inside there was a small white table with a typewriter. Nothing else was different. A new machine, but it stood in the same place. There were still the bed, the scales, the identical gray flannel robe on the door.

What of Dr. Jim's old office? Did the "two internists" occupy that pleasant confusion of knotty pine paneling, oak roll-top desk, peppermint candies — for the children — and the latest thing in chromoscopes? Thoughtfully John hung his hat and coat in the small lavatory. He wondered what had been done with the whites he had sent on from Boone? He would go ask Miss Bean. He did not feel right without a white coat.

With his hand on the knob of the outer door, he heard the laboratory door swing open, and the jingle of glass. Below the loaded tray he saw a white skirt and neat white Oxfords. Above it — "Why, Betty! Betty Mason! What on earth? Gee, I'm glad to see you. What — are you a nurse?"

She pushed past him to set her fragile burden on the dressing cabinet. "No cap," she pointed out. "How are you, John? I'm technician. In there."

John held her hand, looked happily down into her eyes. "Gee, Betty. You work here?"

"Believe me, I work here."

"But —"

"Dr. Jim lent me the money to take a course. I've paid him back — did, before — and I've saved thirty-seven dollars since."

John laughed. "Good girl."

"I'm proud of my job. The hospital has grown, John."

"Yes, I know."

"We've a new wing and —"

"Betty! If you love me, don't tell me about the

two surgeons and the two internists. And John Mallory."

Betty dimpled at him. She was a grand girl, Betty Mason.

"Tell me about Dick. And your mother."

"Mother's fine. Dad — died. You knew that?"

"Miss Lillie wrote me. I'm sorry."

"Yes. Dick is in Washington. Winters. Out in Wyoming, summers. Sometimes he comes home for a day or two. He's married."

"Really? Dick?"

"Don't you write to each other? No, of course not. Girls would. Are you — you aren't married, John?"

John pulled in his lips, took a deep breath. "No. No, I'm not married."

"Miss Lillie said she thought you had a girl. I guess you'd want to get established first."

"Yes. Yes, that's it." He was speaking too hastily, too hurriedly. "Miss Lillie's failed, hasn't she?"

"Since Dr. Jim's death. She'll perk up now that she has you to fuss over."

John nodded. "And how she fusses! I wouldn't be at all surprised to get a report card every five weeks."

Betty giggled. "I have to get back to work, or Bean'll get us both. It's going to be fun having you right next door."

"Yes, it is. My office is small — but cozy."

Betty turned back and looked at him closely. "Dr. Jim's office was sort of lost in the shuffle

— when we reorganized, John. The out-patient room is down there now. And you'll be on the floor so much — in the operating rooms — I don't expect you'll know what size your office is. The staff doctors are all glaring at each other over you. Each one thinks he has best claim on your assistance."

"I thought — I'm a surgeon, and my specialty is pediatrics."

"Well, you know how it is, John. I've seen Gilfoyle give a dose of oil, and O'Connor can cut out a pretty appendix."

"Yes. Yes, sure. And I guess at first I would have to do the leg work. I expected that. If the habit doesn't get too fixed. Look, Betty, can I sometimes borrow your lab? I've been doing a little fussing around with serums. I plan to have some animal cages out at Hayes' and rig up a lab there when I get to it."

"If Wong will let you."

John grinned. "Wong. I'll put him in a cage. I can't afford an ape. Gee, Betty, do you know how old I feel since I've reached Villa Franca?"

Betty nodded. "I can guess. But if I know my John Mallory, you'll grow. And fast."

"O.K. I hope you're right. At that, I'll bet I don't get beyond fifteen in the next year."

His phone rang, and he turned to answer it.

Betty waved a hand. "We'll have birthday parties," she promised gaily.

John's voice was cheerful as he spoke into the phone. It was going to be swell, having Betty so close. He had always liked Betty. She was something like Ellen. Frank. Sincere. Not as pretty, of course. But a swell friend to a fellow.

4

Eight hundred thousand people in St. Louis. Half again as many in the county. It was strange how empty the city was for Ellen. The streets were deserted since now there was no slightest chance of meeting John. Parties were without guests, crowded theaters without audiences. Faces all about her. The phone rang. Invitations lay beside her plate at breakfast. Felix called. Felix sent flowers. Sometimes Felix took her to parties. But Ellen had no friends, no fun.

The city was bad. *Les Grâces* was worse. Last Thanksgiving John had carved the turkey, and Aunt Philomene had scolded him for spilling gravy on the tablecloth. This year the meal was dull. Nothing happened. There was no adventure in tramping the frozen hillside alone, nor in coming back to the chattering little fire, to talk in monosyllables to Felix Watts. Him, with his light hair and *pretty* hands! The piano stood silent, its yellow keys grinning toothily. Ellen hid the glass apple behind a book on the upper shelves of the secretary.

The aunts, her mother, carefully avoided any mention of John. Would it have been better if they had talked of him, had demanded news of him? If they just would not seem so anxious to substitute Felix . . . Ellen sometimes felt a little sorry for the man. He was not to blame.

Aunt Philomene and Cousin Valerie were spending hours every day putting tiny stitches into a quilt they had spent six months piecing. Ellen essayed to help them, smiled at their comments on her stitches. She had a suspicion that Aunt Philomene ripped out whatever she did. She did not care. It gave her something to do. There was comfort in the companionship of these two soft-voiced women. Sometimes Cousin Briand sat in the bay window and read aloud to them. Ellen's thoughts could drift. Thinking did not hurt so much when she was with these people, whom life had also passed by, as it did when she was alone.

Perhaps she would get over her loneliness, her sense of loss. What a goose she was — what a goose she had been. If she could have guessed how badly she was going to miss John, if she had had any knowledge of the physical hurt his going would bring to her — a hurt all the worse because it must be concealed behind a gay smile and careless words, because its tears must be stifled in her pillow at night. Oh, John, John!

"And I think we could very well attempt a wool-filled comforter," said Aunt Philomene one afternoon, when the last "roll" had been made in the quilt and the three of them were again working on the intricate scroll pattern of the border. "What color would you prefer, Ellen, my darling?"

"Me? Oh, were you planning to make a comfort for me?"

The two old women exchanged glances. "What else? With our beds warm, why else should we be pricking our fingers with new quilts? Except for you, and your home?"

"Oh." Ellen stared at them blankly. "Oh. You mean — you talk as if I were planning to be married."

"Are you not?"

"Why, no. Why, of course not, Aunt Philomene."

"You are of the age when every woman plans to marry. And we have seen signs of interest in a certain young man."

Their eyes were beady with earnestness and interest. Ellen wanted to run. To stay, and scream out at them. "Maybe I'll be an old maid," she said hurriedly, her eyes down. "Maybe — I want to be an old maid. If that's what you're making these silly quilts for, you may as well stop."

Spilling thread and scissors to the floor, she hurried out of the room. Oh, she should not have done that! She should not have hurt them, the gentle old souls. It was through no fault of theirs that she had chosen to give her heart to a man who did not want it. Or had wanted it only because of what marriage to her would bring to him. Why, the very fact that John had not stayed on, to work in St. Louis, showed —

Why must she feel — act — this way? Why could she not have taken John's offer of calculating love, married him, and been content with the crumbs of happiness being with him would have afforded her? Or, having preserved her pride — a cold, empty thing, pride! — why could she not now go on with life as if he had never lived? Why could she not? If she had loved John and he had died, would she have not been able to go on, to live, to plan, to hope? Widows loved and married again. There was Felix. And other men.

Yes. And there still was John. Not dead, but alive, only two thousand miles away, working in his hospital, his hair dark and crisp above the collar of his white coat, living in the old frame house he had told her of so often. Had he the dog he had planned to have? Did he help Miss Lillie with her roses? Did he play upon the piano which was exactly like this piano at *Les Grâces*?

Ah, it was the hardest thing of all to know him living, working, without her. If the threads which tied her to John had broken off clean, she might have gone on alone. But they had only unknotted, had drifted off in a sudden gust of wind. There was still a chance that she might clutch them again, and tie them more securely. While there was that chance, she could not go on and plan. There was no life, no future, for her which did not include John.

5

Mrs. Conte's heart ached and bled for Ellen these days. Not once did she attempt to force Ellen's confidence. John's name was not mentioned between them. But she welcomed Ellen's abrupt announcement one morning.

"Isabelle's going to have a baby. Did you know?"

"I'd heard." She and Ellen were dawdling over a late Sunday breakfast. They had meant to go to *Les Grâces,* but the weather had turned cold, and the streets were whipped with flurries of stinging sleet. Their blue and cream dining room seemed much more attractive and warm than a long ride in an old car with smooth tires. Ellen had on a tailored flannel robe that matched the chairs — and her eyes — exactly. She made a pleasing bit of interior decorating, her mother thought. "They've been married about three years, haven't they?"

"Exactly. Isabelle planned to have a baby when she'd been married three years."

"Lucky Isabelle to have her plans work out."

"Oh, they always do for her. She was so logical about it, said she felt it took three years for a bride to get used to being married, and to learn how to keep house and entertain."

"She does a nice job of it," Mrs. Conte admitted. She had always rather wished Ellen had some of Isabelle's practical sense of responsibility.

"Yes. And now she's just as earnest about having her baby. Her health, her mind — even to the flowers she has around her. She says it's all important."

"I'm afraid you were handicapped, my dear."

"I was lucky. But Isabelle means every bit of

this. She's happy, too, about it, and Kurt is positively silly."

"He would be."

"I don't think the Ahnheims have liked their waiting three years."

"I suspect that Isabelle would have concealed the fact that the delay was planned."

"They're old-fashioned. And Vera had two babies in less than three years. They're both alike, Mom. Vera's are. Round and pink, with light curly hair. I'd think she'd like a little variety."

"Some mothers, my dear, regard their offspring in an uncritical haze of maternal adoration."

Ellen laughed, and spread a piece of hot toast with thick white cheese and grape jelly.

"You ought, with justice, to weigh a ton," her mother told her.

"John told me this combination was good. You ought to try it."

There! The name had been spoken. "What do you hear from John?" her mother asked.

"He doesn't write to me. Isabelle, sometimes, tells me about him. He writes to her, of course."

"Why?"

Ellen looked up in surprise. "Why?" she repeated. "Why, he's her brother. Or didn't you know that? It's a sort of secret."

"Brooke Wielande told me some time ago. He was regretting that he hadn't adopted John. He didn't *say* instead of Isabelle, but I caught an implication. John and Isabelle are certainly different types. I wonder why it was a 'sort of secret'?"

"Oh, something about Isabelle's being rich, and John's being poor. He has a stiff pride, you know."

Marguerite murmured something into her coffee cup.

"What did you say?" Ellen asked. Her voice was a little sharp. She wished, almost, that she had not spoken of John. The need to speak had become very pressing.

"I only said, darling, that pride can go a bit far."

"I admire John for his pride. His not wanting to sponge on Uncle Brooke and Isabelle. I admire him for going back to California to work — where he hasn't influential friends, and —" Her cheeks were pink, her eyes sparkling with what her mother thought were probably defensive tears.

"Ellen — my darling —" she said helplessly.

"I don't like your saying anything against John. He — he was my friend."

"I like John, Ellen. You know that. I think he is a remarkably fine young man for the day and age in which we live. But — there is a danger that he may be too fine. His qualities may be the points at which he may be hurt the easiest, or may hurt you. I should hate either of you to lose the substance for the shadow. Human relationships, placed on too rarefied a plane, sometimes perish for want of a little earthy nourishment."

Ellen took an orange from the bowl of fruit. Sat turning it around and around in her hands. Did she know what her mother was saying? There was a sort of pact between Ellen and Marguerite Conte by which both avoided too intimate a probing into the other's mind and emotions. It made for a comfortable existence together. Courtesy, mutual admiration, and a nonpossessive love were the things on which they had built their companionship. Ellen doubted if her mother would speak more plainly. And still, here was Ellen, a woman full-grown, but her mind could get so confused about the strange game of love. How big a part should pride play? What sort of person was the real John Mallory, whom she had thought she knew so well, and yet who now could seem such a stranger? Had she really known what he was thinking when they had walked together out at *Les Grâces*? Granted that she had, there were so many hours of his life of which she knew nothing. The John Mallory in his hospital white clothes lived a life of which she knew little more than the faint perfume of carbolic soap which sometimes clung to his hands. The John Mallory who was Isabelle's brother, who had, however, sought to deny that relationship — even to Ellen, whom he professed to love — that John she certainly did not know. He was, still, not the man she loved, the John who stood laughing at a squirrel and jay bird squabbling over hickory nuts.

"Mom," she said slowly, "tell me something."

Marguerite leaned across the corner of the table and straightened the folds of the white voile curtains which hung at the window behind Ellen's chair. "Yes?" she said, trying to keep her voice at the right pitch of dispassionate interest.

"Are you sorry that I haven't married?"

Marguerite laughed. With relief, partly. She had been afraid Ellen's soberly put question would be harder to answer.

"I can just bear up," she said.

"I mean — I've been out four years. I — Four years ago I would have said my not marrying in that time would mean social failure."

"I daresay you've had opportunities."

"Yes. Some — weren't bad."

"I'm an old-fashioned woman, Ellen. Perhaps you've noticed? But I have accepted the rather modern idea that spinsterhood bears no stigma. Especially when it's a matter of personal choice."

Ellen smiled. "I can see where marriage would be fun, and mean happiness. With the right man it would be rather — rather grand." John's word had been *beautiful*. "Even Isabelle — I can see that what she has is worth having. Especially the baby. You know, Mom, Kurt was the first boy ever to ask me to marry him. I mean seriously. He did it the night of Isabelle's debut."

"Why, Ellen. I didn't know that."

"I know. I was a little ashamed — to have him the first. I laughed at him."

"That wasn't kind."

"No. I was pretty raw at eighteen. But Kurt

seemed the very last thing in Prince Charmings. I — I was shocked when Isabelle told me she was going to marry him. I couldn't understand her doing it. It still seems strange. I didn't want Kurt. I still don't want that — not even when the man is much nicer than Kurt. I mean, not fat, nor — nor —"

"I understand, my dear."

Ellen nodded. "Yes, I thought you'd feel that way. Of course, money would be nice. But — Then there is Felix."

Marguerite nodded. "He's a nice boy."

Ellen looked at her mother appealingly. "I am sure the aunts feel that I ought to marry Felix."

"It would please them if you would. Yes."

"I — It would help you."

"Me? Oh, but, my dear, I'd never want you to marry for any such reason as that. I — you remember your father — you must know the sort of marriage I chose for myself. The sort I would choose for you."

"But that's just it. The *sort* of marriage, I mean. I want you to tell me if I'm foolish to expect, to want, as much as I do from love, from marriage."

The question was not going to be easy to answer after all. Marguerite wished the question — the answer — could be as impersonal as, on the surface, it sounded. But Ellen was thinking of John Mallory, and so was her mother. "I am a bad one to ask, Ellen. You see, for one thing, I am also one of these people who think the beauty of a shadow can surpass the comfort of substance. For another, I selfishly want you to be happy. At all costs. You shouldn't come to me for advice. You really should not, my dear."

Ellen sat looking out of the window, holding her cup of cold coffee in her hand. She was so young. . . .

"Did you and John quarrel?" Marguerite asked calmly.

The teacup chattered against the saucer. Marguerite was startled to see how white the child had gone. "Ellen, darling!"

"Oh, Mom! Oh, Mom, he . . ." The storm broke without warning.

Marguerite rescued the dishes, and drew Ellen's head against her breast. Let her weep. No satin house coat was better than this comforting flood of tears. But what in heaven's name! If it were any man but John Mallory . . .

"Oh, Mom, I love him so much. It hurts so. It does hurt so!"

Marguerite waited.

"I've loved him from the first day I ever saw him. Since I've known John, no one else has ever been good enough, no one ever will be, Mom."

Marguerite smoothed her hair, coppery, clinging, like Jules' hair had been.

"I waited. I was glad to wait. And now — now it's gone."

"What's gone, darling? I imagine John has been waiting, too."

"He has," Ellen agreed. Mopping her eyes, speaking more calmly. "That makes it worse. I could have borne his not asking me —"

"Did he?"

"Yes. Last summer. He — he was so sweet, Mom. So clumsy, and earnest."

"Ellen!" Marguerite spoke with a little exasperation. "I'm probably getting old, my senses failing, but will you please tell me what all these tears are about? If John asked you to marry him, why —"

"But, Mom, you see — I think he was perfectly sincere in wanting to marry me, in *saying* he loved me. The trouble is, our love doesn't balance. I love him, just because he's John. And — and he loves me because I have a lot of ancestors, and some aunts and uncles and cousins who could help him in his profession. His profession is *every*thing to John. He wouldn't marry a girl who couldn't help him."

"Ellen, you ridiculous infant, how can you say that? I don't believe such a thing of John."

"It's true, though. Isabelle told me a long time ago that he was planning to marry me because Uncle Beau and you could help him. I didn't believe her then, but that's the way it worked out. The awful thing is I kept on loving him, and wanting to believe he meant it when he said he loved me."

"But, darling, you still don't tell me why you think John doesn't love you for yourself. Oh, you are ridiculous!"

Ellen looked at her with wide, hurt eyes. "No, I'm not," she said pathetically. "I've tried to fool myself, but — if he'd been entirely honest, wouldn't he have told me Isabelle was his sister? Even if she is married to Kurt Ahnheim — he'd not have lied to me."

Marguerite sighed. "I don't believe John ever thought . . ."

"Mom, you know love has to be based on perfect honesty and trust!"

"Perhaps so, darling. I somehow can't believe John would ask you to marry him for any reason other than that he loved you. He is fine, and honest — nothing of a snob. Why didn't you ask him about Isabelle?"

"I couldn't. I was testing him. It was my only way of knowing if he was honest, if Isabelle was wrong about his using me."

Marguerite shook her head. "I think you've deliberately involved yourself in a trumped-up complication. I think you've been stupid and foolish. And hurt a good many people. John. Felix. Yourself. If you really believed these things of John, you'd give him up entirely. In your own mind. And you'd be dealing more honestly with Felix, who deserves better treatment than he's had from you. I — I'm a little out of patience with you, Ellen."

Ellen bit her lip. "I'm sorry. It's a little hard to figure out what mistake I've made. I didn't mean — but I still don't mean to marry John — or anybody — until I have things straightened out."

"I agree with that, my dear. But if the opportunity should present itself to discuss this again with John — openly, frankly —"

"He's in California."

"Yes. If he loves you, that won't matter. If the opportunity comes, if he makes the opportunity, listen to him, will you, darling? And speak frankly, yourself?"

Ellen wiped her eyes. "I certainly will. I — I'd even help him make the opportunity."

6

John had been too thoroughly trained in a school which considered a year, two years, of intern service little enough preparation for a doctor's striking out on his own now to resent his man-of-all-work position in the Villa Franca Hospital. He was odd-job man, recognized his position as such, and with inspired good sense settled down to learn as much as possible from his apprenticeship.

Dr. Gilfoyle and Dr. O'Connor he knew from the old days. He had used to think Gilfoyle the last word in surgical skill. He had seen other, and better, surgeons since, but he still thought the man able, if a bit overcautious. Dr. O'Connor showed up well through the glasses experience had fitted to John's eyes. He was a conscientious man, well schooled, patient, and likable. Qualities an internist needed. Gilfoyle was often short-spoken to John. O'Connor never failed in courtesy.

John considered the new staff members more

critically. He liked Devaney, the other internist, though the man would probably never be an outstanding success in his profession. Devaney was only a few years older than John. He was a small man, with a shock of bright red hair and a crippled foot. He had been born the son of itinerant fruit pickers, had scrambled for his education, had borrowed money to see him through medical school. Now he went threadbare to repay that loan. He had no breeding, nor charm, and was aware of those lacks. He knew the common people with a brutal thoroughness, and had a fanatic hatred for dirt and disease. He lived in hospital, never grumbled at long hours nor hard work. He could run twenty-five people through a clinic in an hour and a half. John could talk to Devaney about his serums, about his plans for tubercular children.

"You got to get out of diapers first, though," Devaney told him.

"I know."

"You'll make it. I hear Gilfoyle is letting you thread suture needles."

John flushed. "I'm in an odd position."

"Damn odd. Part owner, and all the old grannies telling you how to put on tape."

"I wouldn't want to presume on my ownership."

"You don't. But they ought to let you swab a throat on your own."

"It isn't — I'm not a bad doctor, Devaney."

"Damn right, you're not bad. We all know

you're not. You'd be a good surgeon, too, if Gilfoyle would ever let you touch a knife. I've watched your fingers itching in the operating room."

"Well, I've still a lot to learn. But I could make as good a job of assisting as Stewart."

Devaney's opinion of Stewart was frank and unprintable. "But he used to be a good doctor," he hastened to assure John. "And Gilfoyle thinks he'll reform."

"What do you think?" John wished Stewart did not constantly remind him of Dr. Hugo Marke.

"I think he's a bum — and likes it."

John was inclined to agree. He hated Stewart. He went about his work — taking histories, changing tape, giving a gastric lavage — under the watchful eye of the head nurse — plotting ways to supersede Stewart.

It was Stewart's place John would need to take. He had no craving, at this point in his career, to step into the chief surgeon's shoes. But he wanted to do what Stewart did, or was supposed to do.

It was likely that Stewart had once been a good doctor. Occasionally he showed flashes of true ability, if not glowing genius. The trouble was, you could not count on his being able so much as to hold a knife steady in his hands. When he was unable, Gilfoyle passed over "Johnnie" and called O'Connor or Devaney to assist, or did the job one-handed, as he was well able to do. John resented this ignoring of his ability.

Gilfoyle, he decided, was a little hipped on Stewart. He must know that any doctor who drank as consistently as Stewart did . . . It was not like Gilfoyle to condone human qualities, let alone weaknesses, in a medical man. He bullied Devaney into having his hair cut, made O'Connor address Rotary meetings, because such things maintained "pro." When Stewart was "off his feed," to use Gilfoyle's own term, the day of a bad automobile smashup, John was sent out on the ambulance, and then detailed to "keep an eye on Stewart" — in other words, keep him out of sight of interested onlookers — while Devaney helped set bones and tidy torn flesh.

John hated Stewart, therefore. Gilfoyle said that Stewart's social contacts were good for the hospital. Stewart played golf and bridge at the Country Club; he went to concerts and dinners. He knew how to be charming to old ladies, and naughty with young ones. That was not doctoring, John thought scornfully. Certainly it was not surgery.

He felt his dislike of this man was justified. But, being John, he worried when he discovered that some of that dislike was being turned toward Gilfoyle. That was bad. A junior surgeon would have a tough time if he began disliking and criticizing his superior. Honestly, John had no reason to disapprove of Gilfoyle's practices except a jealous resentment of the older man's tolerance of Stewart. He was afraid some of his resentment might show through — he stopped mentioning Gilfoyle to Devaney, or to Betty.

Betty was too likely to champion John's cause. She was a pretty good technician, but she was also thoroughly feminine and unprofessional in her conviction that John, from the first, should be given his rightful place in the hospital. Once she risked her job, and embarrassed John, by declaring that, Gilfoyle being out of town, and Stewart drunk, it should be John who should perform an emergency operation, not O'Connor.

Miss Bean reproved Betty.

John told her not to be a silly little nut.

Devaney pointed out to her that a man did not appreciate a woman's selfless intervention in his affairs. "Lay your traps for *homo Mallory* outside the hospital, my dear Miss Mason. You may catch your game. I don't mind telling you that I think you will. But don't make the mistake of hunting in the preserve of the hospital. Our Johnnie has an idea that a doctor *per se* has neither eyes, ears, nor heart. Certainly he has no sex."

Well, John did have some such idea, or want to have it. He admired, and religiously trained himself toward, the ideal impersonal attitude. He was fully convinced that such a detachment meant better medicine, better surgical care. His training in a huge plant had strengthened that idea. Now, watching Stewart's cajoling ways, he veered to the brusque, the blunt, side. Gilfoyle was no hand-holder, nor soft-soaper. John comforted himself with that recollection. What, then, was his surprise to have the chief surgeon come into his small office one afternoon, after a long clinic, and reprove the youngest member of the staff.

"I know some of these patients get long-winded, Johnnie," he said. "But you'll have to learn to bear with them."

"You mean Mrs. Hunt."

"Her — and others. They don't like your not showing interest."

"It isn't that. I am interested — in symptoms and reactions. But I can't see anything pertinent in Mrs. Hunt's grandson's I.Q. And in the fact that her sister's husband died because his appendix was on the wrong side."

Dr. Gilfoyle smiled and nodded. "I know. I know. There isn't anything pertinent. Except if you let a patient talk himself into feeling comfortable and confidential, you'll get a better list of symptoms than you will by being rigorously professional and impersonal."

"I see. But it takes so much time!"

"Yes. At this end it does. But it may save trouble in the long run. The thing is, Johnnie, you can't take each case as a unit. You've got to look on the picture as a whole. What Mrs. Hunt's symptoms of gall poisoning are in connection with the fact that all her family have suffered from kidney trouble . . ."

"And eat too much salt, fat pork."

"Pork diet can often account for gall bladder, don't ignore that."

"Ye-es. But isn't it hard to tell where to draw the line? And get any work done? Given a little encouragement, some of these women would talk for hours."

"I know. I know. Given too much discouragement, they'll go to another hospital."

"Business!"

"Business. Again, you'll learn. We can't be noble and save lives unless the lives come to us to be saved. The trouble with you, Johnnie — and it's a fault you'll outgrow — you're too young. Your ideals haven't set into a nice, smooth, eatable custard. Give yourself time. And — about Mrs. Fuelle, too."

"What about her?" Mrs. Fuelle was O'Connor's patient.

Gilfoyle took out his short black pipe and filled it. John did not approve of that pipe in the metabolism room. "You don't look at the whole picture in a case like Mrs. Fuelle. You know there is glandular deficiency, and that thelin slows down her hypernervousness."

"O'Connor's been giving her thelin."

"He has. Carefully. He knows the case thoroughly. She has five children. At thirty-five she is going through what most women put off another fifteen years. She —"

"I followed his regime exactly. It won't hurt her to have to go to bed."

"It won't hurt her. Except — as a young man, you won't recognize the unsymptomatic aspects of her case. If we put Mrs. Fuelle to bed, who

is to take care of her house and children?"
"But —"
"I know. I know. She ought to rest, not worry, not work. But women like this patient are funny, Johnnie. They can worry more, lying in bed, hurt themselves more, than by being on their feet and working too hard. You may not have met up with women of this sort, but a large proportion of our mothers will sacrifice their own health and lives to the warmth and feeding of their children. Mrs. Fuelle needs those shots. They help her. But she also needs to keep on her feet. We have to balance both needs. A doctor can't be a pure scientist, Johnnie. He is dealing with human beings, and the human equation won't fit itself to theory."
John thought this matter over, and had to conclude that Gilfoyle was right. John, the son of his mother, should have had the wit to see such a thing for himself. You could not watch the progress of one case, make your meticulous notes, and then blindly treat a second similar case in the same manner and count on your conclusions coming out even. That truth was so incontrovertible that no one but a sententious ass — such a man as John Mallory — would have needed a demonstration.
Gilfoyle sat watching the younger man, his eyes shrewd behind his glasses. "Another thing, Johnnie — you walk a good deal at night, don't you?"
John stared at the chief. "I — I — sometimes.

I haven't been sleeping well."

"Yes. You're young — and healthy. Ever try to diagnose the cause of your insomnia?"

John colored.

The chief nodded. "You're a smart enough doctor to get an easy one like that. And a cure shouldn't be difficult. You're a good-looking boy."

"I — I — "

"By rights — you being you — I'd say, get married. In the meantime I'd say, get you some kind of woman. You can't buck nature, Johnnie. You ought to know enough not to try. It's bad for you. This not sleeping, walking all night. Makes you cross to the patients. That's bad business. You know it is, and you know you should do something about it."

Well, John did know. Knew when he was cross, and why. If he could only stop *thinking* of Ellen, thinking of her all the time. . . . It was when the realities of life — a patient's foolish question, some trivial duty — intruded on his thoughts of her, interrupted the silent words he called out to her, needing her . . .

Oh, he must stop this sort of thing, climb out of this emotional morass. If Gilfoyle was right, and another woman would help — In any case, there should be enough professional integrity left in John Mallory for him to keep his weltering frustration out of the hospital. He would try for better sleep nights. He would do more than *try* for better work by day. He would *do* better work.

7

Like all resolutions this one did only a part of the good it might have done, but it helped some. Because of it John took a revived interest in the people he met and examined and talked to. He stopped despising his job of history taking, began to enjoy it, to get the most out of it. Sent to the ward schools to give wholesale vaccinations, he exerted himself to make the children appreciate what he was doing. The children went home and dumfounded their parents with what they knew of vaccines and serums. Later, brought to the hospital for a tonsilectomy or with a broken arm, these children asked for "their doctor." Dr. Mallory.

To that extent John had put himself back on the road of pediatrics. Devaney teased him about his popularity. Stewart, nastily, suggested at staff meeting that Mallory might be working up a private clientele.

John met his eyes squarely. "I can remember when the staff doctors here all had their private offices and practices," he said evenly. "And the hospital not hurt."

"Oh, well, if it's a G. P. you want to be —"

"I'd rather never have to do house-to-house work. I'd do it if necessary."

"I like to see Mallory get known," Gilfoyle put in.

"By children."

John's eyes sparked. "It's a well-known medical fact, Dr. Stewart, that children grow into adult — er — patients"

Gilfoyle jumped him for that retort afterward, and with justice. John took this rebuke well. He had paid off a point of his score against Stewart, and was glad he had.

"You're pretty cocky lately, Johnnie," Gilfoyle told him, a twinkle in his eye. "Sleeping better, maybe. But don't forget you're still an assistant, have lots to learn."

"I won't. I don't, sir. I — I would like to be allowed to assist in the operating room, however."

"Don't we keep you busy enough?"

"Yes, sir. But — I'd like to be doing a different sort of work."

"I suppose you could assist — metabolisms and heart records are important, John."

"They are. But — in most hospitals, the technician does them."

"I know. I know. Well, we'll see. I have always thought you'd make a good doctor, Johnnie. But it takes time. However, I'm doing a hernia tomorrow. You can try retracting. If you like."

John's eyes shone. "Are you going to use evipal, sir? You really should — it works to perfection."

Gilfoyle threw out his hand in a gesture of exasperation. "You see? I say you can assist. You turn around and instruct me as to the anesthetic I should use!"

"But — Well, I'm sorry, sir."

Gilfoyle patted his shoulder. He had to reach his hand up to do so. "You'll learn, Johnnie. You'll learn. You know what? Someday I'm going to write a book for young doctors. Tell 'em all the mistakes not to make."

John grinned. "What would some of them be?"

"The one you just made."

"Yes. Two: I quarreled with a fellow-staff member."

"M-hmn. Unprofessional display of temper. Oh, there's lots of things all young doctors have to meet and handle. For instance, I'd have a whole chapter on how to handle booksellers and charity solicitors. All young doctors buy sets of books they'll never read. Then I'd have a chapter on women patients. Tell 'em that every woman patient will sooner or later ask for an abortion, to be prepared for it."

"Do they really?" asked John incredulously.

Gilfoyle laughed. "You see? You need that book right this minute. Yes, sir, I'm certainly going to write it."

"And in it tell us not to buy books like it."

"That's a point. But I've been thinking it over for years. It certainly could give a young doctor pointers he never gets in medical school."

"If he'd read it."

"If — well, maybe you're right. Young doctors today are hatched thinking they know all the answers. Evipal!"

"Are they different from the doctors of your day? And evipal is good stuff. Especially for hernia. You've got some . . ."

Gilfoyle rubbed his chin. "You'd better go get that cardiograph chart on the Bland case," he told John.

8

It had done Miss Lillie good to have John in the house. She did not see a lot of him, but he was there in Jim's room at night. She could get up early and talk with him over his breakfast; there was sometimes an hour or two with him in the evening, in chairs before the fire, later in the rose garden.

Miss Lillie began to work again with her flowers. John's interest, his occasional critical comment on some bush or blossom, was spur enough. She got out her straw-fronted sunbonnet, and directed a young Sicilian boy in the more strenuous digging and pruning. She read the new books so she might discuss them with John. John found time to read, somehow, and she urged him not to confine himself to medical subjects. Just as she urged him not to spend all his free time in the laboratory he had fixed up in the harness room of the barn.

"You ought to go out more," she told him. "You ought to have a girl."

"You'd be jealous if I had any other girl but you." John had achieved ability to talk calmly of such things.

"I would not. I've always hoped you would marry. I had an idea you might bring a bride when you first came."

John turned the pages of his newspaper. "So did I," he said dryly. He could not talk directly of Ellen. He was still trying, without success, not to think of her.

"A doctor needs social contacts," Miss Lillie tackled him again. This was summer, more than a year after Dr. Jim's death.

"Stewart takes care of all that," John told her.

"Stewart?"

"Dr. Stewart. The hospital's official playboy. Gets us patients among the blue bloods."

"I was thinking of you, personally, not the hospital," Miss Lillie said stiffly.

"Oh? Well, I've got all the social contacts I can handle, thank you."

"What are they?"

John smiled at her. "I'm going down to the lab and feed the guinea pigs. Want to come along?"

"John!"

"Yes, Miss Arndt. You've got aphids on your asters."

"I have not. John, I'm going to give a party."

"You have so got aphids."

"In fact, *we* are going to have a party. You should have done it before now. A dinner for the staff."

John stared at her. Came and sat on the wide arm of her chair, put his hand on her wrist. "You feel all right, Miss Lillie?"

She jerked her arm away. "I feel fine! And you're not going to dissuade me."

"No," John conceded. "I guess not. You dissuade harder than anybody I ever knew. But the point is, could I coax? Please, Miss Lillie, don't give a party. Please don't."

Miss Lillie fought a smile. "We are going to give a party. For the staff and the hospital directors."

"My God!" John whispered.

"It's the thing to do," Miss Lillie insisted. "Jim used to . . ."

John nodded. "Yes, I remember. He'd go around in a gloom for days. Wong polished silver. I waxed floors. Remember how I waxed floors, Miss Lillie?"

"Yes, of course."

"Well . . ." John reached out and pulled a leaf from the nearest rosebush. "I was just thinking: so will all the Vere de Vere's of Villa Franca remember. You've got aphids on the roses, too."

"John! Will you be sensible?"

"I'm being sensible. Much more so than you are. Because you're trying to ignore my soapy, scrubby past." A bubble of laughter hung behind his voice. "And it won't work, Miss Lillie. It won't work."

"That's utter nonsense. You're a member of the hospital staff. A stockholder. That's all that matters. The doctors at the hospital have been kind, haven't they?"

John's eyebrows were high. "Oh, yes, they've been — er — kind. But they haven't lost their memories."

"These people would not accept an invitation, and then not be polite. They are the people who should be your friends."

"Sum-average sixty-five," John murmured. "Oh, they'll be polite, Miss Lillie. But, just the same, they will all — down to the last one — be watching to see if I eat with a fork."

"They'll do nothing of the sort. They are too well bred."

John shrugged. "All right. You'll see. If there is one thing you can count on well-bred people having, it's memories. Go ahead and give your dinner party. And if you feel a chill down your back, it'll be Ben Colby haunting the feast."

Miss Lillie's face was grave. "You didn't use to be sensitive, John. Or were you?"

"I hadn't the wit to be, then. In the good old days I thought a man need be only decent, self-respecting, to be the equal of anybody."

"You don't think that now?"

"I've had my error demonstrated." His young face was stern.

Miss Lillie wished she knew of some way she might comfort him, reassure him. "I didn't guess you were sensitive, my dear. But you won't make mistakes. Just be your own sincere self. People are kinder than you think."

John leaned down and put his cheek against hers. "All right, Lillian," he said gently.

The dinner invitations went out, and were accepted. Miss Lillie was busy with menus, plans, spoke distractedly to John of timbales and salt dishes. "Clara Linden says they don't serve bread at formal dinners, John. Will you remember not to ask for any?"

"I'll try. Who is Clara Linden? I thought her name was Post."

Miss Lillie blinked at him. "Clara — Now, John, don't go being — being *masculine!*"

John laughed aloud. "All right. It's a little late to change things, but I'll try to suppress — Who is this Linden person? For days she's been telling you what silver to use, how to seat your guests. Now, it's bread."

"Well, Clara keeps up. She's social. Surely you remember Mrs. Linden?"

John scratched the back of his neck. "Not if she isn't in the history files. Are you going to let Wong serve?"

"I'm having the caterers do it, but Wong won't be kept out. You can't hope for that."

"I don't. I only hope he doesn't tell you your dress is too low."

"He would if I wore evening dress. But I told Clara I'd wear my Chinese-silk suit, as I've always done."

"And what did Clara do? Faint?"

"Oh, she said something about my being eccentric and the town's understanding."

John chuckled.

"But that reminds me. I have to plan on other flowers. Clara is wearing her green chiffon. Red roses won't do."

John gaped at her. "Look here, Miss Lillie, are

you going to let your guests —"

"I'm not letting my guests — Clara is different. She is accustomed to being considered. She's spoiled, I know, but it's too late now to change."

John looked at Miss Lillie sharply. "How old is this — er — influential belle?"

"Clara? Why, I think Clara is about eighty-two. Maybe eighty-three."

She stared with disapproval at John's convulsion of merriment. "Good old Clara!" he gasped. "In green chiffon! A debutante at eighty-two. Whoo-eeee! Boy, am I going to get a kick out of society!"

"You're going to mind your manners, and be nice to the right people," Miss Lillie told him severely.

"Yes, ma'am," John answered, laughter still crinkling the corners of his eyes.

Two evenings later he came home to dinner, tired and feeling sticky from a long, hard day. He was preoccupied with the question of how much say a stockholder had in the personnel of the staff. Something ought to be done about Stewart — He would hold himself open to a charge of professional jealousy — anyway, something ought to be done.

He took a quick shower; pulled on an old thin shirt, white slacks; pushed his bare feet into moccasins; and ran down to dinner, hungry, he said, as an owl. He stopped amazed at the dining-room door. There were candles lighted, glassware sparkled in profusion, an impressive array of silver flanked the two plates.

Miss Lillie looked up at him. "I thought a rehearsal might make you feel — easier," she explained.

"Oh. Oh, I see."

"You seemed nervous about the party. It's really very simple, John. You'll take Mrs. Kiskaddon in — she's the wife of the president of the board. Just offer her your arm — do it for me — that's nice. You really have nice manners, John. You needn't worry. Just seat her as you always do me. Now the silver —"

John let her talk. He was, of course, remembering the things he had done in St. Louis. Should he tell Miss Lillie of Brooke Wielande, the gourmet? Of *Les Grâces*? Of the turkey bonings at Dr. Beaumont Watts'? He said nothing. He never talked of St. Louis and of the people he had known there. Of Ellen. He let Miss Lillie tell him which fork to use, waited for her to show him how to serve himself from a platter. If this gave the old woman pleasure . . . "How about wine?" he asked suddenly.

"Champagne."

"But —"

"That will be enough. I don't really approve of serving wine. Especially to doctors."

John thought of Stewart.

"I'm going to ask you to buy cigars and cigarettes for the gentlemen, John."

John nodded. He would also fill the decanter with brandy, and have the glasses polished and ready. He knew how to play host if the occasion demanded.

". . . but I told her you had a dress suit in your closet, so that would be all right."

John looked at Miss Lillie. "I wasn't listening. I'm sorry."

"Are you tired tonight, John?"

"Yes. A little." All afternoon he had fixed clips to the arteries of a child's throat. Stewart had bungled that tonsilectomy. The kid had not passed out, but the squeak had been close. John was tired.

"I was saying — Clara said you ought to buy a dinner coat. She was a little surprised to find you had a suit. Tails, too."

"Weren't you? Surprised, I mean."

Miss Lillie flushed. "Well, yes — in a way. But I remembered there were probably parties at the school."

"Uh-huh. Only, if it's hot, I'll wear my white flannel suit. Whatever Clara might say."

"Why, she suggested that you might. If it were hot. She said, too, how handsome you are, John. And, oh, yes, she thought you might plan to play the piano — to fill in time."

John pushed back his chair, flung his napkin into his dessert plate. "Look, Miss Lillie. Don't tell me another thing Clara says. I'll do my best not to disgrace you at that damn party; but for heaven's sake, quit telling me things! If you don't, I'll wear a red necktie and suck my asparagus. Now, I'm warning you!"

Miss Lillie watched him stalk down the hall. Wong stuck his head around the screen. "That Missa John?" he asked.

"Yes, Wong. Yes, it was."

"Sound like Doc'r Jim putten feets down. Huh?"

"Well, yes, it did. A little. Hand me my cane, Wong. I'm going out into the yard. You listen for the phone — it might be for the doctor."

She walked slowly out of the room, smiling to hear the old Chinaman's experimental murmur behind her. "Doc'r John. Doc'r John."

9

The party came and went without mishap, or any great mark of success. It was just a party. People were gracious and kind. John talked briefly to the various ones, handled the duties of host easily. This little group of elderly people, excepting Dr. Gilfoyle and Dr. O'Connor, had never possessed any knowledge of John Mallory, nephew of Ben Colby. They knew him only as the protégé of Jim Hayes, and his heir. Jim Hayes had always held an indisputed position among the business and social leaders of Villa Franca.

Miss Lillie, commending John for his social grace, reproved him gently for having expected snobbery from his guests.

"I had 'em wrong," he admitted. "Even your Clara. She's quite a girl, Clara."

"Why, of course, she is. And she said I ought to see to it that you met some of the town's young people. Girls, especially."

John put up his hands defensively. "Don't you do it, Miss Lillie. You give me a chance to settle down at the hospital before you go cluttering up my life with girls."

"That's all very well, John. But it isn't natural, or normal."

"All right. I like being abnormal. You tell Clara I satisfy my sex instincts with guinea pigs. See what she says to that."

Miss Lillie snorted. "I can well imagine what she would say!"

The dinner party had been a lot of fuss and bother, but John felt that, like a thunderstorm, it had cleared the air. Now he could go back to his preoccupation with his own life and work. Without Miss Lillie's fussing at him about social obligations.

He was going great guns with his private lab. Miss Lillie fussed some because he kept part of his mice and pigs in out of the sun, while others enjoyed the luxury of glassed-in runways. It did not seem fair to abuse helpless animals so. How did he dare to set himself up to say what rats should be well, what ones should die?

John shook his head. "I wouldn't dare, if I thought about it. But it's what God does. He lets there be the haves and the have-nots. And He uses boys and girls, not rats."

"That's philosophy — or economics. Not medicine."

"I know it. But I'm just beginning to get the idea that you can't practice medicine and ignore all the other facts of life, Miss Lillie. Economics may well be more important than medicine."

"Now, John. You're a doctor and —"

"I'm a doctor, and I expect to work at that job. But I hope I don't put on blinders so big that I can't see the importance of other social activities, too."

"The old-time doctor just contented himself with healing the sick."

"The old-time doctor is gone. Thank God!"

"John! There never were finer men than —"

"You're right. There never were. But they didn't live today, with today's discoveries, with today's problems. I say, thank God, the old gentlemen are gone. Because they could never have stood the gaff."

"I'd hate to have had Jim hear you talk so."

"Why? He'd have agreed with me."

10

There came a Sunday evening in October, with dampness hanging in pearly drops from every leaf and twig in the garden. John was working in his lab, beginning to think it was getting late and he ought to go up to the house. He had three more slides to ticket and mark up on the proper cards. Betty had offered to come over and help him after hours. If she would take a little pay, he would let her. But Betty wanted to do it for friendship's sake. She honestly wanted to help.

It would be a help, too, not to have to stop and write down his findings, get ink on his fingers. John swore, and wiped his hand on his already smeared smock.

Betty was a swell girl. He had known her always. At the hospital she did her job, was respectful and impersonal to "Dr. Mallory." Not a bit different in attitude toward him from what she was to, say, Devaney. In fact, she joked more with Devaney.

There had been occasions in the past year when Betty's steadfast approval and friendship had done wonders for John's ego and self-confidence. She did not gush, nor call him "wonderful." In fact, it was a little difficult to analyze just how she managed to convey her championship. Something about her always being close, her little smile, her way of saying: "Will you look at this, Dr. Mallory? I think so-and-so, but I want to be sure." Yes, Betty was a swell friend. Perhaps John ought to let her come and help him here. But John knew that the town, Miss Lillie, especially, would begin looking wise if the new young doctor should have a pretty girl assisting him in his lab — a lab which a lot of people looked at as a sort of child's playhouse. No, better not have Betty help him.

He — The buzzer over his head sounded abruptly. John's hand jerked. Damn the thing! He had had it put in as a signal in case a phone call came for him — it saved someone's running down, or trying to yell. He looked about him, made a few adjustments so things could go overnight, took his sweater off a hook, turned out the lights, locked the door behind him. Who in thunder would call him at this hour of night? The hospital? Well, maybe. He hastened his steps. Maybe it was only Miss Lillie thinking it was time he came up for bed. It was only ten.

She met him at the side door.

"What is it, Miss Lillie?"

"There was a phone call. I said you'd call back."

"Yes? Who was it?"

"A farmer up the valley. Mathes."

John was going along to the phone. "What did he want?"

"He said his little boy had swallowed a tractor."

John turned and looked at her.

"I — I suppose it was a toy one."

"Yes. Let us hope it was. Did you tell him to call the hospital? Or to take the child there?"

"Yes. He said —"

"I can't go dashing around the countryside — I'd have to bring the kid to the hospital for X rays and observation."

"He called especially for you."

"So what? Say I'd go out there, and then brought the kid in — it wouldn't go a bit different than if he'd called the hospital."

"This man went to school to me. The father. I've known him longer than I've known you. He — he is a fine boy, John."

John drew a deep breath. Personalities. Before this, Miss Lillie had tried to direct his professional attitude by personalities. Well, he might as well settle the matter now, once and for all. "Look, Miss Lillie. I don't care *who* the patient is. The only thing that matters is *what* ails him."

"John. Don't speak so. It — isn't like you."

"Well, it's too bad for me if it isn't. What's this fellow's name? Did he leave a number?"

"You have to call the rural operator. This baby is all Fred has left. He lost his other three children when his ranch house burned two years ago. The day before Christmas."

John felt his stomach turn. He knew the flimsy siding and tarpaper ranch houses. They would burn like tinder. Three babies. "What's his number?"

Miss Lillie told him, her blue eyes on his face. "You tell him to wrap the baby up and bring it to the hospital, that you'll wait there. If — if you know any way to stop the choking, tell him what to do, John. You explain that doctors today don't go dashing around the valley in the middle of the night. It's foggy. There's a hospital less than ten miles away to care for people. But tell him about the choking. The baby might strangle to death. It would be hard for Fred to drive his old Ford with the baby choking."

John put his strong hands on Miss Lillie's shoulders. "Will you shut up? I want to phone this man. How can I talk with you gabbling away in my ear? Besides, how do you get to know so much? Telling me what to say! Telling me what I will and won't do. Telling me not to go out there. Of course, I'll go out — my car will make the trip faster. That baby may need a tracheotomy. There's one thing you've got to stop bossing me on, Miss Lillie. And that's medicine and professional practice. Now, what's that number again?"

11

The valley heard, and talked, of how young Dr. Mallory had saved the Mathes baby. The hospital heard of it. Devaney teased John about it and hung a horrible lithograph of the doctor and the stork on his office wall. Betty tried shyly to speak of it, and John asked her, please, to shut up.

"O.K.," she agreed. "But I still think it was heroic."

"Rats. Or if it was, heroes must get damn sick of themselves."

Still, Gilfoyle had found the tracheotomy well done when John brought the baby to the hospital and gave the case over to the chief surgeon.

"Must have scared those farmers wall-eyed to see you make that puncture," Gilfoyle told him.

"I chased 'em out of the room."

"Really? That in itself was a major operation. You look after this case, Johnnie. And — I think you could establish a regular routine as assisting surgeon. Speak to Miss Bean. You'd alternate with Stewart, and dress your own cases."

That was great. that, in fact, was swell. Stewart would not like it. let Stewart go straight to hell!

It meant longer hours in the hospital for John. Less time for his lab. He was constantly called out at night, aware that Stewart was throwing the "dirty work" on him. He did not complain. The emergencies which came in at night were a more varied sort of surgery than the scheduled operations. By Christmas, John was being allowed to do a good many things on his own, sometimes with only a telephone council with Gilfoyle, and with Devaney standing by.

"Make him give you the pediatrics," Devaney urged. "And while you're doing it, make him give us an intern."

They needed the intern; John wanted the child cases. It was a way to divide the work more fairly between him and Stewart. He spoke to Gilfoyle. The chief agreed to let him have two afternoons a week for a children's clinic. Agreed that John might assist on all operations on children if he would also care for the medical beds in the children's ward. Dr. O'Connor supervising him. This suited John fine. Again he began to dream of sun porches along the south wall of the building. He was so busy, worked so devotedly, that his eyes began to sink back into dark sockets, his cheekbones drew out fine and sharp. Miss Lillie worried about him, and fed him hot milk when he came in at night. John hated hot milk, but he drank it for Miss Lillie. Sometimes it helped him to sleep. When she protested about his working so hard, he looked at her intently.

"Let me work! Let me know that some of my life is worth while!"

Devaney again brought up the matter of an intern — directly to Gilfoyle. "We need one, Chief. With Mallory filling all the corners with rickety kids from the valley."

Gilfoyle smiled. "He's a worker, isn't he?"

"Yeah, but it's bad business to work a good horse to death. You can get brand new M.D.'s cheap these days."

So they got their intern. Young Dr. Harold Brooks, recovering from a nervous breakdown which was probably accounted for by the brilliant scholastic record he had behind him. John thought he should keep an eye on this young man, even though he did little but take histories and watch the needle of the metabolism machine.

And John got his children's clinic, with results which were not wholly pleasant. The kids were all right. The kids were fine! But John began to work out for himself the truism that, while a doctor can handle the sick, it is the well who often "get him down." If each child who came under his hands did not bring a full set of parents, and often enough grandparents and aunties, John's lot would have been more satisfactory. The children liked Dr. Mallory. They trusted his steady gray eyes, his serious face, his deep, kind voice. The parents guessed he was all right, too. Only — he was so young. They would feel better if Dr. Gilfoyle would look at Jimmie. Too bad Dr. Hayes was gone.

All young doctors must listen to such talk. John hoped to survive it. He knew he was young. Also, he had no doubt of his ability, nor of his readiness to call in a more experienced man when necessary. Meanwhile he hoped to be allowed to work up experience and reputation.

The charge of being young was incontrovertible, but neither so unexpected nor unpleasant as the second attack.

The Villa Franca Hospital was privately owned. It did what charity it could, but had no assistance from the town, no endowment fund. To keep in operation it was almost imperative to get a minimum fee for room and board from each patient. This charge was as small as possible, but, people being what they undoubtedly were, it was necessary to ask for this payment in advance.

John, still edgy on his own account, his raw nerves still oversensitive, did not like the part of a clinical examination which required him to demand such a down payment from the parents of a prospective patient. Disliking the task so much, perhaps his voice and eyes were a little too impersonal, too cold, his demand too blunt.

"I used to know your uncle," one man told him unexpectedly. "He always held money above anything else."

John gasped. Ben Colby. Ben Colby here in this sunny clinic room, his mean little eyes, his grasping claws of fingers. Social Villa Franca had forgotten Ben Colby. But here . . . It is the common people who are snobbish, who resent escape from their ranks.

John got up and went out of the room, the nurse looking after him strangely. He had had a blow below the belt. A foul. Would anyone say that to him again?

They did, of course. And it continued to hurt. Small purpose to remind himself that he was only following hospital practice and routine. He needed no argument so far as he himself was concerned. But these people, whom he had hoped to help through their children! John swore that if a boy could imagine the things a doctor would come up against — things to which his ideals and dedication of self could in no way apply — there would be darn few doctors in the world, and those would all be businessmen!

Well, again he would have to learn. He did not like the job of telling a mother her baby would never walk. He would have to learn to do so, kindly, but without emotion twisting his own heart. Likewise, he would have to learn to state financial facts to these people, and be indifferent to their ingenious ways of evasion and defense. He would have to learn.

He must try anew to calm his own nerves, control in some way his fevered blood. This disturbance, lasting over months, was amounting to an illness. Surely the physician could cure himself.

Should he write to Ellen? He wanted to.

Wanted even such a distant, thin contact with her. But — what should he say? Nothing had changed. She was still Ellen Briand Conte. Desirable and unattainable. He was still plain John Mallory, with only his love to offer her. He would not write. Sometimes he thought separation, time, was healing the wound a little. Better not to probe it open again. Better not.

12

The matter of Harold Brooks was, of course, one which carried on over a period of months and weeks and final, dramatic days. Even John and Gilfoyle — certainly the blond young man himself — were scarcely aware of what it was they were doing until it was over and Gilfoyle stood up before a staff meeting and gave John the full credit for "intelligent observation, and courageous use of advanced medical practices." It was decent of Gilfoyle to say that. Gilfoyle had had his doubts. With Stewart hoping for the worst, O'Connor aloof and watchful, Dr. Gilfoyle had gone around shaking his head, suggesting that they should call in a specialist from Los Angeles and, when John assured him that all was going according to rule, muttering about radical techniques and youthful foolhardiness. So it was decent of him.

John was glad they — he — had been able to help young Brooks. He had felt sorry for the young man from the first day he had come to the hospital, new to a job John had found difficult, tormented by an inward-turning mentality, ragged nerves.

"The guy gives me the jeeps," Devaney told John.

"He's smart."

"Damn smart. I'm scared to death the guy's a genius. Sometimes I wonder if he eats it."

Dope. John shook his head. "I don't think so. It's nerves."

"Golly, and how! Went up to get him to help me with a stretcher last night. He just lay there on the bed, his eyes rolled back."

John looked alert. "Could you rouse him?"

"Not any. I brought the patient in pick-aback."

It was John who mentioned dementia praecox to Gilfoyle. And Gilfoyle snorted. John kept watching Brooks. Back at Boone, after his manner of nosing around beyond the requirements of his medical course, John had spent long hours in the psychopathic clinics and wards. He thought he would know d.p. He would know what to do for it, too. Especially when the patient was a brilliant guy like Brooks. What if it was a risk? If the choice were John's own, death would be a pleasant alternative. Probably the guy would die anyway.

"Maybe it won't help him," Stewart said, and said often.

"Maybe it won't. So what? He's crazy without it."

"If it's praecox."

By that time no one but Stewart doubted its being praecox. Probably Brooks should be sent elsewhere. "I'd like to give insulin a try," John insisted.

"It's such an experimental thing, Johnnie."

"Yes, but I've seen it work. A dozen times. I know exactly how — I have my notes. I — I'll take full responsibility."

"You'd have to have his mother's consent."

"Won't she give it?"

"I don't know. I — The hospital would be responsible in the long run, Johnnie."

"Lord God, what of it? We're responsible for every operation we do. Does that keep our knives on the shelf?"

"I just wouldn't want — You're sure of the process?"

"I'm sure. Look, Dr. Gilfoyle. If we can get the mother to consent . . ."

"You must be perfectly honest with her. Explain the risk."

"I'll do it. Tell her he might die, and he might get well, or he might stay crazy as a loon. The mother of a smart fellow like Brook — I'll bet she lets me do it."

It was necessary to bring Mrs. Brooks to Villa Franca, to let her see her son in the lethargy in which he lay. It was his not recognizing his mother . . . "Will he always lie so?" she asked John. "Without . . ."

John shook his head, his fingers tense on the tube of his stethoscope. "This will give way to what we call agitated depression. Often there are suicidal impulses. . . . Do you understand?"

She looked from the deathlike head on the pillow to the tall young doctor with his glowing, intent eyes. "It must be very hard to explain these things to a mother, Doctor."

John nodded. "It is. I would like to help your son."

"If it were your brother, yourself, would you take the risk?"

"Yes," said John steadily. She believed him.

So, when the case was ready, John, with Devaney to help him, did his job. He had drilled the assisting nurses and Devaney rigorously. For six days a week, for seven weeks, John did not leave the hospital. He himself injected the insulin each morning, twisted the rubber tourniquet around the thin arm each afternoon and administered the glucose. When the convulsions were bad, he repeated the glucose and used caffeine. He never lost faith. So closely did he watch those stiff lips for signs of blueness that he saw Brooks' face on every blank wall before him.

He lived and ate and drank the case. He scarcely slept at all. He spent long nights in that little white-walled room, with a man who might be worse than dead. Life took on a new meaning to John those nights. It seemed very short — its days, its pleasures — to be snatched at and hoarded. A thing like this could strike a man down — especially a man who had weakened his resistance by overwork, overintrospection.

Harold Brooks should have lived a healthier, more balanced life. John Mallory should be living one.

It was during those nights that he began to consider the possibility of someone to fill Ellen's place in the life he had planned, and now must live. Some girl, attractive to him, who would make him a home and thus help his work. Some girl . . .

Yes, once he got this job done, he would see what he could do to help the case of John Mallory.

Devaney stood at his right side through it all. Gilfoyle, O'Connor, Stewart, watched John more critically than they did the case. Gilfoyle, unable to restrain his worry, summoned a specialist, who came, noted how things were going, recommended no change — and offered to tell anyone willing to listen about the use of insulin on schizophrenics. "It's as if it welded the split personality into a sanely functioning unit."

Miss Lillie protested to John over the telephone. Betty made him talk to her about Brooks, explain the disease and the daring treatment of it. She made John walk around and around the hospital court with her for air and exercise. The nurse in Brooks' isolated room could signal from the high window. Neither John nor Betty thought if the hospital might gossip. John needed a pop-off valve. Betty was ready to serve such a purpose.

Then, almost as an anticlimax, came the morning when Brooks opened eyes that were not blank, when his paper-white fingers moved with some purpose on the sheet. The nurse ran for Dr. Mallory.

John walked slowly to the bedside. "H'ya, fellow," he said firmly.

Well, they had done it. Brooks' own interest in the treatment of his case was the life line he used to climb back into a sane world.

"You can't beat a scientist," Devaney chuckled. "He'll cut off his own hand to get a true record of the sensation."

Gilfoyle spoke frankly to John. "I don't mind saying that I thought you hadn't a chance."

Stewart had the grace to keep his mouth shut, which was more than John had expected him to do.

Betty thought more fuss should be made, that people should be told. Over and over she sounded this note. John laughed at her. "You and Miss Lillie. Afraid I won't be appreciated."

"How is Miss Lillie?"

"Fine. Now that I'm home regularly. I've had one hell of a time explaining this thing to her. I think she wants to fumigate me."

Betty laughed. "I haven't seen her in ages."

"Why not? Come and eat dinner with us some evening. She'd like that."

"Oh. Would it be all right? I mean — would you . . ."

"I would. Come tomorrow night."

"Maybe I can talk to Miss Lillie about how

wonderful you are. Honestly, John, it was so *brave!*"

"Stewart is the one you should talk to. He'd tell you only a young medic would be so foolhardy. And what have we gained? Our hospital doesn't get a praecox once in twenty years."

"But maybe we will now." John laughed aloud at the note of bright hope in her voice. A good, hearty laugh was about the best thing he could have had just now.

Chapter Ten

John had given Betty the invitation to dinner casually, casually mentioned her coming to Miss Lillie.

Miss Lillie made a party of the occasion, and so did Betty. There were candles on the dinner table, and a silver bowl of full-blown red roses. Miss Lillie wore her white silk dress; Betty wore dark blue net, the full skirt sweeping the floor. John's eyebrows went up.

"If you girls will excuse me, I'll go wash," he said dryly.

Miss Lillie and Betty smiled at each other. They talked about and around John all through the meal. John felt helpless and out of control. Women were the devil. Just by their being women they could take over the direction of the current of affairs, of small talk, of a man's very life.

Still, it was rather nice to sit here in the soft light, lingering over their dessert and the Spode cups of rich coffee. Miss Lillie told Betty of the struggle they had had with Wong to give John coffee.

"He still does it with his fingers crossed," John concluded. "He has a doubtful look for my medical bag which is a masterpiece."

"But you *are* getting older, John," Betty told him consideringly. "I mean, just these last months, you've seemed older."

"Thanks."

"For nothing?"

John smiled. "Sorry," he murmured.

"John doesn't know," said Miss Lillie wisely — smugly, John thought — "that a person is young so long as he cherishes the few years he has attained. I mean, his sort of young."

"You two talk like you were ninety-six," John cried. "Come on into the parlor. I'll play a piece on the piano."

Playing the Jesse French, after the pleasant meal with the two women, made John think of *Les Grâces* and Ellen. He noted the clinical air of detachment with which he realized that it hurt as much as ever to think of those lost things. His fingers drifted into the "Waldstein" — He broke off abruptly.

"There's someone coming up the front steps," he said, starting for the door.

It was Clara Linden, Miss Lillie's friend. Her old eyes were bright as a bird's to find Betty there. She watched the tall young doctor and this girl — John knew exactly what thoughts were racing through her mind while he evasively answered her questions of inquiry about various townspeople who were patients in the hospital.

"You won't get one word of information out of John," Miss Lillie told her friend. "Jim used to be as bad. I always had to read the papers to find out births and deaths. And now they don't publish the births. Why not, John? I've been meaning to ask you."

"It wasn't my idea — not originally. It keeps the lists of new mothers away from people selling patent baby foods. You see, babies . . . Look. If you give me any encouragement, I'll explain all about the matter of infant feeding to you girls. You may find it embarrassing."

Miss Lillie shook her finger at him. "Now, John!"

He laughed. "I was only warning you. Here, I'll put up the chess board for you two. Betty and I'll go look at the guinea pigs. Can you amuse yourself for fifteen minutes?"

He could feel the two pairs of old eyes following him and Betty out of the door, across the porch. "They're matchmaking," he told Betty.

She giggled. "They're sweet old things, aren't they? I'm still half scared of Miss Lillie."

"Pouf! That's all bluff. She's trying to cover up the disgraceful fact that she's a sentimental woman."

They went down the side steps, along the path of the rose garden. A lopsided moon hung like a golden lantern in the eastern sky. John guided Betty to the bench under the arbor. "If Tut were here, this would be like the party Miss Lillie gave before I went away to school. Remember? You had on a pink dress."

"Why — yes, I remember. That was a long time ago. Six or seven years."

"Uh-huh. I kissed you. Remember that?"

Betty nodded. John's lips brushed her cheek. She was a nice girl, Betty, and one not hard to make love to — if a man put his mind seriously on the task.

"That was the first time I'd ever kissed a girl," he told her, laughing a little at his own youth.

"I know. I knew it then. John —"

"Yep?"

"Do you ever think — I mean, does it ever make any difference to you that I'm three years older than you are?"

John made a long arm and pulled off a stalk of mignonette. "I never thought about it, up to this minute. No. Why should it make any difference?"

Betty turned and looked at him — at the upward sweep of his dark hair, at his fine, strong profile against the half-dark, down at his strong hands worrying the fragrant bit of mignonette. There was not, probably, a grander person in the world than John Mallory. So honest, so sincere, so — so dear. "John," she said on an impulse, "do you realize that you have never told me one word of the things you did in St. Louis, of the people you knew."

He was nodding his head. "I know. I don't talk about it."

"Why? Didn't you like it? Weren't people nice to you?"

"They — people were swell to me. That's why — I don't talk about it."

"Oh. I see. You wish you could have stayed there. Oh. I — we thought you liked it here in Villa Franca."

"I do like it. I wouldn't go back. Only last week I had a letter from my sister urging me to come back."

"Your sister?"

"Yes. She lives in St. Louis. Her name's Isabelle. A rich aunt adopted her, raised her to be a rich woman. Fortunately she married a rich man. They have a baby. He's a year old now. I'd like to see him. That's how — Naturally Belle has a gold-plated baby specialist taking care of her child — I don't suppose he's had a sick minute — and she says she is sure she could get me in with this chap. Ryan's his name."

"The baby specialist?"

"Uh-huh. He has about the trickiest clinic I ever saw."

"Would you like working with him?"

"No. I wouldn't. I couldn't be a society doctor if I tried. I'd speak the truth, and that's fatal. You don't get anywhere telling a rich woman that all that ails her kid is the need of a good, old-fashioned spanking."

Betty giggled. "I can just hear you. But it was nice of your sister to try to help you."

"I don't need her help. Not her kind. Belle just naturally has to think she's managing somebody's life. She's a snob, I'm afraid. Only she calls it diplomacy and cultivating the right people. You see, she's ashamed of having been born poor."

"You aren't a bit like that. How funny for a sister and brother to be so different!"

"Not so funny. We were different to start with. Don't look one thing alike. She's a pure blonde. We were separated when we were kids; our lives were poles apart. Hardly anybody in St. Louis realized we were related; she took the name of the uncle who adopted her. It seemed silly to explain to everybody that I was her brother. Nobody cared about me."

"Nobody?"

She saw John draw in his mouth, the way he did when something unpleasant came up. "Nobody," he said hardily. "I did use to think — But I was flattering myself."

"A girl?"

John nodded. He was pulling the helpless bit of mignonette into fragments. Betty put her small hand on his wrist. "Do you want to tell me about her? If you liked her, she must have been nice. Though, if —"

John threw the stem away from him. Lifted his head, folded his arms across his chest, stared at the moon. The light sparked in the depths of his eyes.

"Ellen. Betty, there never was a girl like Ellen."

Betty made a small sound of — perhaps encouragement, perhaps protest. John was not hearing any sound Betty might make. Staring, blinded, at the moon, he was seeing Ellen — her bright hair, her gay smile, her blue, blue eyes — hearing the laughter that underlay her voice like a deep ripple in a little brown stream. He felt a little warm fire kindle in his breast. For so long he had defended his thoughts from Ellen, had so sternly, so unhappily, fought the hurt of calling her person specifically to mind, that now, letting himself see her so plainly, so clearly remember, was like happy reunion.

"She's so real, Betty," he murmured. "Simple as a lovely strain of music. You recognize its fineness the minute you hear it; you remember it always."

"She — was she rich? Like your sister?"

"Ellen? Like Isabelle? Now, it's funny about that. They were friends — had been since they were both kids — went to school together; were chums, the way girls are, you know. But Ellen isn't one bit like Belle. Belle is beautiful and charming, but it's all veneer. It's all make-up. She's never without it, but it isn't born into her. While Ellen — she's so grand, so real, all the way through. I've always thought of her as a good apple, that you could eat right through, core and all."

Betty laughed aloud, a note of hysteria shrill in the sound. "John, if you aren't the limit!"

John turned to her in amazement. "Why, what . . ."

"Here, I thought you were romantic, dead in love with this girl. I was getting green-jealous about her. And you say she is like a sound apple."

"Well, she is. What's wrong with that? You are, too. Wholesome. No sham."

"Quit it!" She hunted for her wispy handkerchief, dabbed at her eyes. "A girl could sue you for calling her wholesome."

John smiled uncertainly. "I — I meant it as a compliment."

"I know you did, darling. I know you did. And I guess you were giving the last word of praise to your Ellen, too. Maybe I *am* jealous."

John shook his head and sighed. "You've no cause to be. She — Ellen — that's all off."

"You mean" — Betty's voice was truly sorry — "you loved her, and she . . ."

"That's it. She wouldn't marry me. I — I guess I was pretty conceited to be so surprised at her refusing. I'd counted pretty heavily on her marrying me. She did seem to like me — but, when I asked her, she wouldn't consider it."

"Then you must have had the wrong idea of her. She can't be a very nice girl, or smart, if she wouldn't snap at you."

"She's nice. And smart enough. But she certainly didn't snap."

"Then she's a snob."

John shook his head. "No-o, I don't think it's that, either. I did, at first. But — well, I guess love — marrying love — can't be forced. You feel it for a person, or you don't. And because Ellen is so sincere and honest, she couldn't — wouldn't — pretend a thing she didn't truly feel."

"But — are you still in love with her?" Betty felt that she had to ask John that, had to know.

"Yes. I suppose I shall always be in love with

Ellen. I — I don't change easily, Betty. I'm stubborn about a lot of things. Oh, I don't mean that I'll go all my life mooning over a lost love. That I won't ever marry. And be happy, too. I'm not that big a sap. I — I hope I'm not. Don't you suppose it's possible for a person to have different sorts of love?"

"I hope so," Betty whispered fervently.

2

An hour later, undressing for bed, with their hall doors open a way so that they could talk back and forth in the homey companionship Miss Lillie loved, John talked about Betty to the old woman. "She's an awfully nice girl, Miss Lillie."

"She is. Much nicer than most girls are."

"I wonder why she hasn't married. Men are fools."

"They certainly are," Miss Lillie agreed heartily.

"I think Devaney is nuts about Betty."

"I hate that expression, John."

"Well, it isn't pretty. Devaney is self-conscious — about his foot and his humble past."

"That wouldn't make any difference if Betty loved him."

"She likes him."

"That isn't love. And it won't grow into love with you around."

"Me? Why, you're crazy! Why, Betty's three years older than I am."

"That makes no difference. And you know it."

"Well. Well, I told her this evening that you and Clara were matchmaking."

"Indeed? And what did she say?"

"Why — why, I don't remember. Oh, yes. She mentioned her being older, asked me if it made any difference."

Miss Lillie, bundled into a terrific purple dressing gown, came to the door of his room. "And then what?"

"Why — nothing."

"Did you kiss her?"

"Say, what is this? A diagnosis?" John was laughing.

"And what did you talk about after that? Tell me, John. I'm serious."

"I know you are. Why — we — I guess I told her about a girl I knew in St. Louis."

Miss Lillie gaped at him. "If men aren't the most hopeless fools!" she cried, turning back into her room. She slammed the door with an emphasis John could interpret in only one way.

"Maybe she's right," he told the watch he was winding. "Maybe she's right."

3

Isabelle Ahnheim was bored. It was all nonsense for Kurt to insist on their spending Christmas in St. Louis. A German Christmas was a deadly thing, dripping with sentiment, heavy, soggy, with food. St. Louis in December was foul. Isabelle did not mind cold. Kurt had given her a stunning mink coat for Christmas. He had known she was pouty about being held here. But this dreary fog of smoke and low clouds every morning — why, here it was ten o'clock and every lamp lit in her bedroom.

This bedroom. Isabelle had used to think this room was pretty grand. Mamma Ahnheim had had it fixed up before Manny was born so that Isabelle could come here when she left the hospital, and so that Mamma and Papa Ahnheim could have the baby in their own home for a while. They were crazy about Manny, the first grandson. There was no denying that, any more than there was any use denying the richness of this pink and blue bedroom. Blue satin panels on the walls, tufted blue satin on the headboard of the bed, garlands of pink roses, bowls always filled with fragrant pink buds — it was actually *lush*. Only —

Only, last week Hugo Marke had told Isabelle what Marguerite Conte said of her bedroom at the Ahnheim city house. That it looked like a royal German Easter egg. Isabelle had hardly been able to laugh properly. She was not going to let Hugo Marke guess how she felt about Marguerite Conte's catty superiority. Ever since Mrs. Conte had turned down Kurt's generous offer to buy *Les Grâces* — it was not as if Marguerite had not needed the money in 1929 — Isabelle had never got over her disappointment. If you were born a Conte or a Briand, you thought you could get away with anything you wanted to do, or say.

Take Ellen.

Isabelle picked out a letter from those scattered on the satin eiderdown. She reread it thoughtfully. Well, maybe it was just as well for John not to come back to St. Louis, go in with Ryan. Uncle Brooke had been the one to suggest that in the first place. It would not have worked, but John need not be so smug. . . .

> ". . . you don't seem to appreciate that I am very nicely located here in California. Our town is growing very rapidly, and the hospital with it. I'm a bloated stockholder in the hospital, and a respected member of the staff. That is, enough people respect me. I've the sort of work I want to do, and all of it I can handle.
>
> ". . . outside of a natural desire to see you and my nephew, I can think of no good reason to return to St. Louis. My ties are here. I have my home, my work. Yesterday I bought a dog. Any day you may hear that I am going to be married, though I've done nothing drastic yet. A doctor needs a wife. Or his patients think he does. There is a girl here whom I have known for years. She's a little older than I am. She's technician for the hospital — I've reason to think she would be understanding and forgiving of a doctor's peculiar ways. I needn't explain them to you. Betty is a . . . ."

Well. That just showed you — showed Isabelle — how silly it was to fret over things before they happened. A few years ago Isabelle had been *sick* over a silly idea she had had that John and Ellen might be foolish enough to marry. She had done what she could to prevent that. It would have been pure folly, such a marriage. Ellen, with her family tradition and social standing, marrying a mere nobody! It would have been suicidal! For both of them. If necessary, Isabelle would have tried to interfere still further. But it had not been necessary. John had gone off to California. Ellen, of course, had not married anyone else. She was not so awful young any more, either. But she went around town just as she had always done, being sweet and friendly. Only those of impeccable position could be so maddeningly *friendly!* Sometimes Ellen's democracy drove Isabelle Ahnheim to frenzy!

She reached for the ivory phone. She had not seen Ellen in ages. She would invite her for tea — just the two of them. They would have an oldtime talk.

4

"I know why I'm not a social success," Ellen told her mother, coming down through the shop that afternoon.

"Yes? That coat looks nice, darling."

"Doesn't it? Remind me that I think so — because Isabelle is going to compare it with her new mink. I know just what she'll say. She'll say how clever the French are! To think what they can do with weasel! That she's sorry she let Kurt spend thousands on a mink coat!"

Mrs. Conte smiled. "Isn't cattiness a luxury for you, Ellen?"

"Yes. I'm sorry. I — Mom, have I been clever about not showing my feeling about Isabelle? These last few years, I mean."

"Well, I should say so. Yes. If by 'feeling' you mean resentment toward her brother. You were never very fair to blame Isabelle for that. It was a trouble brought on by John, and by yourself."

"How do you mean?"

"Oh — that you used his silence as a convenient doorway by which you escaped marriage to a poor, struggling doctor."

"Why, Mom!"

Marguerite shook her beautiful silver head. "You never loved John, Ellen."

"I did. You *know* I loved him."

"Well, maybe you loved him; but you didn't love him enough. If you did, you'd have a baby of your own by now instead of going to see Isabelle's. Why is it you're not a social success?"

"Oh. Why, I meant because I wasn't able to think up an excuse for not going where I didn't want to go. She called me up and asked me to come over, and I'm going. Mom —"

"Yes? I'm pretty busy, darling."

"I won't keep you. Don't you really think I loved John enough?"

"Oh, no. Of course you didn't. Or such a little

thing like his being Isabelle's brother, and not telling you, wouldn't have mattered. I know, I know. You arbitrarily chose to say it indicated a lack of faith and trust. Did it ever occur to you that he might have *promised* Isabelle to keep silent, or that he might think it could make no difference who his sister was?"

Ellen stood thoughtful. "Do you suppose —"

"I'd suppose that if I were in love with a man, I'd think of ways to get him, not lose him. But, then, I'm not you. Now — run along. Shoo! I've work to do."

Ellen walked the several blocks to Isabelle's. Walked them thoughtfully, not noticing the damp cold nor the sooty snow in the gutters. Not seeing, nor heeding, the heavy traffic on Lindell. Why — why, Mom was right! She had not loved John. She had not! Or a little thing — only, of course, two years ago, it had not seemed a little thing. Almost three years, it was. Oh, it was cruel the way time could shrink and distort a matter. But . . .

The Ahnheim city house was so big, so ornate, that strangers were always taking it for a club. Carl, the butler, admitted Ellen into the huge, glacial hall, with a marble staircase circling its walls. Ellen never went up these stairs without thinking that the music of a Lubitsch picture should accompany her steps. The very large, very bright Christmas tree which stood in the center of the hall added nothing to the warmth and coziness of the place. "It looks municipal," Ellen told herself, smiling at her foolishness.

"Your tree is beautiful, Carl," she told the man who was preceding her.

"Yes, Miss Conte. But the needles fell very badly this year."

"Oh, dear, that's a shame. Did the baby like it? Manny?"

"Oh, yes, Miss. But a small one would have pleased him just as much, and the needles —"

"I can't imagine the Ahnheims' having a small tree."

"No, Miss. I can't imagine that, either."

Isabelle was still in bed. Looking like a bisque doll amid all the satin and ribbons and fluted lace. "Are you ill?" Ellen asked her, having kissed her and listened to the expected comment on her new coat.

"Oh, no. I'm just too bored to get up. And we've a fearful dinner tonight. The symphony committee. So dull. You won't be there?"

"Heavens, no! That's one advantage of being poor. We don't have to go to dinners like that."

"Your mother's on the committee."

"Is she? Well, we don't have to go to these dinners, because there isn't the smallest chance of getting a fat check out of us. How's the baby?"

"Just fine. Or I guess he is. I haven't seen him today. Or — have I? I can't remember. One day is just like another."

"Oh, Izzy!" Ellen's voice sounded her disgust. "You really don't deserve that sweet baby."

"I don't, do I? Is it too early to ring for tea? I

hadn't any lunch. I'm dieting. But I ordered tiny cream puffs for tea. I knew you adored them."

"I do. Thanks. I walked over here, and I'll be able to eat them with a clear conscience."

Tea was brought on a big, heavy tray. The Ahnheim silver was elaborately embossed and garlanded; the Ahnheim linen was thick and shiny. Ellen offered to pour. Perhaps behind this massive urn she could get courage to do the thing she had decided she would do.

"Isabelle," she broke in abruptly on a flood of the other woman's silvery chatter. "Izzy, do you ever hear from John?"

Isabelle looked at her. Had Ellen had a letter, too? "John?" she repeated. "You mean —"

"Your brother. He writes to you, doesn't he?"

"Why, of course, he writes. I had a letter only this morning."

"Oh. What — How is he?"

"Doesn't he write to you?"

"No." Ellen hated to have to admit that truth. If she had really loved John . . .

"I thought he was devoted to you. There was a time when I was afraid he was going to marry you."

"Yes, you were afraid. And did what you could to prevent it, didn't you?"

Isabelle refused to be offended. "It really wouldn't have done, Ellen. I'm glad you were brave enough to see that, though I know you were a little fond of him. Now, weren't you, Ellen? I wouldn't dream of asking — if you hadn't brought the matter up."

Not this matter, she had not. "Why were you afraid we'd get married?"

"Well, your family and John's — you saw that it wouldn't work, yourself. Though I'm afraid John didn't take it very well at the time. But that's all over now. He writes that he is going to be married."

"He —"

Isabelle's eyes were watching her mercilessly. Ellen must keep some shred of pride. She must. Oh, she had never thought of this happening! She knew now that she had not meant to send John away — forever. She knew that she had not loved him enough. Three years ago. But she had not meant to give him up completely, not even then. Then she had been silly and confused. She knew better, now that she was older and wiser.

"Did he say — What did he say — about her?"

"Oh, nothing very much. Her name is Betty, and she's a nurse or something. Anyway, he did say that she understood doctors. And she's older than he is."

"Oh. Do you — do you think they'll be happy? I mean, do you like the idea of his marrying? I mean, marrying a nurse?"

Isabelle dusted her fingers daintily on the napkin. "Oh, I think it should work out beautifully. So much more sensible than his trying to marry you, or any girl above him in social position. Even if he is my own brother, I can say this to you, Ellen. I have never laid any claims to a pedigree. I'm glad John has come to his senses, because I think compatibility of tastes and background are the most important *things* in marriage, don't you, Ellen?"

Ellen stood up. "No," she said flatly. "I don't think a thing in the world matters except love."

5

If the plane had dropped her in a perfectly unknown town, Ellen would have recognized John's hospital. He had described it to her so often that she felt as if she were looking up at the face of an old friend. If John should not be here, she could walk without guidance out to his house. She would know that, too.

The girl at the reception desk was very pretty. Was she the one? Her hair was in shiny red coils under her perky cap. Ellen wanted to ask if her name was Betty.

She gulped, and felt of the lump in her suède bag. "May I see Dr. Mallory?" she asked, her voice a little louder than she had meant it to be.

The girl nodded. Evidently scared young women made a practice of coming in here asking for Dr. Mallory. Ellen wished this place did not smell so. Her head ached; her heart thumped. She could scarcely walk steadily down the hall behind this red-headed nurse. She had freckles — the nurse had — carefully concealed by skillful make-up. But she was a pretty girl, for a nurse. What if Isabelle had been lying?

There was John's name on the glass of a door.

"Dr. Mallory." It looked swell! Real — and scary. There was something strange, unknown about this *Doctor* Mallory. Ellen fumbled hurriedly in her bag. She had to have some excuse . . .

"Just go right in," the nurse was telling her, and smiling. Probably her name was not Betty.

Ellen murmured something and went past her into a very white room with the light from a big window blinding her eyes till she could scarcely see the tall man in his white gown, turning, rising, coming toward her.

"Ellen!"

He shouted so! Ellen pushed back against the hall door. Held out her hand, the little glass apple glowing very blue against her glove. She dared to look up — John's eyes were so gray, so deep. "I — I — brought you this," she said weakly.

He was laughing — the whole hospital would hear him! — he had caught her up in his arms, swung her around, stood holding her, his cheek down against her hair. "Oh, Ellen, Ellen!"

"I —"

"So you brought me the apple?"

"Yes. You admired it. I stole it. From Mom. John, I — I had to come."

She thought he would crush her ribs; it would be ecstasy to die so in his strong arms. She pressed her face against the starched smoothness of his shoulder, smelled the old fragrance that was John. Soap and iodine, and — But he had changed. Not a lot — he was just older-seeming. No one would call him a boy; he seemed firm, assured. Yes, grown up.

"John, do you smoke?"

"I — what? Did you come clear out here to ask me if I smoke?"

"No, I — "

"Well, I should think not. Let's see now. Let's take off this hat — and this coat — and — oh, Ellen, Ellen!" He kissed her then, as she remembered he had kissed her, as she had hoped he would kiss her again. She could feel his heart pump against her cheek. He was trembling almost as much as she was. He was so strong, so dear, so — close to her.

"Don't ever leave me again," she murmured.

"Not me! But — Ellen, what happened? Or does it make any difference?"

She laughed up at him. "It doesn't make any difference. I — Do you smoke, John? You've changed — some. Not a lot —"

"Well, I'm three years older. And, yes, I do smoke. Do you mind?"

"Of course not. Only — it's something I didn't know about you. I'm — I'm just catching up."

"You drove me to it, young woman, when you jilted me."

"I didn't jilt you."

"Did!"

They laughed together happily, rocked in each other's arms.

"Oh, John, I'm so glad I came!"

"You'll forgive a little natural curiosity? Were you just passing the hospital, and dropped in?"

Ellen giggled. "I flew. You'll have to let me stay. I haven't return fare."

John's face was suddenly white. "I — I — Oh, Ellen, let's not talk. You might argue yourself out of marrying me. You did once, you know. I couldn't bear it, a second time. What — what made you change your mind?"

"A nightmare. A picture I had of your marrying that other girl."

John gaped at her. "What other girl? Oh, Belle told you. But, my glory, I told her there was nothing — I just thought it might be an idea, for the future. I was pretty much alone, you see, and I thought . . ."

Ellen nodded. "I know. Because she understands doctors. Well, I'll have you know, John Mallory, I understand doctors, too. Or I understand you, and that's enough. And I decided that if another girl was ready to marry you I might as well do it myself, and not somebody twice your age."

"Here, here! Back up, Miss Conte. Betty isn't twice my age; and unless my memory fails me, you had a very unflattering opinion of marriage to me three years ago. Come June eleventh."

"I know — but then I thought you didn't love me — and I didn't think I could trust you — and there was Felix — and Mom had worked so hard — -and I didn't want to be married because of Uncle Beau —"

John put his big, clean hand over her chattering mouth. "Quit it. You'll be saying next that you thought I was wanting to marry you to get this apple. Aren't you a little — well — upset, Miss Conte?"

"Yes, but I — you asked me. In a way you *were* marrying me for the apple. I mean, for what my family connections could do for you. Isabelle had said you would —"

"Isabelle? Because she plots and schemes for everything she does — how could you believe she'd know anything about my motives?"

"Well, that's another thing. You didn't tell me about Isabelle."

"I didn't tell you *what* about Isabelle?"

"That she was your sister."

"Oh. That."

"You *should* have told me, John. If you were completely frank with me."

"Yes," John agreed soberly. "Except that I had promised her not to. I wasn't very proud of the way Isabelle refused to claim me when I was penniless and — It makes no difference now, though. Now that you're here. Let's forget it."

"John!" Ellen's eyes were cold, angry.

"What is it, Pet? Oh, gee, Ellen, let's not talk. Let's just — Look. I'll change and —"

"John! Do you really mean to say that Isabelle made you promise not to tell me?"

"Not you, especially. Just not tell anybody."

"*She* told me. She said — she said you didn't like her changing her name. I guess she told — or implied — a lot of fibs. Oh, John, John! I shouldn't have believed that you would willingly deceive anybody, or try to marry a girl for any other reason than that you loved her."

"I hadn't any other reason. I told you that. But it didn't seem to be good enough."

"It was good enough — only, I knew you weren't telling me all about yourself, and it fuddled me. Oh, why did you ever let her . . ."

"Stiff pride, I guess. I got the idea she was ashamed of me."

"She *was* ashamed of you. And later — she was afraid you'd marry me. *That* was why she was afraid. She didn't want you — She'd had the best of things — was rich while you had a scrubby time of it, working, doing without things you needed. Then she married Kurt Ahnheim, and it killed her to think I might — that you — Oh, oh, *damn* it! I always cry when I get mad. Oh, John, John! She's such a *pig!*"

John reached for a towel, wiped her face. "Don't, Ellen. Don't."

"I thought — To think of all the time we've lost. And she so smug. And her baby! And you out here, almost marrying a nurse! I — I could scream, John!"

She was screaming, nearly. John pushed against the door into the laboratory where Betty and Dr. Devaney bent over a microscope. He spoke over his shoulder. "Miss Mason, will you get me some aromatic spirits? I've an hysterical patient."

"Yes, Doctor." Betty looked at Devaney. That

was an awfully pretty girl in the circle of John's arms.

"If that's hysteria," drawled Devaney, "I think our Johnnie is developing another of his radical techniques."

Words rattled on Betty's tongue much as the bottles in the cabinet knocked together under her cold fingers. "I'll bet her name is Ellen."